PRAISE

In the Shadows of
Chimney Rock

Nominated for the 2009 SIBA Book Award by members of the Southern Independent Bookseller's Alliance

"Rose Senehi begins her new novel, *In the Shadows of Chimney Rock,* with a scene of such high drama you wonder if she can sustain the intensity. Senehi not only sustains that opening intensity, she ups it in a high-speed tale with as many twists as a mountain road."
—*Asheville CITIZEN-TIMES*

"Both warm and gripping, the book will be best enjoyed by fans of the suspense romance novels that made Nicholas Sparks a household name."
—*Joshua Simcox, WNC Magazine*

"Rose Senehi knows it is essential that we save our Southern Appalachians from pollution and over-development and work for a responsible stewardship of the region. *In the Shadows of Chimney Rock* concerns not only the mountain past, and the all-too-real present, but more important, the mountain and human future. This story will thrill and disturb you by turns, and also inspire hope for the years ahead for the highlands we love."
—*Robert Morgan, Author of Brave Enemies and Boone: A Biography*

"Carolina Mountain Land Conservancy is very appreciative of Rose's support and involvement. We are delighted that she has chosen to employ her wonderful storytelling gifts to dramatize the urgent conservation challenges we face in our mountain region. We hope that through her compelling fiction, she helps to further raise awareness of the need to protect special places like the Hickory Nut Gorge."
—*Kieran Roe, Executive Director, Carolina Mountain Land Conservancy, Hendersonville, NC.*

Also by Rose Senehi

FALLING OFF A CLIFF

CATCHING FIRE

CAROLINA BELLE

DANCING ON ROCKS

RENDER UNTO THE VALLEY

THE WIND IN THE WOODS

PELICAN WATCH

SHADOWS IN THE GRASS

WINDFALL

In the *Shadows* of *Chimney Rock*

Rose Senehi

K.I.M. Publishing, LLC
2015

Published by

K.I.M. PUBLISHING, LLC
Post Office Box 132
Chimney Rock, NC 28720-0132

PUBLISHING HISTORY
Ingalls Publishing Group, Inc. / March 2008

PUBLISHED BY
K.I.M. Publishing, LLC / March 2015

Published in the United States of America.

PUBLISHER'S NOTE

This is a work of fiction. Though there are numerous elements of historical and geographical accuracy in this portrait of Chimney Rock, NC, and its environs, the names, places, characters and incidents either are the product of the author's imagination or are used fictitiously, and any resemblance to actual persons, living or dead, is entirely coincidental.

PUBLISHER'S CATALOGING-IN-PUBLICATION DATA

Senehi, Rose.
    In the Shadows of Chimney Rock / Rose Senehi
        p. cm.
    ISBN 978-0-9962571-6-9(trade pbk. : alk.paper)
    1. Hickory Nut Gorge—North Carolina—Fairview
    —Fiction. 2. Appalachian Region—Southern Fiction.
    3. Habitat (Ecology)—Fiction. I. Title.
        PS3619.E65915 2008
        813/6—dc22

                    2008010315

This too is for Isaac, Katie and Michael

There are places on this earth that touch the soul with the sheer power of their magnitude. The Hickory Nut Gorge in Western North Carolina is such a place. Evident in its people is a distinctive characteristic that has resurfaced over and over throughout generations and echoes within the whole community, for it is the very thing that brought them together in the first place. And even now, this monolithic gorge still has the power to siphon out, from the thousands of people who come each year, those with a certain cast of mind, and draw them close to its bosom.

CHAPTER ONE
July 16, 1916

HAYDEN TAYLOR FELT JITTERY all day. A lot of rain for the river to handle. Eight whole days of it. He tasted the salt in the sweat pouring from his forehead, mingled with the soft rainwater streaming from his hair. The way the river was coming on like a stampede of horses, the cow would perish if he didn't find her right quick. He ran under the black walnut tree for protection and scanned the green ribbon of meadow running between the raging river and the mountain.

It wasn't like Annie to leave the barn door open and the animal untied. The ground quaking the way it did when the giant chestnut uprooted and slammed against the earth would have brought any child skittering back to the house. It was his fault for not going with her to fetch the new kittens.

Everything seemed to be going wrong since the rain started. The corn stood in puddles a foot deep in some places and the small patch of oats, grown from the seeds bought with Mary's hard earned pickling money, lay flat on the ground. The Rocky Broad had already risen from its normal course twenty feet down the bank to where it was almost level with the field; and now the muddy chocolate waters leapt into the air, foaming and spitting like an angry dragon, tumbling the mammoth boulders around like dice.

The giant tree peeling off the mountain like a pick-up stick meant only one thing: the water-soaked forest soil was in a state of movement. The rain began pelting down hard and he couldn't see his hand in front of him. He fixed his pale blue eyes in a squint and roamed the veil of gray. Near dark, it was past time to pack up the family and animals and take them out of the gorge to Mill Spring; they'd head straight off at daybreak. But right now he couldn't leave the cow to be swallowed up by the night.

He discovered her cowering in a patch of giant rhododendrons up against the mountain. If it weren't for the lightning electrifying the sky, he wouldn't have found her at all. He hated to do it, but he kicked her glistening boney rump twice to get her to budge. He wrestled the animal along, guided by the sporadic silhouette of the cabin against the flickering sky.

Suddenly the roar of the river was deafening. Frigid water writhed around his ankles. The Rocky Broad had jumped the embankment!

The rope jerked from his hand as he ran headlong into the dark, a death sentence for their cherished cow, but he couldn't waste a minute chasing it. He had to get Mary and the baby and Annie out of the path of the raging river.

Smoke swirling downward toward the ground from the cabin brushed by his nostrils. He was almost there. Mary knew these capricious mountains. She'd be up and have the children bundled and ready to take to higher ground. All he had to do was reach them.

A sledgehammer force suddenly heaved him up, then a sinister silence swaddled him as the current sucked him under. Mary and the baby and sweet little Annie! He had to get to them! He reached out to grasp something; anything! He sensed the water was surging toward the mountain and braced himself to be slammed against its granite rocks.

Crushed against a web of branches with his lungs about to burst, he grabbed a hefty limb and climbed hand over hand, paying no heed to the stabbing branches until he rose above the water. A bizarre scene flashed in front of him as white lighting streaked across the sky. The giant poplar, entangled in scores of trees, rocked precariously against the icy current as he climbed to a larger limb and shimmied to a crook. He tied himself to the trunk with his suspenders and fell into unconsciousness.

The terrifying thunder of madly rushing water shocked him awake every time something heavy slammed against the clump of trees. Hours passed. Asleep, with his legs and arms numbed from the cold, he saw Mary reach out to him from the water. He strained to grasp her hand, their fingertips touching for a tortured instant. Suddenly, he woke from the nightmare screaming, "God Almighty! Why!? Why this wrath?"

A slight gray glow appeared at the far eastern end of the gorge, and he knew the terror of the night was coming to an end and the horror of the day was about to begin. He scanned the murky darkness as ghost-like images started appearing in the gray of the oncoming dawn, the way a room slowly reveals itself as someone nears with a lantern.

The sight sweeping by awed him. Bloated horses with eyes wide open in terror, chicken coops, wagons, bales of hay, furniture... all pitiful remnants of the humanity that had clung to their meager existence in the Hickory Nut Gorge. He searched the landscape until his eyes ached. Not a trace of the cabin. It had been taken clean away as if it had never been there.

A small boy, arms bobbing limply with the current, bounced along the top of the foamy flood waters. Recognizing the preacher's son from Gerton, he broke into a hymn. *Jesus, Lord, we look to thee...*

He thought about his own boy, the fourth Hayden born since the family left Scotland and made their way along the Great Philadelphia Wagon Road to the gorge and rooted their lives in the shadow of Chimney Rock Mountain. So much strength in that small bundle. Laid him on his stomach right after he was born and not one hour old and the little rascal tried to lift himself up. That's what he needed to think about now... Mary... little Annie... baby Hayden... He comforted himself with an image of his family gathered at the hearth and again allowed his consciousness to drain from his body.

Hayden woke in the daylight and saw that the shadow of Chimney Rock had climbed a third of the way up Round Top. Had to be past seven.

The river had fallen back to the top of the embankment and left a mass of broken limbs, timber and parts of houses and barns and all their contents piled high right up to the foot of the mountain. He tumbled out of the tree and crawled and climbed over the debris.

The stinging, burning and aching drifted apart from him, like a distant tune as he stood up and eyed the endless wall of toppled trees. He took a step and his foot fell through some limbs, scraping his ankle raw. It landed on something squishy and the hair on the back of his neck rose. He was afraid to look. The cow's furry black and white coat appeared almost dry, just splotched with orange clay, her mouth open in a frozen plaint. He leapt onto a log and held back a scream himself.

Nauseous and dizzy, he slogged on through what seemed like miles of mud. Maybe he could quench his thirst from the Freeman's spring that trickled from the face of the mountain. He dropped against an uprooted tree to get his balance and steady his legs, and stared out onto the strangeness before him. The sky was clear and clean and blue. Falls rolled off the top of Chimney Rock Mountain like water casually spilling over the side of a full bucket, while the sun-baked stench of death and dying floated up from the mud and twisted timbers all around him.

He slumped forward and gazed out into the distance, catching sight of a pink ribbon fluttering in the breeze. He locked his eyes on it and climbed and crawled and clawed his way forward. *Please God! Not my little Annie! Not my little Annie.* He stopped breathing as he neared.

She lay motionless, like a doll, big blue eyes wide open. Barely had any mud on her and her golden braids still managing to sparkle in the fading sunlight. He picked up the frail little body with his massive rough hands and cradled her in his sinewy arms, shading her with his shadow. He knew what a body did when exposed to the sun. This wasn't going to happen. Not to his Annie. She was going to grow up to be a teacher, and never do women's work. *She'd told him so.*

He feverishly picked up anything that might have something beneath it, while pressing Annie to his body. The angry waters drowned out his anguished cries. *Please God! Please, don't take Mary and the baby!*

He worked his way downstream with Annie lashed to his chest with his suspenders. Barely able to recognize the river he'd played in, fished in all his life, he waded into the stabbing cold water waist deep to get around a dam of clumped up timbers and debris.

He kept a wary eye on Chimney Rock's shadow steadily creeping up Round Top. Mary and the baby would be getting cold soon if they didn't get their wet clothes off. If it was still standing, he could take them to the Logan House at the bend of the river for the night.

Back on shore, he caught sight of the other side of the river. The drover's road was washed out and the bridge at the McDaniel's place gone, along with their cabin and barn. With the way copperheads were crawling all over the place trying to find cover, he decided to be more careful lifting rubble.

A wave of depression rippled through him, ending in a tormented scream. Then a sudden surge of hope thrust him forward again. Something fluttering from a limb of a fallen tree caught his eye. Looked a lot like the checkered curtains Mary had tacked up on the kitchen window. Apprehension started to get the best of him and his eager scanning of debris turned to wary eye movement directed by the fear gripping his brain. He held his breath as his eyes followed the ins and outs of the jumble, afraid of what he might see.

One of the chairs they got from Sears dangled from a limb. They'd bought two for twenty-five cents apiece when they married, and got another one for Annie when she turned five. Mary had said, with all the work the girl was doing, it weren't right for her to sit on a stool any more. But other than the chair and the curtains, he couldn't find another trace of the cabin.

The shadows were deep on this side of the river by now and

it was getting harder to make anything out, but he spotted a familiar shape up ahead. He could swear it was the cradle he'd carved when Mary was big with Annie. Just sitting there stuck in a sea of mud. As he neared, he could see that the quilt spilling from it was coated with a thick layer of terra cotta colored clay silt. He sank to his knees and sobbed, rocking Annie in his arms like he did when she was a baby.

He'd better wrap her in the quilt. He reached for it and thought he noticed a small place where it moved. He pulled his hand back, slowly rose and laid Annie on the ground. He looked around for a heavy stick to kill the snake with, then carefully took hold of a corner of the quilt. With the club raised ready to beat the viper to death, he slowly pulled it away. He gasped at the sight in front of him. Baby Hayden lay wide eyed, sucking on all four fingers of one hand stuffed into his mouth, his face red and swollen.

He had to move swiftly, the baby needed nourishment. At the very least some water. . . and Annie needed some tending too. He shook out the quilt and gently laid her down, then lovingly straightened her braids down her front the way she always did. He carefully wrapped her, letting out a scream of anguish as he covered her face.

He trudged ahead with a child in each arm.

"Lo, there! Are you alright?" someone shouted.

Two men on horseback waved to him from across the river.

"We've been sent up from Rutherfordton by the county supervisor. Lookin' for survivors. All the bridges are out. Up ahead you might be able to make it over. We'll throw you a rope."

One of the men met him halfway across the river on foot. Easy to tell the bundle held a dead child, he mustn't of thought it right to take it from its father; and Hayden was holding on to the baby too tight to give it up. No grief on his face. Not yet. Just the lean weather worn face of a mountain farmer frozen in shock.

"I guess you'll be wantin' to be leavin' this place for good," the man said.

Hayden looked up at Chimney Rock Mountain and let his eyes roam along the beloved granite faced ridge, then down at the baby staring back at him. Tears ran freely down his lean leathery cheeks. He turned toward the man with his face twisted in defiance. "Us'n Taylors come unto this here gorge in 1784 and this devil of a flood hain't gonna push us out." He looked back at the dreary wasteland, his defiance morphing into a grotesque portrait of grief. He sobbed openly for a moment, then barely eked out, "And I hain't goin' nowheres without my Mary."

CHAPTER TWO
October 2003

MUFFLED CRIES FILLED the dark room. The same unwanted dream—swimming in a blood soaked bed with the bright crimson liquid matting her lacey nightgown to her pale flesh. Hayden Taylor Parks sat up rigid and stared into the darkness until reality overtook her consciousness. She stumbled to the bathroom and splashed cold water on her face. Groping her way to the dresser, she opened a drawer, scooped up a fluffy bundle with both hands and buried her face in it, breathing deeply until the pressure in her chest subsided.

She turned on the lamp with one hand, and put the bundle back with the other. A blotched face reflected back at her from the mirror, along with the image of a bed with only one side mussed. The ornate silver picture frame sitting on the dresser caught her eye, and she slowly ran a manicured finger across a joyous bride and groom walking through a crowd of guests decked out in the flamboyant chic of the affluent South.

Hayden stared blindly at the picture. Memories of friends and family wishing her a carefree life floated through her mind like a disjointed song. She had promised herself she wouldn't do this any more, but she couldn't stop. She pulled up her gown and looked in the mirror at the scar on her abdomen until her thoughts drifted outside herself. Her eyes glazed over and she pictured the pride on Jack's face when he pulled the cradle out of the back seat of the car and held it up like a trophy. A sickening churning started in the pit of her stomach and slowly crept up to her throat. Unable to blot out the image of the frail little hand gripping her finger, hurt throbbed throughout her body.

Something in the back of her mind warned her that she shouldn't keep doing this to herself. A lot of bad things happen to people, she told herself. Some unkind test of the strength of the human spirit. A challenge to absorb the hurt until it runs diluted through every cell of your body. People either get over the pain, or put it some place in their soul that they're careful never to re-visit. Most of these tortured individuals, she told herself, had found a way to turn their back on broken dreams; but, for her, it had already been two years and she still couldn't let go.

Still clutching her gown to her breast, she went to the win-dow and gazed out over the placid moonlit ocean lazily licking the beach. This stillness, just before the world awoke, always sus-pended her in a place where she couldn't lie to herself. She had to stop running soon; there was no place else to go and she was all tired out.

She shook herself out of the trance and let her nightgown drop back down. She crossed the room to the French doors and went out onto the balcony, her depression failing to erase the in-delible stride of an heir to one of the South's largest lumber em-pires. The gentle ocean breeze played with her hair as she gazed thoughtfully at the red glow on the horizon.

She'd watched hundreds of sunrises on this Carolina coast, but something about the bizarre pattern of red streaks in this one telegraphed a warning. She pushed it out of her mind. It was just a reaction to the eerie premonition she had yesterday about her father.

The sun would be up in a few minutes and Jack still wasn't home. His Southern manners will keep him from just walking out on me, she told herself; but then the possibility that he might not be coming back crept back into her mind.

She fished her cigarettes out of their hiding place in the large ceramic urn standing in the corner of the balcony, lit up, and carefully blew the smoke into the breeze away from her hair. Thoughts of her father shot into her head again and she felt sorry for the little girl she once was. The one who had gone to sleep every night fantasizing a perfect existence with a father she had intricately fashioned in her imagination until her Aunt Martha put an end to the fantasy. Seething from an argument with her mother, her aunt had pulled her and her older sister, Barbara, aside and thrilled them with the news he wasn't dead.

Hayden clearly recalled how her mother ran over and put her arms around them. The image of one of the few times her mother had treated them tenderly still burned in her memory. Her mother had gently stroked their hair as she shattered the electrifying moment. *I'm so sorry, sweet things; I had to make up the story of your father dying so you wouldn't get hurt. I didn't want you to know he wanted nothing to do with you when he came back from Vietnam.* Devastating. Like a slap in the face.

Hayden slowly shook her head and remembered how her childhood fantasies became filled with revenge. A favorite scenario had been imagining herself as a famous actress refusing to see him backstage with the cryptic message: *My father's dead.*

Hayden took a deep drag of her cigarette, leaned back against the wall and slowly blew it out. She couldn't believe she was ever that naive. The past two years had taught her enough bitter lessons to almost make what he did seem trivial.

It struck her as strange that every time her depression dragged her down into a dank, dark pit, she yearned to reach out and entwine her arms around her father's neck. Was it because she was named after him? Did she feel that fact obligated him to especially care for her? If only she could prove to him that she wasn't someone to be thrown away.

Maybe it was because her life was at a dead end, but last week, she went so far as to Google him. An art gallery and school in Asheville of all places. It made her heartsick, and then angry to know that all her life he had only been a few hours away. An uncontrollable urge seized her. An urge to capture a love she felt she and Barbara deserved. She thought for a moment. She could get dressed and drive up there today. She wasn't going to confront him, at first, anyway. It wouldn't hurt to meander into his gallery, though.

It'd be easy enough to recognize him from his picture on the site, then she could inquire about taking classes. That would give her enough interaction to find out if he was anything like she had imagined. Some small shred to satisfy her curiosity. Maybe he'd show some interest, invite her to lunch. What a crazy thought. She was starting to scare herself. He could just as easily press a pamphlet in her hand and brush her off.

Why this obsession to find a father who obviously didn't want her? Did she actually think that getting him to love her would help erase the hurt that was paralyzing her? She took a last spastic puff, then retrieved a jar from the urn, tossed in the cigarette, and twisted the lid tight. Watching the mesmerizing smoke curl and fill the jar, her broken spirit arose and leapt across a threshold.

She rushed back inside and grabbed a suitcase out of the closet and slapped it on the bed. The phone rang. She ignored it. Why force her husband to make up another lie, or herself to pretend she believed it. But the endless ringing, screaming it was never going to stop until someone answered, had the earmarks of a call from her mother. She picked up the receiver and glanced over at the clock on the night table. Seven. Early, even for her mother's demands.

"Hayden, come over to the house. Barbara's already on her way."

Hayden threw her head back and stared at the ceiling. Could her mother ever have been young and sweet and tender?

"Well, don't you want to hear what I've got to say?"

"Of course, Mother."

"Then get over here!"

She combed her hair at the mirror and studied the slab of marble her face had become. Colorless. Expressionless. It was as if she were dying from the inside out. Could finding her father keep her from turning to stone? She'd hurry and get over to her mother's, and once that was over with, come back, finish pack-

17

ing and be on her way to Asheville.

HAYDEN WAVED to the guard and waited for a mechanism to read the barcode on her window and lift the gate, then she started through the wildlife preserve scattered with palatial homes. Out of the corner of her eye she noticed a little girl in pink shorts riding her bike on a driveway, pink ribbons streaming from the handlebar grips. Hayden told herself to keep her eyes on the road, but didn't listen to the warning and slowly pressed the brakes.

The child noticed her and waved. Hayden waved back; but it was as if there was a sheet of plate glass between them, locking the little girl out with Hayden pressing against it to get in. She let herself drift into a trance. The nursery had been pink, too. She remembered how Jack showed it off to everyone who walked in the door, especially the mural she had painted on one of the walls—a little girl on the beach with a big straw hat, putting sand in a pail.

Hayden suddenly became aware of a car pulling up behind her, and put her foot on the gas. Her breathing quickened and she squeezed her eyes tight for a moment. She had to stop letting these glimpses of other people's children trigger these memories. Trees whizzed by, but she barely noticed her surroundings as she conjured up what her baby would have looked like at five. It wasn't until she pulled into her mother's brick paved driveway behind her sister Barbara's SUV that the image faded.

She ran up the twenty or so steps leading to the main entrance, opened the door, and followed her sister's call from upstairs. Barbara sat on one of the couches flanking either side of the fireplace in her mother's bedroom, and watched the woman leisurely pack as if life were taking its normal course.

The gracefully aging Elizabeth Burroughs Tarrington put a few things in a suitcase, lit a cigarette, and tossed the pack on the coffee table as Hayden sank into the couch across from her sister.

"Go on, Hayden. Light up. We know you're smoking."

Hayden, from long habit, ignored the remark.

Her mother went over to a dresser. "You might as well know

why I called you. I was going through my mail last night and came across a letter from your father. He intends to include the both of you in his will and wants your addresses." She yanked a scarf out of a drawer, and slammed it shut. "Of all the nerve! After all my father had to go through to make it look like he died in the war."

Hayden swallowed a scream. An aura of light suddenly shone at the end of a dark tunnel in her mind. She'd never dreamt of anything like this ever happening. Hayden studied her mother. Something about her fussing over her father naming them in his will made her wonder how much truth there had been to anything she had ever said about him. But her mother wasn't in the habit of lying. She wasn't afraid of anybody or anything.

Hayden stood up and went over to the dressing table. "Let me see the letter."

"There's nothing to see. He says he wants you girls to know about your legacy. Legacy? All he's got is that shack in Chimney Rock and a hunk of mountain that's too steep for pulling out lumber. What good is it?" The agitated edge on her voice melted away. "I couldn't get Russell on the phone last night, so naturally, I called his secretary at home. What's the good of retaining a family lawyer if you can't reach him?"

Out of habit, Hayden's eyes shot over to her sister and saw her mouthing *naturally* in an exaggerated fashion.

Her mother snapped the suitcase closed. "He's on his way back from Ireland and is expected to get to Charleston sometime late this afternoon while Charles and I are on the boat." She went over, sat down at her dressing table, and started tossing an army of cosmetics into a bag. "Why does God always let these things happen just when you're getting ready to leave on a trip?" She swung around to face Hayden. "I want you to get hold of Russell as soon as he lands and tell him I'll call him from a marina at four."

Hayden barely listened. Chimney Rock? Wasn't that the place that had a huge hunk of granite jutting out of the side of the mountain like a chimney? She'd never imagined her father living

19

in a place like that. She studied her mother. She had taken off her robe and was slipping into a pair of black Capri pants like she was determined not to let anything as trifling as a lie about her first husband being dead upset her social calendar. My mother's going to attack this with all the power she can buy, thought Hayden.

Her mind raced. She couldn't let Russell snub her father's offer. Her breathing became rapid. "Mother, we've got to talk."

"We are talking. And what is there to say, anyway?"

"I want whatever my father's got to give me, no matter how humble it is. Let's not drag Russell into this."

Elizabeth Tarrington's nostrils flared. "I forbid it! Why in the world would we want anything of his? How could you, after the way he walked out on us?" She took another deep drag and blew the smoke slowly into the air as she gathered her thoughts. She opened a drawer, pulled out an envelope, and tossed it on the coffee table. "Here's the damn letter. I want you to give it to Russell and tell him I want this whole thing to end right here; and I want it done before I get back from Florida. He can tell your father to give everything to the poor for all I care. We don't want a thing from him and don't want any of us to be connected to him in any way."

Hayden folded her arms firmly across her chest. "Mother, this isn't fair."

Elizabeth Tarrington flicked a hand in the air. "It's plenty fair when you consider the retainer Russell gets as a trustee of my father's estate."

Hayden's eyes narrowed. "I didn't mean Russell, Mother. *I* want to handle this."

Barbara sat up. "Yes, Mother. He *is* our father."

Her mother's head snapped around to eye Barbara, causing the young woman to catch her breath, then her glare traveled over to Hayden's resolute expression. "Haven't I been a good mother to you? And Charles a good father?"

Hayden threw up her arms. "What has that got to do with anything? You don't make sense! Every time I ask you about my father, you turn things around and accuse me of not loving you!"

Her mother crushed out her cigarette, leaned back with a hand on her hip and looked Hayden up and down. "Okay. You want me to make sense? Well, here it is. You are the last person I would allow to go up there and meet that man. You know nothing about the world. Just look at you. You're almost forty, never had a job other than that decorating thing..."

"I'm thirty-two, Mother, and if it makes you happy, I'll get a job tomorrow!"

"Darling, you simply do not understand how things work. We need someone of Russell's caliber to nip this thing in the bud. Think of it. If anything happens to your father, our names could be smeared all over his obituary. Remember... I know people in Asheville." She picked up a comb, fluffed up her bangs and examined her face from several angles. "Besides, you'd be better off spending more time with your husband. People are talking."

Hayden refolded her arms across her chest and sank against the wall. "Are they, Mother? And just what are they saying?"

"Don't get me started, Hayden. It wouldn't hurt for you to pay more attention to him. For the past year, all you've been doing is putting your head in the sand with all that tennis, golf and charity work. Ever since that baby..."

Barbara jumped up. "For God's sake, Mother! Stop!" She clasped her hands pleadingly and looked over at her sister. "Hayden, please do as Mom says. You know she'll only get her way."

Elizabeth Tarrington rose and dropped her cosmetic bag on the bed next to the suitcase, unflustered, as if the conversation were usual. The sound of the elevator opening in the hall drew her attention, and her face brightened as Hayden's stepfather emerged.

Hayden figured her mother wasn't going to let him in on this awkward situation, and decided it was better that way. Unlike her mother, who had been born in South Carolina but raised in capitals throughout the world, Charles Tarrington was born and bred in Charleston and still retained the genteel manners of the old South. Her mother's cold-hearted attitude would only sadden him.

HAYDEN FOLLOWED HER parent's car out of the driveway and glanced at the clock on the dash. Not even ten. Her mother's words rang in her head: *How could God let this happen just when she was taking a trip?* She had stopped counting on God over a year ago, and the last time she stepped foot in a church was to attend her grandfather's funeral six months earlier. But those casually tossed out words had made her think. And now, alone in the car, they lifted her out of herself.

There was something providential about this freak coincidence of her father's letter coming at the very moment her mother was leaving on her annual trip down the Waterway. Hayden tapped a fingernail on the steering wheel. If it weren't for this coincidence, she was sure her mother wouldn't have let either her or Barbara know their father wanted to make contact with them. It made her angry to think how she would have gotten away with it.

She yanked the map out of the side pocket of her BMW sedan and studied it as she waited for a light. Home was in the next gated oceanfront community down the road, and as she turned in, she prayed Jack wouldn't be there. Nothing was going to break her resolve, and she didn't want to leave for Asheville after a row. She drove past the guard gate, then along the heavily landscaped road sprinkled with ponds on either side, until she reached her house.

She slipped the car into the garage underneath, and felt relieved the space for her husband's car was empty. She ignored the elevator. It was too slow. Instead, she took the garage steps to the first floor hall, then raced up the circular staircase to the bedroom and headed straight to the closet, moving fast without thinking.

She hastily stuffed a few days' clothes into the suitcase lying on the bed, then got a silk scarf from the closet, went over to her dresser and spread it on top. She opened the drawer, tenderly lifted the bundle lying inside, and carefully wrapped it. The phone rang. She froze. The possibility that Jack could be announcing his arrival as he passed the guard gate on his way home made her pick up.

Her husband's polite endearments agitated her. She tried to fight it, but the mellow voice that had catapulted him into relative stardom as a consummate master of ceremonies when he was still in his early twenties, drew her back to the time when he would whisper lovingly in her ear.

"Where were you when I phoned this morning? I didn't want to call after the show and wake you. For Pete's sake, Hayden, do us both a favor and turn on the damn answering machine."

By ignoring the mechanism, she forced him to talk to her instead of burying his lies in a machine; but his needling her about it worried her. Was he sending some kind of message? Not that he was leaving her, but that he was slipping further and further away.

She abruptly changed the subject. "How did the show go?"

"We had a full house. A lot of tour bus people. We were so late cashing out, I just stayed over."

The young thing he probably brought to their condo bothered her, even though she knew she was as much to blame as he. She couldn't stand going backstage after one of the live performances at his Myrtle Beach musical theater any more. Every time she saw a girl with a pretty face, she wondered if he'd slept with her.

"Are you all right, Hayden? You don't sound like yourself."

Her mind raced in another direction and she lost the thread of the conversation. The only thing she remembered was lying to him about going to Charleston for a few days to shop.

"Good idea, baby. Get a new dress for the Pawley's Benefit. I want you to knock them dead."

No matter how much he strayed, she had still managed to remain his prized possession. She recalled all the feverish exercising and near starvation to hang on to her girlish figure. Was it worth it? she asked herself.

She finished the call and hung up, then quickly packed the car. She ran back into the house, slipped into the study and booted up her father's website. While the pages inched their way out, she scribbled a check for the housekeeper, then snatched up the sheets from the printer and stuffed them in her purse. An intense urgency seemed to be taking over, and her melancholia quickly turned into a state of compulsion, as if someone in dire need were calling out to her. That feeling wasn't new to her and it began to put her on edge.

AN HOUR OUT of Georgetown and almost to Manning, the extended beep on her cell phone told her the signal had kicked in again. She punched her sister's number.

Barbara's breathless voice burst from the speaker. "Hayden, I'm so glad you called! I've been trying to get a hold of you for the past hour." Her tone saddened. "I've been thinking. Our father wouldn't be leaving us all his worldly possessions if he had a family, now would he?"

"Hardly."

"This letter he sent sure spooked Mom. I can't believe she's going to sic Russell on him for wanting to be nice to us."

"That's why I'm on my way up there. I've got to get to him before that happens."

"Go, Girl!" squealed Barbara. She laughed joyously for a moment and then turned somber. "Mama's gonna have one heck of a hissy fit when she finds out."

The two sisters started singing spontaneously. *Oh, I wish I was in the land of cotton, Old times there are not forgotten, Look away, look away, look away Dixie Land.* Tears welled in Hayden's eyes. Ever since they were kids, they churned out the anthem's first lines each time they defied their mother.

After a fit of nervous giggles, Hayden imagined Barbara lifting an eyebrow as she spoke. From the pauses and the way some of her words were muffled, Hayden could also tell she was munching on something.

"What on earth did you think... about her worrying about our names being mentioned in any obits? Sometimes I can't believe the stuff that comes out of her mouth. If I hadn't seen them put Granddaddy in the ground with my own eyes... I'd swear he coached her this morning before we got there."

Her older sister's appreciation for the ironies in the human personality made Hayden smile. It gave her a quirky uniqueness, and also, Hayden was sure, her sympathetic nature.

"Don't worry. When our father dies, I'm going to personally see to it that both our names are included in every column from Asheville to Myrtle Beach. Mama might want to live that lie she and Granddaddy cooked up, but I'm plumb sick of it! Our father's not going to leave this world without being acknowledged by his own daughters!"

"Sister Girl, you're starting to sound like the old Hayden!"

After a few moments of silence, Barbara added, "I can't believe you're actually going up there."

"Neither can I. I always pictured our father surrounded by folks who loved him. A family or somethin'. Not someone who had nobody but people who were content to pretend he was dead. Barb, I can't explain it; I feel if I let this chance for us to connect slip away I'll regret it the rest of my life."

"Thank the Lord Mom had to go out of town. Otherwise, she would probably never have let us know about his letter."

That was the second time God was credited for arranging her mother's trip, and Hayden was starting to believe it.

"Have you told Jack?" Barbara asked.

"No. He wouldn't think I could handle it... emotionally, I mean." Hayden felt the familiar overwhelming sadness rise up through her body and grip her throat. She pulled over onto the side of the road, deserted except for her car. Barbara's voice seemed to trail off and Hayden could feel the memories stab at her brain. She drifted back to over a year ago. It was a month after the funeral.

She had turned back to the house instead of going to see the therapist. It wasn't doing any good. When she pulled up to the house, she saw Barbara's car in the driveway. Why? Her sister knew she wasn't going to be home. She walked up the stairs. Sounds came from the nursery. She knew she shouldn't go in, but something drew her toward it. Jack and Barbara looked up. Their faces stricken. She stumbled forward. The crib had been disassembled and Carrie's favorite blanket lay among the piles of baby clothes stacked in boxes. She snatched it up and clutched it to her breast. The screaming wouldn't stop for what seemed a lifetime. Jack held her down on the bed, his tears splattering on her face until Dr. Jacobs came at her with the needle. It was over in a second. She remembered wishing the peace would last forever.

A pickup truck came out of a driveway up ahead. Hayden pulled back on the road. "What... what did you say, Barb?"

"Are you all right, Hayden?"

"Yes. I got into some traffic is all."

"Hayden, are you going to be all right driving in the mountains?"

"Don't worry. These superhighways don't bother me that much. It's just those narrow curvy two-laners with nothing below but clouds that give me the sensation I'm falling off."

"I'll never forget you freaking out on the Blue Ridge Parkway that time Daddy Tarrington took us for a ride in his convertible."

Hayden barely noticed the silence that fell over them. There were always long periods when she and her sister gathered their thoughts. She reflected on the events of the morning. "Barb, thanks for coming to my rescue with Mom. I don't know what I would do without you."

"She can't help it, Hayden. Granddaddy made her the way she is." She chuckled. "Can you imagine being an only child, motherless, and being raised by him?"

Hayden nodded knowingly to herself as they both fell silent again. She finally spoke. "Barb, I don't think she's being totally honest with us. I'd made up my mind to go see our father's gallery before we knew about his letter, but now that he's reached out to us, I'm curious to hear his side of the story. All my life I've been torn between hating him and listening to a little voice in my head telling me there might be an honorable reason he didn't come to see us."

Hayden bit her lip and hoped the reason *would* be honorable. "Barb, as a kid I imagined all kinds of things, like maybe his face was burned off and he couldn't bear to have us look at him. But he might be wantin' to leave us something just because he's ashamed of what he did. If that's the case, so be it; we're not the only people in the world whose father abandoned them. At any rate, I'm going to get to the bottom of this, and accept whatever it is and get on with my life."

She thought for a moment about acknowledging out loud her life was a mess. The emergence from the shadows of a man everyone pretended was dead had flung her into a raw reality.

She reached the outskirts of Columbia and navigated onto Route 77 and followed it to Interstate 26.

The call left Hayden excited. She was actually going to see her father! The letter peeked from her purse. She saw a sign announcing a rest area ahead. She pulled off and parked.

She fumbled through her bag for her cigarettes as she read: *Dear Liz.* Hayden's eyes froze on the words. Nobody ever called her mother *Liz!* She skimmed over the letter, searching for any affectionate mention of her and Barbara. *It's only fair to the girls that they know about their mountain heritage,* was as close as he came.

She had to reach him before Russell! She quickly got back on the road. Not having found her cigarettes, she spilled everything from her purse and pawed through the pile until she felt the soft pack. She zoomed down all the windows before lighting up so her car wouldn't absorb the telltale scent.

Finding herself in a wind tunnel with her hair whipping across her eyes, she started to toss the cigarette from the window, then reluctantly snuffed it out on the pristine ashtray and closed the windows.

She scrolled through her appointments for the day in her head. She had to cancel her session with her personal trainer at the health spa and make a couple of quick calls to get out of her tennis match at two. It amazed her how quickly her intricately woven schedule had become irrelevant.

She mulled over Barbara's comment that she was sounding like the old Hayden, and the thought struck her that what she was about to do might change more than her schedule, possibly the course of her life. But, one thing for sure, she was never going to be the old Hayden again… the girl in the picture who had the world by the tail. For the past year, however elegant the surroundings, she was just being warehoused, and it was her doing.

27

As Hayden drove past Columbia, she started to feel discon-nected from the beach and acutely aware of the changing land-scape. Her thoughts lingered on the way her father addressed her mother as *Liz.* That one word, which her mother hadn't tolerated from anyone else, said so much. How does love wither and die?

The image of Jack putting his arms around her last week flooded over her. The hurt on his face after she pushed him away made her blink back tears. Distant memories of the way he would touch her in the middle of the night swam through her head. She could almost feel the thrill of accepting him with the heightened passion of wanting to conceive. She bit her lip and muffled a cry. That was never going to happen again. They were never going to be the way they were.

She wiped the tears streaming down her cheeks with the back of her hand. All she ever wanted was a little family of her own to pour her love into. Was that asking too much? Jack, please, please, forgive me for what I'm doing to you. I know it's wrong, but I've got to punish someone for what happened to us.

CHAPTER THREE

H E LOOKED UP at the scattered stream of broad-winged hawks dotting the cobalt sky on their ancient fall migration through the Hickory Nut Gorge, but resisted the temptation to stop painting. Finally, Hayden Taylor put down his brush and made his way through the clutter in the cramped attic room to the window. He cocked his head against the glass and glanced up, only catching a glimpse of the far off trail swirling upward on the warm drafts.

Disappointed, he slouched against the window frame and stroked his gray ponytail. He eyed the scissors sitting on his workbench, and for the millionth time felt an urge to get rid of his only act of defiance to a system that let him down. No. Not as long as I remember my brothers offered up in Vietnam like cannon fodder, he told himself. He recalled being brought home on a stretcher in the middle of the night. The thought of this clandestine return for a planeload of wounded warriors still stung. No homecoming. Just smuggled back in the dark.

Out of habit, he languidly reached for the dog-eared snapshot tucked in the window casing. Two baby girls splashing in the ocean surf. He gazed at it until he could hear their gleeful squeals.

He looked out the window again. The shadows cast by a few

of the flock's stragglers along the face of Round Top Mountain looming up on the other side of the river bothered him. That was how he felt. A straggler. If he'd only had the strength to act on his VA doctor's urgings and confronted his wife's lie that he'd died in the war, his life would have turned out differently.

He had to stop beating himself up over this. By the time he was well enough to face the kind of scenes it would have taken to get her to turn things around, the damage had already been done. How could he rise from the dead and disrupt his little girls' lives?

The blazing fall palette creeping down the mountainside put him on edge. Time was running out. He wondered if the two girls knew anything at all about their mountain roots, or if the youngest had any idea her name had been handed down to the first-born son of every generation since the family struck their homestead in the Western North Carolina mountains. It seemed sadly fitting in a way, his having no male offspring, to let the tradition wither unfathomed with the last born of his line.

The uneasiness he had felt all afternoon was starting to get to him. If there was one lesson the war had taught him, it was that at any moment, fate can step in and change the whole course of a life. He was more convinced than ever that sending the letter to Liz was the right thing to do. He had to straighten out the whole mess with his daughters before he died and the story of the Taylors got buried along with him. He owed it to his mother who told and retold the history of their clans in the mountains of North Carolina as she rocked in her chair in the evenings. He smiled inwardly as he recalled how she always captured the poignancy of the Great Flood. His grandfather's endless search for any trace of his wife had sounded romantic to him when he was a kid, but now he understood how much it must have tortured him to not know what happened to her.

A conviction as solid as a slab of granite seized him. There was just too damn much history, too many stories needing to be retold. The lost years with Hayden and Barbara might be gone, but he could still rescue his family's heritage. Leaving them the family's homeplace in his will wouldn't have any meaning if they didn't know the struggles so many generations went through to keep it. This time he *was* going to see them! He felt a calm sweep over him, and went back to his easel.

The sun had arced to the western side of the gorge. Must be around three, he thought. Addie Mae would be coming in another hour to clean. There'd be plenty of time for her to finish up before he left for Asheville to teach his evening class.

He ran a critical glance slowly across the paper's pebbly surface, scrutinizing the image of a man fishing in a stream. The watercolor was complete except for the one stroke that would either make it a masterpiece or ruin it. The paper had to be wet but not watery before he dared to scratch in the fisherman's line being flicked back from the stream.

He'd studied the technique in a Winslow Homer at the Boston Museum, but it was risky business. He didn't want to waste any of the antique sheets he had left. Too much pressure and he'd tear the paper, too little and he'd fail to capture the loose rhythm of the line sailing through the air. Success would also depend upon the move being executed at the very moment the paper held the correct degree of moisture.

He grasped the sable end of the brush and placed the fine wood tip on the fisherman's rod and scraped the paper in a steady sweeping motion, squeezing the color away and exposing the white pulp beneath. He took a deep breath, held it a moment, and slowly exhaled. Perfect! He felt his pallid cheeks flush with exhilaration.

He wedged his heels up against the chair legs, folded his arms and stared at the watercolor and couldn't believe he was actually getting away with it. Shortly, the New York gallery would pass off his fourth Winslow Homer.

A muffled noise broke his concentration. More of a thump than the familiar sound of the ancient floorboards contracting. Couldn't be someone in the house. Addie Mae wasn't expected yet. Nor had something fallen on the roof. The sound came from below. He called out. "Addie, is that you?" Why couldn't he remember if he had locked the door? He focused his ears and listened, then his eyes warily traveled over to the opening in the floor, afraid of whom he might see. No one, so far.

Ever since the glimpse of the trail of hawks, a strange apprehension had crept up on him, like death was hovering overhead. He thought the decision to go see his girls had quelled it, but now the same fear he had felt in Vietnam the first time he was shot at gripped him. The back of his hands tingled and his tongue felt twice its size.

Why hadn't he pulled up the ladder and closed the trap door? He was getting sloppy. He didn't dare move, just fixed his stare. Feeling incredibly thirsty, he was suddenly acutely aware that if he were caught, the disgrace would be a nasty way for his girls to find out he was still alive.

The shrill call from a jay startled him and broke the tension. He felt foolish sitting there like a statue. He drew on his hundreds of hours of counseling with VA psychologists and brushed off the notion that anyone could be downstairs. As he began cleaning his palette, the irony, that the pangs of conscience completely disappeared the moment he felt out of danger, flickered in his thoughts.

A slight, self-satisfied smile spread across his gaunt face as he signed the painting with the famous artist's name. For one ironic instant, the crime he had just committed made him feel enriched and worthwhile.

He went over and opened a desk drawer, picked up a notebook lying next to an army issue .45 automatic he'd bought at a gun show, and flipped it open. All the Winslow Homer sales and dates were carefully noted under a column titled *Therapy* and each painting had a code name. He had already decided to call the new one *Flick.* He carefully printed out the name, wondering how much it would bring.

A tinge of guilt crept up on him and he swallowed hard. He'd never done a dishonest thing in his life, and here he was knee-deep in what had to be grand theft. He had weighed the whole scheme in his head a thousand times. In the beginning, all he thought about was his gallery and the talented students who needed him. It wasn't a crime—more of an accomplishment. But, looking back, he could see pride played a part in his decision to attempt the forgeries. He did it because he knew he could. I can pull this off he had told himself. I'm that good.

His uncle Neb did six months in the Federal prison for moonshining back in the twenties, but that never bothered anyone. After all, they were all doing it. Forgery wasn't a "bloody hands" kind of crime either. Who was he really hurting? He'd been a good citizen and stood up for his country, and what did it get him? The loss of his two kids and a life-long battle with Post Traumatic Stress.

Baby killer echoed in his brain. He slammed his fist on the table. He knew the symptoms. He couldn't keep dwelling on the loss of his girls, or the stress would trigger the Vietnam flashbacks. He couldn't let this happen. It would only put him in that damn hyper vigilant survival mode again and he wouldn't get any sleep for weeks.

Why did he always feel like he was hanging on to his sanity by a thread? All he wanted to do when he got out of the hospital was become a recluse. He couldn't stand to have anyone see how damaged he was. His buddy, Johnny Reb, was different. He got the flashbacks, but from the beginning, recognized what it was and dealt with it. That's okay, Hayden told himself. It took me a while, but I'm dealing with it now.

He went over and stared out the window. Guilt was eating him up too. He had to stop the forging. *Flick* had to be the last. He still had two other finished paintings and could sell one a year for the next three years. By then the gallery would be on its feet, and the two former students he was putting through Pratt, out of school. He'd be all set then, and it would be a good time to get to know his girls.

Then he thought about Johnny Reb. How many times had he heard him swear off drinking? Hayden went over to a portfolio carefully tucked away in a corner and put it on the table, then unzipped it and flipped it open. There were four sheets of the old watercolor paper left. Too much temptation. He picked them up and began tearing. First in half, then in shreds. He rummaged around for an empty can and methodically opened all the tubes of ancient paint and squeezed them empty.

There were still a couple left, but he had to be downstairs before Addie arrived to clean. He'd finish them tomorrow. He gathered up the mess and shoved everything into an empty box, then went over and slapped his accounting book closed and placed it back in the drawer. A conditioned reflex made him check his weapon to make sure it was still in firing condition. He picked up the pistol, released the clip with his thumb, and pulled back the slider on top of the barrel, ejecting the bullet from the firing chamber. He returned the bullet to the clip, slammed it into the handle, locked it and put the gun back in the drawer.

This exercise brought on the bizarre feeling of otherworldliness he'd known in Vietnam. *He had to fight this sickening feeling off!* He looked beyond the room through the window at the endless upward sweep of thick, billowy forest clawing its way up the craggy exposed granite face of Round Top. The awesome sight reignited his hopefulness.

A sharp creak startled him. Hayden froze. His eyes darted toward the floor trap. He was stunned to see his old school chum, Freddy Lucas, standing in the stairwell. As the imposing figure stepped into the attic, Hayden searched his brain for some kind of explanation. Just recently, he'd dropped into the gallery. He remembered thinking then that it was strange for Freddy to look him up. He hadn't seen much of him since he was thrown out of Pratt's Fine Arts Department. Just a couple of drinks when they ran into each other in New York after the war. Damn! He should have been more suspicious!

Hayden backed up to hide the painting.

Freddy strolled past him, then turned with a trace of a flourish. "Don't bother, Hayden. I know all about your lucrative little sideline." He shook his head. "I could never quite figure you out, or what that Burroughs broad ever saw in you. You didn't seem right after Vietnam, but I don't know how you ever let her get away. Think of it, Hayden... *all that money.*"

Dumbfounded that Freddy was casually chatting about their ancient rivalry as if it happened yesterday instead of explaining what the hell he was doing there, Hayden stumbled forward and sank into a chair. For the past year, he'd held his breath waiting for the cops to walk in and arrest him, but this scenario never entered his mind.

Freddy took out his glasses, strolled over to the painting and studied it. "Hell, you nailed this one." He lodged the glasses on top of his head and drifted around the room, fingering odd bits as if he were casting about for what he was going to say next.

"The minute I walked into that gallery of yours, all my suspicions were confirmed." He turned around and looked at Hayden. "Face it, pal, a shop that specializes in student work doesn't exactly belong in the high rent district." He continued casually scanning the room. "When I first heard you had a gallery, I figured Liz's old man forked over a bundle to get rid of you."

"I never took a dime from him," Hayden said, instinctively swiping up a hickory nut lying on the floor. He fell silent and tried to take in what was happening. Why no shock or outrage? There had to be some other reason Freddy was stalking him; and he had a strong inkling he wasn't going to like it any more than facing prosecution. Without looking up, he queried, "How did you find where... I mean, how did you get here? I didn't hear a car pull up."

"I parked in town and walked over the bridge." He picked up a tube of paint Hayden had missed and studied it. "Just as I thought." He looked over his shoulder. "Where did you get this old stuff?"

Hayden felt his tension subside, only to be replaced by a creeping assumption that his life was about to take a turn for the worse. He'd heard Freddy had gotten into trouble over the years. "Right there in the Grove Arcade," he answered. "There was a stash of watercolors and paper that must have been at least thirty years old before someone even brought them into the building. Probably sometime in the twenties. When the government took it over in World War II, they must have crated up everything left behind and stashed it in there."

"I don't get it, Hayden. I would never imagine someone like you attempting such a fantastic scam." His face lit up. "To say nothing of pulling it off."

Hayden felt like he was in a confessional—ashamed, but still hoping for a light penance. "Why not? I had the paper; I had the paint." He smiled wryly. "And then there was my VA therapist who kept telling me to find a hobby. So, for the heck of it, I decided to see if I could replicate the paintings of some old master. Homer was a natural. The mountains and lakes around here look a lot like the ones he painted."

Even though Freddy's intrusion in the attic fell just short of house invasion, Hayden decided to continue with this unnatural conversation and suppress the anger mixed with panic brewing in his gut until he knew exactly what he wanted. There was a pretty good chance a fellow artist might go along with him if he understood his reasoning. Somehow, he had to engage him. "After I got out of the VA hospital, I couldn't take all the walking you have to do in New York. I lost part of my foot when I stepped on a landmine, so I came back home to Asheville."

He looked Freddy in the eye and allowed the wry grin to resurface. "They called them toe poppers." He crumbled the dried nut in his hand and slowly ground it to dust as his grin faded. "And let's set the record straight. I didn't *let* Liz go. It was the other way around. Her and old man Burroughs even had the balls to kill me off in the war." He shook his head. "If I had only fought the divorce, they'd never have gotten away with it. By the time I was strong enough to put up a fight, she'd remarried and things had gone too far. I'd only be hurting the kids."

Hayden looked over at Freddy's broad back and wished he knew what he was thinking. His apprehension was growing, but he was starting to feel some relief in finally sharing his secret with someone. "I started teaching painting, and it grew into a gallery. After all, someone had to sell the stuff. Every once in a while, a really talented character walked in the door, and before I knew it, I was finding them commissions, helping them out with their rent... whatever it took. Hell, I even babysat when their shows opened."

Freddy seemed to be listening intently. A good sign. "I operated mostly in vacant stores, but when the government moved their offices out of the Arcade and the Foundation started leasing space, I figured this might be the ticket to make everything work... more traffic, wealthier clientele. But when I couldn't make ends meet, I either had to ratchet up my therapy to a full-blown forgery effort or move back into an empty store." He slapped his knees. "As you can see, forgery won out."

Freddy adjusted his glasses. "I owe you an apology, old boy. I figured they were being done by one of your brilliant students."

"How in the hell did you find out about them?"

"This whole thing was dumb luck. I looked up our old pal, Sal Valentino, when I was at a sales convention in New York last month." He brushed off a patch of cobwebs he had rubbed against that were now clinging to his jacket. "When he let it slip that he'd been selling some Winslow Homers you found in your attic, I started wondering." An eyebrow arched. "*A find like that?* Hell, you would have run right over to Sotheby's and landed a major auction. Why spoon feed them through a small shop like Sal's unless you had a damn good reason?" He smiled broadly. "It didn't take long to put two and two together... and I decided to look you up."

It was beginning to dawn on Hayden where the conversation was heading. "You don't give a rat's ass about the immorality aspect of this thing, do you?"

"Actually, no." Freddy brought a hand to his mouth and feigned a cough. "Now that we've got that little revelation behind us, let's discuss my cut."

"You're nuts if you think you're getting a cent! This money's helping a lot of talented people."

Freddy's face contorted into an exaggerated grimace. "*Talented?* Give me a break. Half the stuff in that second rate gallery of yours is sheer crap."

Except for the sound of a falling leaf scratching across the window, the room fell silent. Hayden labored for the right words. "How... just how can you be so damn callous? You know what it takes to get to the top of your craft. And when you get there, you drown in a sea of desperation trying to get known."

Freddy laughed as he casually rifled through the sketches on the workbench. "That's one thing you won't have to worry about, Hayden. If this little secret of yours gets out, you'll become known soon enough. You don't want that to happen... *now do you?"* He flipped open a portfolio lying on the table and lifted a large piece of tissue. After examining the watercolor for a moment, he peeked underneath. "I see you have two of these little gems stashed away." He put everything back and zipped up the case. "I'm sure Valentino doesn't care who he does business with. I'll take them with me today."

Their eyes locked.

"Take your hands off those paintings."

The threat in Hayden's voice hovered in the air.

"Don't worry, you're gonna get your share."

Hayden exploded from his chair, knocking it over. Freddy swung around and grabbed Hayden's ponytail with his massive paw. Hayden struggled to get free but Freddy overpowered him, twisting him to his knees and slamming him against the wall.

"I've got a hundred pounds on you, buddy. Calm down or I'll make sure the only thing you'll be painting is bathrooms for the State."

Freddy pressed his knee under Hayden's jaw and wedged him tight to the wall. His voice strained. "When I found out you were blowing another fortune on a bunch of losers, I realized how much I detest you." He pressed Hayden tighter, ignoring the vivid color in his face.

Hayden spit out muffled words from his cramped jaw. He could feel Freddy let up a little on his knee, but at the same time pull the ponytail so tight his face contorted in pain. Freddy was pressing close enough now to look him hard in the eye.

"Buddy, I don't know about you, but it's not too late for me to live the good life. This is the second time a fortune has fallen in your lap; and damn it, this time I'm going to get a piece of it."

Hayden closed his eyes to block out the ugly greed in the two cold blue orbs in front of him. An overwhelming yearning to see his girls rose from his gut, mixed with a sickening fear that he wouldn't unless he allowed his paintings to walk out the door. *A conduit for the arts. That's who he was!* If his paintings were sold strictly for money, he'd be nothing but a common thief!

He had to get free long enough to retrieve his .45 from the drawer. He strained his reach and felt along the floor until he recognized a shoe. If he pulled Freddy's leg out from under him, he could throw him off balance; but that was too chancy with the grip the Goliath had on his hair. Still on his knees, his good leg was tangled in the chair. He could bring up his other knee and plant his bad foot solidly on the floor, then thrust himself upward while he wrestled his head free, then make a rush for the gun.

Could he get enough traction from his toeless foot to pull the maneuver off? Everything he stood for was at stake. He had to take the chance. He snapped into the fatalistic mode that had kept him going in Vietnam, and his training took over. With every ounce of strength he had left, he grabbed the wrist of the hand gripping his hair and propelled himself upward.

His weight shifted evenly onto his bad foot. Good. If only he could keep his balance long enough to kick his other foot free of the chair and release Freddy's grip. Suddenly he started to roll forward off the ball of his foot. In a reflex motion, he desperately flexed his missing toes with all his might to keep from being thrust forward, when a horrible split-second of anguish shot through his brain and he remembered his toes were gone.

AS HE WAS TOSSED to the floor, Freddy kept a firm hold of Hayden's ponytail until he felt the snap. Seeing Hayden in a bizarre pose lying next to him, he eyeballed his open palm in disbelief. He scrambled up, grabbed Hayden by the shoulders and tried to rouse him to his feet, then let the limp torso slide to the floor. He had broken Hayden's neck.

He dropped to his knees and put an ear to Hayden's heart, then sank back on his heels. A slew of horrible possible outcomes ran through his head. Who would believe this was an accident? How was he going to explain what happened without admitting to extortion? And if he said Hayden asked him up there, wouldn't that make him look like an accomplice to his forgery racket? But most of all, what about the fortune in paintings?

Just over an hour ago, he was weaving through the mountains happily considering the perfect place to spend an early retirement, compliments of Hayden, and now he was facing the strong possibility that the place might be prison.

He rose and surveyed the room for his glasses and put them on, then knelt down and checked Hayden once again. He was dead.

He had to act fast. Hayden wouldn't have called out unless someone was expected. It wouldn't be a good idea to be seen carrying anything across the river and along the street packed with shops. If the police ever connected him to Hayden's death, his stealing away with the forgeries could easily lead to one conclusion: pre-meditated murder. He was a gambler, but those stakes were too high. He'd return in the dead of the night and retrieve them after everything blew over. He quickly concealed the board with the wet painting in the last slot of the rack on the floor, taking pains to make sure it didn't get a hundred-thousand-dollar scratch.

He climbed down to the third rung of the stairwell ladder, clasped Hayden by the ankles and pulled him close enough to manage slinging him over a shoulder. The ladder led to the back of a closet at the end of the second floor hall. With labored breaths, he carried the dead weight to the landing between the first and second floors.

Positioning the body correctly would be the most important design decision of his life. If suspicions were aroused, the police would order a thorough investigation of the entire cabin, and they'd find his fingerprints all over the attic. With all his arrests, they'd trace the prints to him within hours. He utilized everything he had ever learned about the human torso in his sculpture classes to place the body exactly as if it had fallen and caused a broken neck.

Finished, he stepped over the body and raced back to the ladder. He climbed up, closed the trap door and descended, but the ladder stared out at him. He noticed an old army blanket hanging from a nail on one side of the opening. He could see there was another hole. He found a nail on the other side and secured the blanket over the ladder, then rearranged the clothes on the rod.

He thought he heard something outside. He made his way to the landing, stepped across Hayden's body, and ran down the rest of the stairs to the living room. His heart hammered as he peered out a window. A woman got out of a beat-up pickup with a bucket of cleaning supplies. He darted into the kitchen, opened the back door, and pressed himself against the wall of the side porch to keep from view.

He saw nothing to fear from behind, since the cabin was nestled against the mountain, but he could be seen from the backs of several houses along the river. The only sign of life was a mutt lying on its doghouse. The animal looked up, yawned and lay back down again.

He had better take a chance and get out of there before the woman discovered the body and called for help. Good thing he hadn't left Hayden at the bottom of the staircase where the cleaning lady would have bumped into him the minute she opened the door.

A vacuum cleaner started, giving the place an unexpected aura of normalcy. A stray cat started up the porch steps looking for some scrap to eat, and seeing him, disappeared in a flash. The vacuum sound moved on to a back room of the cabin. It was time to make a break. He went down the stairs, crossed the lawn to the street in long, seemingly relaxed strides, and made his way to the bridge, all the while surveying the darkened windows beyond for searching eyes. He had lucked out. It was the right time to be leaving. Too early for anyone to be coming home from work, and late enough for anyone in one of these shacks to be busy making dinner.

Next, he had to get over the one-lane steel trestle bridge without someone driving across and noticing him. If he could make it to the street, he'd be absorbed into the crowd of tourists crawling all over the mountains at the height of the fall color season. He ventured across the bridge. The roar of the rapids pounding against the gigantic rocks strewn along the river drew his glance long enough for him to see a hawk swoop down and pull a trout out of the water. This deadly demonstration of the eternal struggle for survival validated his actions and calmed the heaving in his breast.

He was anxious to get off the bridge, but if he moved too fast he'd attract attention. He reached the street and walked casually toward his car, ignoring the benches along the sidewalk dotted with tired people doing the mindless things they do on vacation—licking an ice cream cone, chatting with another tourist about where they hailed from. He crossed the street and got into his car, and as he put the key in the ignition, a police car from nearby Lake Lure silently slipped between the stores and disappeared over the bridge.

CHAPTER FOUR

G ROTESQUE GARGOYLES PEERED OUT at Hayden Parks from the building's frieze as she rolled into a parking space next to a sidewalk filled with vendors hawking everything from fresh fruit to fossils. She fed the parking meter quarters while scanning the terra cotta façade dotted with sculpted hearts, an odd partner to the stone heads lurching from the building.

She opened the brass door of the Grove Arcade, and the vaulted glass ceiling looming three stories above the wide terrazzo concourse took her breath away. Wrought iron staircases, spiraling to the upper levels surrounded by iron-railed arched openings, heightened her feelings of anticipation. The only familiar thing among the flamboyant gothic motifs and gargoyles, was the soft Carolina light streaming down from the ceiling and washing across the faux travertine walls.

A café spilled out onto the hall, waking her stomach up to the fact that it hadn't been blessed with food all day. She slipped into the shop, got the attention of the waitress who was leisurely chatting on the phone, and ordered an espresso to go. A few things in the food case tempted her, but she had no time to waste. She glanced at her watch. Five. A good thing her satellite positioning service had guided her off Route 26 and through Asheville so quickly. Hopefully, the gallery was still open.

She was now worried her mother might have managed to reach Russell by phone from the marina. It was equally possible Russell had called her father and turned down his estate, making any encounter with him that much more awkward.

She went out into the concourse and took a moment to gather her courage. The shops were upscale—handcrafted furniture, exotic décor, chic apparel. The kind of elegance that fit in with the art deco ambience of the place. She pulled out the pages from her father's website she'd run off before leaving Pawleys Island, and checked the address for the third time. *Asheville Arts, Grove Arcade.*

She started down one of the majestic halls lined with shops, each looking pretty much like the other. Her eyes focused on a space at the far end with no lavish decorator items flanking its entrance. Recalling the simple, straightforward style of her father's web site, she checked the wing's directory. *Asheville Arts.* She had guessed right. She took a sip of her espresso to buoy her up, and started down the hall. Nervous, yet joyous.

The gallery seemed out of sync with the style of the other shops—ceramics and small sculptures displayed on folding tables draped with fabrics, a counter that looked like an old bar scrounged from some defunct restaurant, and several large rooms with tables and chairs meant to function as classrooms. A mosaic of paintings blanketed every inch of wall space; but the place was neat and orderly, giving her the impression that the artwork was only a by-product of the gallery's main function: teaching.

Inside, a woman appeared from behind a drape. She was small-framed with a compact figure, but her dark, kinky hair and uneven complexion gave her a rough look. Hayden figured she was somewhere in her fifties, and noticed an air of resignation about her. She could see she hadn't bothered with makeup, and her long linen skirt and loose raglan top were rumpled just shy of looking like she'd slept in them.

The woman's brown eyes peered at her from red swollen hollows. It appeared as if she had been crying. Hayden felt her stare as the woman looked her up and down, her glance pausing for a moment on the diamond and ruby-studded hummingbird brooch on her lapel.

You're Hayden Taylor Parks, aren't you?"

"Yes. How did you know?"

"Your mother told the Troopers you were on your way up here. She wants you to call her."

Fear gripped Hayden. "Something's wrong, isn't it?"

The woman handed her a piece of paper with a phone number. "Your mother's waiting at a marina for your call."

Hayden fumbled around in her purse for her cell phone and dialed.

Her mother answered on the first ring. "It's a good thing you told Barbara where you were going. We got a call from the North Carolina State Troopers. Your father's dead."

Hayden clutched the phone to her ear with both hands. Tears flooded her face. She could hear her mother talking, but the words didn't register. She must be dreaming! Her father was finally going to shower her with all the love she'd ever craved! Validate her existence! Things were going to be different. She was going to be whole. Complete.

"Stop that, darling. You don't even remember him. Pull yourself together, find a hotel, and start back in the morning. I want you out of there. Russell's going to take care of everything."

"Mother, what do you mean, take care of everything?"

"I mean exactly that. I want this thing hushed up. We haven't heard from that man in thirty years. Why is this all of a sudden being dumped in our lap?"

Hayden turned so the woman wouldn't hear, and whispered in the phone. "Mother, death *is* all of a sudden."

Hayden stood pressing the phone against her ear even though the call ended moments ago. Why hadn't she headed for the mountains yesterday when she felt that terrible foreboding? Regret collided with a forlorn feeling of being cheated. Her gaze clouded over as she asked the woman, "When did it happen?"

"Around three this afternoon."

Two hours! She missed him by two hours!

The woman's eyes narrowed into slits. "I tried to find yours or your sister's address to give the Troopers, but the only one your father had in his book was your mother's. Someone at the house got a hold of her." A mournful cry drained from her. "From what the Troopers said, she's planning on nothing beyond a cremation." Her tone turned defiant. "That wouldn't be right. He was loved."

The woman's face distorted into a mask of grief and she sobbed openly. Hayden put her coffee down and folded her arms around her. "Don't worry. I'm not going to let that happen."

The woman slowly drew away and dabbed her cheeks with a tissue drawn from her pocket, the wrinkles around her squinted eyes telegraphing incredulity. Her voice softened. "You're exactly what I had imagined. All the Taylors had blond hair. You look a lot like your dad. Especially the eyes. His were that grayish blue too." She blew her nose. "There's a nice little parlor on Rutherford Street. Do you want to give them a call?"

"Yes. Right away." There was something about her mother's rush to wipe her father's death away with a quick cremation that seemed too much like a conspiracy. He had reached out, and they had been close enough to touch! Don't worry, Daddy, she said to herself, I'm not going to let her lackeys sweep you under the rug.

"By gracious, I'm forgetting my manners," the woman said. "I'm Judy McDowd. I've worked for your father since he got his first place." She motioned toward Hayden's coffee. "Honey, you want to come into the office and sit down and finish that?"

"Right now, we need to call the undertaker."

Judy seemed to respond to the urgency in Hayden's voice. She pulled the curtain aside and led Hayden into a room stuffed with file cases, cartons and the sort of odds and ends that could stretch, hang, paste or hold up just about anything. She flipped through the telephone book and scribbled a number. "Don't you be worryin' none, honey. The undertaker will see to everything." She pulled out a chair and brushed it off. "I don't want to see that white suit of yours get spoiled none."

"When did you find out?" Hayden asked.

"The Trooper called around three-thirty."

Russell's plane had probably landed by four. Hayden was pretty sure her mother had already been in touch with him. She checked her watch again. Five-thirty. Could he have had her father cremated that fast?

Anything was possible. Her mother would move heaven and earth to get her way. Hayden brushed off the tears drying on her makeup. She had to get hold of the undertaker fast. This thing was going to be done right if *she* had to move heaven and earth. An image of a small white casket surfaced in her mind. She pressed her eyelids tight for a moment, took a deep breath and dialed.

Judy stood by as Hayden made the initial arrangements with the undertaker. He promised to call the morgue in Rutherfordton, then go get her father immediately, and let her know the minute he had him in the funeral parlor. Hayden made an appointment to select a coffin in the morning, dropped the phone in the cradle and slumped back in the chair.

Judy burst out sobbing again.

Exhausted, Hayden put an elbow on the desk and sank her head onto her fist. "I'm so sorry, Judy. Were you and my father...?"

Judy waved her tissue in the air. "No. No. Nothing like that. We knew each other since we were kids in Chimney Rock. That's all." She shuffled through some papers on the desk. "Here's an obituary I wrote to give to the newspapers tonight. I don't think I can rightly stand to explain about your father to another person." Her face twisted into a pained expression and she sobbed openly for a moment, then blew her nose. She handed Hayden two numbers and pointed to a fax machine in the corner.

"You can use that."

Hayden started to get up, then slid back down. She'd better read it first. She looked up at Judy. "I'd like to put something in it about a church service."

"It's already in there. I couldn't stop myself from takin' the liberty of callin' the Chimney Rock Baptist Church. Most of his family's buried there. I know he would like that."

This was the first time Hayden had heard her father spoken

47

of with love and respect. "That was so good of you, Judy. I can't tell you how much it means to me, knowing that if I hadn't come, he would have left this world remembered by those who cared about him."

"If I hadn't up and done it, his Vietnam buddies would have. They're a real brotherhood, you know. Specially the guys that have been wounded."

Hayden found the mellow cadence of the woman's voice soothing, and imagined her father's sounded the same, for underlying the pattern of her speech tinged with a Western North Carolina accent, was the message: *Don't sweat it.*

"The evening students will start arriving soon. There was no way to reach everyone this afternoon, and some are coming from pretty far away, so I got someone to come up from Waynesville to teach your dad's class tonight. What else could I do? After tomorrow's papers come out, everybody should know." A stack of bracelets rattled softly as she swept a fluff of hair from her face. She seemed uneasy, as if dreading where the conversation was heading.

Hayden picked up a small statuette of *The Thinker* from the desk and slowly ran her finger along the figure's back. Without looking up, she asked, "How did it happen?"

The woman put her hands in her large, deep pockets, and sank back against the wall. Her eyes lingered on the ceiling for a moment. "Nobody really knows for sure. He was at his house in the mountains. It's only a half-hour away. Addie Mae, his housekeeper, found him. Evidently, he fell down the stairs and broke his neck. Probably lost his balance."

She looked at Hayden. "Maybe because part of his foot was missing. It must have happened just before Addie came in. She's pretty shook up. She was questioned by the Lake Lure police and then the Sheriff from Rutherfordton." Judy shook her head. "Poor thing. I can see her now. She must have acted like a cornered rat."

Something about that statement bothered Hayden. "What makes you say that?"

"You'd have to know Addie. She gets defensive if you ask

her what time it is."

"Where's this house?"

"Chimney Rock."

"Didn't he have any siblings?"

"Just a younger brother that went missing in Vietnam. That's why Hayden... your father... enlisted. He went over thinking he could find him." Judy took out a fresh tissue and blew her nose, then pulled a cell phone from her pocket and scanned through the numbers. "I've got to make a call before I start getting the classrooms ready."

Alone in her father's office, sitting at his desk, Hayden felt his eerie presence. The desktop supplies thoughtfully positioned in a row and neatly printed *Post Its* placed in a straight line on the file cabinet drew a picture of a methodical man, in contrast to the clutter stacked all around the room. A sudden impulse made her collect them and put them in her purse.

Before reading the obituary, she ignored her long-standing rule of not smoking in public, and lit a cigarette, then took a sip of her coffee and read. *Hayden A. Taylor, 59, went home to be with the Lord on Thursday, October 16, 2003. Born in Chimney Rock, North Carolina, he was the eldest child of Hayden and Gertie Mae Taylor... graduate of Pratt Institute... served honorably with the 23rd Americal Infantry Division.* His war record included receiving a Purple Heart and a Silver Star for Valor. *For the past twenty-two years, owner and operator of Asheville Arts located in the Grove Arcade since its reopening in 2001.* A picture of her father began to form, filling in a vacuum that had existed in the back of her mind since she was a kid.

A hum of murmurings rose. She picked up a pen, quickly added hers and Barbara's name as sole survivors, faxed it, then pushed aside the curtain and went out into the gallery. The expressions on the faces peering at her ran the gamut from pained sympathy to blatant curiosity. They obviously knew who she was.

Hayden suspected they were waiting for her to say something and she didn't want to disappoint them. She looked at Judy.

"This here is Hayden's daughter, Hayden Taylor Parks. She's

made arrangements."

"Yes, calling hours are at the Smithfield Funeral Home the day after tomorrow from six to nine," said Hayden, quickly adding, "… and the gallery will be closed tomorrow until Monday."

At least half the crowd drifted out of the gallery stunned and in tears, with Judy shepherding the rest into their classrooms. The hum dissipated, and Hayden blindly skimmed over the art as she slowly moved from table to table feeling like she was trudging through deep water.

Suddenly the door to the concourse flew open and a breathless young man rushed in. He clutched the back of his neck and looked like he'd rather be somewhere else as he approached her.

Hayden managed a smile.

He came up to her and glanced around the room before finally looking her straight in the eyes. "I know you're in a tough situation right now. Your dad dying and all."

Hayden felt uncomfortably overdressed when he brushed back a thick shock of dark hair from his forehead and exposed his frayed cuffs.

"I hate like heck to be asking for anything from you right now, but I brought my wife and new baby home from the hospital this morning and I'm really strapped."

"Did my father owe you money?"

He tossed his head and looked sideways at her. "No. No. Nothing like that. Didn't Judy explain things to you?"

"No. Actually, I just got here."

"I know. She called me a few minutes ago and told me to hurry right over." The young man pursed his lips and looked around the room, seemingly gathering courage to go on.

"Judy called you and told you I was here?"

"Uh huh."

Hayden glanced into a classroom and eyed Judy leaning against a wall staring back at her. Hayden didn't like that she was being set up, but the mention of a new baby gave his plea an overriding urgency that she understood. Noticing the man's white knuckled fists taut against his legs, she motioned for him to follow her to a bench. She sat down and patted the seat, regretting she had put on so much jewelry.

"Come, tell me what you need."

He sat down, back rigid, and couldn't seem to stop bouncing one of his legs. "Your dad's been giving me three hundred dollars every week and I was supposed to pick up a check tonight."

"You're a student of his?"

"I was. Right now I'm working on a commission he got me from the Brevard VFW. It's a Vietnam monument. They're still raising funds to pay for it, but Hayden... I mean your father... was paying me up front so the project could go forward right away." His brow wrinkled and his gaze intensified. "I've talked to the guy heading up the committee and he's going to try to see if they can break into another fund so I can keep working on it. But right now, I'm in a real bind. Heck, I need money for groceries."

"What's your name?"

"Randy. Randy Smith."

"How many more weeks is this going to take?"

"The clay model should be ready for the committee's final approval in a month, and then there's the casting and erection. Not much beyond the first of the year."

Hayden made some quick calculations in her head. She didn't know how much the funeral was going to add up to, but whatever it was she would have to put it on her charge card. She had a nagging suspicion it might be over her limit, but in that case she would split it between two. Luckily, being the first of the month, her husband had just put her household allowance in her account.

She opened her purse, wrote a check and tore it out. "Here, Randy. This is for a month." She reached over and patted his hand. "Let me know if the committee doesn't come through, and I'll see what I can do."

The young man sank into the bench and she noticed his tension evaporate, giving him a boyish appearance.

"I can't tell you how much this means to me. There are two other towns that might hire me to do monuments. They're just waiting to see how this one turns out." He turned toward Hayden and rubbed his rough, cracked hands together. "It's been a real uphill battle getting established. If it wasn't for someone like your dad, and now you, I wouldn't be able to work at sculpture full time. I find a lot of work doing cemetery monuments and I'd be honored to do one for your dad. I wouldn't expect to be paid."

"I'd like that. But I couldn't allow you to do it for nothing."

"I'll put some of my ideas down on paper for you to look at. I'll let you pay for the stone, but that's it."

He rose, folded the check and put it in his wallet. "Thanks again. This means a lot."

"What's the baby's name?"

His face brightened. "Beth."

"Give her a kiss for me."

Hayden went back into the office and said a little prayer that Beth would grow up to be strong and healthy. Then, she sat down at her father's desk, pulled out a cigarette and started to light up when she noticed the butt floating in the leftover coffee. She put the cigarette back, tossed the pack in her purse, and retrieved the stack of *Post Its.*

All short messages in a precise print. Mostly appointments. Either her father going to see someone or someone coming to see him. One said, *Go see Johnny Reb,* and had a telephone number. The one saying *Call Valentino about Flick if it turns out ok* seemed odd.

She'd walked into the gallery a complete outsider, and now it appeared she was not only on the inside, but at the helm. Writing the check to Randy had been like an acceptance of ownership, and now she couldn't resist poking around a little. She wished Barbara were there. How many times when they were kids had they talked for hours in the dark after they were put to bed about what their father might have been like.

The top drawer of the cabinet had files with names neatly printed on the tabs. She looked to see if one had hers, and when none did, got that left out feeling again. Each folder was for an artist. She opened one and flipped through photographs of landscapes done in oil. They weren't bad, but not really that good either. She could see what the artist wanted to do, but they had-n't achieved enough depth. Maybe the shadows weren't deep enough.

She heard the hum of voices again. Probably the gallery was closing down. She looked up and saw Judy in the doorway, slumped against the casing with her arms folded. Hayden resented the squeeze play the woman had just inflicted on her, but then there were all the kind words she'd said about her father.

"Well? What did you do about Randy?" Judy asked.

"What could I do? I gave him the money."

Hayden's answer amazed herself. This morning, the bizarre red-orange sunrise seemed like an omen, but in her wildest imagination she couldn't have thought up the events of this day. But right now she needed to get to the pressing issue of her father's finances before some clerk handed back her credit card with the somber news she'd exceeded her limit.

"Judy, I didn't appreciate being blindsided like that. I want to help, but that means you're going to have to level with me. Can we start off with what you know about my father's finances?"

"I worked for that man for over twenty years and know nothing except that the gallery doesn't bring in enough for him to do the things he was doing. I figured he had some kind of inheritance." Her expression turned sheepish. "Or maybe getting money from your side of the family."

Hayden narrowed her eyes and thought. No. If her mother had been giving him money, she would have thrown it in her face by now. She looked at Judy and spoke with determination. "Do you know who his lawyer is?"

Judy foraged around the office and produced a will with a letter from the attorney.

Hayden studied it. Her eyes glanced up. "Where are his books?"

Judy shrugged her shoulders. "I know nothing about that end of the business. All I ever did was make the deposits."

Hayden couldn't help thinking she didn't know that much about her own finances either, other than her grandfather leaving her a huge endowment. Money was never an issue. She'd just ask her mother and funds appeared in her checking account. Her grandfather's will made her mother its executrix and didn't state his gift in millions, just thousands of shares. She couldn't imagine her mother turning her down; but then she'd never challenged her before.

In spite of a lurking suspicion that money *could* become a problem, cocooned in this cluttered office with people and things her father had surrounded himself with, she couldn't resist fanning the spark of coming alive again that ignited the minute she walked in the place. She tapped the will on the palm of her hand. "We know his bank and his lawyer. That's a start."

CHAPTER FIVE

O NE OF HIS OLD INJURIES having its sweet revenge woke Ben Beckham. He rolled over and gave the football-shaped clock his daughter had given him for Father's Day a quick glance. Just as he thought. Six-thirty. He flicked on the lamp and eyed the vodka left in the glass on the table. He started to reach for it, then fell back grimacing. *That damn pinched nerve!* Fourteen years in the pros as a wide receiver had done a number on his neck. The doctors had operated on it twice, but he could hardly expect them to make up for all the years of abuse.

The little goldfinch that had a nest in the tree next to the house let out a trill. He wondered how soon it would be heading south, and envied it just like he used to begrudge the baseball players who were lucky enough to go to Florida for the winter. He rolled out of bed onto the floor and grunted through twenty punishing pushups.

Stepping out of the shower, he grabbed a towel and caught sight of himself in the mirror. Not bad for forty. He'd hung on to his six-pack and still had the toned look of an athlete. He wiped himself down and smiled wryly at the illusion, remembering the X-ray technician who, seeing all the chipped vertebrae, metal pins and healed cartilage, asked if he'd been in an auto wreck. Looking back, he'd always felt indestructible. Either he wouldn't get hurt, or if he did, they'd fix him up.

Finished in the bathroom, he put on some briefs and flipped through a drawer looking for a shirt. He selected one of his old favorites, a white polo with the Giants' logo on it, then reached for a pair of slacks hanging on the bedpost. The sound of students shuffling through the leaves on the path near the house drifted in. Their conversation was friendly, but tentative like everyone's is when the semester is just getting started. A voice trailed off, telling him someone whizzed by on a bike.

He went around the room picking up clothes from the floor and chairs and stuffed them into the laundry bin in the closet, then fluffed up the quilt. After putting on the navy sports jacket hanging on the back of his late wife's favorite maple rocker, he ran a hand along its smooth headrest and got churned up in the same old turmoil. He didn't belong in this place any more; but leaving would make Jenny a part of his past and he needed to hang on to her a little longer—but it was like the other team was running out the clock.

He needed more time to transfer all his wife's cherished handcrafted furnishings and ceramics to his daughter's custody. That was the one thing he knew Jenny would want, even though she'd never gotten around to asking him. In fact, he reflected, she never got around to asking him for much of anything in the nineteen years they were married.

He gave the room a fleeting inspection, and picked up the glass and took it into the kitchen where he opened the dishwasher and placed it next to six others. Tonight, they'd be washed and put away by Rosita, and he'd be all set for the coming week.

The kitchen table had been pushed up against a large window on the sunny side of the room. A sheet of plastic lay between its precious cherry surface and dozens of pans and cookie sheets dotted with plastic cups of various sizes and colors. He inspected each container, and not finding any sprouted seeds, picked up the spray bottle and gave them enough of a misting to keep them from drying out.

October was way too early to be starting seedlings indoors.

Before it was time to put them into the ground, they'd have to be repotted, and end up leggy and jammed onto every windowsill in the house. Right now, however, all he could picture was the spectacular drift of delphiniums he'd seen at the Ryder Cup last September.

He opened the door that led to the back kitchen entrance where he kept his supplies and flipped through some seed packets until he found the one he was looking for. He blew in enough air to puff it open, and just as he remembered, a couple of seeds were solidly wedged in the fold at the bottom. He took a plastic cup out of the cupboard, scooped up some dirt from a bag on the floor and carried it, along with the seed packet, to the kitchen sink.

Once the dirt was wet enough, he placed the cup on the counter and carefully tore open the packet until the tiny black seeds were exposed. With the tip of a steak knife, one at a time, he carefully lifted them off and laid them on the dirt, then took the cup to the table and pushed things around until he could squeeze it in. Maybe he'd get one more delphinium.

Ever since his days at Penn State, uppers, steroids and alcohol were a fact of life; and in the pros, he added every painkiller known to man—including gorgeous, easy women. When a third concussion abruptly ended his football career, the loss of that money rolling in was no big deal. Jenny had handled their finances from the beginning, so he really hadn't gotten his hands on that much to splash around. There'd been plenty enough in their portfolio to live more than just comfortably for the rest of their lives and still leave a hefty estate to their daughter.

Overcoming his addiction to the high that occurred when he ran out on the field to the screams of sixty-thousand hyped up fans, however, had been a problem. This sheer adoration that made him feel like a gladiator in the Roman Coliseum always made the pain he knew he was going to endure worth it. But, what he missed most was the camaraderie among his teammates who shared the awesome pain and glory of the games along with him; losing that dealt a blow to his spirit he'd never get over.

Football had been his whole life since he was twelve and its sudden disappearance had left him helpless. Jenny took over where his coach left off. Trying to make a new life, he found himself following her around like a puppy.

During that horrible first summer without football practice, they were loading up on shrubs at a nursery and a sign caught his eye. *$1 a Pot.* After spending a small fortune landscaping their larger new house on the Warren Wilson College campus just outside Asheville, he couldn't figure out what in the world would cost only a dollar a pot, and decided, whatever it was, they were going to get plenty of it. When he pointed them out to Jenny, she told him not to bother since they were just damaged perennials that nobody wanted. That offhand comment unleashed all the empathy he had ever harbored for the broken down and discarded—including himself.

He commandeered a flatbed wagon and loaded on every last one of them. He didn't know a damn thing about gardening, but he was going to bring them back to health if it killed him. That was six years ago, and now his garden was spilling over all its boundaries.

The refrigerator yielded nothing that could be passed off as breakfast. Just a near empty carton of orange juice, a bottle of olives, a fresh jar of white onions, and a couple bottles of vodka. He'd pick something up at the cafeteria before he headed out to class. He opened his wallet and pulled out a fifty and tossed it on the kitchen table. He imagined what his illegal must think about the waste when she dusted his seven rarely used rooms, then he pictured his mother's haggard face after a day of cleaning for the summer residents on Saranac Lake. He reopened his wallet and threw down another ten.

A gust of wind brought a sweep of translucent golden maple leaves cascading from above as he made his way down the lane through the campus he'd been lured to by his wife. Jenny had been teaching ceramics there for several years before he was washed up in football. They'd led separate lives most of the time back then, but wherever the sensitive artist he fell in love with on the Penn State campus and their beloved daughter, Heather, lived was where he always called home.

The first fall he was out of football almost killed him. Jenny saved him by getting him a job teaching sculpture at the college, even though his college records failed to mention he earned his degree in Fine Arts by mostly posing. But that's the way things were back then—easy courses that you never really had to attend, expensive gifts from alumni, a new car every year... whatever it took to keep their star athletes happy and stadium seats filled.

Sculpture and ceramics were lumped together at Warren Wilson. With Jenny being one of the foremost ceramists east of the Mississippi, as well as head of the department, the college took him in. There were only three sculpture classes needing to be taught, and it didn't hurt that he was a three time pro bowler and had a coveted ring that could be worn to all the important fund-raising functions.

He'd picked up a lot about teaching since then, mostly from Jenny; but with her gone and he the only faculty member with nothing more than a BA, his position was pretty much a joke. With his contract as a part-time teacher expiring at the end of the semester, it was time to do some serious thinking. He was sure the Dean was praying for the day he'd walk in and tell him he was leaving.

One offer had come in. A faculty member who was on the board of a local land conservancy had approached him about considering an open position as a corporate fund raiser. It had to be his career in the pro league again. He guessed that was the fate of a broken-down athlete with nothing much to offer but name recognition. He'd agreed to meet with them, but the only thing he knew for sure was that he was never going to leave the mountains of Western North Carolina.

He made his way through the throngs of students milling outside the building that housed the college's two dining centers. His two-hundred-pound, six-foot-three physique agilely dodged the dozens of backpacks littering the floor on his way into the upstairs cafeteria.

He smiled inwardly when it was his turn to be served and a student with two rings in his lip dished him out bacon and eggs.

Warren Wilson's triad program, requiring each student to spend twenty hours a semester working for the college, brought them into every function of the school. The place didn't look the same as it would have with a commercial maintenance staff; instead of a cold institutional look, it had a friendlier lived-in feeling, like someone's house when it wasn't all gussied up for visitors.

He tossed some toast onto his plate at a food carousel and began to make his way over to a table in the corner. Someone called out his name and he looked over his shoulder. The three faculty members he used to run with every morning before Jenny got sick were sitting at a table smiling at him. He didn't feel like he wanted company, but gave them a broad grin, went over and pulled out a chair and sat down anyway.

"Have you heard about Hayden?" one of them asked.

Ben nodded.

"The paper said he broke his neck in a fall."

"Is that the guy who runs the gallery downtown?" another one of them asked.

"Yes," Ben responded.

"He was really good to the school," said a woman who taught environmental studies. "We could always count on him to put up a couple of students when we had a two-day rock climbing session and there wasn't enough room at my place in Bat Cave. The paper said he had two daughters. I was kind of surprised. I'd of sworn he'd never been married." She looked over at Ben. "I understand he took in a lot of student work for his gallery. I wonder what's going to happen with that."

Not getting a response, she continued. "They're going to have a visitation for him in Asheville tonight. A couple of us are planning on going. You want to come?"

It had been over a year since Jenny got sick and he stopped running with them, and he was starting to feel melancholy. He said he'd let her know, then got up and told them he had to get to his class.

On the way to the sculpture studio he thought about what might happen to the gallery. It was an institution among the local artists and teachers—one of the only places that gave those who hadn't quite mastered their craft, and who probably never would, a place to at least show what they *had* achieved. An actual sale would be icing on the cake. Mercifully, the worst pieces were usually hung at knee level.

Ben mulled over the operation. A downtown location was good. Lots of artsy traffic all year round. But the mix was wrong. No transition to higher quality work, and too much high rent space allotted to classes. The gallery would have to be moved to a building with a second floor for teaching. What was he thinking? He'd have to get really invested in this thing! No. It wasn't the right fit. He had to find something, but that wasn't it.

When he arrived at the small building that contained both the sculpture and ceramic studios, a couple of students were working outside in the ceramic shed and a pottery class was in progress inside. He puttered around his half of the building for a while, then leaned in the doorway and watched the students working at their wheels. He had loved sharing this space with Jenny. The building was really alive then, with the joking back and forth between the two of them spilling over to the students.

It had all happened so fast. All the stories he heard of women surviving breast cancer buoyed him at first; but she never really went into remission. He tried every technique he had used to win in football and encouraged her to practice visualization of victory over and over again. His last desperate attempt at it ended with the both of them clinging to each other crying, he mostly for the wasted years.

FEELING HIS CELL PHONE VIBRATE, he pulled it out of his pocket and glanced at the name. It was Ricky Jensen, one of his old teammates.

"Well, are you comin' or not?"

"I'm gonna pass, Ricky. Won't be the same without Jenny."

"You gotta get yourself out of this slump, Bud."

"Next year."

"Come on. Everyone's dying to see you. Thursday night's going to be great. You're one of the only guys that won't be at the '86 reunion. Remember those days? I can still hear the roar when you sacked Testaverde at the goal line and we captured the championship! Damn, those were good days!"

Funny how he could always remember the sound of the crowd; every roar was different. But that day, that glorious day, Ben knew he'd connected with his bride-to-be in a way nothing else could have. She was swallowed up in the crowd, but he knew she felt what he felt at that very moment and it would define their marriage for all time. She'd always understand what football meant to him and accept whatever it brought.

"JoePa's looking forward to seeing you."

"Tell the old man not this time, Ricky."

"Aw! Come on, WooWoo! We need you to attract all the babes! Bobby's wife told me you're still the same handsome dog! You know she was the one who gave you that nutty nickname. It used to kill me the way all the cheerleaders sang out *Woooo Woooo* when you appeared on the practice field. It must have been all that blond hair of yours. I envied you, Man."

"Well, you won't have to too much longer. The gold is slowly turning gray."

"Remember Sonja when we were in school? What a pair she had! No wonder Bobby never ran around."

Ben winced. He wished he could do it all over and spend that time with Jenny.

Ricky was the big communicator on the old Penn State '86 team. Never married, he considered them his family. Sports, in some ways, is like war—a shared experience that creates a common bond that will never be broken. Ben was going to miss seeing him and being at the homecoming with all the adoration. There was nothing like it. When he ran onto the field with all the letterman from past seasons, the roar of the crowd always made him feel like he was there again.

"Ricky, why don't you just fly down here next week and we can knock off some beers together."

"*Asheville?* You gotta be kidding."

"Ricky, I'm makin' history here. My garden's got a Mexican sage ten feet wide."

"Geez Louise! Have you gone gay on us? Now I know we've got to get you out of there. It's bad enough you're doing that sculpture thing, but now they've got you tiptoeing through the tulips for Pete's sake!"

Ben laughed.

"Seriously, Ben, I had lunch with your daughter last week. Heather's worried about you, Bud."

"I'm fine. Nobody needs to worry."

The conversation ended with Ben promising to get together with Ricky in New York when he went to spend Christmas with Heather, a tactic they used to escape from a house without Jenny. Maybe that was the reason his daughter never managed to get to Asheville, Ben thought. Could be why she kept urging him to sell the house and find a place in the mountains. He'd buy a paper today, and see what was out there.

CHAPTER SIX

"**I**T'S A GOOD THING MOTHER decided not to come to Dad's funeral," said Barbara. "It would have been a little tricky introducing her as the wife he dumped."

Hayden sat on a bench at the foot of the hotel bed in a lacey slip, smoothing lotion on her feet and legs. She didn't listen to Barbara except for a few snippets. *It was so kind of Jack and George to see us through this unexpected family crisis... Mother made the right choice. It definitely would have been in bad taste for her to come.* Hayden knew Barbara was just reasoning things out so everyone saved face, and her silence was meant to ratify her sister's judgments.

With the drapes pulled aside, the distinctly recognizable view of Asheville covered the window like a breathtaking mural in an upscale Fifth Avenue travel bureau. A spectacular line-up of art deco and neo-classic architecture stood unabashedly in front of tier after tier of hazy blue mountain peaks looming in the far-off distance. The brash contrast of modern hardscape against the millennia-old titans, gave the whole scene an exhilarating edginess.

Hayden took the lid off a slim box lying on the bench next to her and lifted out a sheer pair of dark hose from underneath the tissue. She ran a hand inside one and carefully stretched it over

64

her foot, then diligently eased the stocking over her shapely calf; she repeated the procedure for the other foot while Barbara rattled on about the visitation at the funeral parlor.

Finished with the stockings, Hayden slipped her feet into a pair of black patent leather, strapped spike heels, then put on the black silk suit Barbara had brought, her sister's disjointed remarks floating through the air unchallenged.

Hayden went over to the mirror and fluffed up her hair, then reached into a large cardboard box with ornate gold leafing on the lid and carefully pulled out a large rimmed black felt hat with a pleated ribbon and black silk rose. She and her mother had shopped all over Savannah for the right one for her grandfather's funeral. They'd needed these trappings to put on his funeral rite in the proud tradition of the South. The outfit probably wasn't going to be right for the small mountain community of Chimney Rock, but everything—the suit, the hat, the shoes—were symbols of her Deep South heritage, and when she stood next to her father's casket, she intended to do him proud in the tradition from whence she came. It was who she was. It would be honest and show respect.

Barbara nodded approval. "You look outrageously beautiful."

It was the kind of comment that normally meant nothing to Hayden. Not this time. She handed Barbara a string of pearls, then turned around so she could fasten them.

"You gonna be all right?" asked Barbara.

The question went unanswered. Hayden was used to her older sister fussing over her. More so than her mother. They automatically settled into that relationship every time something troublesome occurred, as if that was the way it was supposed to be. Barbara was childless, but understood Hayden's heartbreak and had been of great comfort.

And now the appearance of the lost but not forgotten father put them in the same position as when they were children, with Barbara consolingly going along with Hayden's longings for a relationship with him. That was the big difference between the two sisters: one lived in the present and the other saw the world from the prism of the past.

The necklace fastened, Hayden went over to the dresser, opened her purse and pulled out her checkbook. "Barb, I need you to get me some money." She tore out a deposit slip. "Put it in there."

"How much are we talking about?"

"Twenty thousand. More if you can get it."

Barbara's mouth dropped open. "Sister Girl, are you going to do something crazy? Jack and George already took care of the funeral." She planted her fists on her hips. "Damnation! I should have known we were heading for trouble the way you were questioning everyone at the funeral home."

Hayden went over and snapped her suitcase closed knowing full well Barbara would come around.

"I guess I can tell Mom I need a new car or something."

"The pricier, the more she'll go for it."

"That's easy for you to say. What'll I do when she stumbles on to the fact that it's not sitting in my garage."

Smoothing down her skirt, Hayden turned her back to the mirror and gave herself a final inspection.

"Did you notice the way all those people were looking at us like we were freaks at the visitation?" asked Barbara.

"Well, aren't we? Hosting a funeral for someone we never even laid eyes on."

Barbara's eyes rested on her sister. "Hayden, look at me. You're all fired up."

"I am, aren't I? And damn if it doesn't feel good."

"You're going to do something, aren't you? *I know you Hayden.* You're scaring me."

"I'm scaring myself, Barb." She pulled her suitcase off the bed. "Jack and I will meet you and George in Chimney Rock."

"Oh no, you don't. *I'm* riding with *you.* The boys can go in their cars. We've got to talk."

ONCE THEY GOT OUT of Asheville and past the plethora of strip centers and convenience stores on the edge of town, 74A ran through rolling pastoral land caressed on all sides by the far off peaks of the Blue Ridge Mountains. While Barbara built up the courage to ask the question hanging in the air, fragments of small talk drifted from the two sisters as the BMW coup approached the mountain range ahead. *I'm glad I got to see what Dad looked like. Not at all the way I imagined. It was worth coming up here just for that. He wasn't as tall as I had thought, but he looked wiry. I could see he was handsome when he was young. His features were fine, but very masculine. I wonder why Mom never showed us any pictures.*

A FOREST CAVERN, embracing the ten-mile Hickory Nut Gorge, loomed ahead, a route carved out before the Indians arrived by bison herds so numerous it took days for them to pass through. The early Cherokee and the Catawba considered this monolithic chasm sacred and never attacked each other while passing through it.

The shaded grotto swallowed the car as it started climbing toward the escarpment. Gigantic poplars, oaks and maples spread their overreaching limbs ten stories overhead, making Barbara feel like they were entering a womb. Occasionally, the sun was able to break through the forest and penetrate the changing leaves—vivid stained glass windows among the undergrowth. Giant drifts of rich green rhododendron hugged the colorful leaf strewn Persian carpet of a road, anchoring the whole spectacular illumination to the earth.

Barbara reluctantly pulled her gaze away from the stunning scene. "Why don't you see if you can pull in somewhere and let me drive?"

"I'll be okay. I'm going to get over this fear of heights if it kills me."

"Let's not fool around, Hayden. Remember the last time we were in the mountains?"

"Yeah. I was *fourteen.*"

Barbara kept looking over her shoulder at the cars behind them, tapping her nails on the armrest before finally asking the question that had been on her mind since Hayden gave her the deposit slip. "You're not coming home, are you?"

Hayden, who seemed to be focusing intently on the road,

didn't answer her.

"Girl, you've seen what Dad looked like. His gallery. What else is there? I know I'm starting to sound like Mother, but we need to let Russell take care of all the grimy details."

Barbara noticed Hayden biting her lip as she took the second steep hair-pin curve. "I can see from the way you're driving you won't even make it back to Asheville."

Hayden's long and deep breaths were audible. "I'm not... going back..." She took another hairpin curve. "... to Asheville."

"Good Lord! Don't tell me you're going to stay at his place in the mountains." Barbara scrunched forward to get a good look at Hayden, her sister's face a study in concentration. "Do you have any idea how weird this is? You know Mom's going to have a melt down when you tell her."

Barbara caught Hayden's eyes flash over to her, and she knew she was going to have to do it. "*Great.* I hope you're not counting on me to break it to Jack, too."

"I'll do that before he leaves."

Barbara sat back and pulled a candy bar from her purse. "Okay. Let's have it. All twenty thousand dollars worth."

"Barb, I might not even spend the money. I just want to settle Dad's accounts and bring his business to a close with honor. He had a lot of financial responsibilities, and yet, I don't know where the money's going to come from." There was a long pause as Hayden took a three-hundred-and-sixty-degree curve. "I went to see his lawyer right after I made the funeral arrangements, and he couldn't tell me much. He's arranging for me to get into his bank account. You might have to sign some papers too, but I don't think there's that much there... from the gallery anyway."

"Hayden, this is your sister you're talking to. We both know there's a lot more to this than his business affairs."

NIKKI WESTERLY HAD BEEN up since six preparing her potatoes and beans for the funeral luncheon. She'd been doing it for five years now. Had to have all the ingredients on hand for her assigned dish, so it could be prepared on a moment's notice; sometimes three or four funerals in a year for members of the church. In her mid-sixties, her slender, small-boned frame gave the impression of the kind of sprightliness that could fracture if too much pressure were applied. Blessed with thick, wavy white hair, her face was almost wrinkleless, possibly because she had so little flesh to wrinkle.

She went around putting out food for her three cats, one of which was patiently waiting at his bowl, all the time careful not to stain her jacket. Being polyester, she could easily toss it in the washer, but there wasn't enough time for that. The other ladies would probably be wearing nice slacks with dressy sweaters, but she wanted to have her best church clothes on when she met the girls. The woman from the gallery had used the word *uptown* when describing them to the pastor, and he had heard the same sort of thing from the funeral director.

The ladies on the dinner committee were bringing things into the kitchen when Nikki arrived at the church; another group was setting up the Fellowship Hall. Three casseroles and some vegetables were set on warming trays in two lines. A couple of gelatin salads along with tossed greens, rolls, and pitchers of sweet and unsweetened tea sat next to rows of clear plastic glasses and a stainless steel bowl filled with ice. Styrofoam plates were stacked at the beginning of each line, the ones with partitions that everyone preferred since they were stronger. Next, the stainless steel flatware neatly rolled in paper napkins.

Since Nikki planned to stick around for the visitation, she offered to help in the kitchen during the meal. That way she could satisfy her curiosity about Hayden's two girls who no one had ever even heard of before. She'd never forgive herself if they got out of town without her laying eyes on them. To look like she was needed, she went around making sure all the plastic lace table cloths were nice and smooth and the new fall season centerpieces with the plastic mums and foliage were placed directly in the middle of each table, even though someone had already done it earlier.

As people started to stream in, she re-straightened the metal chairs with their cushioned brown leatherette seats and backs. Muted yellow tones above and below a chair rail encircling the room, and a practical but realistic looking synthetic wood floor gave the place an aura of sensible good taste mixed with subdued elegance. Nikki was sure, that no matter how fancy these girls were, the newly renovated hall and sanctuary would do their father proud.

While everyone waited, Nikki went out and told the Commander of the Honor Guard they had plenty of food in case anyone wanted anything. Later, the youngest of the five Veterans dropped into the kitchen for a glass of ice tea.

She noticed his Afghanistan Campaign Ribbon, the same one her son wore on his uniform. "Are there any Vietnam Vets in the Guard?"

"All except me, Ma'am."

She noticed he was carrying an instrument under his arm. "Are you the bugler?"

"Yes, Ma'am."

Nikki finally gave up trying to get another word out of him. Everything from his expressionless face to his pressed, spotless uniform and gleaming black boots told her he was too absorbed in the solemnity of the military burying one of their own to make small talk.

BARBARA NOTICED HAYDEN was holding on to the steering wheel with an iron grip as the road climbed over two thousand feet, only intermittently breaking out of the dense forest. Once it reached the Eastern Continental Divide, it started its descent into the gorge.

Barbara took in the scenery with a fatalistic expression draping her face. She always knew that someday it was going to lead to something like this. Hayden just couldn't let things go. The revelations lying ahead could either repair her sister's wounded spirit, or break it so completely she'd never be right.

The mountain ranges rose straight up on both sides with the river snaking along on the right side of the two lane road. Barbara couldn't see a river bed, just layers of massive slabs of rock askew, with rushing water spilling over them, splashing on rocks below or sluicing around and between the mammoths—an endless show of sun-sparkled water dancing on rounded stone. Every once in a while, she spotted a restful eddy the with still clear water and sandy bottom, and it settled her nerves.

At Bat Cave, the road met up with the Rocky Broad and ran shoulder to shoulder with it the whole way into Chimney Rock. They passed through the small hamlet, with its toehold on the base of two mountains, without really getting a good look, since vehicles of every description were parked at an angle to all the shops and restaurants. Scores of sightseers fanned out in every direction and sat on every available bench, porch and boulder. On the edge of town less than a mile down the road, they took a left onto Boys Camp Road and pulled into the church's nearly full parking lot a few hundred yards from Main Street.

THE CHIMNEY ROCK Baptist Church, oddly enough, is located in Lake Lure, a town created when the Rocky Broad was dammed in 1926, twisting its boundaries around the mountains and absorbing parts of what was then known as Chimney Rock Township, including the church and its graves that had been moved to this location before the valley was flooded.

Like the other congregations threaded along the gorge, this one sprang up as soon as settlers arrived in the seventeen hundreds, and over the generations, through sickness and floods and general hard times, remained the bedrock of the community. And because this was a small church in a small community where everyone knew their neighbors, it had always had the closeness of a tight-knit family.

It had been no easy task to keep a congregation intact in this mostly hardscrabble sparsely populated locale, and took all kinds of efforts from all kinds of folks doing whatever they could to keep the church going strong. Over the years, the way in which the congregation reached out to townspeople and the families tucked in the surrounding coves, valley and ridges, mirrored the very character of the people who worshipped there.

Mourners had been mostly milling around outside; but now that the funeral director had everything set up, he gave the signal to the organist and opened the door for viewing the open casket.

NIKKI WAS BUSY in the kitchen, but could tell the family arrived when the dining room doors swung open and she heard the soothing voice of the minister, accompanied by the clicking of high heels and shuffling of feet.

Since the family would be receiving visitors for a while before the luncheon, Nikki waited a few minutes before going out to pay her respects. She'd never seen anyone so dressed up, especially the blond. How in tarnation was she able to walk in those shoes? As Nikki waited in line, she could tell by the friendly smiles on the two sister's faces and the easily offered hands they had genteel manners taught to them. Just like the Taylors, the two girls weren't very tall, but just like the Taylors, they were built like they could spring up fast.

Nikki made her way along the reception. Barbara's husband stood first in line. Stocky. The same height as her. No one can blame him for being so uneasy, she thought. He's never laid eyes on any of us before. She blushed as the other husband shook her hand. His good looks and gracious friendliness made her feel uncomfortably the center of his attention. Folks around here sure are going to be talking about him for a while. She moved on to Barbara. Somewhat plump, but nicely featured. This sister shook her hand and smiled at her for as long as it took for the next person in line to engage her attention.

Nikki proceeded to Hayden. Momentarily awestruck by the young woman's delicate beauty, tears welled when she recognized the familiar gray-blue eyes and the way her eye teeth crossed over their neighbors, just like her father's had. This slight flaw in a stunning face was charmingly appealing and totally disarming. The family resemblance was irrefutable. These were Hayden's girls.

Once they started serving the luncheon, Nikki got busy in the kitchen pushing food through the pass-through to the ladies taking care of the serving lines, and afterwards receiving the empty plates that were sent back. It made her happy to know she was doing something for an old friend.

Since it was getting to be time to start the service, Nikki excused herself and joined the congregation in the sanctuary. She wasn't surprised that every pew was filled.

The Honor Guard and pallbearers sat in front to one side, and the front row on the other was reserved for the family. The casket had been closed and draped with an American flag and the inviting notes of *Shall We Gather at the River* floated from the organ.

Golden fall light streamed in from the stained glass windows as she watched the minister enter the church from a side door next to the altar. Reaching the pulpit, he asked everyone to rise as Hayden and Barbara filed in and settled into the front row pew with their husbands.

Nikki recognized the hymn the minute the lilting voice of the soprano, accompanied by the organ, filled the church. *I come to the garden alone... when the dew is still on the roses... and the voice I hear falling on my ear... the Son of God discloses...*

A latecomer opened one of the church doors, allowing the bittersweet autumn fragrance to waft in as everyone sang. At the end, the minister offered condolences to the family and invited people to speak.

SITTING IN THE PEW, Hayden felt woefully left out, remembering how, the day before, she had told the minister she wouldn't be saying any words about her father. The man had been kind, making it seem like he didn't need an explanation.

A young man approached the lectern, looking uncomfortable in a shirt and tie. Hayden could feel Jack put his arm around her waist like he was getting ready to bolster her up. Barbara squeezed her hand.

As the young man spoke of how her father had helped him with his art studies and been a mentor, Hayden felt a flicker of jealousy. Cheated. Her face twisted as she held back sobs. A baby cried out and she caught a glimpse of Randy rocking his baby in his arms as he made his way to the back of the church.

She couldn't help glancing around at the people in the packed church, sorrow and respect on their faces. How could the man they were honoring have deserted his family? The story her mother had told her suddenly made no sense, and she was ashamed of the part she had played in it. Believing and hating.

She didn't hear that much from the other speakers, just words like *...a good and generous man,* and *...he never turned anyone in need down.*

Hayden wasn't able to get herself composed until the service ended and they were all settled at the gravesite outside the church, but then she broke down again when the minister started repeating the Twenty-third Psalm. *The Lord is my shepherd: I shall not want. He maketh me to lie down in green pastures...*

The sounds of a country setting hung in the air—a goldfinch in a nearby dogwood chirping, the muffled noise of turning pages as someone leafed through a program. A far-off rumbling of a truck barreling along Route 64 seemed out of sync with the serenity of the scene.

Suddenly the Commander's solemn order sounded off to the side. *Honor! Guard! Tench-hut! Present! Arms!* A moment of silence followed, then *Ready! Fire!* Three times the order sounded, and three times rounds echoed across Lake Lure.

By the time taps was played, with each note held for a long moment, Hayden was sobbing openly. Her husband held her in his arms until the Commander presented her with the flag from the coffin, tightly folded in a neat triangular shape. As people rose and placed a rose on the coffin, Hayden caressed the flag as if it were her father.

CHAPTER SEVEN

Hayden was still wearing her large-rimmed black hat when she spotted the crystal chandelier at the foot of the central staircase at the Lake Lure Inn. In spite of being utterly drained, she couldn't help instantly recognizing it as Baccarat. An automatic reflex made her glance over to Barbara, who nodded confirmation. Hayden felt grateful. After the heart wrenching funeral, she could use the comfort of being surrounded by the elegant furnishings of this grand old hotel—along with a stiff drink.

Way past lunch, the place was deserted. They settled at a table in the bar and Hayden ordered a double bourbon on the rocks.

Jack turned to face her. "Do you really want such a strong drink before driving through the mountains?"

Hayden stared blankly at the slightly embarrassed waiter and repeated, "A double, please." She glanced at Barbara. *Dang!* She wished she wouldn't make all those faces! She checked her watch and prayed Judy would wait at the church until she worked up the courage to tell Jack she wasn't going home.

Barbara's husband, George, obviously responding to the tension in the room, made every effort at cordial conversation even though with all the body language bouncing around he was pretty much talking to himself. When the waiter put the drink in front of Hayden, George's monolog slowly trailed off as he watched her gulp it down.

Hayden could see that the way she threw back the bourbon caught Jack's eye, too. He signaled to the waiter, busy setting up for the evening crowd, and asked him to bring some toast and coffee, a remedy she knew he used whenever someone showed up drunk for a performance.

He massaged his jaw for a few moments, then threw Hayden a sidelong glance as he spoke to Barbara. "I think we're going to stay over another night... here at the inn. Hayden's in no shape to drive back to the beach."

Hayden wasn't going to get a better opportunity than this. She casually said, "I'm not going home, Jack. I need to clear up some of my father's affairs."

She watched Jack fiddle with a spoon lying on the white tablecloth and promised herself she wasn't going to let this end in an ugly argument.

In his distinctly mellow voice, with the gently stretched words he owed to his southern roots, he said, "This is exactly what your mother said would happen."

Hayden felt her back stiffen. "So, you've been plotting with my mother again."

"We're all concerned. You haven't exactly been yourself for the past year."

"Well, darlin', it sure is fortunate you had all those sweet girls at the theater to soothe your anxieties over me."

Jack sank back in his chair and spun the spoon around with a finger. "Hayden, I know you're stressed out, but this is uncalled for. Really. In front of your family?" He stopped and looked up at her. "Honey, you've been through a trying couple of days. I'm sure once you get back to the beach and talk things over with your mother, you're going to feel differently about this whole thing."

Hayden slapped her hand on the table. "My mother doesn't have anything to do with this, except that she probably caused the whole damn thing to begin with."

"Hayden, this is not the time, nor the place, to haul out all the family's dirty laundry. To say nothing of that kind of language."

Hayden drew her hand up and splayed her fingers across her chest. "Gracious, me! I'm so sorry if I offended you, Darlin'. It must have been all those generous words I heard about my father that set me off. Why, after listening to Mother and Grandpappy all those years, I was sure he was simply good for nothin'." She turned and looked directly at Jack. "I've been lied to by my mother, my granddaddy, everyone I've ever cared about, and I'm as angry as hell!"

Hayden bit the inside of her lip and tugged. She didn't want an argument, but she wasn't going to be talked out of staying.

George's eyes met the waiter's as he bent down and put a plate of toast on the table. Hayden shoved it aside, but Barbara helped herself to a piece without taking her eyes off Hayden. George wiped his brow with his handkerchief, and no sooner had he folded it and put it back in his pocket, when he pulled it out and did it again.

Jack sat up in his chair, leaned on the table with one arm and reached for Hayden's hand. "Honey, I'm not going to let you do this. I promised your mother I'd get you back home. And where would you stay, anyway?"

"At my father's place in Chimney Rock."

Jack threw his head back and grimaced. "You can't be serious. You won't last two days in that cheesy little town."

Hayden pulled her hand away. "If it was good enough for my father, it'll be good enough for me." She opened her purse and fished out her keys. This is it, she told herself. Nothing they do or say is going to change my mind. "Jack, I'm here, and I'm going to stay here until I get some answers. I've spent the last twenty-five years wondering who in the hell I was and where in the hell I came from, and I'm not going back to that." She softened her tone. "I know it's no secret I haven't been myself ever since… Jack, I'm at the bottom of a deep pit, and if I'm ever to get out, I've got to clear things up here first. There are things I need to know."

Barbara lurched forward in her chair. "That's right, Jack. Ever since she was a kid..."

George signaled to Barbara to hush.

Hayden looked around the table. "I'm sorry I was such an emotional mess today, everybody. I really appreciate y'all coming up here and all the support." She put her hand on her husband's shoulder. "I'm sorry, Jack. I've got to do this." She rose, said goodbye and walked out.

ON THE WAY TO HER CAR, Hayden was thinking she had uttered more truth in the past half-hour than in the past two years. Her eyes landed on the church across the lake. Its gleaming white steeple nestled amidst a spectacular blaze of color looked so innocuous, not at all like the place where she thought her heart would break. She couldn't pull her eyes away until she popped open the trunk of her car. She took off her hat and put it back in its box, then noticing a pair of loafers, kicked off her shoes and quickly put them on. As she peeled out of the parking lot, she caught a glimpse of her faithful sister at the window staring out at her.

Hayden spotted Judy in her Subaru in the church parking lot and noticed she was signaling for her to follow. Hayden trailed her onto Route 74 and was amazed at the traffic jam with cars, campers and motorcycles bumper-to-bumper in both directions. Her car crawled along with the convoy toward the center of the village, passing an array of motels clutching the edge of the highway and hanging over the Rocky Broad in a struggle to hold on to their place in the gorge.

Cars and motorcycles of every description were parked in every available spot and all along the road, creating a hodgepodge of color and chrome. People were spilling out and making their way along tight pathways between the traffic and parked vehicles with kids in strollers, or sitting atop their dad's shoulders, or just being dragged along, all inexorably drawn to the heart of the village like worshippers on a pilgrimage.

Judy had told her to expect these kinds of crowds on the weekends. She said they come for the incredible close-up view of

Chimney Rock's massive bald mountain ridge with its thread of a waterfall plunging over them, as well as a chance to splash around a little in the Rocky Broad and shop the quaint touristy shops lining Main Street. The boisterous scene, with people shouting to each other and every once in a while a motorcycle backfiring, made Hayden nod to herself. She was just like them. On a pilgrimage.

She saw Judy's blinker go on and her car stop in the middle of town, waiting to cross onto Southside Drive. Hayden waited behind her until the traffic in the other lane moved ahead enough for them to squeeze through and rumble across the narrow single -lane steel trestle bridge to a heavily treed dead-end lane lined with small cabins and vacation homes. Judy had mentioned that they were occupied mainly in the summer by Floridians escaping scorching summer heat, or folks from all around North and South Carolina drawn to the overwhelming natural beauty of the gorge and the soothing rhythmic sound of the river.

Hayden followed the Subaru for a few hundred yards past a dozen cabins, until it turned off onto a driveway and rolled to a stop in front of one sheathed in cedar and perched on the side of the mountain among giant poplars and hemlocks. There was no real walkway, just loose gravel leading to the cobblestone porch with two pillars of the same material holding up a tin roof. Other than a couple of pots of wilted marigolds and a few straggly azaleas, there was no landscaping. A dark green Jeep Cherokee sprinkled with colorful leaves sat parked to the side.

Seeing Judy disappear into the house, Hayden got out and decided she better get her suitcase and go in before she changed her mind. Bruce Springsteen's "Lady in a Blue Dress" blared from the cabin, but was quickly silenced. The screen door swung open and Judy reached for Hayden's suitcase as she entered the front room, dark except for some light streaming in from the kitchen beyond.

A solidly built woman stood in the middle of a large, low-ceilinged living room. Introduced as the housekeeper, Addie Mae Hunter, she was somewhere in her thirties, with long kinky blond hair frayed from over bleaching. She wore jean shorts and a baggy navy-blue sweatshirt. Even though she gave Hayden a friendly greeting, there was a suppressed air of furtiveness about her. The way her smile ended in a sneer as it faded, made Hayden dislike her.

"Most people just call me Addie," she said as she took the suitcase from Judy and looked Hayden up and down, the sneer still in place. "You sure you want to stay here all alone?"

"Of course. Why not?" shot back Hayden.

Addie threw her head to the side and lifted one eyebrow as she spoke. "Just checkin', that's all."

An aura of animal cunning that seemed to permeate Addie Mae's every move made Hayden search Judy's eyes the minute Addie disappeared from the room with the suitcase.

"Don't let her upset you," said Judy in a hushed voice. "She comes off a little strange at first, but she's all right. She'll be finished up here in a bit and you can get settled in."

Hayden could see fatigue had gotten the better of Judy, and she had reached her limit of endurance. "Don't worry, I can handle her. You go home and get some rest. Take the whole week off. I'll open the gallery on Tuesday."

Judy appeared to dissolve. Her shoulders slumped, her expression saddened. "Tomorrow and Monday will be enough. I'll be there on Tuesday."

Hayden walked Judy to the door and watched her leave, suppressing an urge to follow her out. She went back in and flopped into a leather easy chair facing a massive stone fireplace. A bearskin mounted above the rugged wood mantle overpowered the room, and the display of the animal's bared teeth and glassy eyes convinced Hayden that it was respected for its ferocity.

Hayden's eyes roamed from the dark shellacked tongue-and-groove ceiling to the worn-smooth oak floorboards in such varying widths they must have been hand hewn. Suddenly Addie's voice startled her. She stood holding an oil lantern.

"I'll put this on the counter for when the power gits off," she said with a slight raising of one side of her upper lip.

Hayden was too worn out to snap back with anything. She just glared at her.

Addie tossed her head toward the fireplace. "I made a bed for you in the back there. Don't want anyone else fallin' down them stairs. Plus, it'll give you more time to get out of here if'n a flood comes on."

Hayden could hardly believe the woman's audacity.

"The minute you hear the sirens goin' off, head on out of here... night or day."

This was turning into a challenge. Hayden put an elbow on the arm of the chair, propped her chin on her fist and flashed an affable smile.

Addie took a rag out of her pocket and got busy dusting. In a friendly, conversational tone, she said, "Flash floods are a common hap'nin around here. And with you being right up against the mountain there's mudslides to worry about, too."

Hayden found herself standing before she knew what was happening. "I think the house is clean enough. I'll let you know when I need you again."

Addie's broad grin seemed to be meant as a taunt. "I don't mind stayin'. My ride won't be here for 'nother hour."

"What about that Jeep?"

"That's your father's. Mine's in the shop."

"Why don't you just take it *and go.* "

Addie lifted a ceramic vase and dusted it as if she hadn't heard. "You prob'ly don't remember me, but I met you at the visitation. Couldn't go to the services cuz I had to get back and ready up the house." She shook her head. "Didn't want to miss that visitation. No way. That's all people around here been talkin' about. I guess the whole town came out to get a look at you. Got a neighbor to take me home so's I could change, and then run me up here. I didn't mean to be pickin' at you. It's just that you don't know what you're gittin' into." She leaned back and examined Hayden's feet. "At least you had enough sense to change them shoes of yourn."

"Listen, why don't you just take my dad's car until yours is repaired?"

Addie threw her head to the side. "That's right nice o' you. But, I could just take off and you'd never see it again."

Hayden wearily flipped her hand in the air. "Please don't do that. I might need it."

Addie gathered up her cleaning supplies and stuffed them into a bucket. "A body's got to be more careful. A lot of people would take advantage of a body like you."

Hayden thought she would run out of the house screaming if the woman didn't stop issuing her veiled threats and get out. Spying what looked like a set of car keys hanging from a nail at the kitchen entrance, she rushed over, grabbed them and after recognizing the Jeep logo on the ring, handed them to Addie.

"Here!"

Addie rose and took the keys. She laughed and shook her head. "You're a glutton for punishment, lady."

Hayden put an arm around Addie's shoulder and led her to the door. Then, overwhelmed with fatigue, she stumbled her way through the living room into an adjoining bedroom and lay down on the quilt-covered bed.

She woke up hours later in the dark. The sounds of the day had disappeared, but the continuous muted roar of the river crashing on rocks drifted in from the open window and the sweet smell of fallen dew-soaked leaves filled the room.

She sat up and turned on the lamp on the bedside table and couldn't resist running her hand over the bed's headboard, masterfully crafted of stripped hickory and inlaid with birch bark. Her eyes wandered the entire room, enveloped in narrow, tongue-and-groove boards, giving her the feeling of being in a carefully crafted cocoon. And as ancient as the room appeared, it had all sorts of brilliantly designed furnishings.

She got up and went over to a rocker sitting in the corner. Every detail of the curly maple, every turn, every curve was matchless in quality. Atop a rough hewn shelf, sat beautifully blown glass vases, and in the corner on a pedestal stood a mannequin bust with a gold necklace built in dozens of tiers of delicate chains. At the neck, was a narrow collar of gold encrusted with gems.

She made her way through the living room to the kitchen with the aid of some light cast from a street lamp in the distance.

An inspection of the cupboards and refrigerator told her that her father was neither a cook nor someone who entertained. A narrow staircase next to the entrance had a landing where it made a turn. Was this where they found her father, she wondered as she climbed the stairs to a long hallway with two doors on either side and one at the end. The bathroom would have surprised her if she hadn't already seen the items in her bedroom. Everything appeared hand-crafted with elegant detailing. Even the shower stall was encircled in copper with a life-sized Adam and Eve etched into it.

She pictured her father's face while she ran the water in the claw-foot tub. Who was this man? His roots went deep into these rugged mountains, yet he ensconced himself in delicate fine art. But, where did he get the money to buy all these things?

Soaking in the tub, she couldn't help reflecting on the past three days. She squeezed the suds from her wash cloth and watched the bubbles dissolve in the water, just like all the anger and resentment had that afternoon in the church. Then a horrible thought entered her mind. If things hadn't happened the way they had, she probably would have been polluted with hurt and hate the rest of her life.

She wondered if her father was thinking of her the day before he died. Or was she just some victim of a fate that revisited her over and over again trying to break her spirit? No matter. Whatever it was that brought her here, she knew being here was a good thing. She felt a strange sensation. Like she was digging her nails into the side of the mountain and hanging on. Maybe, just maybe, she was going to make it.

Then she thought about Addie and laughed aloud. "Honey child," she said as she sank down and rested her head on the rim of the tub, "You don't know *who you're dealin' with*. There is no form of intimidation I haven't been honored with. I'm the fledgling of Elizabeth Burroughs Tarrington who learned it all from her father, the honorable Theodore M. Burroughs. And I do mean *it all*. Darlin', there's *nothin'* you can say to scare me off."

CHAPTER EIGHT

J ULIE GRIGGS DIDN'T KNOW why she made the effort to drive an hour to Cherokee for the drab bunch of retirees perched at the casino's slot machines. She wanted a drink. Damn these dry towns, she said to herself. She put some coins in the slot. Oh, well, I might as well use up my bag of quarters before heading back to the room. Maybe I'll get lucky.

But, so far, luck hadn't been a friend to Julie Griggs. Always attractive, well groomed, and from a nice family, she didn't have enough sense to stay away from the wrong kind of men. Now in her early forties, she still turned heads in a bikini, but years of heartbreaks and mistreatment had left their scars.

A man slipped onto the chair at the slot machine next to her. She turned to face him with a too well practiced smile that sent the kind of message she figured he was looking for. She couldn't stop herself from hoping that somewhere out there she'd find a nice guy as lonely as she was, looking for someone to love. Maybe this one was a second-time-around loser who had learned his lesson, or an indecisive bloke who finally woke up to the fact that it was now or never. He could always be married with five kids, too.

"Having any luck?" he asked.

She noted he had a pleasant enough face, framed with gray

sideburns, and his glasses and sports jacket gave him a professional look. His thick hair was something she was starting to appreciate. Her eyes quickly averted from his shirt tugging at the buttons. Lately, she had learned to accept a potbelly as a fact of life. She couldn't be choosy about looks anymore either, nor get any hopes of raising a family. Those days had passed her by. Too many wrong choices when she had what it took to make a man want nothing more than to be the father of her children.

A promising sign was that he wasn't wearing a wedding band.

"Not so far," she answered. She tried not to think about all the sour relationships that had started this same way, and let a narrow ray of hope bring an encouraging smile to her face.

He stood up and his six-foot frame towered over her like a mountain. He reached for her arm. "Come on. Let me pour you a drink up in my room."

In her job as a receptionist for a contractor, Julie had met a lot of men with a smooth manner and the ability to make fluid conversation, talents developed from spending a lot of time on the road striking up conversations with strangers. She drew her arm away. "What are you doing in Cherokee?"

"I swing through once a month. Do all the promotional set-ups for A. K. Tractors."

"That sounds like a nice job."

"Only if you like staying at third-rate hotels and eating lunch with country bumpkins whose one big dream is to own a brand new trailer."

After hearing that, Julie decided she wasn't going to get through the night cold sober, and the drink started to look good.

He ran his hand down her arm. "Come on. We can have a few drinks and talk for a while?"

"About what?"

"I don't have a wife or family to chat with on the phone at the end of my day. It gets kinda lonely. If we hit it off, maybe we can see each other on a regular basis." He laid a hand on her shoulder. "Come on, honey, let's go on up."

As much as she needed a drink, the idea of going up to his

room felt too risky. A woman came by emptying ashtrays. It looked like she knew him. Called him Freddy and smiled. He had to be a regular. His mention of being lonely touched her; and, you never could tell, they just *might* hit it off. She had second thoughts. No. Too risky.

"If you don't want to sit around and talk, why don't you let me take you out? Do you have something a little fancier to put on?"

She thought for a moment and nodded.

He winked. "I know a nice place in Maggie Valley with a great band." He put an arm around her shoulder. "Let's go to your room. I'll catch the news on TV while you change in the bathroom."

Thoughts of a boisterous restaurant filled with cheerful people out for a night of fun excited her. She grabbed her purse and slid off the stool. Her luck *was* changing.

A crowd of boisterous elderly ladies waiting for the casino's hotel elevator all seemed to know each other, and once the door opened they poured into it like a single body. Julie wanted to wait for the next one, but the giggling mass insisted they squeeze in.

Julie could feel them staring at her, and out of the corner of her eye could see one of them winking to another and pointing to her and Freddy. When a couple of them started to snicker, she remembered the big row she had with her mother before she left. "Please, honey. Don't go out by yourself. I know you're lonely, but it's not right," she had pleaded, nervously scrunching the skirt of her apron in her hands.

The elevator stopped and she and Freddy got out. Julie quickly moved out of sight of the penetrating eyes before the door closed, annoyed at the humiliation.

"Come on, baby, don't let that bunch of old bags throw cold water on our party."

She looked him in the eyes and tried to see his soul, but the deep blue orbs overcast by dark furrowed eyebrows frightened her. She didn't think she could handle him if he got fresh and decided to go back to the casino. As she reached for the elevator button, Freddy covered it with his hand.

"What's the matter, baby?"

"I want to try my luck some more."

"Aw, we've had enough of that. The night's still young. Let's go out and have some fun."

The picture of a cold lonely hotel room that had haunted her all evening, crowded out her fears. She wanted to have a good time. She let him follow her to her room, then foraged through her purse for her key, and as she opened the door and snapped on the light, felt maybe her luck really was about to change. She kicked off her heels, put her purse on the dresser and began fluffing up her hair in the mirror when she saw his reflection and froze. He had taken off his jacket and was unbuckling his pants.

She swung around. "Hey! What do you think you're doing?"

"Listen you little slut, get undressed or I'll rip that cheap dress off myself."

Julie was stunned as she watched him step out of his pants. All the horror stories she had heard about lonely women being treated like a piece of meat materialized in front of her.

She ran for the door. He grabbed her, threw her on the bed and began tearing off her panties. It happened so fast she lost her bearings, but when he loomed over her on his knees, his face red and sweaty, and started to put on a condom, she screamed.

He punched her in the jaw and her head snapped with such a force she was unconscious for most of the rape. She came to in a numb state of shock to see him fully dressed and fastening his belt.

He raised his head and looked over at her. "Don't you dare open your mouth to anyone about this, or I'll kill you."

FREDDY RUBBED HIS SORE knuckles as he raced up the staircase to get to his room. If there was one thing he couldn't stand, it was a slut who acted like she was some kind of virgin. They're all the same. She came on to him the minute he said "Hello." And he gave her exactly what she was asking for.

Damn! He wished she hadn't made him hit her so hard. What else could he do once she got hysterical? He opened the door to his room and went straight to his overnight bag, pulled out a bottle of scotch and poured himself a drink. He strolled to the window and looked out at the Smoky Mountains. He wanted to sock that bitch in the mouth the minute she said it sounded like he had a nice job. She was mocking him. Wanted to make him feel like a loser. He showed her.

He drained his glass and poured another drink. Not just anyone could land a scholarship to Pratt like he had. He'd of gotten his degree, too, if it wasn't for that damn teacher. When she told him to switch his major to commercial art or she was going to recommend they withdraw his scholarship, he begged her not to do it. But she just sat there, coolly telling him he didn't have the talent to make it big in sculpture… like he was nothing. She had asked for it, too. He gulped down the drink, still sore about how the two years of probation screwed up his life.

It was that damn teacher's fault he ended up setting up displays in all these hick towns for the past thirty years. If he had to carry on another one-way conversation through another boring lunch with one more dealership sales manager, he was going to kill himself. He threw his jacket across a chair and flopped onto the bed. He folded an arm under his head and crossed his ankles. Sirens sounded out on the street and he hoped the damn building wasn't on fire.

He decided to get the hell out of there early the next morning. He didn't want to run into that damn broad again. She might try to get him in trouble with the hotel. He couldn't afford any hassles after narrowly beating the rap for assaulting that Vegas call girl. The legal fees put him back almost ten grand and left him on shaky ground with the company. They pretty much told him if he so much as got ticketed for jaywalking he'd be out.

He was too close to getting his company pension to let that happen. Two more years and he'd have it along with social security. Now, all he needed to do to ratchet his retirement lifestyle up from rotting in front of the TV in his two-bedroom condo, to living the good life in an arty community he'd found thirty miles from Mexico City, was get his hands on Hayden's paintings.

Valentino seemed fine with buying them from him when he

called and told him about Hayden's little accident. He'd pick the paintings up this weekend. By now, things had to be cooled down and the cabin empty.

The pounding on the door alarmed him. Maybe the building *was* on fire. He staggered over and flung it open.

"Freddy Lucas," one of the officers said. "You're wanted for questioning in the assault and rape of Julie Griggs."

CHAPTER NINE

Ir was past seven by the time Tom Gibbons pulled into the parking lot. He opened the door to his truck and his blue tick hound, Sweetie, leapt across his lap and out the door before him. He grabbed his clipboard and slid out. His khaki tee shirt was soaked dark with sweat and his slacks crumpled from spending the day walking two farms for their initial evaluation. His hair was mussed and he needed a shave, but he still had his lean, leathery good looks.

He strolled into his office, threw his keys on the desk and snapped on the answering machine, then listened to the calls as he sucked down a fresh bottle of water while Sweetie sniffed every corner of the offices.

He'd been working for the Carolina Mountain Land Conservancy as the Land Protection Director since it started in '94, and there were good days and bad days, and today had been one of the bad days. He got the call from old Mr. Owens on his cell right around five. He had just signed a contract selling his land outside Gerton to a developer who planned to put up a bunch of vacation homes. He sounded heartbroken; but as he said, he was in his eighties and ailing, and the money sure looked good.

Every once in a while the land grab got to Tom—the hysterical race between developers and conservationists to get their hands on as much of the mountains as they could. It was as if there were an undeclared war between the two factions with no one realizing what was happening as they drove through the mountains with a carload of kids enjoying the scenery. Hadn't they noticed the zigzagging roads scarring up the slopes? Or the big white condo complex on the ridge of Sugar Top Mountain that looked like a remote TB sanitarium? So far the conservancy had been able to protect over 18,500 acres from wanton development, but that was a drop in the bucket compared to what was being swallowed up by sprawl.

He was still kicking himself for not moving faster to close the deal with Hayden Taylor. His four hundred acres on the top of Round Top were essential to make the dream of a continuous hiking trail through the Hickory Nut Gorge a reality. But Hayden had been so slow with all the paperwork. Damn! The survey alone took two months. Now, from what Hayden's lawyer told him, the estate was going to his two daughters. Luckily, one of them was staying on at his place in Chimney Rock.

He heard the name of Ben Beckham coming from the answering machine and rewound the message. Last week the office manager hinted they were offering Beckham twice what they were paying him. Oh well, what did he expect; no one forced him to leave his father's law practice and go to work for the conservancy.

He believed if he worked in this specialized field from the ground up, some day he'd be able to really make a difference in Washington. All the interfacing he'd done with folks over conservation easements gave him an insight into the deep-seated connection these mountain people and flat land farmers had with their land, especially those who'd had it handed down through several generations. It seemed that the beauty and the hardship of these places had shaped their character and the character of those who came before them, and they were finally coming around to the idea that something had to be done to save it.

The message was from the office manager. "Tom, wait till you get a load of this Ben Beckham. All the girls in the office are gaga over him. And I think he's got all kinds of money. The director told me he's giving half his salary to the conservancy. What do you think of that?"

Tom hit the delete button, a little ashamed for begrudging him his overblown salary. Name recognition is how the director had presented their new development guy. All he had to do was call some bigwig on the phone, and the minute he dropped his name they'd be all ears. But did he have the passion it took to make people believe? If not, he wasn't going to last a month. They'd shake his hand, have a few drinks, maybe lunch, and he'd never hear from them again, or be fobbed off on their corporate giving director. From what he gathered, this Beckham didn't know the first thing about easements, but the way the director put it, he was supposed to give him a crash course, and from there Ben would send his donors to him for the legal work.

He was coming on board in a couple of days. Maybe he'd take him with him to see that Taylor woman.

BEN KEPT TOSSING the keys to his new house in the air as he left the closing attorney's office. He felt a little guilty about making such a major move without Heather's approval, but hell, he couldn't hang on at Warren Wilson past the end of the semester and had to do something! The place came with the homestead's original twenty-five acres, but the cabin had been added on to over the years, with two-thousand square feet put up just two years back.

He laughed to himself remembering the real-estate agent two weeks before looking like she won the lottery when he walked in and showed her the ad he'd clipped out of the Sunday paper. Before the day was out she'd written a million-dollar contract and gotten the listing for his campus house.

The truck was coming with Jenny's furniture in a couple of hours and he had just enough time to pick up some lunch and get over there. He'd been in a frenzy the day before, sheathing every piece in bubble wrap. Heather refused every offer from him to ship things to her in the dozen or so phone conversations they'd had over the past two days. Thank goodness a friend of Jenny's came over and went through all of her things for him when he wasn't there.

Maybe he could find something to eat in Chimney Rock. He passed Bearwallow Road on his way in and almost decided to ditch lunch and run up to his new house, but he needed to have some food in his stomach to tackle the job ahead.

He swung his Ford 250 in at an angle to the Riverwatch Café and went in. The nostalgic posters of everyone from James Dean to John Wayne plastered on the walls, basic pine booths, worn oak floors, and a few large carved bears sprinkled around the place mirrored the rustic atmosphere of the town. He ordered a Reuben sandwich, then sauntered outside to a deck overlooking the Rocky Broad and waited for his order.

How he wished his mother was still alive. There were certain times in his life when undeniable emotions surfaced; and this was one of them. Not a single night had gone by when he was growing up in the Adirondacks outside Saranac Lake that he didn't lay with his head on his pillow dreaming of owning a place like the one he just bought. He'd tell his mother when he grew up she wasn't going to have to clean lodges any more, and he was going to build her a place on the mountain where the spring floods wouldn't touch her. Unfortunately, her hard life and hard smoking got to her before he graduated from college and had the money to do it.

Distracted by the sound of his name being called, he went back inside to pick up his order. The woman at the counter, heavy, somewhere in her fifties, gave him a familiar look. The only thing that had changed about the suggestive smile over the years was that the age bracket of his admirers had crept up. He winked at her and took his food back outside.

As he sat eating and gazing up at the flag on top of the Chimney Rock and listening to the white noise of the river, a strange feeling overcame him and he allowed himself to pretend his mother was sitting across on the picnic table. He'd never been able to discuss his promise to buy her a mountain house with anyone, not even Jenny. It was a kind of sacred pact that had taken on a life of its own when he was a kid. A special glue that held him and his mother together, and put a glow around their simple existence.

He had looked at some of the new mountainside developments just for the heck of it and was startled to see how much of the mountains had been carved up by their roads. Ironically, a salesman at one of these places used the fact that their property was bordered by land protected by the conservancy as a major selling point.

Ben had thought a lot over the years about a solution to runaway development and felt it all narrowed down to the people on all the planning boards, zoning boards and town councils in the spider web of little hamlets and townships sprinkled throughout Western North Carolina putting the brakes on high density construction and steep slope stripping. But until the urgency of the situation trickled down to the folks who elected all these people, it was going to be up to land conservancies like the one he just joined to make sure their side scored the most points. He knew if he was going to succeed in this new effort, he had to unleash his passion for saving the beauty of the place, yet he couldn't ignore the strong desires of people like himself to own a piece of the mountains.

"WHAT ARE YOU staring at?" Hayden asked Judy as she strolled into the gallery.

"That outfit."

"I intend to make the most of my time here, so I went over to Bubba O'Leary's in town and got some jeans and put on some work clothes."

"I wouldn't exactly call 'em work clothes, but they're a sight better than those fancy duds of yours."

"Where's our handyman?"

"On his way."

Hayden asked Judy to come get her when he arrived and went into the office.

Just then, Ben Beckham, dressed in jeans, walked in carrying a box of small sculptures. He'd called Judy and told her a new sculpture teacher was coming on board at Warren Wilson and he was starting to wrap things up and wanted to deliver some pieces he'd promised his students he'd bring down.

Judy was filling out a consignment sheet when Hayden walked back out. Her hair was wrapped in a silk bandana and she was wearing straight leg jeans and a close fitting turtleneck sweater, sleeves pushed up to the elbows.

"Good. I'm glad you finally got here," she said to Ben. She wrung her hands and looked around thoughtfully. "I want you to start by removing everything from all the tables. Put them in one of the classrooms."

Ben recognized the troubled grayish blue eyes in the delicately chiseled face from the visitation at the funeral parlor and offered his hand. "I'm Ben Beckham."

"Forgive me, I'm forgetting my manners." She gave him her hand and introduced herself. "I'll be in the office straightening things up. Please let me know when you're finished." She left, leaving Judy grinning.

Ben got the picture right away. Judy wasn't exactly thrilled taking orders from an outsider and was enjoying Hayden's blunder.

Judy finished the inventory and handed him a copy.

He folded it and put it in his billfold, saying, "What's she going to do when she comes out and finds ..."

A crash and a scream broke the air. Momentarily stunned, they looked at each other for a split second before running into the office. Hayden had put a chair on the desk, and it must have slipped off as she was reaching for a box on a high ledge, and she was hanging with one hand gripping the ledge and the other a pipe. Ben jumped on the desk, got hold of her and lifted her down to the floor.

"I wouldn't try that trick again any time soon," he said as he jumped off.

Hayden rubbed her hands on her jeans and after eyeing her nails, shut her eyes and squealed.

Ben took her hands and examined them. "It doesn't look like anything's broken."

Clearly distraught, Hayden yanked them away.

Judy laughed openly. "Only them manicured fingernails of

hers, I reckon."

Hayden's back went ramrod straight. "Well, will everybody just get back to work!"

Suddenly a man peeked in the door. "Sorry I'm late."

Hayden stared at him for a moment in disbelief. "Who are you?" she asked, flustered.

"The handyman."

She turned and looked questioningly at Ben who was smiling at her confusion. "Then who are you?"

"I teach at Warren Wilson. Came to make a delivery."

"Well, why didn't somebody say something!" She clamped her jaw and glared at Judy.

"I guess I'll be getting along," said Ben, his eyes catching the handyman's as he walked out the door.

On his way to his truck, Ben couldn't help thinking about Hayden and Judy. He knew the way it was between them and didn't think it was fair to Hayden. When he first saw her across the room at the funeral parlor, her striking beauty excited him. He figured it would be a long time before the likes of her would be seen in these parts again. But when he shook her hand and looked into those strange gray eyes he saw the same thing he'd seen in his own when Jenny was dying, and had to fight off the return of the sickening remorse he'd lived with for more than a year.

He pictured Hayden hanging from the ledge like nothing was ever going to make her let go and couldn't help smiling to himself. It looked like she had more than just looks—the kind of grit he'd seen in the old-timey mountain people.

He smiled to himself once more, remembering her attempt at looking casual in a pair of jeans topped with a two-hundred dollar cashmere sweater and silk scarf around her hair; but he liked her for the effort. He also liked her for trying to breathe some life into her father's gallery. Talk was she never knew him. There had to be a story in there somewhere. The whole notion of this elegant Southern belle staying on, rolling up her pricey sleeves and diving into Asheville Arts was both fascinating and puzzling.

THINGS IMPROVED in the gallery as the day went on. The five oak tables Hayden had wrestled from an antique dealer arrived along with the antique tablecloths, Judy was beginning to respect her judgment, and the handyman actually stayed until five.

Thankfully, there weren't any classes that night. When Hayden said goodbye to Judy, they hesitated for a moment then spontaneously gave each other a hug—the kind they couldn't let go of because it was saying so much. And, naturally, Judy couldn't pass up the chance to get all teary-eyed. Hayden deflected the emotion by changing the subject. "I'll be coming in late tomorrow. A man from a conservation group is coming to see me."

Her father's lawyer had set up the appointment, but at the time, she had been in such a stupor she hadn't really taken it in. The lawyer had also gotten her access to her father's bank account, and she was surprised that there was enough in there to cover the normal overhead for a couple of months. She still couldn't find his books or cancelled checks, but the bank was sending her copies for the past six months and statements for two years. That would give her a good idea of what was going on.

She'd already been at the mountain house for eight days, but had spent most of the time getting the gallery in shape or shopping. Her father must have lived on the air in the place. No salt. No pepper. She was now stocked and ready to take the place apart room by room, starting tonight in his bedroom.

Inviting Addie Mae to help on Saturday had been a bitter pill to swallow, but being on borrowed time she had to swallow her pride. There'd been numerous calls from Jack, but so far, silence from her mother, and every time a car pulled up or someone came to the door, she half-expected it to be her.

She was hoping she could hold out long enough to resolve the riddle of her father and decide what to do with the gallery even though Jack had demanded, "Close it!" during their last call. She wondered what he was going to say when he got her charge card bill riddled with cash advances.

She stopped off at a home improvement store and picked up some needed hardware, then started toward the gorge.

HAYDEN SPOTTED THE FIRST indication of the coming approach to Chimney Rock—a "Welcome" sign on the village's boundary. Then she swung around the next curve and spied one welcoming everyone to "Small Town Friendly" Rutherford County. Below it, another sign with a large ominous eye warned: "Neighborhood Crime Watch."

It seemed to her that the town and county fathers didn't want to waste any time indoctrinating anyone coming into their realm, and posted every possible warning or annoyance. Tonight she decided to stop and find out what they all said. She pulled into one of the many parking spots along the river, got out, and strolled over to the type of sign she noticed was posted all along the route. "The Broad River is capable of flash flooding with little or no warning. Be alert to changing weather conditions and evacuate during severe weather or rising water. If you hear an air horn tone siren, evacuate immediately!!" Evacuation routes and shelter locations appeared below.

She walked a few more yards and read another one pointing out that the town's noise rule was enforced, and adding a degree of authority by mentioning *Village Ordinance Section 84.04.* She smiled. Too many people must have asked, "Who says so?"

She got back on the road and waited for the final curve before she saw her first glimpse of the Chimney poised four hundred feet above the town. At night it was lit and visible for miles around. It jutted upward from the mountain below the ridge, and from that distance the Stars and Stripes on top resembled the miniature flags they put on cupcakes. She could finally handle the drive without getting scared if she didn't go too fast, and was becoming more determined to overcome her fear of heights. Tonight, eyeing the Chimney, she made up her mind to start by giving it a try some weekend.

The Esmeralda Inn was coming up ahead. Judy had told her stars like Clark Gable and Mary Pickford had been guests, and the script for *Ben Hur* was written there. Across the street were some rentals. The only notoriety they had enjoyed was someone getting shot in a poker game.

Past six, the town was deserted with all the shops closed and just a couple of pick-ups parked in front of the Riverwatch Cafe. She had quickly learned that Chimney Rock had two distinct personalities—by day a bustling day-tripper destination, and by night a quiet, "dry" hamlet that pulled up the sidewalks after the stores closed.

A little stray kitten was waiting in the bushes as she parked in front of the cabin. She examined the dish she left out with some salmon the night before and saw it was empty. She went in and turned on all the lights in the dark living room, and giving the bear's bared teeth a second glance, got a sheet, stood on a stool, and threw it over its head. Her next effort to liven up the place was to put on a Rod Stewart disk.

As she stood listening to the strains of *Embrace me, my sweet embraceable you*... her mind wandered to the man she met in the gallery that morning. She'd thought about him a couple of times that day. More than she cared to admit. She used to think about Jack like that, and had hoped that after being away from him she'd start to get that old feeling back. But there was nothing but sorrow. It was as if the loving, playful couple had died along with their baby, leaving two hollow beings to remind themselves of the loss so the wound would never heal. If only they could have had another one.

She was doing it to herself again and had to stop. The romantic music was putting her off. She quickly shuffled through the disks and found a Bruce Springsteen. Must have been what was playing the day she came. She folded her arms and meandered over to the window. The sill, with its chipped paint, was pocked with hundreds of scratches and dings from its years of use. How many Taylors, she wondered, had stood at this window and watched Chimney Rock's shadow crawl up Round Top as the sun sank in the west?

Listening to the music, she pictured herself as the lady in the blue dress and felt joyous. She was going to be all right tonight. Snap right out of it. A quick shower, a glass of wine, and then she'd make dinner. She found some clippers in the bathroom, held her breath, and trimmed what was left of her nails. She chuckled remembering that afternoon when they were taking a break and Judy saying with a hint of pride that it took a Taylor to hang on to that ledge the way she had.

She came down the stairs in her pajamas with a towel wrapped around her hair after the shower, and went into the kitchen. A few pieces of asparagus were drizzled with olive oil and put in the oven to bake, then she sprinkled three scallops with salt and pepper from a new grinder and seared them in an iron skillet she'd discovered stuffed in a closet. She took off the towel, shook her hair loose and sat down at the round oak table in the living room and ate heartily, saving a part of a scallop for the kitten peering through the screen door.

The dishes done and kitchen straightened, she climbed the stairs and entered what had to be her father's room. A shiver ran through her. She went over to a small neat desk and picked up the picture she'd come in every night to look at of two little girls posing on a sand dune. Her grandfather had one just like it. She thought back. She and Barbara were still toddlers. Must have been before he went to Vietnam.

Other than the picture, there was nothing interesting, except for a worn wallet sitting there inviting her inspection. She'd save that for later, when she got into bed.

The desk's only drawer revealed a stack of papers and cards. She reached in and pulled a bunch out. Mostly articles on artists or gallery shows, often with *Asheville Arts* underlined. She lifted an old newspaper clipping and her eyes froze on the headline. *Debutante Weds Jackson Parks in Pawleys Island.* Her eyes filled with tears. He cared! He had to have cared or he wouldn't have cut out her wedding announcement! Thrilled, she wondered just how much he knew about her.

She pulled the drawer out and went through every sheet and scrap, dividing them into piles, with the biggest one being letters and documents from the Asheville Veterans' Hospital. When she found Barbara's wedding announcement along with a clipping from a glossy magazine showing her and Barbara at a fund-raising banquet, she picked up the phone and dialed.

"Barb! Item number one: he had both our wedding announcements clipped out of the *Post.* He was following our lives!" She rattled on about some pictures she found around the house of people who had to be Taylors. "If you want to know where your roots are, Barbie, you've got to take a look at this picture of everyone sitting on this very porch. There's a little girl in a flour sack dress that looks just like you!"

They grew silent.

"You sound good, Hayden."

"I'm finally getting out of my grog. After you left, I slept for two days, and every night I can't wait to hit the sheets. I haven't slept like this… in a long time."

"But, aren't you getting lonely?"

"How could I, with l'il ole Smokey the Bear hanging over the mantle and a rabid ole cat lurkin' outside? Listen, I'm just getting started here in the cabin. I absolutely had to put a Band-Aid on the gallery. That place was just crying out for a woman's touch. Heavens, most of the people who come into that shop are women."

"I hope you're not out buying *a lot* of Band-Aids. Mother didn't swallow the story about the new car."

"Do you think she's going to tighten the purse strings?"

"Uh huh."

"See if you can get a cash advance on one of your credit cards. Five thousand or so."

"Don't worry. I'll just get it from George. But, what are you doing up there? I mean, do you have some kind of exit strategy?"

"Item number two: we have to figure out what to do with this house, but we can't until I go through it with a fine-tooth comb."

"How long is that going to take?"

"Maybe another couple of weeks." Hayden bit her lip. "Barbie, I want you to come up and stay for a few days. Just you and me. There's something about this place and the mountains looming up over it that's kind of arresting. You've just got to come."

"I'll try. By the way, Mother's acting strange."

Hayden was too filled with resentment to respond with any sort of civility.

"I mean it, Hayden. It's like she's scared. Every time she lights up a cigarette, she phones me. And I'm getting a real sense of meanness in some of the things she's saying. Face it, sooner or later we're both going to run out of money."

They chatted for a while about the gallery and goings on at Pawleys and then hung up. Hayden took a moment to straighten all the piles and noticed a sympathy card she'd tossed on one of the stacks. Something warned her not to pick it up, but she couldn't resist. The pink tones and delicate bouquet of flowers made her stop breathing. She started to open it, then hesitated. But she knew she'd never be able to sleep if she didn't.

Her baby's obituary had been carefully cut out of the paper and tucked inside. She blinked back tears as she read the short note: *My beloved daughter, my heart goes out to you. Your Adoring Father.* She slid down onto the bed. No matter what happens in the coming days, she thought, discovering this sweet secret gesture would make it all worthwhile. She carefully laid the clipping back in the card, turned off the light and went downstairs to her room. She opened the drawer of her dresser and pulled out the delicate fluffy blanket and tucked the card between the folds.

CHAPTER TWELVE

"HAVE YOU SEEN THIS?" shouted Hayden. She slapped the sheet of paper she was holding with the back of her hand. "Pratt Institute is asking for tuition payments in December!"

"I'm glad you're in a good mood," said Judy as she worked at the copier. "They're for two of your father's students."

"What in the world was my father doing sending kids to school?"

Judy glanced up. "He never intended for it to happen. He got drawn into it kind of gradual like. He gave these kids lessons since they were in grade school. And they were good. But not good enough to land scholarships to Pratt like your father. You got to remember, they were competing with kids from all over the country."

Crouched on one knee, Judy tore open a ream and continued stacking paper into the machine. "Billy Bath was the first one. Comes out of one of those coves near Gerton. His mother used to bring him in Saturdays for lessons." Judy looked up. "She knew Billy had something in him that needed to come out. A real talent."

Judy ran some more sheets and brought two piles of papers over to the desk and started collating and stapling. "Once your father discovered it, too, he took Billy under his wing... setting up rides for him to get in for after-school classes... bringing him in himself on the weekends. Your father matted all his submissions for Pratt and personally took his portfolio up to New York; but the most he could get for the kid was a little help on the tuition and a job in the cafeteria to pay for his room and board."

Hayden couldn't keep the slight sardonic expression from spreading across her face.

"Marilyn was pretty much the same story. She wasn't as all-around talented as Billy, but she can do watercolors like nobody's business. Even portraits. Your father had her do them of anyone he could talk into it so she could buy clothes and supplies for school. She's starting to get a real following. We already have a couple lined up for her to do over the Christmas holidays, and a friend of your father's who owns a gallery in New York has gotten her some work, too."

Hayden drummed the eraser end of her pencil on the desk. There was no way she could afford to put two kids through school. "For starters, I want you to get a hold of these two and have them look for as many student loans as they can get their talented little hands on."

Judy stopped collating. "These old timey mountain people don't trust the banks or the government that much, and your father was of the mind that their parents might keep them home before they let them do that sort of thing." Judy started stapling. "Remember the kid that spoke at the funeral? Well, that was Billy."

Hayden drummed the pencil, and thought. The expenses grew by the day. Boxed in. That's how she felt. What else could Judy be keeping from her? She tossed the pencil on the desk and looked at her. "You don't like me, do you, Judy?"

Judy stared at her. A little frightened.

Hayden stood up, folded her arms and managed to pace in the tight space. "You knew about these kids all along." She stopped and flung a hand in the air. *"But did you tell me? No!* You weren't going to be happy unless it snuck up and grabbed me from behind, were you? I'm just getting in deeper and deeper. And just where do you think I'm getting all this money?" She pulled her wallet out of her purse and yanked out four credit cards and threw them on the desk in front of Judy. "There! That's where! And it's just a matter of time before my husband turns off the tap!" She threw up a hand. "Ha! I can hardly wait!"

One of the gallery's volunteers pulled the drape aside and peered in. "Are you guys okay?"

Hayden folded her arms and tapped her foot on the floor impatiently. The volunteer quickly said she was sorry and closed the drapes.

Hayden hunched her shoulders and hovered over Judy, her voice just above a whisper. "How could you sit here day after day and not tell me what my mother and grandfather did to my father? I had to get the truth myself last night from practically a stranger!"

Judy's face twisted into a mask of bitterness. "How could you and your sister not look him up all these years? Sure, your mother told you he was dead. But didn't you ever wonder where he was buried? Or where he came from?" Judy put down the stapler and sank into a chair. "Once, when you girls were around nine, he went out and bought you presents and asked me to wrap them. Pink sunglasses and a beach ball for each of you. He said he was going to drive down to Pawleys Island and go see you."

Hayden's eyes became large orbs. "Did he?"

"Oh yeah. He pulled up to that big beach house of yours and couldn't get up the nerve to get out of his beat-up old truck and knock on the door. He felt he had nothing to offer you but embarrassment. His limp was still pretty bad; he had no money. Nothing. But he couldn't leave without at least seeing you two. He parked down the street and took a walkway to the beach, thinking he might catch a glimpse of you kids playing in the ocean."

"Did he?"

"He said he saw two little girls who were just about the right age tossing a ball to each other. The little one missed the catch and the ball rolled to his feet. He picked it up and handed it to her. He told me he recognized the Taylor eyes and teeth the minute you gave him a big smile."

Hayden racked her brain trying to remember if she had ever seen such a man on the beach. "Did he talk to me?"

"No. In fact, he liked the way your older sister came over and pulled you away. Protective like. He just kept on walkin' down the beach and came home. He told me he was glad he went. It did him good to see you were both doin' so well." Judy shook her head. "If only you had tried to find out what happened to him. It would have changed his life."

Hayden went over and dropped back against a file cabinet, her arms loosely folded. She bit at her lower lip. So it was finally out in the open. Judy was giving her a hard time because she blamed her for what happened. This realization made her numb.

"We knew he wasn't dead from the time I was eight. That's when my mother told us he walked out on her and didn't want anything to do with us. For years, I was so hurt, all I could feel was hate. Hate's a bad thing, Judy. It tears you apart. You may not believe this, but I was finally tired of hating, and wanted nothing more than to lay eyes on him. That's why I drove up here."

The two women fell silent, with the only sounds drifting in from the gallery. Finally, Hayden picked up her keys and grabbed her purse. "I'm all worn out and I'm going home. What Johnny told me about my father, kept me up all night." She avoided making eye contact with Judy. "And I'm not coming in tomorrow. People from the conservancy are taking me for a hike in the mountains."

JUDY SLUMPED OVER the desk, her head buried in her arms.

The volunteer entered the office quietly and tugged at Judy's shoulder. "I can stay until closing, Judy. You should go home, too."

Judy rose and silently gathered her things and left for her house, just a couple of miles from downtown at the foothills of the mountains overlooking Asheville. Her cat, waiting on the porch, rubbed against her leg as she unlocked the door. She entered and went over to the mantle and picked up her husband's photograph. "We sure are having a beautiful fall, honey. You should see that maple you planted out front," she said.

Joe had been dead two years now, but that didn't make any difference. She felt as close to him as ever. She wondered why she hadn't cried over his passing as much as Hayden's. Maybe, because her husband had enjoyed such a full and happy life and died surrounded by those he loved. Her eyes skipped along the photos on the mantle—her daughter and Joe beaming their identical grins, then her son, standing in front of Joe's old Camero. They'd been good years for all of them.

Maybe guilt made her do all the crying. Why hadn't *she* gone down to see the girls and told them what happened? It wouldn't have been any skin off her hide. So what if they didn't believe her and it caused a big rumpus? Things couldn't be any worse. And, why didn't his therapist at the VA do something? The whole damn thing was a mess that never should have happened.

Judy walked over to the window, pulled the curtain aside and looked out at the maple tree. Her thoughts scrolled back to the fall, more than thirty years ago, when she ran into Hayden on Main Street in Chimney Rock. They'd hung out together all through high school. She didn't know who looked worse, her or him. She had just left her first husband who was little more than a drifter, and come back to the mountains from Florida. With her parents dead and the homeplace sold, she was crashing out at a succession of friends' places. Thinking back, she didn't know how she survived it— living out of a duffel bag; no education; no money.

Hayden saw her pain straight away and invited her to stay on with him. She started off cleaning and cooking; and then one night he got home and pulled a dress out of a bag. He told her to put it on in the morning *'cause he was taking her to Asheville to work in his gallery.*

She couldn't help thinking how in all the years she worked for him, he had nothing but his students during the day and that eternal yearning for his children at night, while she met Joe and built a good life for herself. How many times had she watched him go down to the newsstand and buy the *Post,* and then over a cup of coffee scan it for any mention of that dang blasted Burroughs family and his two girls. She just knew when he was taking that fall, that's who he was thinking about.

With the mess his life was in, it was a credit to him that he'd still made a name for Asheville Arts, and so many of his students had gotten to where they were considered collectable.

No matter how much that girl gussied up the place, she wasn't going to replace his passion. All those years and not a damn word from her, and now out of the blue she walks in and takes over. Her hysterics this afternoon weren't all that bad. It was about time the cool little aristocrat showed some emotion.

But there was something wrong with her. She was hiding something, almost like a runaway. It was obvious her family was against her being there. Otherwise, with all their money, why would she be living off her credit cards? And then there were all the hushed conversations with her husband on the phone that always ended with her running out to buy cigarettes, lighting one up, and then crushing it out. She didn't know how many packs Hayden had twisted and tossed in the wastepaper basket.

Judy went into the kitchen and took out the tuna casserole left from the night before. She always made too much when her daughter came over with her two little boys. She started to put some in the small microwave on the counter, when her cat stretched its front paws up against the cabinet next to her begging for a morsel.

She put a chunk in its dish, and as she watched it eat, thought about a plan Karen and Terri had mentioned. Maybe the gallery could be saved by turning it into a co-op. They'd both belonged to one before and were calling around so they could put some numbers together to present to Hayden. She sure hoped they'd come up with something before it was too late.

HAYDEN DIDN'T REMEMBER being so sure of herself in years as she rushed out of the cabin into the glorious fall sunshine, looking forward to a day away from her problems. She had put on a pair of jeans and a pullover and braided her hair.

She took a long look at Round Top, a habit she'd fallen into. It gave her the same feeling she got from looking out at the ocean. On an overcast day when the thick forest surrounding the cabin looked uniformly drab without the benefit of shadows and light from the sun, she could look up and see the cotton candy white clouds floating across the mountain, or the mountain hidden behind a veil of smoky haze with only the crown of Round Top peering out, and for one brief moment feel like she was nothing but a speck on the earth and her troubles insignificant.

Excited to be doing something different, she struggled with the convertible top, then jumped in and pulled onto Southside Drive. A couple walking their dog threw her a wave, and she smiled and rolled along down the street. She stopped midway on the bridge, pushed herself up and looked out over the inviting boulder-strewn river. It was early in the day for children to be wading or playing on the rocks below; it had to be all the warm weather.

Being Saturday, bumper-to-bumper traffic was pouring into Chimney Rock from both directions, but a man in a pickup gave her a big smile and let her scoot out in front of him onto 74. Finally starting to appreciate the rhythm of mountain curves, she enjoyed the drive to Gerton, and was surprised to see so many people in the lot next to Nita's as she pulled off the road. They all must have known each other quite well by the way she got stared at as she pulled in.

BEN BECKHAM STOOD in the gathered crowd wearing a pair of khaki shorts, a white tee and his favorite hiking shoes that were nicely settled into, like old friends. He had spent the whole morning at his old house digging up some of the perennials that needed dividing, and bringing them back to a small sunny strip he had fitted out as a garden in his new place in the mountains.

At first, he had thought he would keep his twenty-five acres of woodland strictly in its natural state, with only native plants, but he found the allure of his English border so seductive he couldn't let it go. Every time he had to teach a class at Warren Wilson, he shot over to his old house and dug a few more perennials up; and every night spent time in the new garden planting.

Before joining the conservancy, he had been on several of their outings and knew a lot of the volunteers. One of his old running mates, Kate Decker, was there to lead the walk. When she wasn't teaching classes for Warren Wilson, she was one of the conservancy's strongest volunteers.

A major goal of these jaunts was to make people fall so much in love with the mountains that the conservancy could either recruit them as volunteers or get them to join their cause. Ben had noticed their membership levels had carefully chosen names denoting the donor's concern for the land: *Steward, Protector, Conservator, Friend,* and wondered what category they had put him in.

Ben smiled at Hayden's open convertible and walked in her direction. He greeted her with a friendly smile as he opened the door and helped her out. The gold braids falling over her shoulders sparked in the sunshine and her hair being pulled back from her face showed off her perfect features. He noticed how different her eyes looked. They seemed full of hopefulness.

One of Ben's eyebrows rose when she put a foot on the ground and he noticed she was wearing loafers and no socks. From over his shoulder he thought he heard someone say, "How is she going to go for a hike in them?"

"Pop open your trunk. I'll get your bag," Ben said, hoping she had a pair of sneakers or something more substantial in the back.

"Bag? What bag?"

Ben winced. "Darn. I forgot to tell you to bring your own water and some lunch. Don't worry, I've got you covered." He should have called her and given her more information. With the new house and juggling two jobs, he was really messing up.

By now, everyone huddled around Kate who was introducing the volunteers and staff. With her special welcome to Ben, it was apparent she was thrilled over him joining the team at the conservancy.

She continued by telling about the Hickory Nut Gorge, speaking with casual familiarity about the Appalachian woodrat and green salamander, two of fourteen rare animal species found in the gorge, and rare flowers like the granite dome goldenrod and white irisette, two of the thirty-seven rare plants.

The names of the mountains framing the gorge that begins at Hickory Nut Gap and drops down 1800 feet to its end in Lake Lure, rolled off her tongue—Rumbling Bald, Shumont, World's Edge, Sugarloaf, Chimney Rock, Round Top, Cane Creek, The Pinnacles, Little Bearwallow, Little Pisgah. She ended with a nicely concise description of the conservancy's work.

The group piled into a few vans and drove to the foot of the Little Pisgah where the conservancy owned six hundred acres donated outright by Glenna and Tom Florence and known as the Florence Nature Preserve. Given in two separate gifts, probably for tax reasons, it had miles of trails, many laid out by the donors themselves.

Hayden got separated from Ben when a friendly husband and wife team coaxed her into one of the vans. The group spilled out at the foot of the trail with everyone strapping on their backpacks and snapping open collapsible walking sticks that resembled ski poles. Hayden looked over at Ben, comforted a little that he had neither.

"Listen up," shouted Kate who had jumped up on a large rock. "Stay on the trail. Don't lose sight of the person in front of you. If you can't keep up, don't worry. Ben Beckham is going to bring up the rear and will always be the last person on the trail. This climb will be two hours up. We'll stop for lunch before heading back. Ben and Charlie Evans here on my right can answer most of your questions on plants. Have fun everybody!"

She jumped off the rock and landed in front of Hayden. Kate ignored a barrage of questions, and instead, looked Hayden up and down and pointed her walking stick at her shoes. "Do you really want to try this trail in those?"

Ben made his way over to them. "She'll be all right. We'll take it nice and easy." Darn, he thought. Another mistake. He should have told Kate how important Hayden was to the conservancy. If she'd known, she would have taken off her shoes, put them on Hayden and laced them up for her. Heck, he was willing to carry her on his back if he had to.

As she walked away, Kate turned and said, "Watch out for the poison ivy," and pointed to a three-leafed plant a couple of inches from Hayden's bare ankles.

The group, chiefly made up of experienced mountain hikers, attacked the trail like they were running from a posse. Hayden kept up for a while, but finally fell back against a tree to catch her breath until Ben, walking with one of the older men, caught up with her.

The three talked about the vegetation along the trail. Ben pointed out a flypoison plant in a small clearing and explained how it was on the threatened species list. He told her that the now green spike-like flower had beautiful white petals in the spring and that the Cherokee used its root to poison crows, and the pioneers to poison flies.

Hayden said she'd like to learn more about mountain plants and might get a book to study, and it seemed to Ben that she meant it and wasn't just making polite conversation. He crouched down and pushed aside some foliage to reveal a small clump of downy oval leaves with white veins arranged in an interesting pattern and explained how it was an orchid called rattlesnake plantain that grew in isolated colonies throughout the mountains. The flower spike was intact, but spent. Ben said the Indians believed it was a cure for snakebite, but it had never been proven.

Hayden laughed the soft lilting way he found appealing, and said she was glad she finally knew the cure for flies and snakebites, but wasn't going to be happy until he showed her a granite dome goldenrod. He laughed to think she'd remembered Kate's little talk and promised her before she left for the beach he'd show her one.

Before long, Hayden had gotten up to speed and was, he thought, doing pretty well on the trail considering her shoes gave her ankles no support. With the straight leg jeans and braids over her shoulders, she looked more like a mountain woman than an heiress. He noticed she had shed all the rings he'd seen her with before... with the exception of a wedding band.

He liked listening to the sound of her sweet Lowcountry accent as she walked ahead with the man accompanying them.

"You should have been here in the spring," the man told her. "There are pink ladyslippers all over this here mountain." He went on about the rhododendrons and mountain laurel, pointing them out, with Hayden quickly learning to identify the shrubs by their leaves.

The three finally caught up with the rest of the hikers who were seated on ledges on a rock outcrop overlooking a spectacular view of Bearwallow Mountain on the north facing slope across from Little Pisgah.

Ben helped Hayden down to a ledge that formed a bench, and didn't notice her move to an enormous rounded boulder at the edge of the outcrop as he went to find her something to eat.

He found Kate sitting on a rock and asked her if she had any extra food. She readily reached into her backpack and handed him a sandwich and a bottle of water, saying she figured he wouldn't bring anything so she packed two lunches. As he turned to go, she tugged on his shirt. "You're not going to give this to that China doll, are you?"

"Go easy on her, Katie. It's my fault. I didn't give her enough information and she's really being a good sport about everything." He crouched down and spoke under his breath. "Katie, she's Hayden Taylor's daughter and I'm supposed to be showing her a good time here on the mountain. I don't know if you know this, but her father was set to sign an easement agreement for his property on Round Top before he died. We're hoping we can get it from her."

"Damn!" She quickly reached in her bag and pulled out an apple and a snack bar. "Here, give these to her, too."

Ben took them, stood up and started to go, when Kate pawed through her bag and retrieved a pair of socks. "Have her put these on before she gets poison ivy, if she hasn't already."

The scream made them both freeze. This wasn't the first time Ben had heard that cry and his heart jumped to his throat. God help us; a fall could kill her. They both rushed to the front of the outcropping fearing the worst. Everyone was standing by the huge granite boulder that gradually sloped downward a good twenty feet before it dropped off.

"I saw it happen," someone said. "She turned real fast and started sliding with those leather shoes. She tried to stop by dropping to the ground, but then just slid on down and over."

Kate ran over to her backpack and pulled out a nylon rope. "I'll find her. Maybe she's all right. You call 911."

"I'll go after her," said Ben.

"No! I'm the best climber here. I'll do it!"

Ben, knowing she was right, quickly tied the rope to a tree and Kate started rappelling down the rock. Suddenly, a gasp rose from the shocked crowd. Kate's mouth fell open as she watched Hayden clawing her way up on the side of the boulder next to a clump of trees. Kate, holding onto the rope, bounced adroitly across the massive rock. "Easy now, don't move. I'm coming for you."

With the fingers of one hand dug into a crevice, Hayden seized the trunk of a sapling with the other. A muffled cry rose from the crowd. Ben cautiously made his way toward Hayden. She was breathing hard as she swung a leg up and over the sapling.

"Oh my God," someone shouted. "She's like a monkey!"

Before Kate or Ben could reach her, Hayden was on her hands and knees crawling to safe ground with whoops and hollers all around. Ben was amazed to see her stand up and brush herself off. His eyes darted over to Kate's shocked expression. She caught his glance and rolled her eyes.

Ben rushed over to Hayden, her pale face now flushed and sweaty. "Are you all right?"

"I think so," she said as she continued brushing herself off. She looked up at him and swept away stray hairs from her face with the back of her hand. "I landed on a ledge a few feet below. I wasn't thinking. I never should have worn these shoes."

She was married and Ben knew better, but he wrapped his arms around her and squeezed. Just then, he looked up and saw Kate standing there, her mouth slack.

The crowd became jovial, leading Hayden to the same safe

ledge Ben had left her at, and offering her water and all sorts of food. Ben smiled inwardly as he watched her eat a sandwich, nonchalantly answering everyone's questions. He didn't know why, but at that moment, he thought about her father. He had noticed how much the two looked alike at the visitation and noted that they both had the same sad look in their eyes, like their spirit was broken. But in the few weeks she'd been in the mountains, he'd seen a change. She didn't have that look anymore, and sure as hell there wasn't anything broken about her spirit.

Kate was now kneeling in front of Hayden putting salve and Band-Aids on her worst scratches. Ben was touched when Kate took off Hayden's loafers and helped her put on a pair of her socks, even though he knew she was only doing it for the conservancy.

The trip down the mountain was a relatively easy trek with everyone in the kind of giddy mood that surfaces after a close call. Hayden, although walking a little stiffly, seemed okay to Ben; however, he'd been hurt enough times to know that in the morning she'd feel like she'd been hit by a ton of bricks.

CHAPTER THIRTEEN

ALL SHE HAD WANTED to do was step a few feet out on the boulder so she could get a peek at the view, and now, here she was sitting in the tub counting her bruises and fuming over the way her fear of heights caused the whole humiliating fiasco.

The minute she had sensed the endlessness of the expanse off the mountain, she felt she was about to spiral into space, and spun around to run off, when her smooth leather soles slipped on the slick rock and she took the fall. Even at that point, if she had stayed calm and kicked off her shoes, she could have worked her way off the bald granite with her bare feet.

On the trek down the mountain, she had wanted to tell Ben that's why she went over, but he worked so hard at being amusing to lighten up the mood that she never got the chance. Now she worried that he considered her foolish, especially after the episode in the gallery.

She had to admit she liked being with him and had to keep telling herself the hug he gave her didn't mean anything. She remembered feeling a tingling sensation all over her body when he bent down to uncover a plant and she got a good look at his long, broad-shouldered back. It was easy to picture him in a skintight uniform running across a football field.

She got out of the tub and examined herself in the full-length mirror, her hair tumbling over her shoulder. She was finally starting to feel like a woman again. Even the scar didn't seem to bother her tonight.

Patting herself dry, she felt a little guilty about taking the day off, and remembered she hadn't taken a thorough look at the closet at the end of the hall. She decided to slip into her pajamas and poke around in there while she waited for Barbara to return her call.

The door was made of tongue and groove planks held together by a crisscross grid of boards on the back. Had to be original to the building. Just like she remembered, there were some musty clothes on hangers. She pushed them aside and saw a few cardboard boxes in the back on the floor she had missed in her first inspection. It was too dark to see anything, so she dragged them out into the hall with every muscle in her body telling her to leave it for another time.

Ignoring her sore fingers, she tore open the first one. Nothing but a bunch of old files—school records, army papers. The other box held a stack of old bills. She fanned through them and found they were at least ten years old. She shoved the boxes against the hall wall and closed the closet door. She'd go through everything later. Right now, she needed a drink. The phone rang and she ran down the stairs in her bare feet.

Hayden wedged the phone between her shoulder and jaw and chatted with her sister while she went into the kitchen and got a glass out of the cupboard. She put in some ice and filled it three-quarters with quinine water and the rest of the way with vodka. She carried the drink into the living room, then gingerly sank into a leather easy chair. Now she was ready.

"You've quit smoking, haven't you?" asked Barbara.

"I'm trying. How did you know?"

"Come on, girl. I've been listening to you inhale in my ear for the past two years."

Hayden wanted to say that she had been listening to the crunching of candy bars for longer than that, but didn't have the heart. She almost didn't have the heart to tell her about their mother. Barbara, being the peacemaker, forgave her for everything. This time she was going to have to call a spade a spade.

Barbara read her mind. "Okay, sister girl. Out with it."

"Barbie, I went to see one of Dad's friends who told me Dad never wanted that divorce. Mom and Grandpa forced it on him right after he got back from Vietnam when he was in the hospital. They made up the whole story."

"I always figured it went something like that. Think back before Aunt Martha told us he wasn't dead. Didn't it seem strange to you that Mom never showed us any pictures and changed the subject every time we mentioned him, like she was trying to forget he ever existed?"

Try as she may, Hayden couldn't remember ever suspecting such a thing at such a young age. However, now and again in recent years she'd wondered if her mother was telling the whole truth.

"That must be why she freaked out over the letter. She's afraid we're going to find out what she did," said Barbara.

"How could she and Grandpa have been so despicable? I could never imagine anyone doing such a thing to someone."

"It's best we never let her know we know the real story. Let's just bury it with Dad. Hayden, she's all we've got. If it helps any, she's been a mess since you left. Why don't you come on home and let Russell finish up there. Mom hinted that she would authorize him to take care of Dad's obligations."

"Barb, have you turned into some kind of fool? How could you trust anyone who could do what she did to an injured soldier? The father of her children no less? If I come home, she's going to sic her lapdogs on this place and heaven only knows what havoc they'll reap on everything he cared about. I'm telling you, Barbara, she's messed with him as much as I'm going to let her."

"Hayden, I've talked to George and if you come on back, we'll be behind you one-hundred-percent and help you handle everything from here. And if we have to, we'll sashay right on down to see Russell."

Hayden bumped her elbow on the table and moaned. When Barbara asked her what was wrong, she didn't dare tell her about the fall. She grimaced and continued. "It's not that easy. I've already talked with him. Barb, I can't explain everything to you over the phone, but our father was getting a lot of money from somewhere. And since his bookkeeping is missing, I can't figure from where. I need more time."

The two women were quiet as they gathered their thoughts.

"You'd like him, Barb."

"Dad?"

"Uh huh."

They were silent for another while until Barbara asked, "What's Jack saying?"

"Naturally, he's in mother's corner."

"Darlin', please come on home. I promise you, we'll get everything straightened out. This is where you belong."

For one insane moment, Hayden almost believed her, but that last phrase made her stop and think. Is that where she belonged? The lowcountry was in her blood, but these mountains tugged at her soul.

They chatted a while longer. "I sent you some information on an easement Dad was going to give a local land trust on his four hundred acres here in Chimney Rock," said Hayden. "Take a look at it. But we're not going to be able to make any decisions until you get up here and see the situation for yourself."

Barbara agreed to come up the following weekend, and begged Hayden one more time to come home soon. It made Hayden wonder if getting all tangled up in her father's problems was just a way of running away from Jack.

As the call ended, Barbara spoke softly, "Hayden, if you don't watch out, you could lose him."

JACK GOT OUT of his car, filled his lungs with ocean air and smiled at the Mediterranean blue sky spread out before him. How he loved Myrtle Beach in the morning. He noticed a bunch of cars in the lot. Must be Cal going through the new Christmas numbers with the chorus. He ran up the steps, unlocked the door, and went in.

The janitor greeted him with, "Hello, Mr. Jack," and pushed

on past him with his wide broom.

Jack listened for a moment. It was Cal, all right. He'd know the sound of his piano playing anywhere. His fingers tap danced on the keys. The girls' voices drew him toward the stage and he peeked in. They had worked up a sweat, but they looked like they were confident they had the routine down. Cal would probably have them run through it with the full orchestra at the afternoon rehearsal.

He pulled himself away and strolled into the lunchroom, poured a cup of coffee, and took it to his office. Boards illustrating all the new sets lay on the floor, on chairs, up against walls... anywhere they could be viewed. Three mannequins wore skimpy, but not too skimpy for the Bible belt, versions of a red velvet Santa's helper outfit fringed in imitation ermine.

As he made his way to his desk, the bank of framed photos hanging on the wall caught his eye. It had been a long time since he took a look at them. With Hayden being gone all these weeks, he felt a yearning for the ways things used to be. He had his arm around her in the photo they took on opening night. God, how he loved that grin of hers.

From the moment he laid eyes on her at the frat party, she captivated him. How could anyone that beautiful be so down home? It wasn't possible this debutante from one of South Carolina's most distinguished families could ever fall for a guy whose only goal in life was to own a live musical theater. It didn't fit in with her genteel Southern upbringing. Heck, it didn't fit in with his. He remembered how his parents ignored his dreams and pinned all their hopes on his two younger brothers' careers in medicine and law.

A surge of love washed over him, remembering that Hayden didn't seem to notice how no one took his career seriously after they married. His own mother glossed over his stint in Branson, Missouri, by telling everyone he was "between jobs." He thought back and couldn't believe he was ever that driven. Nothing could stop him. He only felt alive on stage. He connected to the aura of an audience at his feet. He fed on it.

He studied the picture. Elizabeth Tarrington stood next to

Hayden. You'd think she'd be the last one to make his dream come true. He recalled the way she hopped on his career once Hayden became pregnant. He could hear her on the telephone as if it were yesterday. "Bring me that proposal for a theater in Myrtle Beach Hayden says you're shopping around to investors."

What a whirlwind. She and her father paid a consultant almost what he was making in a year to analyze his proposal. He couldn't sleep for two weeks. The day Elizabeth called and said they would finance the theater, was the happiest in his life.

That's when he started feeling guilty. In all the excitement, Hayden began to recede into the background. But with the baby coming, she didn't seem to mind.

The road to developing a successful theater had been bumpy at first, and because of the nature of the business, still was. He'd had a rough time right after his opening. The Palace Theater came on the scene and gave him stiff competition. He managed to regroup and hang on to his theater, but swore he'd never let that happen again.

He went to his desk and took a sip of coffee. He straightened the stacks of files on his desk, and mulled over why Elizabeth was coming to pay him a visit. Anything she had to say, she could do over the phone.

He marveled at her ability to keep emotion out of business, and he suspected, out of any other sort of experience as well. For a woman who never ran a company, she had a piercing knowledge of all kinds of strategies. She had to have learned them from a lifetime of manipulating and being manipulated by her father. In observing her, he came to the conclusion that she wasn't as pleased to have someone's blind obedience as she was to succeed in deftly maneuvering them to her way of thinking without them knowing. Sorry, Liz, thought Jack. In due time, everyone figures you out.

Elizabeth Tarrington walked in without knocking. Pretty much what he had expected her to do. She was stunning in a sky blue dress, but not as stunning as Hayden would have been. Her face was narrower, and instead of the perfect nose, hers turned up a little too much so as to make her nostrils prominent. Jack hid his smile. If anyone ever had stage presence, it was this woman.

She took a chair like she owned the place, and technically she did. It would be at least another twenty years before he paid off the mortgage.

As he expected, Elizabeth got straight to the point. "Jack, you're going to hear about this sooner or later and I wanted to give you a heads up."

Her remark surprised him. He anticipated she was coming to demand that he press harder for Hayden to come home, and now it seemed like it was a little more than that, like she was letting him in on some confidence.

Jack settled back in his chair. This was going to be good.

"You're a real Southern gentleman, Jack, and I know you're not going to reproach me. But that girl is. I need your help."

He waved his hand with a flourish. "Mother, you have it."

"I knew I could depend on you. I've never told you this before, but you've been like a son to me, Jack."

The remark sent a chill through him.

She glanced around the room, her eyes pausing at the mannequins for a moment, then she looked straight at him. "I don't know how much Hayden's told you about her father, but I lied to her and Barbara about him asking for the divorce and refusing to see them. Once she starts nosing around, she'll find out and it's liable to distress her, especially where I'm concerned."

It startled Jack to see how coolly she could disclose such facts.

"I know now what my father and I did was wrong, and not up to the Burroughs standards of deportment, but at the time the whole marriage was a disastrous mistake we felt we had to correct... as painful as it might be to all concerned. I warned Hayden that if he left his family to go to that godforsaken war in Vietnam of all places, I wouldn't be there when he came back. He chose to go look for his brother over taking care of his own family.

She brushed something from her dress, and Jack figured she couldn't look him in the eye.

"I was humiliated. If it weren't for my dear father I don't know what I would have done. I married Charles as soon as Hayden came back from Vietnam and my father's lawyers were able to get the divorce." She looked up at him. "My father didn't want the girls to have the baggage of my failed marriage in their background, so he thought it would be best to wipe the slate clean by telling everyone Hayden died in the war, and let us get on with our lives."

Jack was amazed with how impersonally she had rationalized the deed, until her voice started to quiver.

"I never knew the extent of his injuries until he called me from a hospital a year or so later." She looked away. "He wanted to see the girls, but my father would have none of it."

Her eyes met Jack's, and he detected a flicker of pain.

"You knew my father. He had an iron will. He raised me single-handedly after my mother died and was all I ever knew. What could I do? I just went along."

"Why don't you drive up to Chimney Rock and tell Hayden all this?"

She stood up. "No, Jack. I want you to do it. When she comes back, I intend to make it up to her as best I can, but first, she's got to come home... here to the lowcountry where she belongs." She started to leave, then turned. "I don't want you financing this idiocy. Do you understand? *Not one penny.*"

After all she'd done to Hayden and the poor guy who married her, it astonished Jack that the woman only showed a flicker of remorse, and only for an instant. Talk about an iron will. At that moment he was proud of Hayden. In an awesome display of southern manners, she had never said a word against her mother. Not even a "Bless her little heart" every once in a while.

He reached for the picture of Hayden he kept on his desk. Angel Face, he always called her. What must it have been like for this sweet-tempered girl who always wanted to please to be brought up by this woman? No wonder she fell apart after little Carrie died. All Hayden must have wanted was a child of her own who she could shower with all the love she'd never gotten.

He turned the frame over and carefully slid out the cardboard backing to reveal a photo he'd taken of Hayden and Carrie right after Hayden came home from having her operation. Carrie was a month old. He ran a finger over the two deep dimples she inherited from him.

He fixed on Hayden's endearing signature smile with the two crowded eye teeth and remembered how ecstatic she was over their little treasure. It seemed to get her past the tragedy of not being able to have any more children. But after Carrie got sick, he noticed a change. Desperation clouded her eyes, and she refused to have sex.

If only he could have focused her on adopting a newborn, she'd have snapped right out of it. Twice he had to stay home from the theater for a few days because of all the scratches and bruises on his face after he tried to talk to her about it. When Hayden wallowed in deep mourning for over a month, Barbara started to panic and came up with the idea of packing away Carrie's things so Hayden would move on to thoughts of adopting. He could see now what a big mistake that was. After having to call in a doctor to settle her down, he stopped trying.

He shook his head. Why did he turn his back and let her win this battle? His eyes roamed over all the costumes and illustrations. He got what he wanted, but what price did he have to pay for it? He was never there for Hayden when she needed him. Now, where was the passion to keep her? Maybe he just didn't have what it took to fight a battle on two fronts. Or, maybe he couldn't get over the painful way she rejected him.

It made him sick to remember the night he finally let himself slip away from her. As usual he had buried himself in work to keep from going home. He heard a knock on his office door. One of the girls from the chorus invited him over to her place. He winced recalling the epic bout of philandering that lasted almost a year. Thinking back, he couldn't remember all their names.

It had already been a couple of months since he decided he'd had about as much of it as he could stand, and went to see a lawyer to start divorce proceedings. He could still find some kind of a life. But he couldn't sign the papers. Even though the marriage had died, he wasn't going to be the one to pull the plug. Sooner or later Hayden had to realize the only reason she was holding on to him was because he was her last link to her only child. He was convinced she'd never leave him until she was ready to let Carrie go. Maybe someday she'd be able to, and maybe she wouldn't. Meanwhile, he was staying away from the nicer girls, lest he fall in love and ruin someone else's life.

He dug through a stack on his desk until he found the credit card bills neatly fastened with a paper clip. *Okay, Angel Face. Those five minutes I spent with your mother bought you another month.* He pulled out his checkbook and paid them.

CHAPTER FOURTEEN

T HE LIVING ROOM screamed out a welcome the minute Hayden walked in the door. Hayden's eyes roamed the room. She never dreamt the place could look so good. Addie Mae's "transformation" was more like a miracle. Hayden smiled to herself thinking that she must have picked up the term from one of the home furnishing magazines.

Addie emerged from the back bedroom. "I went and got us a new rug. Now if you ain't likin' it, I'll take it back." She nudged Hayden, "I got good credit with all the stores in Asheville. They know I'm decoratin' and stuff."

Hayden liked the rug. It lit up the room, as did the colorful pillows and lacey café curtains. She especially liked the way Addie had repositioned all the furniture and opened the room up.

Addie presented Hayden with a bill scrawled on a paper bag. No receipts, just a dollar amount. Hayden took it and glanced at the figure. Addie had obviously marked everything up. This was a customary practice amongst her interior decorators back home, so why shouldn't Addie. Hayden wrote her out a check and watched the sneer morph into an expression of self-satisfaction as Addie folded the check and tucked it in her bra.

Hayden went around examining all the nice touches. She would have paid anything for the way the place looked. Everything sparkling, the warmth of the blazing fireplace, vases of wildflowers here and there.

Addie, who never mentioned borrowing the Jeep any more and just drove it around like it was hers, readily agreed to fetch some ornamental cabbages in Hendersonville the next morning, and then work one more day to finish getting everything ready for Barbara's visit. She didn't seem put out that she would be there. This accommodating attitude left Hayden wondering if it would last through the weekend.

The next day, Hayden slid onto a stool and watched Addie finish the last window in the downstairs bedroom. Addie stepped back every once in a while to examine the glass from a different angle and talk to it as she gave it another buff, like she was sorry it had been neglected.

Addie asked a lot of questions about the reason for Barbara's visit, and Hayden answered with questions of her own about her father. As the day went on, the answers became less and less guarded, as did the questions, and they were both forming a pretty clear picture—Addie of Hayden's life at Pawleys, and Hayden of her father's mountain roots.

Addie seemed to know a lot about the Taylor family. Not so much first-hand information, more as if it were local lore. Every once in a while Hayden felt like asking her if she knew anything about her father getting large sums of money, but if in the three weeks she'd been there she couldn't find anything out, how would Addie know.

Hayden decided to take some clothes up to her father's room so Barbara could have the downstairs bedroom. She opened a dresser drawer and gathered a few of her things.

Addie stood over her, the sneer firmly etched on her face. "I see you've got a baby blanket in there."

Hayden gasped for air and slammed the drawer closed. She froze with her hands on the drawer pulls.

"Did it belong to your baby?" asked Addie.

Why did I let this woman in my life! Hayden screamed in her head.

"I figured somethin' was wrong with you the minute I looked

in them strange eyes. Just like your father's."

A pained cry of indignation escaped from Hayden.

"That's always been the trouble with you Taylors. Too sensitive. You let life eat you to hell up."

Hayden turned, and leaning against the dresser, studied the sneering face in shocked silence.

"Why don't you just go out and find yourself another one," said Addie. "You've got the money."

Hayden put her hands over her face and screamed.

"Shoot! I've gone and done it now!" Addie put her hands on her hips, shifted her weight and looked down at the floor. "Lady, you've got to get a grip on yourself. Heck, you're not the first woman to lose a young'un."

Hayden removed her hands from her face, now a picture of stone cold hate. She pushed Addie aside, left the room and headed straight for the kitchen where she filled a glass with ice and poured vodka over it, her hands shaking uncontrollably.

Addie grabbed the drink and splashed it in the sink. "That ain't gonna solve nothin'. Believe me, I've been there."

"Get out of here! Get out!"

Hayden stumbled to a chair and plopped down. Defeated.

Addie went over and gently took her arm. "Come on, now. I'm sorry. Anyways, your sister's comin'. Let's go finish up. I'll get your things out of the drawer and take them upstairs."

Hayden jumped up, fire in her eyes. "I'll get them!"

A clap of thunder echoed through the gorge. Rain started hammering on the tin roof over the front porch. Addie shook her head and watched as Hayden wrapped the delicate yellow blanket in a silk scarf.

Once upstairs in her father's room, Hayden opened a drawer and placed it inside. In silence, the women made the bed and straightened the room to the deafening sound of thunder booming through the two mountain ranges. Finished, Hayden went over to her father's desk, sank into a chair, and stared in wide-eyed silence.

Addie pulled up a stool and took Hayden's hands. "Tell me about it. It'll do you good."

Hayden stared ahead unblinking.

"She was the sweetest little girl you ever did see. We called her Carrie." This was the first time she had uttered the name since the funeral. "It all started when she was around two months old. A fever that wouldn't go away. Leukemia. After all the blood work, they hospitalized her. In her whole little life, she was only home for a total of four months. Died before her first birthday. We brought her home for Christmas and Jack and I slept with her in our arms. That night I thought it was a dream at first. But when I woke up and turned on the light I could see I had blood all over me. Carrie was bleeding from the nose. I knew then the end wasn't far off."

"How long ago was that?"

"One year and three months." She turned to Addie, her face placid, emotionless. "After she died, not one single night went by that I didn't have that same nightmare." She looked up at Addie, wonderment on her face. "Until I found a sympathy card my father bought for me but never sent. It was the most healing thing that anyone said or did."

"Why didn't you have another child?"

"When Carrie was born my uterus came out with her. Uterine inversion they call it. I remember the pain mostly, then being tipped upside down while they put everything back." Her words began to pour out in a rapid stream. "They let me go home after a week. I developed a fever, abdominal pain. I was bleeding way too much. Every time I called the doctor's office, they'd phone in another prescription."

She took a deep breath and slowly exhaled. "A lot of it was my fault. Jack was in the middle of constructing his theater and I didn't want to be a bother. I knew how much it meant to him. My mother and sister were in Europe and didn't expect the baby to come for another three weeks.

When my mother finally got in, she took one look and drove me straight to MUSC in Charleston. I'd gotten endometritis. The infection had spread to my ovaries, my tubes, every place down there. They performed an emergency operation and found a tear in my uterus. They recommended a hysterectomy but my mother

153

wouldn't have any part of it. They patched me up as best they could, but because of all the scar tissue holding the uterus in place I can't have any more children."

The room had gotten cold and Hayden shivered. Her thoughts lingered on how her mother personally cared for her for two weeks in the hospital, sleeping in the next bed. She wasn't tender or loving, more efficient and alert, like nothing bad was going to happen to what she considered hers. She remembered lying on the bed holding Jack's hand and listening to her mother talk with the doctors. "You've done enough to this child, absolutely no hysterectomy!"

The rain on the porch's tin roof sounded like it was being pelted with bullets. Suddenly a siren went off. Addie looked at Hayden. "That means there's a flash flood rollin' down the gorge. Let's git out of here!"

"You go. I'm staying."

"What are you talkin' about, girl? The bridge could be washed out any minute."

"I'm not leaving. How many years has this li'l ole cabin been here? It's too high up for the river to touch it."

"Well, I'll be damned. You got the makin's of a real mountain woman. But I'm not goin' to leave you here by yourself. I'll sleep on the couch."

"That won't be necessary. You can sleep in the next room."

As they moved on to the bedroom down the hall, Addie shook her head. "Girl, you're either very brave, or too stupid to know what a flash flood in these here mountains can wrought."

She pointed out the boxes on the hall floor and asked Hayden where she wanted them. Hayden said to shove them back in the closet and she'd get to them once Barbara left. Addie opened the door to the closet, and after glancing around, said they might as well toss all the clothes while they were at it and ran downstairs for a plastic bag. "It'll keep our minds off the river."

Hayden carefully checked the pockets and threw each item on a pile on the floor. She noticed an army blanket hanging on the far end of the closet and yanked it away as Addie returned.

"Where does this ladder lead to?" Hayden asked as her eyes

traveled up to the hatch in the ceiling.

"Beats the shit out of me."

"Is there some kind of a room up there?"

"How should I know? Your father was very secretive. I never knew what was goin' on in this house."

Hayden looked at Addie through squinted lids. She was getting suspicious of the way she went on the defensive every time she was asked a simple question about the house or her father. It made her wonder. "From outside, I didn't notice an attic room."

"It's set way back from the front. You can see it from my place on Terrace Drive. Some nights I seen a light on."

"Why didn't you tell me about this?"

Addie shrugged and threw up her hands.

Not wanting this to escalate into another argument, Hayden decided to say no more. She would go up there with Barbara. They shoved everything in the bag, put the two boxes back, and went into the bedroom.

After they finished making their third bed for the day, Addie sat down and bounced on it, remarking that the mattress wasn't all that bad and saying the room was nice too. She repeated it several times.

Hayden felt obliged to ask, "How much longer are you going to live in that room over the garage."

"Till the baby comes."

Hayden was mildly astonished.

"Haven't you noticed?" said Addie. "Everybody in this gossipy old town has." Addie pulled up her shirt. "Look! Why do you think I've been wearing this oversized sweatshirt in this dad-burn heat?"

Addie had to be more than six months pregnant. Hayden sank down on the bed next to her. How could she have missed it? She was getting so wrapped up in the gallery she was becoming blind to everything around her. She slowly shook her head. "You can't stay in that place in your condition. Something could go wrong." She bit the inside of her lip and thought. "Tomorrow, go get your things. You can stay here until the baby comes."

Addie rocked back and forth nervously rubbing her thighs

with tense fingers. "There you go again, lady. You don't know me from Adam. I got no right expectin' you to do this for me. I'd be takin' advantage."

"You took care of my father's house for him. That entitles you to some consideration in your hour of need."

"Why, if I went home right now and told my father about my condition he would put the heel of his boot on my rump and shove me out the door so fast I'd land on my face. Nobody's ever been this kind to me. Lendin' me the car and all. Half the people in this town ain't gonna have nothin' to do with me no more, 'cept to look down their noses. And you wanna go and take me in."

"I doubt if that will be the case. There's always room in someone's heart for a baby and its mother."

They finished stocking all the bedrooms with towels and toiletries, all the while Hayden wondering if Addie was genuinely appreciative of her offer, or just thrilled at finally getting her foot in the door. She'd been angling for a caretaker position from the start. But the thought of this baby was starting to intrigue Hayden and she found herself staring at Addie's stomach and wondering who was the father.

By now the power was off and the house in darkness. While Addie bustled around in the kitchen lighting all the lanterns, Hayden went out onto the screened porch. It was eerily black and the noise almost deafening with the roar of the thunderous river, the pinging on the tin roof above, and the muffled sound of rain pelting the forest. She pressed a cheek against the screen, letting the misty droplets spray across her face and the smell of wet decaying leaves fill her nostrils.

The door opened and Addie was silhouetted against the soft glow of the living room lit by lanterns. "Don't you have enough sense to git out of the rain, gal. Come on in before you catch somethin'."

As she came in and lay down on one of the couches, Hayden noticed Addie was nervous.

"Didn't I tell you we was gonna need these here lanterns?"

"I need a drink more," responded Hayden.

Addie scurried back into the kitchen, boasting she had worked as a bartender for a while. "Vodka and tonic with a slice of lime?" she called out.

"Perfect! But go easy on the tonic."

"It's okay to have a drink now," said Addie as she brought it in. "I just didn't want you using it as a crutch."

The fireplace was snapped on and they lay on couches watching it flicker and listening to the drumming rain. Hayden, too tired to cook and not wanting to mess up the kitchen, just had an apple with a slice of cheddar. Addie made herself a sandwich.

Every once in a while someone would say something, but mostly they both tried to absorb all the information they had traded through the day.

Addie suddenly snorted out a laugh. "You was right about the river. During the 1996 flood, the bridge got washed out, but it never touched this place. Your dad told me after his grandfather lost the original homestead along with his wife and daughter in the Great Flood of 1916, he was bound and determined it would never happin' again and rebuilt way up against this here mountain."

The dancing flames from the fireplace made shadows flicker across Addie's face. "Tell me about your little girl."

Hayden couldn't believe she actually wanted nothing more than to do just that. "She looked exactly like Jack. Deep dimples, golden brown hair, dark blue eyes. As sick as she was, she always smiled so nice and easy like her father. I went to the hospital every day, and with all those tubes and tape, she'd give her mama that big ole smile of hers."

Hayden decided she'd better think about something else before the hurt took over, and asked Addie to tell her about the gorge. The sound of her voice would be comforting if she didn't have to look at that sneer. Hayden closed her eyes and listened intently as Addie's voice eased into the rhythm of a storyteller. Hayden imagined homespun stories in simple unadorned language had been told by mountainfolk in front of this hearth ever since the cabin was built. An old timey art Hayden felt Addie didn't show too many people.

"Hiram Hunter was the first of us. Arrived here from the flat-lands over two hundred years ago. The Cherokee were still usin' the gorge as huntin' grounds back then."

The storm suddenly let up, but Addie continued the story. "Ole Hiram heard tell of this gorge while sitting around camp-fires when he served in Washington's Continental Army; and once the war was over, became one of the earliest settlers. My cousins are still sittin' on the old homestead in a grand house. I hear tell they take good care of the original log cabin Hiram built, even though it ain't used for much."

Hayden envied Addie's knowledge of her family's history as she listened to her story unfold.

"My grandpa was the black sheep of the family and threw away ever'thin' ever handed him. Maybe that's why my father's so mean. When we was kids, he wouldn't give us a cent. Not even for milk to go with the lunches we brought to school. My two sisters hate him to this day. The youngest one works in a bank in Charlotte and said she found out the bastard's got thou-sands in CDs."

Addie's voice trailed off and after a while Hayden got up and saw she had fallen asleep. No need to get her up and into her room. She retrieved a quilt from the downstairs bedroom and covered her, then lay back on the couch and stared into the fire.

In spite of all the conflicts and tensions of the day, with the glow of the fireplace and oil lanterns, Hayden felt mellow. She liked the idea of Addie staying on at the cabin. If she suddenly had to leave for the beach, she would be there to take care of things. Plus, it hadn't been but a couple of hours, and she was already concerned for the baby. And, just when she was thinking she'd reached a dead end in her hunt for her father's books, she found out about the attic room. All in all, this had been a day of discoveries.

CHAPTER FIFTEEN

S WEETIE PRANCED into the conference room behind Tom Gibbons for the conservancy's weekly meeting. Then the hound curled up on the floor next to him. Ben smiled as he reached down and gave the dog a pat.

This was the second staff meeting Ben had attended and his esteem for the place was growing by the day. He sat amongst the best and the brightest and hoped he could measure up. He'd spent last week at a conservation symposium in D.C., but was still finding some of the terminology tricky.

Suzanne, their P.R. gal, kicked off the meeting. Articulate, precise and charming. Next, Tom Gibbons began his report on lands they were in the process of protecting. He went over to a map-covered wall and pulled down a screen, announcing that today he was going to give a comprehensive update on concerns specific to the Hickory Nut Gorge. He looked at Ben and mentioned, that even though the conservancy operated mainly in Henderson and Rutherford counties, sometimes their projects spilled into the three bordering counties.

Ben had heard of Tom's reputation at the conservancy for putting his passion into words and he wasn't disappointed. The urgency in his voice sparked Ben's team spirit. The only time he had felt this kind of energy during his years at Warren Wilson was when the Giants dashed across the TV screen in his den.

Tom flashed a disturbing slide on the screen of the south facing mountain across from Chimney Rock Park's Exclamation
Point, the park's highest peak. Several people gasped at the yel-
low-orange scar gouged out of the forested mountain to access
the Prism Falls development. It dominated the landscape and
inspired the same gut reaction as watching someone walk into
the Louvre, take out a knife and make a snake-like scrape on a
priceless Van Gogh.

Next, Tom showed a surprising number of other recent large
tract developments in the gorge, then proceeded to outline major
parcels that could fall victim to this kind of development and
where the conservancy stood with protecting them. Ben liked
Tom's plain-spoken, yet knowledgeable delivery, more like he
was used to in pro football. Different from the university-speak
he'd had a hard time with, where they went around and around
in politically correct terms, leaving everything to the imagination.

Ben listened intently to the low-key discussion that played
out like a battle plan, and took notes on the various strategies
kicked around; everything from trying to get money together
from every available source so they could buy some of the parcels
outright, to, at the least, getting easements that would allow a
narrow corridor for hiking trails.

Tom put up a few aerial shots of the Taylor tract. "We're in
contact with the two sisters who have inherited the four hundred
acres; and contrary to rumors, the one who's staying in Chimney
Rock didn't jump off Little Pisgah to get away from Ben."

Ben threw up his hands and grinned, and everyone laughed.
He was grateful they were finally past that and appreciated
Tom's light approach.

Tom continued. He'd received a phone call from the other
sister, a Barbara Johnston, who lived in Pawleys Island. He'd
spent an hour with her on the phone answering questions and
going over the proposed easement agreement. From what he had
gathered, the family owned large tracts of timberland throughout
the whole of South Carolina and she seemed to have a keen in-

terest in conservation efforts. She also mentioned that her sister, Hayden, had heard from a developer, but as yet, was too busy with their father's gallery to talk with anyone.

The director interrupted. "You've got to get both sisters to promise to let us know before they agree to any kind of sale. The clock's ticking on this property. You and Ben are going to have to move fast. I don't want to have to go out and look for money to buy that tract at top dollar. That woman may be too busy to pick up a phone and return a call, but these guys will buy up everything in her gallery if that's what it takes to get her attention. Boys, we've already got all the paperwork to make this easement deal, all we need now is the signatures."

DURING HIS PRESENTATION, Tom decided to hold back from disclosing something else about Barbara. It was only a hunch, but it sounded like her mother controlled the family business, and this Chimney Rock property was the first time she and her sister were in a position to make a difference. He was pretty sure she was going to be the key to preserving this mountain, especially after she appeared so eager to go along on a tour during an upcoming visit.

Tom wound up the talk telling the group he and Ben were going to take the girls to the World's Edge property on the weekend. He noticed that when he mentioned that Kate had said Ben seemed to have established a good rapport with the sister working at the gallery in spite of the unfortunate fall, it put a smile on Ben's face. Her comment had pleased Tom, too, since it was clear Hayden's interest lay mostly with the gallery. This deal would hinge on the other sister; he would concentrate on her. It was good Ben was on board to help, since they were working with two principals. They'd just have to get together and work out an approach.

FREDDY LUCAS SNAPPED off the TV in the dark, cramped motel room. The grungy air conditioner jutted out from the window, leaving barely enough space for the bed. He hated the dump, but it was the only motel in Black Mountain where people minded their own business. He glanced over at the letter from the company's personnel director lying on the dresser. He'd read it a dozen times since he picked up his mail at his condo in Charlotte. Some kind soul had sent her the clipping from the newspaper. There was no mention of his indictment; they were too smart for that. Just an offer of early retirement. Made it look like a standard option. They evidently wanted to pull out all the stops to get him out before the trial came up.

If A.K. Tractors wants to save their lily white reputation, they're going to have to cough up more than that! He riffled through his suitcase for a pair of walking shorts and a tee shirt. He had to look like a tourist if he didn't want to call attention to himself in Chimney Rock. He'd walk over the bridge and see if the cabin looked empty, then when he was sure no one was around, drive up and get the paintings.

He folded the letter from the personnel director and shoved it in his briefcase. The sooner he started working on his pension payout, the better. The lawyer's fees were draining his savings, and he had to put up his condo for the bail bond. His fake passport put him back another thousand. He'd probably have to spend every dime in his savings account to get the lawyer to stall the trial date until he got the money for the three paintings and could take off for Mexico.

The lawyer said he could beat the rape charge, but he'd probably have to do time for the assault. Shit! He had to stay off the sauce. He must have been drunk out of his mind to hit that tramp hard enough to fracture her jaw. At least she was going to have her big mouth wired shut for a couple of months.

Good thing he had the paintings to fall back on. He had to demand a bigger cut from Valentino when he took them to New York, and if he resisted, ruff him up a little. Hayden died over a month ago. By now, everything should have quieted down in Chimney Rock.

All he could think of on his drive south from Black Mountain on Route 9 was how close he was to screwing up his retirement. He really counted on getting that house in Lake Chapala. But how in the hell could he swing it without selling his condo? He'd have to kiss that money goodbye once he jumped bail; and then, how, as a fugitive could he collect the goddamn social security he'd been paying into for the past thirty years?

He could feel his ears getting hot. Keep you head screwed on, Freddy Boy, or you're going to blow the whole deal. You can still pull this out of the fire if you keep your cool. A hundred thousand dollars apiece. That's what you've got to get for the paintings. He laughed to himself. And he wouldn't have to pay income tax on them either.

He recalled the real-estate lady showing him a nice two-bedroom condo overlooking Lake Chapala. If he remembered right, it only ran around a hundred and twenty thousand. There was at least that much in his pension fund. If he kept out of trouble in Mexico, the money from the paintings could last him long enough to find a rich widow. He'd take his time. Make sure she didn't have any family.

First, he had to get the paintings. Then, he had to negotiate the lump sum pension payout and accept early retirement before his trial date came up, or he'd lose that, too.

A good idea would be to have a little conversation with his pal who covered the next district. He could tell him his lawyer felt he might be convicted on both the rape and assault counts, and let him run right over to the personnel director with the story. That ought to soften them up for the negotiations. He'd give him a call tonight once he got back to the motel. Then tomorrow he'd call in sick, drive up to New York with the paintings, and be back at work on Monday.

Being Thursday, there weren't any tourists out on the road and it took less than a half-hour to get to Bat Cave. He found Route 74 just as deserted. He drove his white Taurus through Chimney Rock and passed Southside slow enough to glance across the bridge. Still too many leaves on the trees to see much. He turned around in a motel parking lot up the road and came back into town.

Good. No one on the town's main street except a lady pushing a man in a wheelchair in front of a gift store. He swung onto the bridge and started up Southside. Slowly. Didn't look like anyone was around. Just a short distance more to go before Hayden's place. A cat bound in front of the car and he slammed on the brakes.

Damn! Hayden's Jeep was sitting in the driveway and it looked like the door beyond the screen was open. Who in the hell could be there? He drove down the road until he could turn around in a driveway. On the way back, a large-boned blond in jeans and a sweatshirt came out of Hayden's cabin, shook out a rug and went right in again.

It was the same cleaning lady who came when he was hiding on the back porch. She'd be gone in a while. Meanwhile, he'd get some lunch in town. He swung onto Route 74, the town's Main Street, and spying a small white cinderblock post office with a sign in the window saying *Copies - 15¢*, got an idea. He'd put money on it that the postmaster knew all the town gossip. He pulled into one of their parking spaces, and instead of going in, walked down the street a short distance to Bubba's General Store.

An elderly couple sat on a weathered bench out front that looked like a recycled church pew. They commented on the old gas pump nestled against one of the porch's stone pillars. They read the old gauge, *Thirty-five cents a gallon,* and shook their heads.

The smell of age mingled with the sweet aroma of fudge and penny candy of every conceivable type greeted him as he opened the door. The tinkling of a bell on the door brought an elderly clerk scurrying down from the balcony in the rear.

"Can I help you?" she asked.

"Do you have any cards?"

She pointed to a small rack. "Those make nice birthday greetings if you know the year the party was born. Has highlights of hapnin's at that time."

He went over and spent a few moments as if he were really interested, picked one out along with an envelope and took it to the counter. As she rang it up, she mentioned that they also sold stamps. He shook his head; he had something else in mind.

The post office next door was a basic bunker with a room no

larger than twenty by six feet. It had one wall dedicated to postal boxes and two others to bulletins, including flyers of the FBI's most wanted that hung from a nail. A door on the left led into a smaller room with a worn counter proudly displaying a large glass bowl filled with candy, an amenity no doubt provided by the rotund postmistress who sat smiling behind it.

Freddy Lucas felt at ease. One thing he was good at was making friends with country folk, a skill he'd learned in his thirty years of bumping around farm stores in the Carolinas.

"How ya doin', Ma'am?"

"Jess fine," she answered.

He gave her a wink. "You wouldn't might have a stamp, would ya?"

"Sho 'nough," she said with a big, friendly smile.

He pulled the card out of the bag and wrote something, stuffed it in the envelope and addressed it to Mrs. Lucas at his condo. "It's for my mother. Not her birthday or anything. Just wanted to give her a tickle."

"By gracious, it's gettin' so most folks now days ain't that thoughtful. Just passin' through?"

"Yes." He leaned on the counter and looked out the window at the Chimney Rock. "Nice town you got here. How many residents?"

"Permanent. I reckin' we got about a hundred."

He heard the door in the adjoining room open, sucking the door to the postal area shut. When the outside door closed, the rush of air opened it a crack again.

"I used to have a friend, that if I remember right, lived here."

"Really?"

As Freddy talked, the man who must have just come in entered the postal room and began thumbing through the Priority Mail envelopes in a rack in the corner.

Freddy pulled his gaze away from the window and looked at the woman. "Hayden Taylor. Do you know him?"

She shook her head and a sigh escaped. "He up and died a few weeks back. Fell down some stairs and broke his neck. A body can't never tell when their time is comin'."

"What a shame. He was a really nice person. Did he leave any family?"

"Two girls. Right smart, they were. Met 'em at the visitation. One's stayin' at his place."

"Permanently?"

"I don't think so. Least ways, that's how it looks to me. She's probably just settlin' up his business. She's got a housekeeper in there with her now."

Freddy paid for the stamp, thanked her, and left.

JOHNNY REB STROLLED over to the window, and while careful not to let the man see him, watched him get into his car. He took out a small spiral notebook from his breast pocket along with a pen and jotted down the North Carolina license number.

CHAPTER SIXTEEN

R OUTE 64 RUNS with Chimney Rock Road between Hendersonville and Bat Cave through what is known as the Apple Valley. At one point it crosses the Eastern Continental Divide at an altitude of 2,236 feet above sea level. One could say that the story of this road is in many ways the story of the mountains and its people. Before it was an Indian trading path and later a drover's road, it was gouged out by the great herds of bison that had the brute strength to barrel through the virgin forest, followed by bear, deer and other large animals that roamed freely to and from the flatlands below.

This twisting, steep road, lit at dawn by the sun rising above Sugarloaf Mountain, was the doorway to early settlements like Henderson County's own Lost Colony that disappeared in the 1930's, and historic battlegrounds like the Slick Rock Road area where a wandering band of Chickasaw Indians fought the settlers in 1776. At Fort Point Lookout, Polly Stepp, a pioneer woman, ended a daylong battle with a renegade band of Cherokees by grabbing a musket, and with the dead aim she was famous for, shot and killed the chief.

Settlers with names like Lyda, Edney and Owenby cleared patches of land along the trail and built log cabins from hand hewn virgin poplar and chestnut logs.

In the early nineteen hundreds, this dirt road was traversed summers by horse-drawn carriages that carried visitors to Bat Cave from Hendersonville for a day of picnicking and sightseeing. Today, roads branch off from this mostly winding mountainous route with names like Ole Blue, Bald Rock, Hominy, Hogs Rock, and Apple Dumplin.

Descendants of the early settlers still live along the route, selling apples from their orchards and mountain cabbage from their fields. And even today, the rugged beauty of this place still has the ability to draw modern-day settlers, like a couple from Texas who opened an emporium on the Slick Rock leg of the route offering many of the old-time handmade articles—two young people who wandered through and couldn't leave.

Barbara decided to drive to Hendersonville and take Route 64 to Hayden's. She pulled into one of the several vegetable stands and picked up some heirloom tomatoes and sweet mountain cabbage. "The last of the season," the lady told her.

HAYDEN HAD BEEN WAITING for Barbara all morning, and when she heard her pull in, ran out, banging the screen door against the house behind her. Hayden ran over and hugged Barbara, then excitedly broke the embrace and thrust both arms upward toward Round Top. "Look! Have you ever seen anything so gorgeous in your whole life!" Then she tugged at her sister until she was in the house, stopping abruptly in the middle of the living room.

She threw up an arm with a flourish and sang out, *Ta-dah!,* then ran around pointing out family portraits and some of her father's treasures. She snatched up a framed photograph and thrust it in Barbara's face. "Look! That girl in the gunny sack dress is your spitting image!" Hayden paused to catch her breath and read her sister's reaction to the photograph.

Hayden watched Barbara study the photo, then place it back on the table. Her sister came over to her, cupped her face in both hands, and looked into her eyes. "I can't believe it. You're back, baby. You're back." Then Barbara hugged her tenderly.

Addie walked in holding a tray with two glasses of wine and hors d'oeuvres.

"Gracious! Where are my manners?" Hayden proclaimed. She quickly introduced Addie, then scurried into the kitchen and came out with another glass of wine. "Ladies! A toast!"

Addie rolled her eyes and reluctantly took a glass from the tray.

Hayden lifted hers toward the bear over the fireplace. "Here's to Joe! May he rest in peace in this house for another hundred years!"

Addie Mae took a token sip and went out to fetch Barbara's bags while the two sisters chatted about doings at the beach. When she came back and headed for the bedroom toting a heavy suitcase and a garment bag, Hayden grabbed the suitcase, then took her sister's hand and the two followed Addie. Hayden smiled as she watched Barbara's eyes roam over the beautiful furnishings and art objects, aware of the effect they were having.

Barbara ran a hand under the necklace draped around a bust, saying it was the most beautiful piece of jewelry she'd ever seen. She looked at Hayden. "This was made for you. You're the only one I know who could dare compete with its beauty."

The women hugged again, with Barbara stroking Hayden's hair. "Baby, I don't care how wild and crazy this scheme of yours is; it's brought you back to us."

Barbara opened her suitcase, and Hayden noticed a pair of well broken-in hiking shoes.

"Whose are those?"

"Mine, of course. I wear them when I go out with our forest manager to inspect our lumber tracts."

Hayden remembered her mention of visiting the tracts, but never realized she was that involved.

While arranging some personal items on the dresser top, Barbara went on about how she had led a group into several of their tracts, trying to sight the ivory-billed woodpecker everyone feared might be extinct. "Hayden, do you remember Grandpappy telling us he sighted one back in the forties on our property above Spartanburg?"

The question surprised Hayden. She'd never seen this side of Barbara before. She'd been so wrapped up in her sorrow that she hadn't really gotten to know what her sister did outside the family. Then not wanting to be outdone, she told her to wait right there, and ran out of the room and up the stairs. She returned proudly dangling a pair of brand new hiking boots.

"You mean you're not going on that trail in a pair of high heels?"

Addie, who was bringing in another bag, piped up with "She ain't rightly goin' to be doin' that kind of thing no more… but a body can never tell."

Hayden followed Addie out of the room and tapped her on the back. Addie turned. Hayden held a finger to her lips and whispered *ssshush*. Addie smirked from one side of her mouth and said *okay, okay*.

Dinner was as elaborate as Hayden could make it, with everyone in a jovial mood. With all the excitement, Hayden had almost forgotten about the attic room, and they decided she and Barbara would explore it after they finished the tour the next day.

Throughout the meal, Barbara and Addie kept looking up at each other and Hayden could tell they hadn't exactly hit it off. Hayden had warned Barbara that she had to make allowances, but it didn't help. Especially that afternoon, when Addie called her sister to the staircase and pointed to the landing halfway up, declaring, "That's where I found him. Dead as a doornail. Cleaned the whole downstairs before I got to him."

THAT SAME AFTERNOON, Bill McAnnis pulled into a parking space at the Bat Cave Post office and waved to Ben who quickly jumped into his Jeep. As one of the conservancy's board members, he was frequently asked to take people on a tour of their projects, and was looking forward to taking Ben out today in advance of his and Tom's trip with the Taylor girls. They could grab lunch at the Lake Lure Inn afterward.

Bill drove down Route 64 toward Hendersonville and turned off onto Pilot Mountain Road, then onto Sugarloaf that climbed and curved like a serpent along the ridge. After a mile or so, he turned onto a deeply rutted dirt road. He couldn't wait to show off the pristine World's Edge property to Ben.

The road ended with a spectacular view, and they both jumped out. Bill smiled at the awed expression on Ben's face. He was awed all over again himself. No matter how many times he'd been up to this outlook point along the mile-long ridge of steep slopes contained in the World's Edge property, the view always conjured up an imagine of a Cherokee scout shading his eyes from the sun, and looking out for miles for the great buffalo herds.

"This is fantastic," said Ben. "How many acres is it?"

"Fifteen hundred."

"Wow. How long has the State owned it?"

"Over a year now."

Bill stood next to Ben at the edge of the lookout point thinking that capturing this place would probably be one of the biggest deals the conservancy would ever achieve. He was proud of his part in it. He looked over at Ben.

"Getting this property into the hands of the State of North Carolina is one of the most exciting sagas I've ever lived through. Hell, it could have wiped me out."

Ben raised an eyebrow.

"Yep. We had our eyes on it well before the owner died in 2005. It's hard to believe. In a matter of days, a developer offered the executrix of the estate sixteen million for it. We jumped right in and got her to agree to sell it to us instead. The kicker was that we had to match the offer and come up with the funds in thirty days."

Bill smiled inwardly. He'd never imagined his love of the mountains would move him to such an extreme. "We ran right over to the State's Division of Parks and Recreation and got a verbal promise that if we managed to keep it out of the hands of the developer they'd eventually buy it back and make it a part of the then-proposed Hickory Nut Gorge State Park."

"Did you get it in writing?"

"No. We had to take one hell of a leap of faith."

"How'd you get the money?"

"The Nature Conservancy came up with ten million, but we had to go look for the other six. We got three from the Open Space Institute, but the last three were quite a struggle."

Bill wondered if anyone would ever know just how much stress he and everyone else on the board went through to make this thing happen. He continued, careful not to make himself out as some kind of hero.

"We'd heard about the Self-Help Credit Union headquartered in Durham. They were lending money to those who couldn't find conventional mortgages... minority and women-owned businesses, rural residents... that kind of thing. Their branch in Asheville agreed to lend us the money if our members would gather up three million dollars of their personal assets and take them over to the bank so they could put liens on everything for collateral."

He remembered how gut wrenching it was for him to put up all the cash he could get his hands on. "About a dozen of us cobbled the money together. Some of us put up our life savings, and John Humphrey let them put a lien on his North Carolina farm that had been mortgage free since he bought it in 1968." He shook his head. "Can you believe it—all on nothing more than a verbal promise from the State?"

Bill filled with pride. This extraordinary accomplishment had created a momentum that coalesced efforts from all the conservation agencies operating throughout the Blue Ridge Mountains, and not only led to North Carolina purchasing World's Edge, but also the one-thousand-acre Chimney Rock Park abutting it, and changing the name of the proposed park to Chimney Rock State Park.

Before starting back, Bill got a bag out of the Jeep and started picking up trash. He looked over at Ben who bent down to pick up a beer can. "Folks sometimes illegally use this spot for partying, and I pick up every time I come up here."

They finished gathering the trash and got back in the Jeep. Before Bill put the key in the ignition, he turned to Ben. "Son, you and Tom have got to get that easement on the Taylor land tomorrow. Round Top's an important connector between the Rumbling Bald and Rainbow Falls ranges. We're going to need it if we're ever going to build that hiking and rock climbing trail along both sides of this gorge."

THE NEXT DAY, Ben looked at his watch and saw he was forty-five minutes early. He didn't want to show up at Hayden's place too soon, but was anxious to get into the game. He needed to get her to take her focus off the gallery long enough to embrace her father's wishes for the mountain. He had to admit, he didn't mind seeing her again, either. He drove his new SUV into Chimney Rock and ordered a coffee at a small restaurant. He finished in less than ten minutes and decided to run out the clock on the town's River Walk.

His tires finally thumped over the bridge deck across the Rocky Broad and swung onto Southside. A green Jeep and SUV were parked alongside Hayden's coupe. He pulled in and went up to the screen door. It slowly creaked opened and a bleached blond with the kind of long crimped hairstyle that went out in the eighties stood with a salacious smile, her eyes roaming his body.

"Miss Hayden said I should watch out for a nice lookin' gentleman, but darlin' she ain't even close."

Ben would have sworn he was beyond the point of blushing, but the fact that Hayden had mentioned him in that respect hit him unexpectedly.

"Come on in. They've been waitin' for you."

She didn't budge as Ben entered, and he couldn't avoid rubbing against her a bit to get through the doorway. It was the kind of move women had practiced on him for years, only now less often. The hardness of her abdomen made it clear to him she was well along in pregnancy. Addie sauntered toward the back bedroom, and he wondered what in the world she was doing there.

Hayden appeared with her sister, and Ben concealed a quick glance at their feet. Both wore sturdy trail shoes. Hayden made the introduction and mentioned the blond stayed with her. This was not a good sign. Had to be someone she was setting up to act as a caretaker once she left.

They piled into the SUV with Barbara in the front seat and made small talk as they drove up 74 to Bat Cave. Passing the Prism Falls development, Barbara asked if that was the road she spotted as they drove over the bridge. An eyesore she called it.

"What road?" asked Hayden.

"You mean you never noticed it? You can see it running up the mountain plain as day as you cross the bridge," said Barbara.

Ben glanced in the rear-view mirror. Hayden looked as if she felt left out.

Barbara brought up that she had told Tom that Hayden was afraid of heights, and asked if he had mentioned it to him. Ben responded that he had, then thought back to his last meeting with Tom. They talked about it, and figured Hayden must have panicked on Little Pisgah and that's probably what led to her falling off the rock. It was decided Ben would make sure she felt comfortable at the overlook.

Hayden scrunched forward as far as her seat belt allowed and said Tom had called her about it, too, and she assured him she'd be just fine. To Ben, Hayden sounded more like she was determined not to be frightened than convinced that she wouldn't be. He turned onto Route 64 in Bat Cave and drove toward Hendersonville.

As the vehicle climbed the twisting, heavily forested road, Barbara pointed out some hemlocks starting to die. "It looks like the Wooly Adelgid's pretty advanced around here. Most of our timberland is in loblolly pine but we expected to lose any hemlocks we do have."

Ben glanced in the mirror a couple of times and kept noticing a bored look on Hayden's face. The first chance he got, he asked her how the gallery was doing. She said it was coming along and invited him to come see for himself.

He then glanced in the mirror with an obvious gesture, so she would know he was looking back at her. "Only if you promise not to order me to rearrange the place." He could see a grin appear. There was something about the crowded eye teeth that made her smile look playful. Like they were playing a prank on her perfect face.

He turned off Route 64 and the vehicle climbed until it reached the ridge. They bounced along until they spotted Tom on the dirt lane in the four-wheel open Jeep used for viewings over rough terrain. They managed the introductions without too much small talk, and everyone hopped in with Tom.

As planned in advance, Tom sat up front with Barbara, and Ben in back, with Hayden sitting directly behind her sister so Tom could get a look at the both of them.

The Jeep bounced along the deeply rutted narrow road until it came to a clearing that was all blue sky. Ben jumped out, ran around, and helped Hayden down. She took his offered arm readily, but her smile appeared forced, and instead of walking with him toward the view, she stood on her tip-toes to get a better look.

Barbara, on the other hand, went to the edge of the lookout and took in the stunning view. The land fell away from the ledge and swept straight down two thousand feet into a bed of color.

Tom pointed out Kings Mountain in the far distance and explained there were twenty-thousand feet of streams and waterfalls in the parcel as well as habitat for rare flowers, endangered bats and salamanders, and birds such as the peregrine falcon.

Barbara turned to him. "That's quite an array."

"The forests of the Southern Blue Ridge are the most ecologically rich in the temperate world"

Ben cajoled Hayden. "Come look. I promise I won't let you fall."

She smiled and stepped forward, but he could feel her firm grip on his arm. When they got close enough to catch sight of the entire panoramic view, she must have dug in her heels, awestruck, for he couldn't budge her any farther.

Ben and Hayden silently listened to Barbara and Tom chat as a hawk sailed across on a draft. After a while, they got back in the Jeep and Tom slid around, positioning himself so he was able to make eye contact with both sisters.

His voice rang with deep sincerity. "All the land trusts in Western North Carolina are in a race against time to preserve what you're looking at. This decade is our last chance to raise a hand and say, 'Halt!' These mountains have taken millenniums to form and millions have been drawn to their spectacle. They're our national heritage. We can't sit by and let them be defaced to the tragic point that we'll only be able to tell future generations how proud and beautiful they once stood."

Everyone was silent for a moment.

"Would our property be the only parcel up on the Round Top ridge to be protected from overdevelopment?" asked Barbara.

From the sound of that question, Ben had to agree with Tom that Barbara leaned in their direction.

Tom answered enthusiastically. "Oh, no. We're pretty much working with everyone that owns on the ridges from Lake Lure to Gerton."

Ben noticed Hayden wasn't as fully engaged as her sister, and decided to take a hand at getting her drawn in. At the first pause, he put a foot on the axle hump on the backseat floor, hugged a knee and said, "If I could, I'd like to tell you ladies a story. It's part of the lore in these parts and I believe it's true. There's a plaque on the Blue Ridge Parkway at Bull Gap Overlook marking the spot."

Ben could see Tom straining to face him. He seemed slightly taken aback, but Barbara and Hayden looked on with interest. Ben cleared his throat and put on his smoothest storytelling voice. "It all happened on a morning in the early fall. The old buffalo bull plodded along the same mountain trail his ancestors had for generations as they went back and forth through the gap from the mountains to their favorite grazing lands in the flat lands."

Ben noticed that even Tom looked engrossed. Good. He'd let himself get more animated. "He was in a *surrrly* mood. For days he'd been searching for others of his kind. The old buffalo would eat a few mouthfuls of grass, raise his head and sniff into the wind for the telltale smell of other buffalos. The lonely old bull just couldn't understand it. In his youth he had wandered this same path with so many of his kin it took days for them to pass through.

"Each time the bull raised his head and rolled it back and forth sniffing the air, he poured forth a rumbling series of deep bellows that echoed throughout the gorge. It was the mating call."

Ben raised an eyebrow. "These bellows drifted into the narrow creek valley below where a young Joseph Rice was hard at work. Hearing the rumbling, he dropped his ax and reached for his musket, then waded the creek and started up the trail. He knew he didn't have to be cautious, for he was down-wind from the bull. He rounded a bend and caught sight of the raging animal pawing dust in the air. He got within shooting range and squeezed the trigger. The mournful mating call ended in a blood-curdling death scream."

Ben shook his head. "It was in the fall of 1799 and this was the very last buffalo to be seen in the Blue Ridge Mountains." He took a moment to look each woman in the eye. "We can't help thinking of this gorge as that old bull bison bellowing out for help, and we don't want to see it shot."

CHAPTER SEVENTEEN

THE TRIP TO THE WORLD'S EDGE had been a sobering experience for Barbara. Once they arrived back home, she looked over her shoulder at Round Top on the way into the house, and cringed at the thought of it being pockmarked with houses and gouged with roads.

Addie wasn't there, so she and Hayden ate lunch and decided to rest a while on the porch before tackling the attic. Barbara foraged around the kitchen until she found some peanuts, then went back onto the porch and sat adding more comments on the margins of the easement papers. It made her smile to see Hayden kick off her shoes and sprawl on her new wicker couch. Barbara hadn't seen her sister this relaxed for over a year.

Barbara reached for a handful of peanuts. "Well, Sister Girl, what do you want to do? I've studied this document and I think I know what it says."

"What do *you* think?" asked Hayden.

Barbara didn't want to come on too strong. She wanted Hayden to buy into her plan on her own. "I'm definitely in favor of doing something with the conservancy, but I don't know exactly what. After all, it's what our father wanted." She noticed the familiar squint Hayden always displayed when she was thoughtful. "But we're in a different financial position than he was. I've looked over the appraisal and it might bring us a lot more tax benefits if we give them the four hundred acres in segments over a period of years. I'm going to ask George to have our accountant get in touch with Tom Gibbons and go over the various options. And then he's got to get together with Jack and his accountant to see how this can best benefit us all."

Hayden lifted her head from the pillow. "Look at you, girl! I don't know a thing about taxes." She put her head back down and added that she didn't know anything about trees, the environment, or their forest holdings either, sounding as if the whole day had humbled her.

"Barbie, it's good you're into all this, but let's not act too hastily. We haven't heard what that developer has to offer. I know I've talked your ear off about the gallery, but tomorrow I want you to spend a couple of hours there. The kids will be in classes and you'll get to see the place. How it works... the energy. It's really quite wonderful."

Barbara took off her glasses and laid them with her papers on a nearby table. The gallery was starting to worry her. "Hayden, you know we can't subsidize that place forever. You've got to accept the fact that you might have to close it down."

"We know Dad was getting money from somewhere. If I can only come up with his books. Maybe he's got stocks or a Swiss bank account," said Hayden.

"For the sake of argument, what if you do find this pot of gold. Are you going to continually pour money into that place?"

"Listen Barbara, it's come a long way in the past two years. Besides all the money, Dad put in a lot of sweat equity. If I could get enough funds together, I could endow the place. You know. Just enough to keep it going until it's up on its feet, then maybe provide scholarships after that."

Barbara took a deep breath. It was starting to look like Hayden was never going to be able to let the gallery go. "You've torn everything apart. Where else could these papers be?"

Hayden sat up. "The attic!"

Barbara collected her thoughts and remembered Hayden's unsettling comment about the developer. Hopefully, a fruitless search of the attic would end in her taking a more realistic look at the gallery.

"You're not serious about making me crawl around in some dusty ole attic. I'm going to leave that to you after I go home." She looked at her watch. "I'll give you a half hour to rest, then, darlin' we're going shoppin'! I bet you anything there's something in that li'l ole town with my Georgie's name on it."

Barbara put on her glasses, announced she'd like to go to the Lake Lure Inn for dinner, then picked up her papers and continued making notes, while Hayden fell into a deep sleep.

AFTER A WHILE, the Jeep rolled in and Addie got out. She started toward the front door and Barbara quickly got up and slipped into the living room as quietly as she could, then rushed across the room to head her off, lest she waken Hayden. Addie swung open the screen door sending out a screech, with Barbara catching it just before it hit the side of the house. Barbara responded to Addie's quizzical expression by whispering Hayden was asleep on the porch.

Addie sighed that she'd cleaned three condos and was going up to take a shower. The way she gripped the banister and threw her weight on it for support as she climbed the stairs made Barbara wonder if she should be working that hard in her condition.

Actually, everything about Addie troubled her. She didn't like the insidious way she had glommed onto Hayden. First the Jeep, then the cleaning, followed by the redecorating, and finally her move into the house. But, most of all, the baby. Hayden may of had no idea what was motivating her to harbor this brash, greedy woman who was apparently trying to see how much she could get away with, but Barbara did. It was just a matter of time before she dangled the baby before Hayden's outstretched arms. Addie'd be set for life if Hayden took it.

Then she had Ben Beckham to worry about. The chemistry between him and Hayden had her mildly concerned, but she sensed he understood how troubled Hayden was by the way he took care of her on the trail. A little more than the professional courtesy extended to someone afraid of heights. And, when he was telling them about the old buffalo, she saw something in the lines of his artfully sculpted face that reflected heartache. These were two fellow travelers on the same road, and she believed they would never do anything to harm each other.

Barbara calculated. She was leaving on Sunday. That gave her tonight and all day tomorrow to find out exactly what was going on in Hayden's head.

She strolled through the room examining some of the items scattered about. Hayden was right, the place had the kind of character that comes from an authentic and intriguing past. She went over to the window and looked up at the mountain. She had done that over and over again while sitting on the porch. Something about this section of the monolithic range with Round Top as its promontory kept drawing her out of herself, and she could see how this relaxing mindlessness could give Hayden enough respite from her sorrow to start to heal.

BY THE FRIENDLY way everyone in the restaurant greeted Hayden, Barbara could tell breakfast at Genny's in Chimney Rock was a habit.

"Is that religious music?" Barbara asked.

Hayden barely gave her a wink and nodded toward a couple in their sixties who sat stonily, not saying a word to each other. Barbara could see by the expression on Hayden's face that she was thinking she'd rather die than end up like that with Jack.

The hymn coming out of the speaker reminded Barbara of the game they used to play since childhood. They would read all the signs on church lawns as they sat in the back seat watching the scenery go by on the way to their Aunt Martha's house in Greenville. "Have you read any good ones?" she asked Hayden.

"How about, 'Life is a test… are you ready for the final?'"

"Not bad. Where'd you see it?"

"Route 74, on the way into Rutherfordton." Hayden finished the one scrambled egg she had ordered and pushed the plate aside with the toast untouched.

"What was up on the barn?" Barbara asked as she picked up a piece of toast from Hayden's plate and dunked it in her coffee.

The ominous messages that someone always painted on banners hung on the side of a barn midway between Georgetown and Manning were some of her and Hayden's favorites. At the end of every trip to Greenville they'd pick the best, and that one usually won. By the location, they had figured the owners were black and members of a Baptist church. They swore that they'd find it some day and go to a service, but never got around to it.

Hayden put down her coffee and responded to her sister's query. "One of his best ones, actually." She leaned toward Barbara, an impish smile on her face. "Hell is no joke. Find Jesus now."

Barbara couldn't help notice how Hayden's eyes twinkled. She hadn't seen them sparkle like this since before the baby got sick. After breakfast, she was equally impressed with the ease in which Hayden handled the drive to Asheville as she rattled away about the gallery. She took the curves slowly, but it was a far cry from the way she hyperventilated on the way to the funeral.

"I can't wait for you to meet Ruth Summers," said Hayden, excitedly. "She's the executive director of the Grove Arcade Public Market Foundation. They run the place. Actually, all the shops and restaurants on the first floor. Oh, Barbara, you should have been there. I walked into that plush office of theirs on the second floor and expected to meet up with some pompous ole bureaucrat, but this woman was wonderful. She's been in the arts business for years and knows her stuff."

Barbara was incredulous. Hayden wasn't only better; she hadn't been this enthused about anything since she was expecting Carrie.

"I went to see about a couple of things. I wanted to know if they could possibly lower the rent and let me assume the lease."

Barbara caught a quick glance in her direction.

"On a month-to-month basis of course," Hayden quickly added.

"Well?"

"You've got to remember, Barb, this is a group of people who really want this historic arcade to serve the community in a really nice way. Ruth was very sympathetic and I think she sees the true value of Dad's gallery... the way it transitions a lot of its students to being recognized artists, and at the very least, future patrons of the arts. I'm tellin' you, kiddo, Asheville Arts is an institution in itself."

Just as Barbara had feared, Hayden was more involved than just putting on Band-Aids. "And what did she say?"

"Before they consider anything, I have to come up with a business plan so the foundation can see how the gallery's going to move forward." Hayden laughed. "I didn't get the answer I was looking for, but I sure as heck got a good feeling, especially when I left and she patted me on the shoulder and said 'We always try to work things out.'"

Hayden's interest in talking with the developer began to make sense to Barbara. This gallery had gotten hold of her and she was evidently willing to consider anything to keep it afloat. Barbara's eyes roamed the cliffs of the gap as the car twisted around the range. She remembered the metaphor Ben had drawn of the bison calling out, and hoped that pot of gold would turn up fast.

ON THE DRIVE IN, Hayden had warned her about Judy. *She hates me,* she had thrown out rather casually, *but don't worry, I'm working around it.*

Hayden had exaggerated Judy's attitude, but not the energy of the place. Kids of all ages skittered about between classes, calling out, laughing, then earnestly plunging into their work. Mostly painting. Barbara wouldn't have missed seeing the maternal look on Hayden's Madonna-like face for anything when one of them came up to ask her a question.

Barbara's throat tightened when a little girl with dark hair and a deeply dimpled smile ran up to Hayden and impulsively hugged her legs. She held her breath for a moment, frightened for her sister. But Hayden simply grinned with delight.

That split second of joy on her sister's face won her over. Whatever it took and wherever it led, she was going to help her hold on to this place. She crossed her fingers and hoped it wouldn't be at the expense of the gorge or Hayden's marriage.

CHAPTER EIGHTEEN

F REDDY CAME OUT OF HIS MOTEL room in a casual pair of walking shorts and tee shirt, slid into the Taurus, and headed straight for Route 9. The leaves were starting to fall, but there still was enough color splashed across the mountains to draw hordes to Chimney Rock, making it easier for him to go unnoticed. He expected Southside would have its share of weekenders, too. He could park his car on the street, cross the bridge and see if it was safe to stroll down the lane past Hayden's house. Then, maybe he could get a better idea of what was going on. He'd already gotten a glimpse of the daughter in the gallery. A real looker. Classy.

If luck was with him today and no one at the cabin, he would drive up, jimmy the door open, and get the paintings.

He couldn't think straight any more; probably the reason he had the big argument with the company's personnel director over his payout. As soon as he got his hands on the paintings, he'd be able to make concrete plans. That should settle his nerves.

He drove into Chimney Rock, and just as he thought, the place was packed. He scanned the street for a parking space. Good. Someone pulled out of one in front of the John Bull Trading Company. He put on his blinker and couldn't believe his luck. A car in the oncoming lane stopped and let him go in.

He reached for his camera and hung it around his neck, then snapped the tinted lenses over his glasses. Next, he grabbed his cap off the back seat and carefully adjusted it on his head. The expressionless black lenses reflected back at him from the mirror, masking the anxiety in the deep creases around his eyes. He had to get the paintings today. Time was running out.

DAMNATION! HAYDEN SAID OUT LOUD. Where was Addie when she needed her? She and Barbara had driven to breakfast in town, and when they returned there'd been a fender bender just before the house and she had to park at the end of the next driveway. When they finally got into the house Addie was gone. How many condos were there in Lake Lure anyway?

Barbara headed for home right afterward, so Hayden changed into some jeans and decided she had no choice but to venture up to the attic alone.

There was barely enough light to make out the hatch as she climbed the ladder. It flipped up easily enough, and from the expanse of the ceiling she could tell the room was bigger than she had thought; but looking around, she couldn't see much past a heavy easel lying on the floor.

She stiffened at the disarray. It was as if some kind of disturbance had occurred. She continued the rest of the way up and into the room, cautiously. Light streamed in from a large window and she could make out a sink that had to be right over the half-bath on the backside of the house. She had second thoughts about going any further. Maybe she should wait for Addie.

BY THE TIME Freddy got to the bridge, a family was milling around, enjoying the view of the river. Their dog barked as he neared, but no one bothered to look his way. Just the same, he picked up his camera and looked through the lens as if he were planning on taking a picture.

There were a lot of cars parked along the tree lined street, but no one out and about. He walked past several houses, and just as he was coming onto Hayden's place, a big black Lab came galloping down the street.

A door slammed and a woman ran out screaming, "Lucy!"

The dog jumped up on him and started licking his face, knocking his glasses to the ground.

The lady finally caught up and grabbed the dog by the collar and yanked him off. "I'm so sorry. Are you all right?"

"I'm fine," he said as he picked up his glasses and brushed himself off.

"Are you staying here on the river?"

He pointed to his camera. "No. Just taking a stroll and getting some pictures."

The woman got a good look at him and it made him upset; but seeing there were no cars in front of Hayden's cabin tempered his angst. He'd go get his car, drive back in a few minutes and pull right into Hayden's driveway. The house was far enough back that he could pull in behind a drift of giant rhododendrons and no one would notice him.

If I get the chance, I'll kill that goddamned dog, he thought as he walked back to the bridge. The tourists were gone, but he could see scores of people passing on the street ahead. He walked across, turned the corner and started toward his car.

HAYDEN SPIED A DESK near the window in the attic and decided she'd burst if she had to wait for Addie to see what it held. She wrestled with the big heavy easel lying on the floor until she got it upright, then hurriedly made her way around the clutter to the desk. She swiped her finger across the top. Barely any dust. This room had evidently been used until just recently. She looked around and got a creepy feeling the place was trying to tell her something. It was as if time had stood still... or abruptly ended.

A dusty mannequin in the corner wore a brown uniform with medals pinned on its chest. An MIA flag hung from nails in the rafters overhead, seemingly fastened to the air by spider webs.

From what she knew about her father, it wasn't like him to leave such a mess. Maybe he was having a stroke or something, and on his way down, collapsed on the staircase. But that wouldn't account for how carefully the ladder was disguised with the blanket.

She picked up a chair lying on the floor and dragged it to the desk and sat down. A shriek from a blue jay startled her. The oak desk was too big to have been brought up through the hatch. Must have been raised through the floor. She could see where the boards had been cut over the back bedroom.

She pulled out a long narrow drawer and gasped. Light reflected off the gun's gray steel—cold, treacherous, lethal. It lay next to a ledger like a guard dog. This is what I've been looking for! She wedged the book out of the drawer, careful not to jar the gun, placed it on the desk, and flipped open the cover. Everything was neatly printed and she could see it went back two years. Had to be when he opened the Arcade gallery.

Thirteen columns ran across each pale green sheet. At the top of each column her father had noted a category: rent, wages, supplies. It all seemed regular and in order. She flipped over the pages to a red plastic index tab and could see the heading *INCOME* at the top of the page. She felt her cheeks flush. First a wide column for the item description, then three others: one marked *Gallery,* another *Consignment* and then *Classes.*

Another disappointment. There was nothing out of the ordinary, just weekly totals. She turned the page. The seventy-five-thousand-dollar figure made the hair rise on the back of her neck. It was listed under an added column: *Therapy.* How strange. Her finger traced the line from the amount to the description keenly anticipating the solution to the riddle of where the money came from. But, oddly, there was just one word: *Canoe.*

She ran her finger down the Therapy column on the next page. Nothing. She turned the page. Two entries, both for seventy-five thousand each. Her finger raced across the line to the descriptions. *Dandelion* and *Ship.* She had to catch her breath as she looked for the last entry: *Flick.* No amount, just the word. She searched the column and found two other entries with no amounts, only identified as *Surf* and *Rowboat.*

She felt sick. Her father wouldn't use codes unless he had a good reason for secrecy. She knew something wasn't right about this room from the moment she peeked in from the hatch. Things strewn around, the gun, and now his accounting in code. What was he doing that he had to be so secretive? No one was ever going to find this room unless they were searching for it. She'd been in the house for four weeks and would never have discovered it at all if she hadn't stripped down the closet. It was probably the reason he didn't want Addie to do a deep cleaning. Just like she said, he wanted her in and out quickly.

A good thing Barbara and Addie hadn't come up. She had to figure this out by herself. Was he some kind of thief? She put her fingers to her temples and held her head. *Oh Daddy, I love you so much. I feel so badly for what they did to you. Please, please don't be a thief.*

FREDDY HADN'T GONE too far past Bubba's on Main Street when he stopped, suddenly. He could see a mountain man with a huge mane of gray hair and mustache inspecting his license plate. He had a pad in his hand and was comparing numbers. Freddy swung around and walked in the other direction. He'd seen this guy before. But where?

He ducked into the first door he could find. The last thing he needed was motorcycle paraphernalia, but he hung around Heavenly Hoggs with his back to the door for at least a half-hour before daring to go out on the street again. Motorcycles roared by, wrapping up the weekend with as much noise as they could blow out of their pipes.

The damn mountain man worried him. Could be an undercover cop checking out license plates of dangerous felons or people on bail. Maybe he was following him? A splitting headache stabbed at his brain so strong he could hardly think. He had to get a grip on himself. He could blow everything with another stupid move like going ballistic on the personnel director. He'd get the paintings another time.

He walked as casually as he could to his car, smiling at folks he passed, even petting a dog. If that cop was watching him, he wanted to look harmless. Just someone out enjoying a nice fall day.

HAYDEN FORCED HERSELF to snap out of the turmoil she was going through wondering if her father was a thief, and jotted down the names, amounts and dates from the ledger on a pad she found in one of the three side drawers. Nothing except odds and ends in any of them.

There had to be more clues. She got up and foraged around all the art supplies and found a carton, took it over to the desk and opened it. The checks! By now, she knew how most of the money was being spent and nothing in the cancelled checks told her anything new except that they confirmed he had deposited the three seventy-five-thousand dollar sums into his account.

If only she could find his taxes, there might be a clue in them. She shoved aside some open cartons of dusty odds and ends, and made her way over to a file cabinet. She pulled open a drawer and flipped through the files. Ah, ha! State and Federal taxes. She quickly pulled out the last two years and studied his business forms. By the amount of his income, he had obviously included the large deposits as part of his total sales. At least he wasn't guilty of tax evasion.

She stood up and pondered. What did all this mean? Where was all this money coming from? She knew the answer was in that very room and she was going to find it if she had to examine it inch by inch.

The big, lumbering easel kept drawing her eye. Why would he come all the way up here to paint? She recalled Johnny saying he was making some extra money doing watercolors. Then she remembered the *Post It* she took off her father's file cabinet. It had said *See Valentino about Flick if it turns out.*

"Flick" was her father's last ledger entry. Then she remembered Judy had told her Sal Valentino was a friend of her father's who had an art gallery in New York City. She didn't like the path her mind was traveling.

She went over to a rack holding a dozen or so boards of the kind the gallery's students used to stretch watercolor paper on and remembered Johnny Reb saying her father was making extra money from his watercolors. She paused for a moment to gather the courage to pull one out. Nothing. Nothing on the next, only

189

remnants of wide tape used to hold down the paper.

By the time she got to the last board, she was starting to relax. What kind of craziness was she thinking? She pulled it out almost as an afterthought, and a chill ran up her spine. Even from an arm's distance away, she could tell it was a masterpiece. The fisherman had waded into a stream and was flicking back his line. Trembling, she took it over and propped it up on the easel and kept repeating, "I don't believe it," as her eyes froze on the Winslow Homer signature in the lower right-hand corner. She took a deep breath, nervously exhaled, then stumbled over to the chair and collapsed.

Her glance wandered over to a portfolio leaning against the wall. A stab of apprehension made her get up and bring it to the desk. She unzipped it, then carefully lifted a tissue lying on top. The painting of a fisherman in a rowboat took her breath away. She searched for the signature, her eyes steely, like razor blades. There it was. She placed the painting aside and was almost afraid to lift the next sheet. A young girl in a swirling pink dress was portrayed wading in the surf. Again the Winslow Homer signature.

Hayden gazed ahead not seeing anything except the words that had appeared on the ledger: *Surf, Rowboat, Flick.* She shuddered.

She was suddenly aware that she had landed in the middle of a conspiracy. If she didn't go straight to the police, would she be culpable? Surely... not if she didn't try to pass them off as originals. But, then again, she knew there were three people out there who owned very expensive fakes. If she didn't do anything, wouldn't that make her an accomplice after the fact? Her first instinct was to destroy everything—the paintings, the ledger, whatever she could find. She could burn them in the fire pit outside when Addie wasn't around.

What if the police were already on to him? She remembered the man who Judy said had come into the gallery a couple of times and seemed so interested in her. He might be a detective.

She couldn't talk to anyone about this... except... maybe Johnny Reb. No. Then she'd be implicating him too. She folded her arms and strolled to the window and looked out over the roof of the front of the house at Round Top. The setting sun had layered a veil of pink over the mass of fall colors and Chimney Rock's deep, dark shadow was creeping upward.

A photograph tucked in the casing caught her eye. She pulled it out. The finish was cracked in several places and the corners tattered. Her father must have stood at this window and looked at this picture of his two daughters a thousand times. Suddenly all the wonderful things people had said about him at the funeral came flooding back to her. Tears ran freely down her cheeks. He'd done it for his students. Hers and Barbara's surrogates. It was all so sad. All the love he had for his daughters never returned.

She wiped the tears off on the shoulders of her sleeves. Somehow, she had to keep him from being disgraced and put an end to this whole hideous circle of hurt; but right now, she had better get back downstairs before Addie showed up. She zipped up the portfolio and started to take it down with her, but changed her mind and leaned it up against the wall next to the ladder. She gave the place a long look before descending. What other tragic secrets, she wondered, were entombed in this room.

CHAPTER NINETEEN

BEN TRIED RICKY for the third time, then checked the drawer for the key to Ricky's New York apartment. There, just where he left it. His daughter, Heather, shared an apartment in Forest Hills with three other girls, but he mostly stayed with Ricky ever since the night he crashed on Heather's couch and woke with three giggling pajama clad young ladies standing over him, purring about how cute he was. Made him feel old.

He worried about not getting any kind of answer from Ricky's cell phone. His new girl friend, Bianca, didn't answer at the apartment either. He checked to make sure he had everything to go with his tuxedo, zipped up the garment bag and took a long look at the Super Bowl ring on his hand. It had been over a year since he put it on. He let himself relive the thrill of the night it was presented to him. Jenny and Heather were there. The smile on his face slowly faded as he realized they paid a higher price for it than he had.

A pair of freshly polished black wingtips got shoved in his tote along with a bunch of toiletries and some underwear. He wouldn't need much since he'd be back the next day.

The two-and-a-half hour drive to Charlotte gave him plenty of time to think about his conversation with Bill McAnnis who he hadn't seen since he toured him through the World's Edge property. They were to meet at six at the New York Yacht Club on 44th as guests of Howland and Sara Auchindelf who owned a significant tract of mountain property.

Bill had run into Howland on the golf course in Flat Rock when he and his wife were in town vacationing for a couple of weeks. Bill had served under Auchindelf when he was an Admiral in the U.S. Navy, the first member of his illustrious New York stockbroker family to do so, and they had kept in touch.

"Boy, was he excited about you joining the conservancy," Bill had said. "Hell, he remembered you back from when you were at Penn State."

Howland had insisted Bill bring him to his club for dinner the next time they were in the City, and that next time was tonight. Ordinarily, Ben wouldn't give a dinner of this type a second thought, but Bill's enthusiasm over it showed he was counting on the occasion to reap instant results. And then came the comment that slipped out about Bill's vote being the deciding one to hire him after a rather contentious debate. *This'll show 'em,* he had said.

The Auchindelfs owned one hundred acres on the northern boundary of the DuPont State Forest, and the conservancy had been working with them for the past two years about adding it to the park, but couldn't get Howland to take the final step. Ben took a deep breath and slowly let it out, remembering what Bill had told him. *I'm counting on you, son. I know this dinner is going to clinch the deal.*

Ben tried to get a hold of Ricky and his girlfriend once more before boarding the plane but didn't have any luck. He was glad Bill had gone up to New York ahead of him since he'd upgraded the seat the conservancy bought to first class, paying for the increase himself. The cab ride from Newark, with a foreign national behind bullet-proof glass with sitar music blaring from a boom box, reinforced his decision to live in the mountains. The only good thing he could say about the trip was that the driver demonstrated heroic calm during what resembled a suicide mission.

Ricky's doorman gave him a warm welcome as he opened the cab door, probably because his face was more familiar than Ricky's. He glanced at his watch. Plenty of time. He didn't need more than two hours to shower and shave and hop a cab over to the club.

The newspapers stacked in front of Ricky's door figured. Probably out of town again. He put down his bag, fumbled for the key and opened the door. The reek of puke hit him. The place was a wreck. Liquor bottles, glasses, a pizza box lay open on the coffee table. Ben ran into the guest bathroom, grabbed a towel and buried his face in it. He strained to keep from vomiting himself as he struggled with the jammed sliding balcony door, finally forcing it open. He ran to the railing and sucked in a lungful of air and looked down at the traffic twenty floors below.

Rickie suddenly appeared in the doorway in a pair of boxer shorts, his mussed sweaty hair lying in ringlets around his swollen face. He'd put on quite a belly, bringing to mind how he must have looked as a baby.

"She left me," he wailed. His almond shaped eyes were more hidden under puffy folds than usual, as if he were looking inward and facing painful facts.

Ben went over and put his arm around Ricky's massive shoulders. "She'll be back, Buddy. Meanwhile, let's get someone in here to clean up this mess."

Ricky elbowed Ben in the chest. "No she won't! She said we're through!" He gripped his head with a giant paw. "I can't live without her. I'm going to kill myself."

He suddenly charged for the railing and just as he was about to lift a leg, Ben grabbed him and threw him back against the wall. Ricky had been one of the Giants' powerhouses and had to be over three hundred pounds, and in spite of the rolls of fat was still strong as an ox.

Sitting askew on the balcony floor, Ricky looked up at Ben and spoke in a dazed tone. His voice trailed off as he stared out at the skyscrapers in the distance. Then it was as if his brain had snagged some endearing moment that suddenly ended, and he fell into a pathetic crying jag.

Ben wedged his hands under his arms and wrestled him into the apartment.

Ricky suddenly appeared wild-eyed. "I'm gonna kill myself, and nothing's going to stop me!"

"Come on, Ricky, an aging pole dancer isn't anyone to kill yourself over."

Ricky barely managed to roll onto his knees, and with the aid of a nearby couch, stand up and collapse on its arm. He languidly reached for an open bottle of whisky and started to take a swig. Ben grabbed it out of his hand, and as he strode into the bathroom, picked another bottle off a table. Ricky lunged at him. They wrestled in the bathroom until the contents of the bottles were splashed across the room.

Ricky put his head in the crook of his arm and collapsed against the wall crying. Ben had seen plenty of grown men cry, plenty of times, but not with all this blubbering. It had to be the booze. Ben patted him on the back. "Buddy, you've got to get a hold of yourself."

"I can't. She took our baby?"

"What baby?"

"Jo-Jo."

Ben grimaced. "You mean that ratty little dog of hers?"

Ricky turned. His face was solemn, his back arched in indignation. "He might be a ratty dog to you, but when he licked my face I wanted to cuddle him in my arms forever." His face broke up. "He's the only one who ever gave me unconditional love." He stood crying, helplessly.

Ben had to make some decisions, fast. He was counting on building a new life with his job at the conservancy, but he and Ricky went too far back to leave him in this state. He might do something crazy. If he could only get him sobered up, he could be quite charming. Ben looked at his watch. Only an hour and a half until he had to be at the club.

He got Ricky to sit down on the toilet and told him not to move, then ran into the kitchen and put on some coffee, loading the filter to the brim with grounds. Thank goodness the doorman answered the phone quickly. "We've got a problem," he told him. "Get the super up here *pronto.*"

He found some bread, and while he was waiting for the toast to pop up, ran into the spare bedroom down the hall and checked it out. Thankfully, Rickie hadn't polluted it yet. He quickly brought in his things, opened the windows, and closed the door.

The doorbell rang, and Ben rushed to open the door. The super spit out the wooden match from between his teeth and choked. Ben pressed two Franklins into his palm and told him to find a company to clean the place up and send Ricky the bill. He'd move him to a hotel until it was finished. His instructions to "Ditch all the booze" cast a shadow of a smile across the super's haggard face.

The coffee and toast started to bring Ricky around and Ben got him into the shower in the spare bedroom suite. The layer of flab around Ricky's midriff made Ben determine to add five more pushups to his morning routine.

After Ricky showered, Ben parked him on the toilet seat again, plugged in his razor and told him to start shaving, they were going somewhere. Finished in the bathroom, Ben found Ricky's tux and made a quick call to Bill's hotel as he watched Ricky bumble his way into his clothes.

"Sure. Bring him right along," said Bill. "I'm sure Howland will be delighted. I'll give him a call. Hell, he's getting two for the price of one."

"I'm just a screw-up, Ben. You're right about Bianca. The cellulite was starting to show on her ass." His face crunched up like a sheet of foil in someone's fist. "But... Jo-Jo was so...."

Ben grasped Ricky's shoulders and looked him square in the eyes. "Get a grip on yourself, Buddy, and don't think about that dog. Right now we've got to find your ring?"

Ricky jumped up. "Oh my God! I hope she didn't take that too!"

He shot out of the room with Ben trailing, careful not to step into anything unpleasant. Ricky's hands shook and he had to try the combination to the safe in the corner of his walk-in closet several times before he finally retrieved his super bowl ring.

"Shit! I can't get it on!" said Ricky.

Ben pawed through the dresser and found some of his girlfriend's hand cream, spread it on Ricky's finger and shoved on the ring. Within an hour they were riding down in the elevator. Ben didn't know if the smell of puke had saturated their clothes or was just clinging to the hair follicles in his nose. He was hoping most of all Ricky hadn't stepped in any. He checked his watch. Just enough time to make it to the club.

"I'm a mess, Ben. Maybe you should have let me go over the railing and end all my suffering. I thought Bianca was finally the one, and then she went and called me a pig. Can you believe that?"

Ben reached over and straightened Ricky's tie. "Hell, you've been called worst than that by chicks, you should be use to it by now."

The doorman whistled for a cab and Ben wrestled Ricky in. "You've got to get your head screwed on and forget about Bianca tonight. The game is about to start."

"Where are we going anyway?"

"To the New York Yacht Club to have dinner with some very nice people. They're going to love you. All you got to do is be your usual charming self and remember to clean up your language."

The cab stopped for a light. A Budweiser sign blinked in a nearby bar. Ricky put his hand on the door handle. "Just let me off here. I'll be all right."

"Oh no, you don't. I'm not letting you out of my sight. We're going to make it tonight. Good food, good company, then I'll check us into a hotel."

The cab dropped them off outside the limestone exterior of the New York Yacht Club. After having their names checked by the doorman, they went up the steps and entered a massive heavily marbled lobby.

Bill came rushing over. "Good. Good. You're here. The Auchindelfs are really looking forward to meeting you. They're waiting for us in the Model Room."

Ben noticed Ricky seemed calm and interested in the place,

looking around like a kid on his first day at school, impressed with the obvious strength of the institution. Ben just wished he wasn't sweating so much. In the rush, he hadn't put a handkerchief in his pocket.

They entered an enormous room resembling the inside of a galley ship with arched trusses sweeping to the ceiling and details of the sea's history and traditions splattered all around. There had to be over a hundred fully rigged models in glass cases and over a thousand half models. Sea monsters of limestone swept down on columns from the balcony, and an expansive Persian carpet ran down the center, dotted with comfortable chairs and tables.

Ricky nudged him. "Is that Ted Turner over there?"

Ben looked over to a huge fireplace with an ornate marble surround that had to be fifteen feet tall. Ted Turner was holding a drink and talking animatedly with four men, a haunting "ship at sea" echo trailing his words. Ben gave Ricky a wink. Atta boy, he thought. Everything's going to be just fine.

The Auchindelfs were a well matched couple. Somewhere in their early eighties, they were both tall, bone thin, and blue blooded. Sara Auchindelf gave them the kind of graciously confident smile she must have flashed since her debutante days, now just a little more toothy.

Howland stood up and shook everyone's hand. His jacket hung from his shoulders as if there were nothing inside but bones. He still had some of the bearing of an Admiral of the Fleet, but his Dutch New York stockbroker roots that went back to before the Revolutionary War overshadowed everything else. He was a man who knew who he was and enjoyed every minute of it.

Sara was happy to sip her wine and chat with passersby as Howland showed the men around the club's pre-eminent model collection, explicitly mentioning that over fifty percent of the club's members owned yachts.

"Except for the absence of motion, one might fancy oneself at sea," said Howland as they settled at a table in the club's oak paneled grill room, again resembling the hull of a sailing ship.

"Do you sail?" Sara asked Ricky who was seated next to her.

"No, madam."

She waved a hand. "Of course. I forgot. You're a footballer, aren't you?"

Ricky nodded.

"How quaint. I'm finally seeing two of you in the flesh. It's *soooo* tiresome to watch those little figures scurry around on Howland's television screen. All the whistle blowing and waiting around. I just don't know what all the fuss is about."

Howland ignored her comment as if they were in two separate spaces having conversations with different people. "Well boys, what are the Giants' chances?"

Ricky was suddenly in his clime. He'd done a stint on *ESPN* but didn't want a permanent position, and was happy with being invited on from time to time as a commentator. The lively conversation soothed Ben's fears and he started to relax, until Howland ordered the wine.

Ben told the waiter he didn't want any and put his hand over the top of Ricky's glass.

"Nonsense," said Howland, and motioned impatiently for the waiter to pour him some.

Ben gave Bill a quick glance and detected a wink and a nod.

Sara captured Ben's attention for a while, rattling on about how most of their friends were dead and how difficult it had become taking care of all their homes. Ben listened to her with one ear, responding with the appropriate interest, and to Ricky with the other. Howland motioned for a second glass of wine and Ricky gulped it down.

The courses kept coming along with the wine. Ricky was holding his own right up to the dessert, then it was as if someone pulled the plug on his enthusiasm. He sank back in his chair, his huge round shoulders drooped, and he stared ahead as if some sad scenario were running through his brain.

Concerned, Ben ordered crème brulée, excused himself and stood up. He went over and nudged Ricky up off his chair and said they'd be right back. In the men's room, Ben said, "You've got to knock off the wine, fella. You really made a hit with these people. Let's not spoil it."They relieved themselves with Ricky promising not to touch another glass. Back at the table, Ben asked for coffee for the both of them, only to have Howland insist on another glass of wine. Ricky looked over at Ben and shrugged his shoulders, then raised his glass to Howland with a wink and drank it down.

Ricky grew increasingly sullen and Ben had to pick up the conversation.

With Ricky fading from the stream of football talk, Sara latched onto him. "Are you married, young man?"

"No, madam."

"Well, I declare. Surely, a nice young man like you should have a loving wife. Do you at least have a girl friend?"

The long, tortured moan interrupted Howland's replay of one of Ben's Penn State touchdowns in mid-sentence. Ricky was holding his head in his hands, his back bouncing up and down. Ben jumped from his chair, grabbed Rickie and said they'd be right back. Ben caught Bill's concerned glance.

The minute Ricky walked in the door of the bathroom and collapsed crying on a bench, the attendant, a dignified black man, slapped his knees and slowly rose as if he was about to embark on the usual drill. "I'll go get the coffee."

Ben rushed over to the sink and ran a neatly folded hand towel under cold water, wrung it out and wiped Ricky's face. "Come on, buddy. We're on the five yard line."

"Nobody loves me."

"Sure they do, bubba. You're downright adorable."

The attendant appeared with the coffee.

Ben quickly poured a cup. "Here, let's get this down you."

"Why didn't you just let me jump. I don't want to live without little Jo-Jo."

"Keep your mind off that dog and everything's going to be okay. We can still score a touchdown if you lay off the booze."

"Ben, you're the only one who's ever taken care of me, and look what a mess I made."

He rushed to the urinal and puked.

Ben got him over to the sink and held a towel while Ricky

rinsed his face.

Ricky took the towel and rubbed the back of his neck dry. "Reminds you of the old times. Doesn't it? Remember New Orleans after the big game with the Saints? I almost choked to death puking."

Bill appeared at the door and sized Ricky up. "We've got to keep him out of the sauce."

"That's what I tried to tell you," said Ben.

Bill neared Ben and spoke under his breath. "What's the matter? Family troubles?"

"Something like that."

"Don't worry. Howland's okay with this whole thing. Actually, he's happier than a pig in shit and can't wait to get to the Atlantic Club in the morning to tell his golfing buddies about meeting you two, especially Ricky." He tossed his head in Ricky's direction. "Clean him up and get him back out there."

Ben made his way to the table with an arm around Ricky so his staggering wouldn't be so evident. "We're heading for a touchdown," Ben whispered in his ear. "Keep your hands off the booze and whatever you do, don't think about that damn dog."

Bill must have mentioned something to Mrs. Auchindelf for her face was a portrait of sympathy. The waiter served the dessert and Howland motioned for more wine. Bill waved the waiter away from Ricky's glass, but Howland said the young man looked fine and insisted the waiter pour. Ben noticed the waiter throw a quick glance at the maitre d' before he filled Ricky's glass.

By the time they finished dessert, Ricky had consumed two more glasses. Ben said a prayer that they'd be able to get out of there before something else happened.

Mrs. Auchindelf announced she'd heard enough football talk and looked over at Ricky. "There now, you poor boy." She patted his hand tenderly. Don't worry about anything. I'm sure things are going to get better." She looked into his eyes. "Son, maybe what you need is a dog."

Ricky burst out crying loud enough for those in nearby tables to look around alarmed.

Howland threw his napkin on the table and gave his wife an angry scowl. "Now see what you've done!"

She looked around at the people seated nearby, and in a defensive tone, remarked, "All I said was that he needed a dog."

By now Ben had his arms under Ricky's and was lifting him out of the chair with the aid of the maitre d' who had rushed over to the table. Ricky blubbered uncontrollably about Jo-Jo and begged Ben's forgiveness for fumbling the ball. Bill followed them out of the room and whispered in Ben's ear that he'd take care of Howland and Sara and for him to get Ricky the hell out of there.

IT TOOK THE super until two the next afternoon to send Ben's bags over to the hotel along with some clothes for Ricky. Ben had called the office and told them he'd be at least another day in New York. Showered and shaved and in fresh clothes, he was looking forward to seeing Heather who was coming by after her last class. He'd ordered dinner from her favorite Chinese restaurant and expected it to arrive any minute.

Ricky was propped up like a zombie in a chair in the bedroom watching reruns on TV.

Bill had left a message on Ben's cell. "That buddy of yours got us that easement. The Auchindelfts are big dog lovers and the whole thing really touched them. Howland wants Tom Gibbons to contact his lawyer and draft a proposal for adding his land to the DuPont Forest."

It amazed Ben that his and Ricky's fading gridiron triumphs could still override the fiasco of the night before. A chit they had for all the pain. He wondered how many more years it would last.

A knock at the door. No matter how many times he'd laid his eyes on her, Heather never failed to stir his pride. She flew into his arms and he twirled her around. "Oh, baby, it's so good to see you."

She stood in front of him wearing a cashmere car coat and filmy boa that picked up the color of her hair. He nodded approvingly as he studied her. "You look great."

"So do you, Daddy."

She peeked around him so she could get a look in the bedroom. Ricky hadn't noticed she came in and was still staring blankly ahead at the TV. Heather shook her head. "He looks like hell."

"He'll be okay," Ben said as he grabbed his wallet off the dresser and answered a knock at the door. The delivery man handed him a box, took his money and left. Heather got busy setting the table and putting out the food while Ben leaned against the counter and watched her.

Twenty years ago, when the nurse presented her through the hospital nursery window and he spotted the red hair, he knew she'd grow up to be feisty, and it didn't take long for her to prove it. When she was almost three, they were all in the living room watching TV. She had dragged her rocker tight up against him, and when he asked her to move forward a bit to give him more space, she abruptly stood up, grabbed the arms of the chair and lugged it across the room next to her mother, and plopped down again, obviously put out. He remembered catching Jenny's eye and sharing her smile. Then he went over, picked up the rocker with her in it and put it back tight up against him.

"A hangover?" Heather asked as she placed some napkins. Ben nodded. Heather shook her head. "When is Uncle Ricky going to learn? Maybe we should just give him a bowl of rice and some tea tonight."

Ben watched her fill a bowl with her dainty pale hands and slide on her knees next to Ricky. Ben watched them hug and then Heather sit up on the arm of the chair with her arm around him as he ate. She came back in the room with his plate and dished him up some more.

"This ought to hold him," she said with a wink.

Ben didn't talk much during the dinner, just listened to Heather's sweet lyrical voice float through the air with tidbits on her classes at Pratt and Columbia. Her conversation was laced with the same exciting, yet delicate wit her mother had.

Ben just kept looking at her. His mother was a redhead and it hurt him to think she'd never laid eyes on his only child. Every time he saw a woman light up a cigarette, he wanted to take it and crush it to bits; but of course, he never did.

By the time they finished, Ricky was flopped over to the side asleep. Heather helped get him into bed, then Ben cleared the table while she made some coffee. Her shoes off, she tucked a leg under as she slid onto the leatherette couch. This was the signal for Ben to brace himself for the lecture which had been stirring in the room all evening like a gathering fog.

"I'm proud of you, Dad. Goin' out and getting yourself that mountain house you've talked about since I was a kid."

He gave her a devilish wink. "You still *are a kid.*"

She laughed and reached across and squeezed his hand. "You had to get out of that house. It was time."

Ben put some cream in his coffee and stirred. "When are you coming down to see my new place?"

"I'm thinking about coming in the spring. One of my roommates has a sister who wants to move to New York and she can take my place in the apartment." She ran a finger along the edge of her cup. "Actually, Dad, I'm thinking about transferring to Warren Wilson. Not to study art. Now that I'm in art school, I can see that I'll never be as good as some of these kids. I kind of did that because that's what Mom always wanted. I've been talking with some of Mom's friends and I want to end up as a lawyer working in conservation. Kate said she could still get me into their Environmental Studies Department if I make up my mind right away."

Ben couldn't believe it. The last thing he had ever expected was for he and his daughter to have anything in common other than family matters.

They were quiet for a moment. "I've got to get over to that place of yours and stake my claim on a bedroom before your girlfriends start moving in."

"You don't have to worry about that, baby."

"Why not? It's time."

"Hey, if you want to play cupid, find someone for Ricky."

"He's not ready, Dad. In fact, I don't think he's ever going to be ready. What is it this time? Another breakup?"

"Yeah." He looked at her and cracked a deep grin. "And she took the dog."

Heather put her coffee down, pulled her feet up on the couch and hugged her knees as she listened to her father.

"I'm glad you're coming. I was a lousy father, and I intend to make it up to you."

"Dad! What are you talking about? You were the greatest father in the world."

"Yeah! Sure."

"You were gone a lot, but you were always there when it counted. Remember when I was the spider in *Charlotte's Web* and you flew in minutes before the play started and had to turn right around and fly back out after it ended? Mom said you paid a fortune to charter that plane."

"You liked that, huh?"

"Yeah, I liked that." She reached across and patted his hand. "In your own way, you were there for mom, too. I can see her now behind her loom with that little TV set looking up to see you on the field. She never missed a game and watched every time you were on *ESPN*. We've got them all taped."

"I know. I ran across them when I was packing."

"She understood about the whole football thing. It had to have hurt, but those last years you had together made her so happy. She was like a kid."

"So was I. Those were the happiest of my life."

They talked about the conservancy on the cab ride to Heather's apartment. It was the first time their conversation amounted to anything other than the casual kind of remarks a father makes to a child he never connected to in any other way than that of parent who spent most of the time on the sidelines. She'd been the strong one during Jenny's illness. He couldn't count the times she'd made him tea and gotten him to sleep after he returned from the hospice only to dissolve into tears.

Heather's roommates squealed when he peeked in and threw them a wave. Heather gave him a wink and whispered that he still had his old rock star appeal. He stood at the door for a while after it closed, mulling over this new dimension to their relationship and her wanting to come back home. As luck turned out, his decision to stay in the mountains had been a good one.

On the way back, when the cab neared Grand Central Station, he decided to get out and walk the rest of the way to his hotel just off Times Square. He loved New York in the evening with its warm inviting light spilling out from bars and shop display windows in the dark tunnels of its skyscrapers. A Greek grocery store was open with fresh produce lining the sidewalk. He bought a small bottle of pomegranate juice and drank it down.

A group of fashionably dressed people erupted from a restaurant. He suddenly yearned to be on that street arm in arm with Hayden, her sweet laughter dancing in the air. He hadn't had these kinds of stirrings since Jenny's health started to fade. Maybe it *was* time like Heather had said.

But Hayden wouldn't be the one. He'd committed enough crimes against the institution of marriage and was never going to be guilty of that sin again. Yet, there was something about her staying on in the mountains and the sadness he'd seen in her eyes that didn't add up to a happy home life. And other than at the visitation, he hadn't seen her husband around.

He pictured the spunky way she crawled up the rock face at Little Pisgah and laughed out loud. Then he remembered his promise to show her a granite domed goldenrod before she left for the beach. He'd see if he could find one in the woods, and at the very least enjoy her playful smile when he showed it to her.

CHAPTER TWENTY

H AYDEN WOKE and hit the alarm button before it went off. Addie had looked a little haggard the night before and she didn't want the sound to wake her. She ran her hands through her hair and shook out all the snarls. The sound of squirrels scampering across the porch's tin roof drifted in the window, and what she called the Judy bird started up its staccato: *Ju-dy, Ju-dy, Ju-dy.*

A damp chill held a grip on the house and the heat pump started to hum outside, not quite overpowering the sound of the river. Since the developer wouldn't be there for a while, she slipped out from underneath the thick down comforter, closed her window and put on a sweater and a pair of jeans and went outside. Moist leaves covered the ground and a bright golden glow rose from the east. The gorge was about to wake up, and she decided to walk to the bridge and watch the sun rise.

Everyone on the street was still asleep. The weekend folks had left their garbage cans out on the side of the road before they left, with remnants of recent purchases piled alongside. An empty box for a toaster oven jammed up next to a rusty tricycle had a couple of deflated inner tubes stuffed inside. Further on, the cat she'd been leaving food out for was sitting on a porch on a cushioned chair. Evidently, it had found a home.

As she neared the bridge where the enormous boulders were dense, the roar of the river cascading over and around them enveloped her. She walked to the middle of the steel trestle structure and looked out at the rising sun's reflection dancing all along the wide twisting rock strewn river. A pair of blue herons waded in a small eddy. She got a whiff of frying bacon. Someone in the village had to be cooking breakfast.

Hayden closed her eyes and listened. The river had the same endless sound as the ocean and made her feel disarmingly insignificant, like a grain of sand on the beach. She looked up at the Round Top range, now lit by the sun's horizontal beam, its undulating rock outcrops casting shadows on its depths.

Its granite face wasn't smooth like Chimney Rock's. More chiseled and craggy with long dark streaks, and in the morning, not at all the bright orange it turned when the setting sun shown on it. Without the jarring sound of traffic along Route 74, the landscape took on a serenity that made her understand why the Indians believed this gorge a sacred place.

PETE REYNOLDS JUMPED out of his truck and knocked at the door. He looked forward to meeting Hayden. Everyone in town was talkin' about this pretty gal. He took off his cap and ran his fingers through his flattened hair. The door opened and he wasn't disappointed. He clutched his cap in one hand, and shook her hand with the other. "Thanks for letting me come and talk with you, Ma'am."

"Come on in. I've made some coffee."

As he sat at the dining room table, he couldn't help noticing how much the place had changed since he met there with her father, and hoped he wasn't on another fool's mission.

Hayden brought the coffee and settled in a chair across from him. "Well, now. Why don't you tell me what you have in mind."

"To come straight to the point, I'll give you three million for your four hundred acres on Round Top."

Hayden's lips were set in a firm line. "I don't know. My sister wasn't too impressed with the Prism Falls development, and I don't think she would want our mountaintop defaced in that way."

"Oh, that's not going to happen with me. The guy that developed that tract runs a family owned business in South Carolina and was a novice to building in these parts. I'm much more experienced, and I was born and raised here. Though, I will give him that he never intended to impact that mountain the way he did. He never realized the severity of that grade would require such an invasive road until he got into it, and then there was no turning back. That's the kind of project you get when they let some guy learn at the community's expense."

"What guarantee would we have that you wouldn't do the same? Maybe even turn around and sell it to someone like him."

"Just call the chairman of the Chimney Rock Planning Board. He'll tell you. They just passed a steep slope ordinance that calls for a maximum building grade of 18 percent. It also provides for larger lots on the slopes. We're talking ten to fifteen acres each, not two or three like they have at Prism Falls."

She sure was a pleasure to look at, thought Pete, but on the cool side. He had no idea what she was thinking. "Another thing, I'd leave a canopy over any roads and my restrictions wouldn't allow trees to be cut except for the footprint of the homes, and just enough limbing for a view."

The way she left everything he said hanging in the air worried him, yet he could tell she was thinking the offer over. "There's a private road off Route 9 that winds to the top of your land. If you want, I'll take you up and show you what I mean."

"How fast could we get the money?"

This response surprised him. "Thirty days. Sooner if you need it."

She took his card and walked him to the door.

CHAPTER TWENTY-ONE

Hayden could smell fresh brewed coffee wafting out of one of the classrooms. Unusual, she thought, since Judy never made any. It was as if at one time in her life she was forced to wait on people and swore she'd never do it again.

Hayden picked up the new cell phone she had bought the day before, and started to dial the number Judy dug up for Valentino. Terri and Karen appeared at the door dressed less flamboyantly than usual, like they meant business. Hayden, remembering they wanted to meet with her, reluctantly snapped her phone closed.

Hayden sensed something was afoot when Judy peeked in and announced everything was ready. She gave Judy a squinty stare meant to say, "Now what have you been up to behind my back?"

Judy appeared undaunted and led everyone into a classroom that had been set up with a table and chairs for the occasion. A coffee maker sat on a small table along with a stack of Styrofoam cups, one haphazardly stuffed with packets of sugar. A few flattened donuts were piled on a paper plate looking as if someone had accidentally sat on them.

Hayden found a chair and waited while everyone poured their coffee.

Terri held a cup of coffee in her ring-laden hand with her

pudgy little finger thrust straight out. She placed the cup in front of Hayden. "Here, *Sugah*. What do you take with it?"

Hayden smiled and said black was just fine.

Karen took command. She proceeded with the kind of polished professional manner she must have used in meetings when she headed up the Public Relations Department at the community college in Spartanburg.

"Assuming that you'll have to be going home sooner or later, we have a proposal we want to present to you so your father's legacy can continue."

Terri jumped in. "That wonderful man burned himself out on this place, and we certainly don't want to see it go for naught." She patted Hayden's hand. "And, Sweetheart, from what we observe of you, we don't think you want that to happen either."

Hayden stared hard, first at Terri, then at Karen. What would they say if they knew about his legacy as a master forger? Her attitude softened as she surmised they probably wouldn't give it a second thought as long as that was what it took to keep the gallery alive and classes going.

Karen cleared her throat. "If this place is to succeed on its own, there's got to be some changes. Since your father isn't here to subsidize it any more, we're going to have to do it cooperatively."

Hayden put an elbow on the table and stroked her chin. "What sort of changes do you have in mind?"

Karen opened a folder, took out a few sheets of paper and pushed them toward Hayden. "We figured, if the gallery charges all co-op members one-hundred dollars every quarter and splits the sales, seventy percent to the artist and thirty for the gallery, it could work. That is, if we have enough members and can get the rent reduced. At least for the first year."

Hayden folded her arms and sat back in her chair and studied the two women for a moment. They were settled, comfortable, confident, and looking for trouble. Hayden was pretty sure a scandal wouldn't shake their resolve. Maybe, she thought, this might be the best way to save the gallery. Hayden picked up the sheets and examined the column of figures. She asked, a little sheepishly, "How would a co-op work?"

Terri rubbed her hands excitedly. "Volunteers would be a big part of it... *after all, it is a co-op.*" She tossed her head toward Judy. "Of course, Judy would stay on as a paid employee, but that would be it."

"What if someone can't afford the quarterly fee?" asked Hayden.

Karen cleared her throat again, as if it were a signal for Terri to let her do the talking. Terri, looking a little shamefaced, pursed her lips.

"That's where volunteerism comes in," said Karen. "Then they would have to work at the gallery four hours each week for the quarter. The gallery would be re-hung four times a year with everyone pitching in."

"How would the teachers get paid?"

"Give them seventy percent of the income the class takes in. If they get a lot of students, they could do a lot better than they are now. And it'll be a real incentive for them to whip up business and satisfy the students." She pointed to a column on the sheet. "See. We've taken the past year's class income and used thirty percent of it in our budget figure."

Hayden put her elbows on the table and rested her chin on her tightly interlocked fingers. Handing over the management of the gallery to a committee was hardly what she had in mind, and the proposal, based on the premise that she wasn't able to keep the place going by herself, was humiliating. But she had to swallow so much pride in the past weeks she was getting used to it.

She straightened her back and folded her hands on the table. If this plan was going to be the gallery's salvation, she meant to be a big part of it. "I've already talked to the foundation about renegotiating the rent structure and they said they needed a business plan. Possibly this might work."

Terri let out a gleeful cry and quickly covered her mouth.

No one seemed to know what to say next.

The gallery door opened and the noise of the hall drifted in. Judy strained to see who it was. "Just a woman with a baby in a stroller. She'll be all right by herself for a while."

Hayden studied the three women staring at her expectantly. One thing she knew for certain, they all had a deep respect for her father and seemed willing to do whatever it would take to keep his legacy alive. She was also convinced they'd be one-hundred-percent behind her plan to get the paintings back, if only they knew.

Hayden raised an eyebrow. She slowly looked from one woman to the next. An impish grin surfaced as she said, "Ladies... I'm in."

Terri jumped up and gave her a hug.

That bit of camaraderie went a long way with Hayden. "We can all go talk to Ruth Summers in the Foundation's office next week, after I've had time to study your proposal." One thing she knew she was going to insist upon was a clause stating that if the co-op failed, she would have the first right of refusal to gain the gallery back. She also intended to be named as a permanent member of the advisory board.

The two ladies bubbled out of the gallery.

If this meeting had taken place last week, Hayden would have been overjoyed, but right now the looming challenge of getting the money to buy back the three paintings was all she could think about. She had to be out of her mind to even consider it a possibility.

Valentino needed to be called; but first, she was going to have a little talk with Judy.

"You knew I would go for it, didn't you?" asked Hayden.

Judy barely shrugged and continued clearing the table.

Hayden leaned against the doorway, arms folded. "How long has this li'l ole plan been in the works?"

Judy ignored the remark.

"Why in the heck can't you level with me? I've had to put up with this kind of manipulating from my mother all my life and I don't intend to do it with you, too. I'm in a tight squeeze right now, and I need you on my side, not over in some corner plotting your next move." Hayden put her head back and stared at the ceiling. "I'm surprised you didn't wait until this whole place collapsed around me before offering to take it off my hands. How is it, that every time I think we're getting somewhere, you pull something like this?"

"I'll get everything set up for the ten o'clock class." Judy dropped the last Styrofoam cup in the wastebasket and left the room.

Damn! It had taken hours to get herself psyched for the call to Valentino, and now she was stressed out again; but there was no point in stalling. She went back in the office, picked up the new cell phone she had bought just for this purpose, and dialed.

"Mr. Valentino isn't expected until after lunch," said an over-polished voice.

Hayden hung up, then booked a flight to New York for early the following morning.

Two classes had started and Judy was working on papers at the counter. Hayden slipped out of the office, her arms folded, and strolled nonchalantly in front of her. "I won't be in for a couple of days. I'm going to New York."

Judy looked up, puzzled. "Are you going to see Valentino?"

Hayden kicked a dust ball lying on the floor. "Wouldn't you like to know."

Judy laughed to herself; purposely loud enough, Hayden thought, for her to hear.

"You know, Judy, this works two ways. Maybe you should fuss and fume about what I'm doing in New York and see how it feels."

Judy shook her head. "You're a real work of art."

"Sho 'nough. Just a rich little girl without a care in the world." Hayden meandered over to a wall of paintings and perused them with a blind eye. "I wonder if my father would approve of the way you've been treating me?"

Judy slammed her fist on the counter. "How dare you! You, didn't give a damn about him until you thought you could be entertained with a little diversion for a few weeks!"

Several people came running out of the classrooms. Judy shooed them back in with an agitated gesture. She came out from behind the counter and skulked toward Hayden, speaking in a guttural tone barely loud enough to be heard. "That's it! I'm out of here. I'm not going to take this from you."

"Oh yes you are. You want to be here so bad, and want me out of here so much, you can taste it. Why else would you have engineered this li'l ole co-op deal? Well, you're not going to get me out of the picture that easy. I intend to be on the board *in perpetuity."*

Hayden went face to face with Judy. "I'm hanging on by my fingernails, Judy, and I want you to be nice. *Do you think you can be nice?* I certainly hope so, or I'm going to burst into a million pieces and take this whole place down with me!"

Hayden suddenly realized the doorways were crowded with concerned faces. She took a deep breath, put an arm around Judy and smiled. "Gracious me, where are my manners! Everything's fine. Please go back to your work."

BY THE TIME TWO o'clock rolled around, Hayden had smoked two cigarettes and Judy had sniffled her way through a package of tissues. Hayden picked up the special cell phone and dialed.

A man's voice answered. "Valentino's at the Ritz. Sal Valentino speaking." His voice was just as affected as the woman's who had answered earlier.

Hayden had already decided to use a fake name. "Mr. Valentino, my name is Melody Smithe, and a friend of mine who's been in your gallery suggested I come take a look at what you've got. Will you be in tomorrow morning?"

Valentino said he would be, then cordially asked a host of questions that Hayden skillfully sidestepped, other than saying she was from Charleston since there was no way she could disguise her drawl. She no sooner put the phone back in her purse when the land line rang. It was Ben Beckham asking if he could drop by to explain the revised conservancy agreement.

"My sister's handling all that."

She instantly regretted her vexed tone.

"I know, but I just wanted to go over some of the main points and see if you're comfortable with them."

Hayden dropped her head in her hand. The last thing she

cared about was this agreement. Besides, she had no intention of signing anything right now. Ben's face flashed across her mind and it was impossible to push it out. She didn't listen to what he was saying, just to the sound of his comforting deep voice. She pictured him standing in her doorway the first time he came to the cabin. He had the same bone-deep confidence Jack had that only comes after it's proven to you over and over again you're desirable to be with and to know. A chosen one.

That's the way she had felt up until when Carrie got sick, and she was never going to get it back. She understood, for the first time, the appeal these blessed individuals had. The beauty of their looks and easy goodness of their nature simply engenders a feeling that all is well with the world.

She interrupted him in mid-sentence. "Come on over. I'll be here."

The afternoon had some rough spots. First, the teacher who ran a sculpture class called in sick and told them to have everyone continue working on their projects and he'd add a half-hour to next week's session. Then Judy finally worked herself into a meltdown. Hayden ended up calling Terri and asking her if she could handle the evening shift so Judy could go home early. The guilt didn't help Hayden's mood.

Ben showed up, but Hayden couldn't break away from a problem some student was having with her account. She couldn't find the payment book and the woman wouldn't let it go. While she tried to get Judy on the phone, she watched Ben out of the corner of her eye drift around the sculpture class with a sleek co-ordinated gate that reminded her of a tiger casually prowling the jungle.

By the time she reached Judy and straightened out the woman's account, Ben had taken off his jacket, rolled up his sleeves and was moving from student to student commenting on their work. Two people came in the gallery and miraculously bought something, and the phone kept ringing. This was one of the few times Hayden had handled the gallery on her own and she chalked up all the confusion to God paying her back for the way she had treated Judy.

Ben pulled up a stool next to a shy, painfully thin nineteen-year-old girl who found it hard to look anyone in the eye. Over the weeks, Hayden had found herself paying the girl the same kind of attention, once even coaxing her to join her for lunch at the deli down the hall. Ben's obvious rapport with the timid girl touched Hayden. With a phone to her ear while waiting for a supplier to look up their last order, she meandered into the room close enough to hear.

"Don't be afraid to make the ear a little twisted like the model's. It gives him character." He swiped off the clay ear, massaged it in his warm hand, spread it flat with his thumb and deftly pressed it back on the head. "Go on. Try it."

The girl self-consciously tweaked the piece of clay.

"Go on. You can do it."

She worked tentatively at first, then became absorbed in shaping the ear, bending the upper half outward. Ben gently patted her on the back.

"Atta girl. I knew you could do it."

The girl turned and looked him directly in the eye, and for the first time, Hayden saw her beam. Judy had said he was a good teacher, but Hayden hadn't been able to visualize it; he was too self-possessed, too confident. But now she could see he took on a different persona in the classroom. Giving of himself in a disarming way that erased the student's fear of failure.

Hayden had heard about Jenny Beckham's work for years and thought her sister had a few of her pieces. If she remembered right, they had a whimsical flavor. One of his former students had mentioned that Jenny and Ben had a great chemistry together, he in his sculpture studio, her in the adjoining ceramics lab. The sensitive fanciful artist and the masculine laid-back sculpture mentor. It must have been a beautiful thing to watch.

She thought of how akin she was to Ben. They had both lost someone. His former student had also told her Ben was so broken up over his wife's death she didn't think he was ever going to get over it.

A wave of regret washed over her. She'd been ugly to Jack for over a year now. So many hateful words that could never be taken back. Would he ever be able to forget them? Then there was the condom floating in the toilet when she stopped in to check out their beach place in Myrtle Beach. It still made her sick to think about it.

Terri arrived as the class was ending. This was the first time Hayden could take a moment to talk with Ben. He chatted for a few moments with a couple students, then washed his hands, threw his blazer over his shoulder and came toward her.

"I hope you didn't mind my taking over your students that way. They told me their teacher was sick, and I could see how busy you were."

"No. I appreciated it."

"Can I take you to dinner so I can go over the agreement with you." He grinned. "After all, I've got to do *a little work* for the conservancy."

Hayden reminded herself about her meeting the next morning with Valentino. The last thing she wanted to do in her frame of mind was sit in a restaurant stressing out over whether the food would be any good. Besides, she was itching to cook herself. Probably the only thing that would keep her from climbing the walls tonight. She glanced up at Ben and studied the optimistic expression on his handsome face. Even though it teetered on over confidence, she still wasn't going to be the one to change it to disappointment. He had earned a listen. "Why don't y'all come on over to my place. I'll cook you dinner and then you can tell me all about it."

BEN HAD NOTICED the agitated state Hayden was in from the moment he had called her. This was the first glimmer of cordiality all afternoon and he decided to work it for all it was worth.

"Don't tell me you can cook, too?" he said.

"Why, darlin', I live to cook."

Her sweet Southern accent melted him. There was nothing like it.

She had put her hands on her hips and was making a point of looking him up and down. "By all appearances, I'd say you're a Frogmore stew kind of guy."

"How *did* you know?"

"And, what's with the *too?*"

"I don't know how to tell you this, but they're gonna be talking about the Monkey of Little Pisgah for the next twenty years." He slowly nodded. "Yep. A genuine legend in the making. Just a matter of time before there's some kind of plaque on that boulder."

Ben waited for the lilting laughter and wasn't disappointed. By now they had reached the parking lot in the back of the building. Hayden stopped short. "This dinner might not be a good idea, Ben. You remember Addie Mae? The woman who's staying with me? She can be pretty intrusive at times. Before you can say Jack Robinson, she'll have you hiring her to clean the house and rearrange your furniture. Maybe we can get together another time." She seemed genuinely disappointed.

He raised his hands, palms facing her. *"Wait a minute.* I happen to know a kitchen at the end of Hog Rut Road praying to be rescued by someone who *lives to cook.* Heck, if it gets insulted once more with mac and sleeze, I think it's going to blow itself up."

A breeze swirled her hair around her head and the late afternoon sun behind her created a glistening golden halo. "Do you have pots, pans? That sort of thing?"

"You bet."

"Okay. You win. How do I get there?"

Ben gave her the instructions and was relieved she insisted on stopping by the grocery store and personally picking up the ingredients. It would give him a chance to straighten up the house.

He rushed home and threw himself into the job. *Rosita, darling, where are you when I need you?* Don't get any ideas, he told himself as he put a couple of bottles of wine in the fridge. She's just coming over to cook you a meal out of gratitude, and give you a chance to pitch the easement.

He hadn't cooked much since he moved in, and there still were boxes of dishes and utensils stacked all over the place. He quickly got things in a semblance of order, then went in and stocked the guest bathroom with towels and toilet paper. He hated himself for doing it, but he quickly made his bed with fresh sheets, then he collected all the clothes hanging from the bed-posts and chairs, and tossed them in a closet.

He heard her pull up to the house, and ran out. Once they hauled in all the bags from her car, he got the feeling the dinner preparation wasn't going to be the leisure experience he had visualized. She kicked off her spiked heels, then fished around in her purse and pulled out a large clip and put up her hair, the ends fanning out over the top of her head like a senorita's comb. She asked him what he was staring at, and he was quick to say, "Nothing."

Hayden unpacked and thoughtfully positioned everything like she was planning a war. "I suppose you don't have an apron handy."

He ran into the bathroom and brought out a towel, which she wrapped around her waist. The sleeves on her grayish blue silk blouse were already rolled up and a considerable pile of jewelry lay on the counter.

She thrashed through the pots and pans until she found a large one. She poured in a bunch of new potatoes, and covered them with water and beer like she was on a mission. He mainly tried to stay out of her way.

She snapped her fingers and pointed to the pot. "Watching the clock is your job. Seven minutes, once it boils."

It didn't seem to bother her that he watched her more than the clock. This was the first chance he had to really study anything more than her face. She was small framed and a little on the thin side, but solid. "Do you play tennis?" he asked.

She didn't look up. "Yes. Actually, a lot."

His eyes traced her slacks down her nicely formed figure to her feet. They were long for her body. Especially the toes. It was as if God had thrown in the imperfection to apologize for making someone so perfect.

She chopped the onions like a professional chef, every so often giving him a wink that said, "Wait 'til you taste this." Once she cut up the corn and sausage and added them along with the crabs she picked up from a man who sold them from his truck every afternoon, she rubbed her hands together like something magical was about to happen. "Now we let this simmer for ten minutes." She made quick work of cleaning up the counter and threw in the shrimp. It went off like a well rehearsed half-time performance.

Not until she removed the pot from the heat and started to set the table did he get a chance to offer her a glass of wine. She strolled with it over to a table in front of the wall of glass framing his mountain view. "What do we have here?" she said as she lifted one of the seedlings.

Ben felt himself inflate with pride. "My delphiniums." He lifted an eyebrow. "Actually, you may be looking at the next generation to completely blow away the lovely and charming belles of the Western North Carolina Garden Club."

"You? Garden club!? *Bless your little heart.*"

He picked off an imaginary piece of lint from his shirt and tossed it in the air. "I'm on their board."

Hayden raised an eyebrow and gave him a sly look, like she was thinking the only reason was that they wanted the pleasure of looking at him. "I'm genuinely impressed." She delicately ran a finger under a fringed leaf. "Ben Beckham, you don't cease to amaze me... football hero, teacher, conservationist... gardener."

He scooted over to the bookshelf, grabbed a small trophy and held it up. "Please. Make that prize-winning gardener."

Ben folded his arms and took her in as he listened to her laugh. She reminded him of a beautiful wild animal—quick and resilient, yet fragile enough to be destroyed by one brutal act, and he was sure something of that sort had happened to her.

Ben enjoyed watching her eat as much as he did the meal itself. "Do all South Carolina girls know how to cook like this?"

"Heck, yeah."

Ben loved the way she sang out those words, stretching *heck* to three lyrical syllables like she reveled in her accent. Sweet was the only way to describe it.

"From the time I was five, our cook would send my sister and me out on the creek to fetch fresh crabs. Ole Martha worked for us every summer doing the cookin' at the beach house, but by the time I was twelve her ankles got so swollen she could right hardly stand, so I'd whip up this lowcountry boil myself at least once a week."

Hayden started in on a piece of corn. "That's how I learned to cook. I was always so afraid if she didn't get the meals up in time my mother would let her go, so I'd come in early from the beach to help out, and she'd sit and rock in that tired ole thing we had in the kitchen and tell me what to do." Hayden flapped a hand. "Heck, cookin' was the least she did. She was like a mother to us. When she died, the place never felt the same."

Hayden's gaze drifted off. "Those summers seem so wonderful to me now. I'd always imagined I'd go crabbin' with my kids some day and teach them how to cook all those meals." She tossed her head. "It's funny how things don't work out the way you expect them to."

After they cleared the table and stacked everything in the dishwasher, Hayden insisted on tidying up before strolling out on the deck. When she started to take off the towel she had wrapped around her waist, he wanted to help but didn't dare. He didn't think he could stand it if he touched her.

There was a nip in the air and a whippoorwill's haunting call sounded in the distance. The sun had set behind them but they could still make out the veil of blue misty mountain tiers floating in the distance.

Ben stood close enough to Hayden to smell the perfume of her hair. She looked up and he managed to meet her gaze. They stared at each other for a moment; then, he had to turn away.

Hayden shivered. Ben wanted to put an arm around her, but knew if he did, he wouldn't be able to stop there. Not only was it wrong, it would kill him if she rejected him. He quickly led her into the great room and lit the fire.

"This is nice," she said, her spirits somewhat subdued.

Ben scratched behind his ear. "I guess it's time for me to explain the easement."

Hayden threw her head back and groaned. "Please don't. It's the furthest thing from my mind right now."

Ben laughed. It was the furthest thing from his, too, and he had a hunch she just wanted to talk. He got two fresh goblets and poured some wine. Laced within the things she had been saying all evening were hints that she had something pressing on her mind. But she was so uptight, he knew one misstep and she'd take off just like the little doe that morning when he opened the door to get a better look.

"Are you worried about the gallery?" he asked as he handed her a glass, careful not to appear like he was prying.

"Yes, but there's something else that's troubling me even more."

Ben recalled one of the board members phoning him about seeing her at lunch with the developer at Carmel's sidewalk café in the Arcade. It was possible she might be struggling with selling the four hundred acres.

"Why don't you tell me about it?" he asked.

"I'm afraid it's one of those things I've got to figure out for myself."

Ben knew he'd kick himself after she left if he didn't ask her the question that had been on his mind all night. "Is it your husband?"

"No. Jack's a great guy. Anything that's wrong with our marriage is my fault." She hugged herself tightly and stared into the fire. "We lost our baby just over a year ago and I can't have any more. I guess I couldn't accept it. Our little Carrie was the spitting image of Jack, and every time I looked at him my heart got torn out. Though, now I think I'll find peace in it. It's all that's left of her." She came out of her trance, slapped her legs and looked at him. "When I finish what I have to do here, I'm going to go home and see if we can get a new start."

Ben had felt all along things weren't right between Hayden and her husband, but nothing this tragic. He couldn't help imagining what would have happened to Jenny if she had lost Heather. Not knowing what to say, he put another log on the fire and cast about for something else to talk about.

Why were her hands shaking through the whole meal? Something was very wrong, and if it wasn't her husband, what could it be? He was convinced the only reason she came over tonight was because she needed someone to talk to. It was evident it wasn't because she had any interest in him. He decided to take a chance.

"Hayden, are you in some kind of trouble?"

She frowned. "Not yet, but I will be."

"Maybe it'll help if you tell me about it."

"It's a long, sad story, It's not fair to put you through it."

"Try me."

She tensed up, all fidgety, and it suddenly appeared as if she had been waiting all evening to spill out what was on her mind.

"Something my mother did years ago started a whole chain of horrible events, and I need to make things right."

He hunched forward. "Go on."

"Do you promise that you'll never tell anyone, no matter what?"

"I promise."

As he listened to the story of what her mother and grandfather had inflicted on an injured war veteran, Ben found it hard to believe Hayden had turned out so well. And then he thought back to all the times he'd been with her father and couldn't remember ever hearing him laugh.

"There are things I've run across at the house that would break your heart," she said, her voice cracking. "He followed our lives... bought us cards that he never sent." She wiped a tear trickling down her cheek. "I'm convinced that's why he was so generous to his students... scholarships... free lessons... you name it."

The cadence in Hayden's voice sounded ominous, like she had come to terms with an ugly reality. Ben figured this story wasn't going to have a happy ending.

She looked up at him. "I don't know if you want to hear any more of this. It could put you at risk."

"Believe me; nothing could be riskier than pro ball."

Her face twisted into a quizzical expression like she was having a hard time believing what she was about to say. "My father was a forger."

"Checks?"

"No. Nothing like that." Her gaze was intense. "Paintings. Winslow Homer."

Ben strained forward to make sure he was hearing right.

"I discovered three of them in his attic." She looked him in the eyes. "They're masterpieces." She took a deep breath. "But I'm afraid three others have been sold through Valentino Galleries in New York City."

"Are *you sure* about all this?"

"Quite. He had to get the money from somewhere for all the things he was doing. The gallery never even brought in enough to pay the tuition bills for the two kids he was putting through Pratt."

With Heather attending the school, he had a pretty good idea of the kind of money she was talking about. "So, what are you going to do?"

"Sooner or later someone's going to catch on that those paintings are forgeries and my father will be disgraced. Nobody will remember all the good things he did with the money. I'm going to New York tomorrow to see Mr. Valentino and try to buy them all back. Our family did this to my father and I'm going to make it right no matter what it takes. And there's another reason I want to get the paintings back. I don't want to see anyone else cheated because of what we did."

Ben stood up and strolled over to the wall of glass. Lights were twinkling off in the distance. He wasn't prepared for this fantastic revelation. He suddenly remembered changing the sheets on his bed and wanted to kick himself.

Finally, he came back and sat down, then looked at her earnestly. "Take my advice and destroy whatever paintings you've got, get rid of all the evidence, and forget you ever knew anything about this. If your father were alive right now, he would tell you the same thing. If you go to New York tomorrow and confront this guy you'll be implicating yourself. And if there are any problems getting the paintings back, this whole thing could come back to bite you."

"I know that, but I'm going to do it anyway. If there were… say… ten of them, I'd agree with you. But there's only three.

Even if I don't get them all, I can narrow the exposure by taking as many out of circulation as possible."

"Hayden, this could get dicey."

"It boils down to a business deal right now. We can try to buy them back for a little more than they were purchased for, and if that doesn't work, explain they're fakes and hope the people will take their money and run."

"This Valentino hardly sounds like the kind of guy who would care much about your father's reputation. Besides, I don't think he's going to pass up an opportunity to double-dip. Once he finds out how much you want them back, you can bet he's going to put the squeeze on you."

"I'm prepared for that. He just better be prepared for me. While other kids were hearing down-home gossip at the dinner table, my sister and I were listening to strategies for some of the biggest land deals that ever went down in the South. I know how much Valentino gave my father and can imagine how much his gallery took in. What's more, it's *his* reputation he's got to worry about. If this gets out, he's out of business, if not in jail. He had to know they were fakes. Where was the provenance?"

Ben couldn't believe she was actually going to go through with this. "All this could be very costly."

"I'm sure it will be." She wrung her hands. "Just keeping the gallery going has been a struggle."

"I don't understand. I thought you and your sister were quite the heiresses."

"I can't get my hands on any of my estate. My mother's got it tied up. I've been pretty much living on my credit cards since I got up here."

"Then how are you going to buy back the paintings?"

She looked at him through slitted eyelids. "I've got a plan."

They both fell silent. Ben didn't have to spend much time thinking through her options. She was talking big money getting those paintings back... more than a credit card company was liable to advance her! If only she hadn't met with that developer, he wouldn't worry so much.

"Hayden, let me go with you to New York. I'm flying out to

California tomorrow for a Nature Conservancy conference, but I'll be back Sunday night. We can go together next week."

"No. I have to do this myself. I feel bad enough dragging you in this far. Like you said, if you come with me, you'll be implicated."

"I've got a friend. He's a big guy. I want you to take him along with you."

"I'm no fool, Ben. I'm hardly going to meet Valentino in some dark alley in the middle of the night. I have another cell phone strictly for contacting him, and it's the only number he's going to have for me. No matter what phone he calls from, I'll know it's him or someone he gave my number to."

Hayden had become so calm the thought crossed Ben's mind that she was making up the whole story. But it was too fantastic. He wrote down her cell phone number and gave her Ricky's. "Promise me you'll call him the minute your plane arrives. I talked to him just before I came over this afternoon. He's sitting around in a hotel room waiting for his apartment to be recarpeted." Ben jotted down her flight number. "I'll have him meet you just outside the terminal."

"Actually, it'll be good to have someone drive me around. Thanks."

Hayden rose and looked at Ben. "I can't believe I told you all this. You must think I'm reckless. First the fall in the office, then the slip off the boulder, and now this. And I didn't even listen to your proposal after you spent practically the whole afternoon helping out." She put her arms around him and squeezed. "Ben, I really needed a friend tonight. Thank you so much."

Ben became aroused by the nearness of her body. He put his hands on her waist and held her at arm's distance even though he wanted to pull her back close to him so much he ached. He walked her to her car and didn't want to take his hand off the door. Not reckless. Strong like the mountain women he'd always held a deep respect for. Even though she was from a different world than his mother, she had the same resolute single-minded idea of fairness, and he was counting on it.

"Hayden, will you promise me one thing?"

"What?"

"Promise me you and your sister won't do anything with your land without giving us a chance first."

"I promise."

He watched her car lights fade as she made her way down the mountain, then went into the house and called Ricky.

"How will I know her?"

"Don't worry. You'll know her. She looks like an angel. Drive her wherever she wants and stay with her until she gets back on the plane."

"Do you want me to bruise anyone?"

"No. But I do want you to stay completely off the booze."

"Don't worry. I don't touch the stuff anymore."

"Sure, Ricky."

Ben went around turning off the lamps, then made himself a drink and meandered out onto the deck. He could see the glow from the lights in Hendersonville on the dark horizon. Whadda ya know? Hayden Taylor of all people. A big time forger. He had to call Tom and give him a heads up that Hayden might be planning on selling her land, so he could line up alternative plans before it was too late. It didn't look like there would be much time. She would probably need to get her hands on money fast.

Somewhere in the back of his mind he had thought something might happen tonight, but nothing like this. He recalled the sound of her voice as she begged off her invitation in the parking lot that afternoon. He must have sensed she desperately needed to reach out to someone, and was now glad he didn't let her go. The way she had confided in him tonight made him wonder if his life was destined to be intertwined with hers for as long as he had breath.

He couldn't shake the look in her eyes as she talked about her baby. The same empty stare he saw at the visitation. He rolled the glass around in his hands and mulled over what she had said about going back home and getting a new start. Her remark, that seeing her baby in her husband would be a comfort, bothered him. He didn't know that much about psychology, but enough to surmise that wasn't healthy. And how would a man feel if he knew the main reason she was staying with him was that he was the only link between her and her dead child?

A shrill call from the whippoorwill sent a shiver rippling through him. This steely little lady was definitely a lot more confident in dealing with the seamier side of the gallery business than he would be; yet, at the same time she appeared emotionally scarred. His throat tightened. A cold-hearted mother, a father she never knew, and finally the only child she was ever going to have taken away. No wonder she couldn't let it go. But, judging from the change in her over the past weeks, he knew some day she would, and wondered if he'd be around.

CHAPTER TWENTY-TWO

HAYDEN BREEZED THROUGH the terminal clutching a large shoulder bag, ignoring all the eyes turned her way. Wearing heels and a flowing trench coat over a creamy silk pantsuit, the electricity of New York pumped her up as she quickly made her way through the throngs and eventually onto the sidewalk outside. It teemed with security and the discord of honking horns, screeching brakes, and police whistles.

Wind streaming through the terminal's tunnel-like loading zone, ironed her hair flat across her face. A big red F250 pickup truck swerved in front of a taxi and screeched to a stop. A man jumped out and shouted her name, his baby face in sharp contrast to his mammoth physique. She waved and he ran around, opened the door and helped her up.

Once he jumped back in the truck and slammed the door shut, the quietude made her feel like she'd just escaped from a war zone.

Hayden offered her hand. "I'm Hayden Parks. Ricky, I really appreciate you coming to pick me up."

A policeman tapped on the window, and he quickly pulled away. "Happy to do it for you, Hayden. Where can I take you?"

She gave Ricky the address and was surprised when he said he knew the place.

"Sure. I've been to Valentino's. Bought one of my girlfriends a painting that her hairdresser did. He's quite well known now."

Ricky's thick forearms fused with the wide paws gripping the steering wheel. The truck stopped for a light and he turned toward Hayden and studied her face. "Ben said you looked like an angel. He sure as heck got that right."

Hayden smiled.

"Gonna buy some paintings?"

"Yes. You could say that."

By the time they pulled into a parking garage near the gallery, Hayden was feeling nervous about the meeting with Valentino and grateful to Ben for arranging to have Ricky along; especially later when pedestrian traffic on the sidewalk seemed to clear a path for them. His blasé attitude convinced her Ben hadn't told him the purpose of her visit.

Once they reached the gallery, Hayden took a moment to look around. Typical for New York, she thought. Hung with artwork of the abstract type that fits in well with current decorator trends—plenty of splashes of color and geometric shapes. Hard to picture a Winslow Homer being sold off its walls.

A woman emerged from a hall and approached them. Her dress was as affected as her manner. She was too young for the black crepe and too classic looking for the elaborate antique jewelry. Hayden told her she had an appointment with Mr. Valentino. She turned and said she'd go get him.

Sal Valentino's limp handshake made the same impression. As agreed in advance, Ricky said he'd wait in the gallery. Valentino shepherded Hayden with a sashaying gait into an office with damask-covered walls and a reproduction of a Louis XIV desk. He kept glancing at Hayden's rings as he conducted the perfunctory small talk about how much he loved Charleston. Finally, with a receptive smile on his face, he pulled a legal pad out of a drawer and asked, "What sort of paintings did you have in mind?"

"Watercolors."

"Something to go in your home?"

"Winslow Homers."

The smile faded.

Hayden put her purse on a small side table, folded her arms and crossed her legs. "I'm Hayden Taylor's daughter. Are you aware that my father passed on?"

"Yes. Please accept my condolences." His eyes darted around the room and avoided hers, making him appear to be thinking fast. Finally, he looked at her with a slight squint. "Has Freddy Lucas been in touch with you?"

"No. I don't know a Freddy Lucas."

He nodded and then spoke. Cautiously. "Do you have something you want to sell?"

She couldn't believe it. He hadn't the least tinge of shame or guilt and was apparently ready to deal with anyone who had their hands on her father's forgeries. Good. His total lack of morality would make it easier to keep this on a business level. "No. I had more of a joint purchase in mind. I want you to get back the three Winslow Homers you sold."

He stared at her. "I don't know what you're talking about."

"Well, I hope your memory improves before I'm forced to go to the police."

The blood drained from his face.

"Mr. Valentino, I'm doing you a favor. I'm willing to put up my father's end of the sale to get those paintings back before someone discovers they're fakes and smears his name all over the newspapers—and may I add, yours too."

"I'm shocked! I never knew they were forgeries!"

"Please. Save your indignation for the six o'clock news. I found three more paintings in his attic along with his bookkeeping and I know exactly how much you paid for them. I have no choice but to go to the police and expose this fraud or I'll become part of it. But if we can get them all back... let's say... in the next couple of weeks, and save my father's reputation, I'd be willing to take that chance."

His accommodating posture evaporated and he sank back, making the elaborate chair look too large for his small frame. "The instant I looked in your eyes, I knew I'd seen them before."

He opened a drawer, pulled out a file and nervously flipped

through it. He shook his head. "I don't see where you have anything to worry about. We shipped two out of the country."

"And the third?"

He looked up at her, his face pinched. "The decorator who took them does a lot of boardrooms here in New York... banks... Fortune 500s. That's probably where it is."

"I want them all back."

He put his elbows on the desk and slowly ran his hand through what was left of his wispy dark hair, then massaged the back of his neck. His voice took on a conciliatory tone as he looked up at her.

"Sweetheart, let's be realistic. Right now, if someone discovers they have a forgery, I can claim I didn't know it was a fake, and it'll be impossible for them to prove otherwise. And as far as you're concerned, you're not even in the picture. On the other hand, if just one of these buyers suspects what's going on, this thing could blow up in our faces." His voice rose. "Talk about being implicated! There'd be no claiming we didn't know they were forgeries then. Hell, we'd be caught red-handed!" He fell back in his chair and shook his head. "We're better off letting sleeping dogs lie."

"Come now, Mr. Valentino, if you sit and wait for someone to make the discovery, do you really think they're going to believe you didn't know they were forgeries. Three paintings all by Winslow Homer showing up out of the blue? Where was the provenance? Why not go to Sotheby's and sell them for top dollar at a well-publicized auction. You'd look guilty as hell. On the other hand, you'd appear more innocent if it looks like you just discovered the misrepresentation and were trying to set things right."

She tapped her fingernails on the desk. "And if the police didn't think they'd have enough for a conviction, you'd probably be slapped with a civil suit by the buyers and end up paying the whole amount plus attorney's fees. Ask yourself, where would your credibility be then? With a scandal of this sort, you'd be washed up. Right now, you're in the best position since I'm prepared to kick in my father's share to get them back."

"My dear girl, where do you think I'm going to come up with the money to buy back my portion?"

"I'm afraid that's your problem. It's all I can do to come up with mine."

She opened her purse, took out a pen and a slip of paper and wrote down her cell phone number. "Here. I'll expect a call from you in the next couple of days." She looked at him. "Mr. Valentino, there's only three. We can do this."

VALENTINO COLLECTED HIS THOUGHTS for a moment after Hayden left, then dialed and asked for Andre. "I don't care what the hell he's doing! Get him on the phone!" He drummed his fingers on the desk.

"Darling! What's the big rush?"

"I can't get into it right now, Andre, but I've got to get those goddamned Winslow Homers back."

"Ca-ching, ca-ching, sweetheart."

"Don't go there with me, Andre. You're in this shit as deep as I am. If it wasn't for you, I'd never have let Hayden talk me into this harebrained scheme to begin with. Now his damn daughter wants the paintings back or she's going to the cops."

"Oh, stop your whining and let me figure out how we're going to get them back. The one I put in Pepco's board room will be a cinch. But we're going to have to give them their money."

"What was it? One-fifty?"

"I marked it up another thirty," said Andre.

Sal thought for a moment. "I've got a Toulouse-Lautrec sketch here I haven't been able to move. Do you think they'd take that instead?"

"It had a lot of color in it, didn't it?"

"Yes. Yes. Very colorful."

"I'm redoing the vice president's office, so I'll be there tomorrow. Get it over to me before ten and I'll talk them into a switch. That boardroom needs a little perking up."

"Are you sure?"

"Darling, they love me!" He snickered. "Especially that hunk of an operations manager."

Sal was thinking he'd have to give his client the one hundred thousand he wanted for the sketch and forget about any commission, that is unless he marked it up another ten or twenty thousand. He'd get it from her in cash when he handed over the fake. Parting with that kind of money might be exactly what that bitch needed to knock some sense into her.

"Are you listening or not?" pouted Andre.

"I'm sorry. What was it about the other two?"

"They're in Dubai. I had to spend a weekend with that crazy Arab. He almost killed me."

"How much did you mark those up?"

"Believe me, darling, I earned every penny."

IT WAS HARDLY AN HOUR later when Hayden was dropped off at the departure lane at Kennedy International; and by five-thirty she was standing at a counter in the Myrtle Beach airport renting a car. On the way to the lot to pick it up, she pulled out her new cell phone and checked for messages. Just one from Valentino asking her to call. He'd located the painting in New York, but needed one hundred and twenty thousand from her to buy it back.

She phoned and they haggled back and forth, finally settling on a hundred thousand. She said she'd call him in a couple of days when she had the money, then come to New York to make the exchange. He told her to bring cash.

Her next call was to her mother. "It'll take me an hour to get to your house. Will you be there?"

Her mother was silent for a moment, then answered, "Yes."

Hayden snapped her phone closed without saying another word. Everything that needed to be said had to be done face to face.

Hayden pulled into her mother's driveway, and just as she had expected, found her upstairs in her sitting room. All the windows were open and a warm ocean breeze ruffled the drapes. Elizabeth Tarrington lay on a lounge chair in a pair of slacks, slowly blowing out a puff of smoke like she was looking forward to hearing Hayden either beg for money or for forgiveness, and if she were really lucky, both.

Hayden gave her a solemn greeting, then went over to the fireplace and stared at the pictures on the mantel, not seeing them. She was about to attempt something that would change the whole character of her existence and she had to get it right. She turned and faced her mother.

"I want you to call Roger and arrange to have my share of Grandpappy's estate turned over to me."

Her mother exploded in a laugh. "You're as loony as your..."

Hayden cut her off. "It's payback time, Mother. You ruined my father's life and now we're going to do right by him."

"What are you talking about? Do right by him? He's dead for heaven's sake." She took out a fresh cigarette and lit it with her old one. She spoke flippantly, in spite of her shaking hands. "So, what does he have... a couple of kids or something. I'm sure we can put funds aside..."

"No, Mother. He didn't have any kids. Just me and Barbara. Remember?" Hayden leaned back against the fireplace, her arms folded. "Besides, he was too busy forging Winslow Homer watercolors."

Elizabeth sat upright.

"Three of them have been sold through a gallery in New York and I intend to get them back."

"You're out of your mind."

"That's possible. Who wouldn't be with a..." Hayden stopped herself.

Elizabeth inhaled and watched as Hayden went over to her desk, dug a checkbook out of a drawer, and handed it to her.

"Write one out for a hundred thousand," said Hayden.

Her mother slapped the checkbook out of her hand. "I'll do nothing of the sort!"

Hayden's eyebrow rose. "All right, Mother. Just be sure to get your roots touched up before the photographers arrive."

"What are you talking about?"

"Can't you see; we're both implicated. If I can't get those paintings back, I'll have to report this fraud to the authorities."

She strolled around the room. "And then, I think... right after that... have the press conference. I can see the headlines now... *Heiress' Ex a Big Time Forger.* But you don't have to worry, Mother. Just stay out of the grocery stores and you won't see them. I'm sure all your friends at the club will be very sympathetic."

"I can't believe you're capable of blackmailing me with your father's thievery just to get your hands on that money?"

"What do you expect, Mother? I had a good teacher."

Hayden bent down and picked up the checkbook and handed it to her. "Here. *Now.*"

Elizabeth took it and looked up at her. It was one of the only times in her life Hayden had actually looked in her mother's eyes and seen her looking back. No anger, no hate. Just a cool calculating stare.

Her mother studied Hayden's face. "You may have learned a lot from us, but you were never a Burroughs. I saw your father in you from the very beginning." She looked blankly into Hayden's eyes. "I should have known once I told you about his letter, you'd take off just like he did." She took a deep drag of her cigarette and looked off across the room. "What are the chances you'll get these goddamned paintings back?"

"I already have one."

Her mother nodded to herself. "Get me something to write with."

Hayden handed her a pen, then picked up the phone. "What's Roger's number?"

Without looking up from writing the check, Elizabeth answered, "Number two on the automatic dial."

Jack had to be number one, Hayden thought as she waited for someone to answer. She was surprised it was Roger himself. Her mother evidently had the number to his private line. "Hello, Roger. It's Hayden. My mother wants to speak to you." She pressed the phone to her chest and looked her mother directly in the eyes. "And that goes for Barbara, too."

Elizabeth tore out the check, handed it to Hayden, and took the phone.

Descending the stairs, Hayden could hear her mother tell Roger she felt her girls were ready to handle their own affairs. Hayden smiled inwardly. She knew Roger would know better.

SHE DIDN'T THINK she should risk going back to her house. Too many memories that might draw her into another depression. There was too much at stake. She didn't want to see Jack either. Not until she resolved everything in Chimney Rock. So she decided to stay the night at the summer house in South Litchfield. Aunt Martha's grandkids were back in school, so no one would be using it.

She got the key hanging from a nail on a joist under the porch and opened the door. Tokens of over a hundred years of cherished memories were scattered about the ancient rooms or plastered on the cypress walls—shark teeth, baskets of Indian pottery chards collected on the barrier islands, photos of happy, sun-tanned faces. She spotted a rag doll carefully tucked in a toy bed, and smiled. She liked that Rosie was still being lovingly played with by her cousin's children.

There was some food in the fridge and the hot water was still on. Martha's daughter probably planned on coming back for a couple more weekends before it got too cold. She got a bottle of beer out of the fridge and put a bag of popcorn in the microwave, then meandered out onto the porch and sank into a weathered Adirondack chair. The ocean breeze was soft and warm. The tranquil ocean lapped gently on the shore, and a flock of pelicans sailed across the cloudless blue sky. There was nothing like the beach, and no beach like Litchfield's.

She got up, found her purse and came back out, then dug out Ben's phone number, flipped the phone open, then shut again. It wasn't a good idea to talk to him. In her present mood, she was afraid of what she might say.

BEN WAS GLAD The Nature Conservancy conference had shut down at three. His plane was leaving at six and he'd have time to talk with Hayden. He'd reached Ricky during a five-minute break, but needed more time with her. He rushed up to his room, took a shower, and put on a polo shirt and slacks for the trip back to Asheville. He grabbed a bottle of water out of the fridge and lay down on the bed with his cell phone in hand, calculating the time zone change in his head.

Tom had trusted him to deliver Hayden and he didn't want to disappoint him, but mostly he didn't want to see her make a big mistake. Tom handled the news about the possibility of Hayden wanting to sell pretty coolly, and swung into high gear with mind-boggling scenarios that Ben worried he might not be able to handle. When he told Tom, "You better take over," he dismissed the offer.

"No, she trusts you. I'd have to start at ground zero. I'll put my efforts on the sister. If that developer wants that mountain bad enough, he'll take it with the easement. Just keep me posted."

Ben finished off the bottle of water, then made the call. Hayden answered as if she were sitting with the phone in her hand. "Ricky tells me you got on the plane all right. How did everything go at the gallery?"

"Good. Valentino was what I expected. Sort of a nervous twit who doesn't want to be hassled. I'm sure he's going to do everything he can to find the paintings. In fact, he's already got one. He tried to shake me down for a lot of money, but we cut a deal. Like I said, he doesn't want to be hassled... *and darlin', can us li'l ole Southern Belles hassle when we have to.*"

There she goes again, thought Ben. He wondered if she knew how that accent of hers affected him.

"Heck. He's getting twenty-five thousand more than he gave my father. All I have to do now is get him the money and he'll hand it over. He wants cash, Ben. Once I've got it together, can you get Ricky to go with me again?"

"Sure. And if he can't, I will." His mind raced. How much time were they going to have to lock in the conservation easement?

"When do you think you'll be ready?" he asked.

"As soon as my check clears."

It wasn't possible she would have gotten an earnest check

without Barbara's knowledge. Surely, the developer knew both sisters owned the property. He'd have to call Tom and give him a heads up. Meanwhile, he'd have to work harder at getting Hayden's confidence. He invited her to lunch at Carmel's the next day and was surprised how easily she agreed.

Ben hung up. He wasn't handling this situation well. Normally, he would have met this new development head on, but he couldn't confront her. This mission she was on had brought about such a change in her that he couldn't snuff it out, or utter a word that might dampen her spirits. He admitted to himself that his feelings for Hayden were getting in the way, and he had to level with Tom before he blew the whole deal. He couldn't rein her in, and worse yet, remembering her sister's concern for Hayden, he didn't believe she could either.

CHAPTER TWENTY-THREE

AFTER AN UNCOMFORTABLE NIGHT on the red-eye from California, Ben barely had enough time to shower and shave before leaving for the office. Last night, before phoning Tom, he had decided it would be insane to tell him that his feelings for Hayden made working with her difficult. He wasn't a teenager, and this wasn't high school. What's more, it would probably trigger a suspicion that there was more to the story. But he did manage to convey Hayden was pressed for money, and get Tom to agree to set up a morning meeting with the director to hash out all their options.

They were both in the conference room waiting for him when he walked in.

"Well, let's have it," said the director as he raised a cup of coffee to his lips.

Ben sank into a chair and fingered a pen someone left behind. "The other night, Hayden Parks told me she needed to get her hands on a large sum of money quickly to cover her father's obligations and keep the gallery going, and that she couldn't get it from her estate. Then last night, she told me she's got the money." He tapped his fingers on the table and faced the director. "She had lunch with Pete Reynolds last week, and we all know he's out looking for large tracts of land in the gorge."

Ben felt badly when he saw Tom wince at his reference to the Owens' tract that Reynolds stole from underneath him.

It was Tom's turn next. He reviewed his conversation with Barbara the day before, asserting that she definitely appeared to be on track with the easement and even went so far as to say she and her sister were considering gifting the entire property over to the conservancy rather than just giving them an easement. All she was waiting for was their accountants to come up with the best way to proceed.

The director rubbed his chin. "I tend to feel that's the way they're headed. Why else would her CPA be carrying on an almost daily dialog with us?"

Ben responded quickly. "Hayden went to New York yesterday morning to wrap up a business deal, and might not have had time to talk with her sister until late last night."

Ben, seeing Tom wasn't impressed with that argument, decided to try another approach. He was walking a fine line. He couldn't break his promise to Hayden and tell them about the forgeries, yet he owed it to the conservancy to warn them about the urgency of the situation.

As much as he hated to do it, he said, "This woman is coming out of a major depression from losing her only child. There's no question her emotional state has improved since she's gotten wrapped up in the gallery. Frankly, I think her sister will do whatever it takes to keep her on the mend?"

Tom looked like he was considering the point. "Actually, there's merit in that argument. When we took them up to the World's Edge, I could see her sister was overly concerned for her."

Tom looked at Ben. "Did you get a promise from Hayden that they wouldn't sell without letting us know?"

"Yes."

The director turned to Tom. "Didn't you get that same kind of promise from Mr. Owens?"

Tom nodded.

"Okay, Ben. I want you to confront her about her intentions straight out during this lunch. We've got to know what we're facing before it's too late." He took off his glasses and rubbed between his eyes. He looked up at Tom with a weary expression on his face. "These parcels can slip through our fingers in one afternoon."

THE BEAUTIFUL FACE with the playful smile put a lump in Ben's throat as he watched Hayden study the menu. He didn't know how he was going to broach the subject of her selling out to the developer.

"When did you get back to Chimney Rock?" he asked as he gave the menu a quick glance.

"I didn't come back to Chimney Rock."

The coyness in her tone made him uneasy. "Where did you go?"

"Pawleys Island."

He knew it! She'd gotten her sister's signature on the sales contract last night! Had she already delivered the signed contract and deposited the earnest money check?

"When did you get back in town?"

"Five minutes ago. I had to leave the beach at seven this morning to get here on time."

Ben could feel his ears get warm. She seemed pleased with herself as she took a bite of a breadstick from a basket the waiter brought to the table. He'd never understand women.

He was getting a little annoyed watching her grin at him, but he couldn't let his emotions get in the way. She obviously hadn't had time to deposit the check, and if it was the last thing he did, he was going to talk her into signing the easement, and then get her to hold off closing this deal until it was registered in the courthouse.

Ben couldn't believe he had actually abetted her in this travesty against the mountain. Which side was he on? Instead of helping her get around in New York, why hadn't he just told her that her father would rather have suffered any kind of humiliation before sacrificing that mountaintop?

If she hadn't felt so guilty about what her family had done to him, she probably would have just shrugged the whole idea of a scandal off in the first place. But then he remembered what she had told him: *I especially want to get the paintings back because I don't want to see anyone else cheated because of what we did.* If that were the case, why wasn't she being fair to all the people who loved the beauty and nature of the gorge, and everyone who would come to this sacred place in the years ahead? He felt betrayed.

"Aren't you going to ask me about the money?" she asked, with a big grin.

You bet I am, he said to himself. He had to fight an urge to wipe the smile off her face.

She didn't wait for him to answer. "My mother!"

The triumph on her face dumbfounded him, but the waiter coming and taking their order gave him a chance to clear his head, only to find himself wanting to push the man aside, lift Hayden out of her chair, and hug her. He made himself calm down, and once the waiter left, leaned forward and whispered, "I thought she had a lock on your estate and was hell-bent on keeping it from you?"

She leaned forward, gave him a meaningful wink, and whispered, "Just let's say she's had a change of heart."

Ben thanked God he hadn't confronted her with selling out to the developer. He'd never forgive himself for insulting her, and didn't think she would either. As he watched her finish off the breadstick with the impish grin on her face, he knew it would kill him if he never saw her again. He'd fought with his emotions in the past few days, but right now he felt a warmth toward her that he didn't think he could stand.

Hayden gave him another wink and said with glee, "One down and two to go."

Ben couldn't help chuckling his way through the meal. Hayden's pride in herself filled him with joy. They discussed getting the cash once her mother's check cleared. He wanted to offer to go with her to retrieve the first painting, but if he were alone with her in New York, could he hold himself back? Ricky was probably a safer option. He would let him know what was going on. Ricky would take the proper precautions.

As he watched her sip her wine, he thought about being in

New York with her. He was a lot more experienced than she was, and she still had the down home friendliness and readiness to accept people on face value you only seem to find in the South. Yet, even though he could be pretty smooth if he wanted, he wasn't quite sure he would be able to break down her resistance. Suddenly he hated himself for thinking such thoughts.

Hayden continued in high spirits. "Do you remember meeting Addie Mae at my house?"

"*Oh, yeah!* She made quite an impression."

Hayden's smile was a mixture of curiosity and triumph. "Well... I've got a funny feeling about her."

Ben cocked his head, his fork frozen in midair.

"I don't mean anything bad. I don't know if you know this, but not only am I named after my father, but the name goes back to before the family came over from Scotland. It was given to the firstborn son of every generation. My mother didn't want any more children so my father ended up giving it to me." Hayden picked up her glass and swirled her wine around. "It's funny. I never felt comfortable with it." She looked up at Ben, a perplexed expression on her face. "I always felt like I stole it. Like the name wasn't meant for me, and belonged to someone else."

Baffled, Ben asked, "What has this got to do with Addie Mae?"

"That's the crazy part. I don't know why, and I have nothing to base it on, but I have this feeling she's carrying my father's baby... the very person my name was meant for."

"Hayden, do you think it's a good idea to dwell on these kinds of things?"

Her high spirits seemed to return. "No. But I'm dwelling on them just the same."

"You don't think anything's going to come of this, do you? As far as you're concerned?"

"*Maybe.*"

"You certainly don't think she's going to just hand this baby over to you, do you?"

Hayden's finger traced the rim of her glass. "She keeps dropping hints. Not much. A word here and a word there is all."

"What's her last name?"

"Hunter. Addie Mae Hunter."

Ben could easily picture someone like Addie taking advantage of Hayden's loss. Tomorrow he was going to check her out.

"How would your husband feel about it?"

"He wanted to adopt, but I couldn't stand the thought. It was so... final." She was silent for a moment, then her voice took on an intensity. "Ben, something's going on here. Call it serendipity, Divine intervention. Whatever. I never would have known my father was reaching out to me if his letter hadn't arrived just as my mother was taking a trip. This one incredible coincidence has changed my life. All the questions I've had about my father... questions that were like a festering sore... are pretty much answered now and I feel like I'm starting to heal."

She shook her head. "I'm about to pay a considerable retribution for what my mother and grandfather did to him. It won't erase their crime, but it will keep the wound from getting any deeper."

She looked off in space. "And why shouldn't I have this baby if Addie wants to give it to me. I've made up my mind. If I get it and it's a boy, I'm going to name him Hayden." Her expression was as resolute as her tone.

They both finished their meal in silence.

Hayden wiped her mouth, and tossed her napkin on the table. "And, now that I'm on a mission to straighten out my life, I've decided to walk the Skyline Trail in Chimney Rock."

Ben was caught completely off guard by her decision about the baby and her vow to climb to the top of the Chimney Rock ridge. This woman's life was moving in fast gear and he was caught up in it. Ever since she told him about her father's forgeries, he asked himself if he had wanted to be drawn into her life all along, or had *she* wanted him to be drawn in; and as wrong as it was, he hoped it was what they both wanted. "Do you think that's a good idea?" he finally asked.

"Definitely. This fear of heights almost got me killed on Little Pisgah and I'm going to beat it, Ben. I'll really be proud of myself if I can do it." She twisted her mouth and looked downward. "I haven't been too proud of myself for the past year."

"When are you planning to go?"

"In a couple of days."

"All right. If that's what you want, I'll go up there with you."

"That's really kind of you, Ben, but this is something I've got to do myself. Tens of thousands of people have walked that trail in the one hundred years that park's been in existence. If they can do it, so can I."

He reached over and held her hand, "You'll wear your hiking boots?"

She nodded.

"Promise me you'll be careful, and if you don't think you can handle it, you'll turn back."

She nodded again, and let him hold her hand for a moment longer before she pulled it away.

Ben walked Hayden to the gallery, then headed for the office. Driving down Route 26 to Hendersonville, he looked forward to telling Tom the good news in person, but was still in a state of bewilderment, especially with Hayden's mention of the baby. Just when he thought she was moving on with her life, she turned and ran back to her past. He shook his head. At least she wasn't hoping for a girl she could call by her child's name. That stood for some progress.

JOHNNY REB READ THE REPORT AGAIN. The owner of the license plate number he took off the Taurus had a rap sheet that included arrests for assaults going back forty years, but so far no major convictions. He was out on bail for the latest, which included rape. A Vietnam buddy who headed up the Sheriff's Department had the plate number pulled for him, then talked with the DA in Cherokee. He told him the guy's trial couldn't come up until the State's witness was well enough to testify. Freddy Lucas had done a real number on her, he had said, and this time he was going to get five years.

Johnny had never felt comfortable with the story of Hayden breaking his neck in a fall. He'd been born and raised in that house and could take every step on that staircase blindfolded.

Why was this thug asking all those questions at the post office? Why all the interest in Hayden's daughter? And what was he doing hanging around town?

Hayden had told him about running into some guy from his past a couple of days before he died. If he remembered correctly, he had said he'd known him at Pratt. Said he was a bad ass that got kicked out of school for throwing a punch at a teacher. Could this be him?

He picked up the phone and called the gallery. Hayden said she'd be home by six. He didn't want to alarm her, but pressed hard enough for her to agree for him to come over at seven.

Impatient, he got over to Hayden's house well before then. Addie, knowing who he was, let him in. They got to chatting with Addie mostly telling him about her transformation business and suggesting that he ask her to come and take a look at his place. He was too disconcerted to carry on a conversation, to say nothing of gabbing about her decorating business.

She finally gave up and said she was exhausted from all the weekend cleaning, and would it be okay if she went upstairs while he waited for Hayden. He had to stop himself from telling her nothing would please him more. As she started up the stairs, she turned and asked him to tell Hayden she wouldn't be eating and was going right to bed.

Hearing water running in the shower upstairs, he went into the kitchen and got a glass, then sank into a leather easy chair. He took a flask out of his shirt pocket, and after pouring himself a drink, looked around and noticed the place had changed. All the furniture seemed to be put at an angle, and scattered about were the kinds of things you see in the magazines lying around in waiting rooms—pillows, throws, candles. The last thing he'd ever go for was to let that woman come over and do that sort of thing to his place. Thank goodness they didn't take down the bear Hayden's brother shot. It was the prettiest thing in the place.

It was dark enough that Hayden's headlights streamed through the window. He rose to greet her as she walked through the door, looking tired but still stunning.

"Sorry, I got here a little early. Addie let me in. She's upstairs taking a shower and told me to tell you she's going to bed."

Hayden came over and gave him a kiss. When she pulled away and smiled, the two overlapping eye teeth reminded him so much of her father he gave her a hug.

She breezed into the kitchen and looked in the fridge. "Have you eaten?" she said loud enough for him to hear.

"Yes. But you go right ahead." He settled back in the chair and waited until she returned with a plate. A boiled egg and a small salad. She even picked at her food like her father.

"Yesterday, I went to New York and then to Myrtle Beach," she said. "I didn't get back in town until today."

"You do look a little worn out." He hesitated for a moment. He didn't want to get her worried, but he needed to find out if she knew Freddy Lucas. "There's a guy kickin' around town that kinda worries me and I wondered if you've seen him."

Hayden looked up, her eyes wide open. "Is he tall, wears glasses and has dark hair? Somewhere in his late fifties?"

"Yes. Have you seen him?"

She put her plate on a nearby table, stood up, crossed her arms and paced. "I wanted to come over and talk with you before now, but things have been happening so fast." She came back to the chair and sat down. She leaned forward and wrung her hands. The flickering fireplace cast eerie psychedelic shadows on her face. She hesitated for a moment, as if she wasn't quite sure she should go on. "I might as well just come out with it, Johnny."

The whole time she narrated the story of finding the paintings in the attic, all he could think about was the fall her father had taken, especially when she mentioned that the room looked amiss with the easel and chairs tipped over. Her discovery also solved the mystery of the money.

"Has all this got anything to do with your going to New York?"

"Yes. I went to see the dealer who sold my father's paintings. I'm going to buy them back."

"Won't that take a lot of money?"

"I'm afraid so. But I'll die if I see my father disgraced." She stood up and started to pace again. "I'm worried that man you were talking about might be from the police. I've never seen him myself, but Judy described him to me. He came to the gallery a couple of times asking questions. It's possible one of the people who bought my father's paintings might have discovered it was a forgery, and now the police are conducting an undercover investigation."

Johnny took the flask out of his pocket and raised it toward Hayden. "You want some?" She shook her head and he poured himself another drink. "Have you ever heard of Freddy Lucas?"

She started to say "no", then wrinkled her brow and looked at him questioningly. "Yes. Valentino asked me something. I think it was, 'Had he been to see me?'"

"What did you tell him?"

"That I didn't know him."

Now that he had gotten all the information he was looking for, Johnny decided he might as well ask Hayden outright if she was getting the money for the paintings from the sale of her father's land. Word around town was that she had met with Pete Reynolds. Johnny didn't want to hurt her feelings, but his loyalties were with her father, and if he were looking down on them right now, he'd want him to do it. "Hayden, are you getting the money for the paintings from selling Round Top?"

"Oh no, Johnny! I wouldn't dream of it. The way I see it, it's only fair that my family buys them back."

"I don't understand. You told me your mother held all the purse strings. I can't imagine her going along with this."

"Think about it, Johnny. Why *did* she divorce my father?" She let out a cynical laugh. "The Burroughs couldn't handle having a broken down, shattered war veteran in the family. It didn't fit in with their image of themselves. Now, imagine the scandal about my father being a forger coming out in the papers. The tabloids would have a field day. I knew that once I told my mother I was going to the police and giving the story to all the newspapers unless she gave me the money to buy back the paintings, she'd crumble. That's her Achilles' heel, Johnny. Her pride."

CHAPTER TWENTY-FOUR

As if Sal's nerves weren't shattered enough from trying to wrestle the paintings from the Dubai sheik, the next call came from Freddy Lucas. "I don't want to talk to him," he told his assistant.

She made a face. "I already said you were here."

By now, Sal was tired of Freddy, and getting rid of him was the only silver lining on this wearisome business. He picked up the phone. "Freddy, our deal's off. Hayden evidently has a daughter who knows about his little sideline."

"What are you talking about?"

"The cold-hearted bitch was here. In my office. Just a few days ago. She's got a nutty idea that old Hayden's reputation might get tarnished if anyone finds out they're fakes, and she wants to buy back the three paintings. She's even threatening to go to the police. If she does, I'm done for. I tell you, there's nothing worse than a stubborn bitch when she gets a bug up her ass."

"What did she look like?"

"A delicate snow-white Alabaster statue... and just as cold."

"That's her all right. Did she say anything about the three that are left?"

"No. All she cares about is getting back the ones I've sold."

"You didn't mention me to her, did you?"

Sal didn't know what to say.

"You did, didn't you? *Damn!*"

They were silent for a moment until Freddy said, "Stall her. I think I can get my hands on the other three in the next couple of days."

"What are you talking about!? How are you going to do that without killing her or something?" Sal stopped short. He wished he hadn't said that. "Listen here. All I did was mention your name once and she said she didn't know you. *That's all!* I'm through with this deal and don't want anything to do with the rest of Hayden's stuff." He held the phone away from his ear and shouted into the mouthpiece, "Don't contact me again!" then slammed the phone in the cradle.

REPUTATION? WHAT REPUTATION? Freddy screamed in his head. No one had ever heard of Hayden except that snooty band of phony artists that hung around his gallery. He slapped the lid of his cell phone closed, then checked the time. It was already three. He had to get those paintings out of the house tonight. She might do something foolish with them. He could get on Route 9 and be in Chimney Rock in half an hour.

What was that rich bitch doing there in the first place? She was just like her father who couldn't have done anything more stupid than to walk away from that gold mine he married and run off to Vietnam thinking he'd find his brother. But, judging by the way she shook Valentino down, she had a lot of her mother in her.

She wouldn't be home from the gallery until around six. Plenty of time. All he had to worry about was the broad who was staying with her. By now he had her routine down and knew she did most of her cleaning at the Bald Mountain Resort in Lake Lure until late in the afternoon.

After he had the paintings, his mind would be clear enough to figure out a way to get rid of the daughter before she caused any more trouble. Once she was gone, everything would be back on track and Valentino would have to deal with him. The dumb sap was in too deep to get out.

He remembered following the daughter home one night and noticing how slowly she drove, like she was afraid of heights. Tomorrow morning he could park on Terrace Drive, wait for her BMW to go by, and then follow her to Asheville. There were so many hairpin curves on the way down the mountains, he'd have plenty of opportunities to force her off the road. He'd grab her, and throw her in the trunk; or better yet, if he were lucky and no one was coming, just knock her out and let the car go over the cliff.

She better not have destroyed the paintings or she was going to be real sorry. If she had, there'd be no point in risking a murder charge, but he'd make sure she never wanted to look in the mirror again.

Damn! He had everything set to leave for Mexico, and now he had to deal with this. It was all Sal's doing. He was careless. Too many slips of the tongue.

As the car swung around a sharp curve on Route 9, a solid wall of granite loomed on one side, and what seemed like a bottomless pit lay on the other. It struck him how much he had messed up. A few weeks ago he was sailing through the mountains thinking he was set for life, and now he had his back to the wall with nothing ahead but a deep abyss.

He'd never meant to hurt Hayden that day in the attic. It was his fault for coming at him in such a rage. Then if that slut at the casino hadn't freaked out, he never would have hit her. And if that weren't enough rotten luck, this snoopy broad, with no damn business being here, was ripping his whole escape plan wide open. With her forcing Sal to get the paintings back, why in the hell would he want to buy any more?

He hadn't had one good night's sleep since his lawyer met with the DA. It looked like the best deal he could get if he pleaded guilty to the assault charge was five years in prison. He might as well be dead. He'd be pushing seventy by the time he got out. He had no choice. He either had to get rid of the bitch or go to jail.

Just as he entered the center of town, the big blond passed him in the Jeep from the opposite direction. Traffic moved slow enough to give him a chance to glance at his rearview mirror and see her make a turn. It took a good five minutes to find a place to turn around, and then another five to make it back to where she had veered off.

Terrace Lane climbed up behind the shops on Main Street, and was dotted with mountain cottages gripping the steep slope, all looking like they had been cobbled together with odds and ends by various generations over the years. No one was out, so he coasted along and looked up and down the driveways gouged out of the heavily forested mountainside until he spotted the Jeep.

The woman was pulling a pail of supplies out from the car. Seemed pretty intent. Didn't even look up at him. Freddy checked his watch. It would take her at least an hour to clean the shack. Hopefully, she was going to head out for the resort after that and not get back to the cabin until after five, but if she walked in on him, he'd just do whatever he had to. He didn't like the idea that she was pregnant. They were the broads who fought the hardest.

If he could only get over to the cabin and get the paintings, he'd be able to think more clearly. Then, all he had to do was get rid of Hayden's daughter, and he'd be through with this godforsaken dump. Hell, he'd be through with North Carolina!

He drove down the twisting lane until it spilled back onto Main, then he turned onto the bridge. He cruised down the deserted street, slipped into Hayden's lot, and tucked the car behind a clump of giant rhododendrons.

Can't leave the place looking like it's been broken into. If I remember right, the door to the back porch didn't have a dead bolt. He reached under the seat and pulled out a pair of gloves and put them on. Next, he took a screwdriver and knife from the glove compartment, then got out of the car and plowed through the ankle-deep leaves. A breeze shook off what was left on a giant ash, and the yellow oval shapes slowly drifted down like snowflakes.

He decided to try the front door before going to the side. At least he could see what kind of lock it had. When he opened the screen, the inner door rattled. He smiled and gave it a try. Just as he thought. It creaked open. The living room was dark, but he could still see it had been rearranged. He suppressed the rage creeping up on him. That damn daughter better not have moved the paintings, too. He hurriedly searched the rooms downstairs, careful not to disturb anything. Not a sign of them. He sprinted up the stairs.

A new runner lay in the hallway. The room on the left had to be the daughter's. Neat, with pricey pieces of art scattered around. He went over and picked up the top to the silk pajamas lying across the foot of the bed and brushed it against his cheek. He thought back to the night when he was still at Pratt when he went to visit Elizabeth Burroughs. She wore silk pajamas, too, but was nowhere near as beautiful as her daughter. It still angered him to remember her flirting with him all afternoon in class, and then refusing to let him in and slamming the door in his face.

The bathroom directly across had a faint smell of perfume. He picked up a bar of soap and sniffed its delicate scent and pictured the daughter's porcelain flesh. It would be a real shame to kill her without getting a little pleasure first. He knew of a gravel road that twisted way up off Route 9. The best thing would be to grab her and put her in his trunk and take her up there for a couple of hours for some fun. There'd be plenty of places to bury her after he was through.

As he continued down the hall, he pushed open another door. Must be the big blond's room. The small bed resembled a military cot with the blankets tucked firmly under the mattress. A row of shoes were neatly lined up underneath. The only personal item in sight was a tattered rag doll lying on the pillow.

Good. Now he knew where everyone slept. If the paintings weren't up in the attic, he'd have to remember to leave the kitchen door and the windows in the downstairs bedroom unlocked before he left. I'll drive around until dark and come back on foot after they've gone to sleep. I'll slit the cleaning lady's throat straight off before she knows what's happening. The daughter's going to tell me what she did with the paintings, all right. Then I'll spend a couple hours teaching her a lesson before I finish her off.

Maybe he could make it look like a robbery gone bad and get away with it like he did Hayden's death. Everything he touched had to be wiped. He'd have to remember to bring the denatured alcohol and rags he used to clean off his fingerprints from the plastic displays cases.

He made his way down the hall to the closet. The blanket still hid the ladder. Good. That meant the daughter hadn't told anyone about her discovery. He yanked it away, swiped off the sweat pouring from his forehead with his sleeve, and climbed the stairs. He opened the hatch and saw the place had been straightened. Anger boiled inside of him.

He entered the attic, went straight to the rack holding all the boards, and pulled the last one out. The fisherman in waders flicking back his rod took his breath away. He closed his eyes and breathed deeply until his heart stopped hammering in his chest. He rummaged around for a flat tool and eased the tape off the board and lifted off the painting. He threw the board aside and looked around for the portfolio with the paintings. It wasn't leaning against the wall where he had left it! A rampage around the room produced nothing.

Keep calm, Freddy boy. He took a deep breath and slowly let it out. I need a moment to think. He collapsed on the chair next to the desk and gazed ahead. Something on the edge of his vision caught his eye. A black leatherette portfolio leaned against the wall next to the hatch.

He ran over and grabbed it, then swept everything off the desk and laid it down. His hands shook so violently he could hardly get it unzipped. The tissue inside fluttered as he swung it open. Both paintings were there! He quickly added the one he pulled off the board, and zipped up the case.

His pulse throbbed at his temples. He remembered Hayden hadn't heard him come in, and he didn't want the cleaning woman to give him the same sort of surprise. If he had to kill her, it would mess up his plans. He checked his watch. Almost five! He had to get out of there! He picked up the portfolio and made his way down the ladder, swiftly closing the hatch and reattaching the blanket.

His hearing became acute. Five more minutes and he'd be on the bridge and safe! He ran down the staircase and peered out a window. No one! He raced to his car and stood the portfolio on the floor against the back seat. *Mexico, here I come.*

A low guttural growl sounded behind him. A tingle rolled up his spine. He turned. Slowly. The black Lab he'd seen on the street last week bared its teeth. Moving stealthily, Freddy edged over to the trunk. He reached behind and held down the lid as he hit the button on his key ring for it to unlatch. He slowly let the lid rise, then carefully felt behind for his crowbar. "That's okay, boy," he kept repeating.

Suddenly, the dog sprang forward barking. Freddy swung the crowbar and struck it on the side of the head. The bark turned to an interrupted scream and the animal dropped to the ground, its eyes and mouth frozen open.

Freddy's eyes roamed the street. Nobody! He hurriedly grabbed the animal by its collar with one hand, put his other arm under its torso, and lifted the limp body into the trunk. Hopefully, the lady would think the nosey mutt had finally run away. He'd take off its collar and throw it off a bridge in Black Mountain tonight.

He quickly put the crowbar back in the trunk and slammed it shut, then jumped in the front seat. He wiped his forehead with the back of his hand. If anyone shows up before I get back on the street, I'll tell them I'm just looking for someone. He backed the car up and started out, half expecting to see the woman out looking for her dog. All he needed were a few more seconds.

By the time he hit the street, his tight throat started to relax, and a sensation that he was decompressing descended upon him.

As he rolled over the bridge and waited for the traffic on Main Street to let him in, a mud-covered black pick-up slowed in front of him. His eyes jumped to the driver. The mountain man he'd seen checking out his license plate stared back at him.

The pickup passed and Freddy shot out in front of on-coming traffic and made a quick left. He drove as fast as he dared out of town, all the while glancing in his rearview mirror to see if the mountain man had turned around and was following him. He swung around a curve, and noticing the Esmeralda Inn, made a quick right into the parking lot. He spotted a huge catering truck parked at the far end of the lot and pulled in next to it, out of sight. He didn't dare get out to see if the truck followed him, lest he be spotted.

His nerves were shot and he needed a drink. He reached down and fumbled around under the seat for his flask, took a couple of gulps and put it back. After a moment, it started to sink in that he actually had the paintings. Now he had to focus on getting rid of the daughter. He had to grab her in the morning on her way into work before she discovered the paintings were gone.

It was almost an hour before he let his car creep out from behind the truck. He saw a few vehicles scattered around the lot, but no pick-ups. He slowly made his way onto the road. The mountain man was starting to worry him. He had to be an under-cover cop keeping an eye on Chimney Rock. He must have run his plate by now, and knowing he was out on bail, was probably keeping an eye out for him. Maybe he should just take off for Mexico tomorrow with the paintings.

That didn't make any sense. Who was he going to sell them to but Sal. And Sal wasn't going to buy them as long as Hayden's daughter was on his back. Itching to have another drink, he held on to the steering wheel with one hand and reached under the seat for the flask. He secured it between his legs, unscrewed the cap and took a long swig, not noticing the truck hidden in a driveway just before the turnoff onto Route 9.

ONCE HE'D SEEN LUCAS turn off Route 74, Johnny didn't think he had to worry about him any more that evening. He ran into Addie in the post office that morning and she seemed pretty excited about Ben Beckham coming over to the house for dinner.

The fact that Freddy Lucas had hid out for an hour after he was caught coming out of Southside Drive, confirmed Johnny's suspicions that he was up to no good. There was no question that Freddy's visits to Chimney Rock had something to do with the forgeries still in Hayden's possession.

Freddy's rap sheet troubled him; the offenses had gotten progressively more brutal, especially the recent rape. A good thing he had talked with his friend who owned the cabin next to Hayden's. He'd move in tomorrow morning and keep a closer watch.

IT HAD BEEN TWO DAYS since Ben had lunch with Hayden, and her invitation that morning for him to come for dinner to discuss her upcoming trip to New York had intrigued him all day. They could easily have talked things over on the phone.

Finding it hard to concentrate, he left his office early. Driving home he thought about the coming evening and knew what he wanted was wrong, but he couldn't fight it any more.

He took a shower and shaved, then examined his face in the mirror from several angles. He could hear the cheerleaders singing out *woooo, woooo,* and laughed. He winked at himself in the mirror. Evidently, he still had it. Suddenly an idea struck him. He quickly burrowed in his closet until he reached his safe, then got out his Super Bowl ring and put it on. He dressed, mulling over his hunch that Hayden wanted him to come over for more than discussing the trip.

On the drive to Chimney Rock, all kinds of possibilities floated in and out of his head. He remembered her voice had that playful lilt. Possibly she was getting a divorce. Hadn't she told him she was going to make some changes in her life?

He knew he looked good after five minutes checking himself out in the mirror. But as elated as he felt, nagging thoughts kept disturbing him. The situation of getting back the paintings was highly inflammable, and in a matter of seconds could turn into something beyond a "simple business transaction," as Hayden had phrased it. Her interest in the baby was worrisome. He'd asked around about Addie and didn't like what he heard.

He pulled up to the cabin. The light spilling out from the open door silhouetted an enthusiastically waving Hayden. A warmer welcome than he was used to. Things were definitely looking up. He strolled to the door in a confident gait, almost a swagger.

Hayden pointed to a collection of bottles on the counter, and invited him to make himself a drink as she went about preparing poached salmon.

Ben considered Hayden the quarterback calling out the plays. If she had arranged for Addie not to be around, he'd be pretty sure they were heading for a touchdown.

"Where's Addie?" he asked.

"Upstairs resting. Today was her last day cleaning until after the baby comes, and she overdid it."

This promising answer brought a smile to his face. "When is she due?"

"Two months. I tried to get her to stop working the minute I found out she was pregnant, but she wouldn't listen to me. Bless her heart, she told me later she was afraid she'd lose her clients if she did. Now that the fall rental season is winding down, she's basically done until spring."

"How long are you planning on letting her stay here?"

Hayden stopped tossing the salad and looked up at him. "I don't know, Ben. She's got no family to speak of, if you know what I mean."

Ben knew exactly what she meant. It seemed everyone in the gorge knew what a nasty brute her father was. Ben, however, didn't like the way she had insinuated herself into Hayden's life. Then there was her reputation. From what he understood, no serious man in these parts would have anything to do with her. Her indiscretions didn't bother them as much as the scars her hard life had left on her personality. She had no friends to speak of and was only hired by people who were willing to ignore her combative nature. Then there were all the rumors of run-ins with clients.

Hayden brought the food to the table. "I know what you're thinking, Ben; but trust me, she has a good heart." She squeezed his arm. "I'm going to get her down for dinner. Please give her a chance." Reaching the staircase, Hayden stopped and turned. "It wouldn't hurt you to let her take a look at your place. She's done wonders decorating this house." She laughed. "And I'm sure she can tone it down a notch."

Ben picked up a velvet pillow from the couch and shook it until the beaded fringe crackled. "How about five notches?"

The meal would have been a lot more enjoyable if he didn't have to listen to Addie tell him how much one of her "transformations" could do for his place, especially when she reassured him that in the event he died, his house would be easier for those left behind to unload.

He detected Hayden's amusement in Addie's solicitations; in fact, she looked like she was downright enjoying seeing him squirm, and kept winking at him every time Addie brought up the subject of him hiring her.

He couldn't tell if Addie finally broke him down or he just wanted her to stop talking about it, but he agreed to let her come over to his place and take a look. When the two women's faces morphed into a picture of self-satisfaction, it suddenly dawned on him that Hayden's only reason for inviting him over was to give Addie a chance to sell him on one of her redecorating jobs.

Hayden stood up, clasped Addie's shoulders and said, "You can go on up now. Ben's going to help me with the dishes," like their mission was accomplished.

He rubbed his ring and flushed with embarrassment; then, the first moment Hayden wasn't looking, he took it off and put it in his pocket.

As Addie started to ascend the stairs, she looked back and said, "I'm gonna be so spoilt by the time this baby comes I won't hardly be good for nothin'."

Ben did the drying while Hayden washed; however, the third time the rubber gloves slipped off her petite hands, he took over. She tied her apron around his waist and he closed his eyes and held his breath every time he felt her touch.

She made coffee and served it in the living room. With all the wine, the warmth of the fire in the hearth, and the wonderful dinner, Ben couldn't stand to be sitting ten feet away from the woman he wanted to hold more than anything in the world. He either had to break this mood or go home.

"Why don't you show me your father's watercolors?" he asked. "I'd like to see them."

"They're up in the attic."

He slapped his knees and started to get up. "Let's go."

"Ben, it's too late to be digging around up there. I don't even know if there's electricity."

"Heck. You've got a flashlight haven't you?"

She shrugged. "Okay."

When she reached the stair landing, she paused and turned to Ben. She put her hand on his shoulder. "Please don't ask me go up there, Ben. I'm feeling too good and that place gave me such bad vibes. Plus, I'm going to climb the Skyline Trail tomorrow and I need my rest."

Now that he was standing two steps down, he wanted to run his hands down her face and smell the perfume in her hair. He reached over and twirled a soft, blond curl around his finger.

"Remember... you promised to be careful."

She nodded. "I'll be okay."

She looked so vulnerable and trusting he felt ashamed of his feelings. "You can show me the paintings later. It's about time I hit the road." There was no point in hanging around to discuss Addie Mae's baby. It was evident by the way Hayden was taking care of Addie, she had her heart set on getting it.

Winding through the mountains on the way home, Ben felt completely different than he had on the way up. Glumness fell upon him and he had to fight off feeling like a chump. After all, he couldn't blame Hayden for trying to help Addie develop her business when she was getting her child. And giving Addie a chance to prove herself was the kindly thing to do. His house wasn't going to be the way Jenny would have wanted. But that's okay. Heather can set things right when she comes home.

He remembered putting on his ring and his face flushed. What had he been thinking? Hayden wasn't a cheerleader looking for a few laughs before she settled down with some nice guy and raised a bunch of kids. Heather was right. He was ready. Why else would he have gotten so excited over a dinner invitation, for Pete's sake? He took a steep turn and remembered the old bison who hollered out for a mate. He laughed to himself. He was lonely too. Tomorrow he'd call Kate and ask her out.

CHAPTER TWENTY-FIVE

Hayden curled up in bed and hugged her pillow, recalling all the times she woke up gasping for air and couldn't get back to sleep. It wasn't that long ago, but it seemed like a lifetime away. The terrifying image of her nightgown soaked in blood hadn't visited her for a while. She wondered if the mission she was on for her father had crowded it out. A mission she could do something about, not just sit idly by wringing her hands in torment with no solution or cure.

She could tell the heat pump was on by the way the curtains ruffled over the floor register. The sounds of the birds were less than when she first came and the nights too cold to keep the windows open. She slipped out of bed and tiptoed into the bathroom, careful not to make a noise and waken Addie. She pulled the rug nearer the sink with her foot and stepped off the icy floor onto it.

The shadow of Chimney Rock cloaked the house most of the day now since the sun was so low in the sky. She looked out the window and saw the morning light stream down the gorge from the east. Had to be around seven. The park would open at eight-thirty. Plenty of time to get ready and have breakfast at Genny's. Maybe the religious music would do her some good. Being Wednesday, there shouldn't be many tourists in the park, and if she got an early start, not that many on the trail either. She knew she could do it if no one rushed her.

She put on the silky long underwear and running outfit she'd bought at Bubba O'Leary's especially for the climb. She pulled on her hiking boots, making sure the laces were even and firm, all the while wondering if this was how astronauts felt when they were suiting up—impassioned yet fearful. They said it might take up to two hours to climb the Skyline Trail to the top of Hickory Nut Falls and then loop back down on the Cliff Trail. No matter. She was going to do it if it took all day and she had to crawl on her hands and knees to keep from panicking.

She'd been thinking about her fear of heights a lot since falling off Little Pisgah, and vaguely recalled being on a swing when she was very young. She screamed as two of her cousins pushed her higher and higher. She kept slipping off the wooden seat, and the only thing keeping her from falling was her steel grip on the ropes. She remembered Barbara pulling and tugging on the girls until they stopped. Years later, Barbara told her everyone at the picnic laughed at them because of the way Hayden had hung on to her by the hem of her pinafore the rest of the afternoon, afraid the cousins would put her back on the swing.

She was a big girl now, Hayden told herself as she drove to Genny's, and it was about time she let go of her sister's pinafore.

FREDDY LIT HIS LAST CIGARETTE, then twisted the pack and threw it on the dash after spotting Hayden's car coming out of Southside. He checked his watch. If she followed her usual routine, she'd have breakfast at Genny's and be on the road in less than a half hour. He'd spent the better part of the early daylight hours taking the turns on 74, and chose two places that would be the best bet. Once he got rid of her, he'd be on his way south of the border. He could almost hear the inviting sound of a concertina drifting out from a friendly bar.

After dumping the dog's body late last night, he left the company's car in a client's parking lot, a tractor dealership in Black Mountain. He'd talked the personnel director into letting him keep it until he had a chance to go out and get another one. She was so worn out from negotiating his final payout, she talked management into allowing it. Then he walked over to the back of a nearby garage where he had arranged to leave the used car he'd bought with part of his pension money. He'd gotten a Georgia license with his new identity two weeks back and registered the car in that name, using an address he found on a vacation home in the mountains on all the documents. He hadn't planned on using it until he was on the road for Mexico, but the nosey cop was too familiar with the Taurus.

He spotted Hayden coming out of Genny's. As she got into her car, he quickly started up his engine and began to pull out. Just then, she took a U-turn and swung into the park's entrance.

HAYDEN'S CAR THUMPED over the bridge and began the one-mile climb to the park's ticket plaza. The narrowness of the road and series of hairpin curves didn't seem to bother her, and she suspected it was because of the dense carpet of forest hiding the view and her familiarity with all the turns on the way to Asheville.

The road finally leveled out onto a large plateau with a ticket booth. She paid her entrance fee and the lady told her it was another two miles to the tunnel entrance where the elevator would take her up to the Sky Lounge.

The steep road had a thread of a shoulder and rarely a guard rail; but she hardly noticed since she kept her eyes glued to the asphalt directly in front of her. She kept as close to the center as she dared until a blind curve appeared up ahead. She carefully nudged the car to the right and crept around. Once safely around, she let the car drift back to the middle of the road.

Her eyes started to burn, and she realized she had hardly blinked the whole way up. She turned a sharp corner and saw that the twisting road ahead seemed to be clinging to the side of a cliff with nothing but a low stone abutment separating it from open sky beyond. The feeling that she was about to float out into space made her back tingle. She swallowed hard and inched along the center. She began to tremble and it took all her will to summon the strength to keep driving.

She bit her bottom lip. *What am I going to do if a car comes from around the curve up ahead?* She didn't think she had the courage to move close enough to the barrier wall to let another vehicle pass. Luckily, before anyone came from the opposite direction, the road made a turn and led to the parking lot.

There were less than a dozen cars in the broad lot with parking either against the bare granite mountain looming skyward, or in front of a low stone wall framed by an endless sky. She pulled up against the mountain and got out. Her legs wobbled. She'd have some water and settle down a bit in the lounge before attempting the trail.

She took out a twenty dollar bill, tucked it in her pocket, and slung her camera around her neck, then locked her purse in the trunk. She crossed the lot and gripped the side of a pick-up and worked her way to the front until she was looking out at Lake Lure and the start of the gorge.

A familiar sensation began melting her legs. She pulled her eyes away, determined not to let this feeling run away with her. Across the lot, the rock face ran straight up twenty-six stories to the chimney. The Stars and Stripes rippled in the wind on top as if it were proudly laying claim to one of the most singularly unique and overwhelmingly beautiful scenes on the face of the earth. Like a sentinel watching over a sacred place.

FREDDY DRUMMED ON THE STEERING WHEEL. What in the hell is taking her so long? If I go up now, and she turns around at the ticket booth and passes me on her way down, I probably won't be able to turn around and follow her until I hit the ticket booth. If that happens, she's going to get too damn far ahead of me. I've got to be right on her tail for my plan to work.

He looked at his watch again, trying to absorb the situation. It had been a half hour since she went up. This looked like more than just paying a visit to the ticket booth. But why would she go up to Chimney Rock of all places? It was obvious by the way she drove she was afraid of heights. He kept looking at his watch and thinking. If that *was* where she was headed, this was a real opportunity. In the whole time he had been waiting, only three other cars had turned in. That meant there wouldn't be many people on the trails. This might be the perfect way to get rid of her.

He quickly pulled onto Main Street and slipped through the stone entrance and over the bridge. As his car wound upward, he kept an eye open for a place to turn around in case she came down, but there were none all the way to the booth.

He handed the ticket taker the money, careful not to let her see his face. He couldn't see a camera mounted on the underside of the canopy, but that didn't mean there wasn't any. He took the brochure handed to him and pulled away, hoping they didn't have a camera recording his license plate. Damn! He wanted to take off for Mexico absolutely sure no one could connect him to his new car and identity. Anger made him grip the steering wheel until his knuckles turned white. How could one woman cause so damn much trouble? She was one little lady who was going to get what she deserved.

He passed a couple of picnic areas on the way up. Good. Maybe he could turn around somewhere if he saw her doubling back. His mind raced as he tried to remember all the trails. It had been at least fifteen years since he walked them with a client, a widow who owned one of the biggest dealerships in Buncombe County. He had figured he could marry her, slide into the sales manager position, and eventually take over.

He recalled hauling her two hundred pounds up the steps to the Skyline Trail. He wanted to kill her when he came back in town a month later and a stock clerk she married the week before was sitting in the sales manager chair waiting for him to take him to lunch.

He reached the top parking lot and spotted Hayden's car. She must have gone up in the elevator. He backed into a parking space to hide his license plate, then rifled through some things he had thrown in a box for the ride into Asheville. He stuffed a pair of gloves in his pocket, then pulled up a pant leg and strapped on his knife, just in case.

A couple of cars with senior citizens pulled in. Their out-of-state license plates made him smile. With a crowded elevator, the operator would be less likely to remember him; and these folks would be long gone by the time anyone discovered the body.

The seniors took forever getting things out of their trunks. He waited at the entrance to the tunnel while they looked at the view, then he kept behind them on the walk through the long dark cave to the elevator shaft. He thought about what he would do if the doors opened and Hayden walked out. He could stall for time by reading some of the placards telling the history of the tunnel until she was out, then follow her down the mountain and onto Route 74.

The elevator opened, empty except for the operator. Freddy got on last and stood close to the door, facing away enough so the operator couldn't get a good look at him during the thirty seconds it took the elevator to zoom up the twenty-six stories.

The door opened to a tightly packed gift shop. When he couldn't find Hayden there, he went through the small restaurant area beyond, and stepped out onto a fifteen-foot-wide platform bridge ending in a series of staircases. The route to the chimney consisted of a flight of stairs hung in the open air between the platform and the top of the famous landmark fifty feet above. There was another narrow staircase twisting its way down a trail to the park's Needle's Eye, and then one leading up to the Skyline Trail.

Two people sipped coffee at a small table on the bridge, a little dog by their side, and another couple leaned over the railing up on the chimney's platform. Other than the occasional clanging of the hardware of the flag's wind tossed ropes against the pole, an eerie silence hung in the air.

He squinted and looked around for Hayden. Not seeing her, he worried she might have been in the bathroom next to the elevator and gone down already. He started to turn and go back in when he spotted her coming off the chimney. He was right. She was afraid of heights. Her shoulders were hunched over and she was clasping the railing with both hands as she slowly descended. There was no way she'd be able to climb a trail. Better wait in the gift shop so he wouldn't be noticed, then ride down with her.

He casually perused the items on display, fingering the key

chains and flipping through tee shirts like he was looking for something in particular, all the while keeping an eye on the door. Minutes passed and she still didn't appear. *Where in the hell did she go!?* He wanted to find her and throttle her to death on the spot. He slammed a picture postcard in its slot and went back outside. His eyes slowly traced the scene in front of him, starting at the chimney, then traveling along the soaring rock face to the staircase leading to the Skyline Trail.

He stopped cold and stared for a moment in disbelief. She was midway on the massive bank of stairs reaching up to the Skyline Trail. A slow smile spread across his face. She couldn't have made it easier for him. There'd be dozens of places on the mountain ridge to throw her off.

JOHNNY REB MOVED into his friend's cabin with the basics: field glasses so he could get a good look at what was going on at Hayden's place, a couple of changes of clothes, and a few bottles of vodka. He'd pick up his meals in town.

He decided to check out the view straight off and went over to the window with his binoculars. Hayden's car was gone but the Jeep sat in front. His sights moved slowly along the contours of the house, first to the door and then the windows. He focused in sharp and could see Addie Mae moving around inside. The first precaution he wanted the women to take was to secure all the windows. He'd go over and do that right now.

He noticed Addie's face looked a little puffy when she let him in, and he asked how she was feeling.

"You're starting to sound like Hayden. I don't want to be fussed at."

"Hayden's gone to work, I assume."

"No. That foolhardy gal's gone up to the rock."

"Chimney Rock?"

"Yessiree," said Addie as she tugged on the bottom of her shirt and dusted a table with it. "She's feared to death of heights. Thinks it'll cure her. Almost killed herself fallin' off Little Pisgah." She shook her head. "They don't never learn."

"When did she go?"

"She said she was gonna be there when it opened at eight-thirty. Says she's gonna walk the Skyline Tra..."

The door slammed with her voice trailing off.

Johnny hopped in his truck and eyed the clock on the dash. If she got to the ticket booth right at eight-thirty, she already had a ten-minute lead. He thanked God he'd put on his compression stockings, for the climb in his condition was going to be a real challenge, especially since he had to go fast enough to catch up with Hayden. He was worried about his heart, but there was no way he was going to let her roam that trail alone with Lucas on the prowl.

The thought that his old friend might have met his death at the hands of a creep like Freddy made him sick. He kept asking himself why he didn't tell the daughter about Lucas. Damn! He should have let her in on who he was so she'd be on her guard. He could have done it without mentioning his suspicions about her father's death.

He cruised along the upper parking lot looking for Freddy's car, and not finding it, pulled in next to Hayden's. Freddy's car not being there calmed a major portion of his fears. His health being the way it was, he wondered if he shouldn't sit and wait for her there. He started to think. If Hayden was as afraid of heights as Addie had made out, she had no business on the Skyline Trail. He checked his watch again and got out.

On the way up in the elevator he figured she had twenty minutes on him. Hopefully, she'd gone up to the chimney and looked around a bit before she started the trail. Maybe even had something to eat. He shook his head. Somehow, he couldn't picture her doing that. He rushed through the lounge to the platform outside and hurried across the bridge to the staircase going up to the ridge.

"HELLO, THIS IS Ralph Jackson. Please leave a message..." Buddy Reister snapped the phone shut. If he had to hear that message one more time he was going to throw the darn cell phone right over the cliff and let it smash on the rocks 430 feet below. He'd been trying to reach his boss on it ever since the girls at the ticket

plaza told him he had taken the park truck into Hendersonville to pick up some supplies, and now the charge on his battery was almost drained, since he forgot to plug it in the night before.

That wasn't the only mistake he had made. In the one and a half years he had worked at the park since graduating from high school, he had never disobeyed an order or gone against park safety rules, but last night he was in such a rush to get home in time to shower and shave for a date, that he didn't put his park radio in the charger in the office either. It was almost dead when he talked to the girls in the booth.

There was no way he could get the pipe to stay in the ground, no matter how far he pounded it in. Without a bag of quick setting cement the pipe that stabilized the fence couldn't be secured. Plus, the fencing had been kicked apart and he'd need a lot of wire to get both sides reattached to the lead pipe once he did manage to get it solidly in the ground.

A cold breeze kicked up and he wished he hadn't left his jacket in the truck when he went down to get the sledgehammer. The tape was a lucky afterthought. They ought to shoot the kids who wrecked this section of fence, he said to himself. He'd found remains from a campfire on the top of the dome above the trail. They must have snuck into the park last night, hiked up the trail and vandalized the fence after they partied. Now, there he sat on the Chimney Rock ridge at Exclamation Point with no way to fix it and nothing but a roll of yellow *Caution* tape. Oh well, he told himself. He'd just have to do the best he could.

He tied one end to a section of the waist-high chain link fence that wasn't damaged and stretched it across to a still-intact section beyond the gaping opening. He turned around and didn't like that the massive boulder about ten feet back rose from the ground and ballooned upward forming a huge rounded platform a good thirty feet deep. If someone ran off it real fast, there wasn't much room to stop them before flying over the cliff. The tape certainly wouldn't do it.

He tried his phone and the park radio once more, but just as he had feared, they were both dead. He suddenly felt very stupid for not at least calling the office and letting them know what was going on, but this problem had him befuddled. He had a few jobs to do after his morning check of the trail, and they wouldn't be looking for him until around noon. He'd been waiting for someone to come up the trail so he could send them back with a message, but he hadn't seen a soul. Maybe it was too cold and too early for anyone to be on the trail.

He picked up the roll of tape and decided to walk down, turning back anyone he met, and closing off the landings as he went along. When he reached the Sky Lounge he'd use their phone to call for help.

HAYDEN DECIDED the cabin-like rain shelter a few yards before Exclamation Point was a good place to take a rest, have some water, and study her map. She nestled against a corner in the dark enclosure, drew her feet up onto the bench, and hugged her legs. So far, so good, she told herself as she rocked in self-satisfaction. Except for a few rough spots, she was doing well.

The worst leg of the journey had been the dozen or so flights of stairs that started near the Sky Lounge bridge and ran up against the granite outcrop and finally connected to the trail above that led to the ridge. The huge structure seemed to be hanging in mid air. Her hands shook so much when she stopped to take a picture of the chimney and the gorge below, she wondered if the shot would be out of focus.

She heard someone shuffling in the leaves and looked up just as a man passed by, going back in the direction she had come from.

JOHNNY REB FELT A LOT BETTER since Freddy's car wasn't sitting in the parking lot, and figured he could catch up to Hayden as long as he took the trail in a steady stride.

Once he got up the initial series of steps traversing the cliff above the chimney, he doggedly trudged the rugged trail, little more than rocks and boulders of all shapes and sizes lying askew in a dirt path with splotches of coarse asphalt that had to have been brought up by pack mules years before. Rustic staircases, mostly created out of various sized rocks, kept appearing to raise the path on its climb to the top of the ridge. There was no view to speak of since the trail was cloaked in trees that were approaching the final hues of fall with less than half their leaves blown to the winds.

Johnny kept along the trail and could see open sky up ahead as he climbed what looked like a final series of wooden steps. Thank goodness, he thought. The pain in his chest was beginning to worry him. As he neared the top he could see someone ahead tying a wide band of yellow tape onto a handrail.

The man looked down at him and waved. "Hey! Johnny! Ain't you too old to be climbin' this ridge?"

Johnny recognized his neighbor's son, but was too breathless to do anything but throw up a wave. His lungs felt like they were going to burst. He fell against a railing and tried to catch his breath. "Why... are you... closing off the trail?"

"Some smart-assed kids kicked out a section of fence on Exclamation Point last night. Have to close it until we get it fixed."

"How bad is it?"

"Wide open at the top of the cliff. I strung some tape to block it off, but heck, some kid running off the big boulder above could go right off if they couldn't stop in time."

"Did you see... a woman go by? Real pretty? Blond?"

"No. Just a guy. He asked me about a pretty blond too. Said his daughter went ahead of him and said she'd wait for him at the falls, so I warned him about the fence and let him go." Buddy scratched his head. "I don't know how I could have missed her unless she went through when I went to my truck for the sledgehammer."

Johnny tensed up. "What... did this man look like?"

"Around your age. A big guy, but I wouldn't call him heavy. He was wearing sunglasses and a cap so I didn't really get a good look at his face."

"How long ago was that?"

"Five minutes at the most."

"Buddy, I've got to go through, too."

"Sure." He held the tape and moved aside. "Is something wrong? You look worried."

Johnny didn't answer. Just waved him off and sped up.

THE MINUTE HAYDEN SPOTTED the caution tape ahead she stopped dead in her tracks. Up until now, she hadn't really caught sight of the view from the ridge, but could now see open sky up ahead. She didn't want to go near the cordoned off area and yet didn't want to turn back. To her left, was a slope of slick rock rising up to a large rounded outcropping of granite. She decided to give that route a try, and was pleased with how her hiking boots gripped the smooth stone as she climbed.

Upon nearing the top, a cool wind on her back told her she was in the open, and she was afraid to turn around. She crouched low, put her palms on the stone, then slowly turned on them. The view was spectacular. She could feel her heart pulse in her neck.

She sat down on the rock to calm herself. The dreaded feeling seeped into her muscles and made them weak. She closed her eyes and shook it off. After a while she began to feel at ease enough to look around. The crown of color on Round Top faced her straight ahead across the gorge. It was in front of a pristine series of mountain tops that rose above it, but were back far enough so as not to be visible from the ground. No wonder her father never wanted to see it developed.

She scooted down a few feet on her backside, breaking with her boots, to see if she could get a view of the town or the gorge below, but she couldn't. After a few moments when she felt comfortable again, she scooted down a few more feet. She kept repeating the maneuver until she was on the edge of the outcrop in front of the cordoned off area and could see some of the gorge to the west. She looked ahead and suddenly realized the fence was torn open, leaving a gaping section at least ten feet wide.

She pulled her camera off her neck and took a few shots of their property on Round Top to show Barbara. She figured if she stood up and stepped down onto the path she could get a good shot of the gorge toward Asheville and maybe even the town below. There were at least ten feet between her and the tape, but she couldn't build up the courage to do it.

A man came from around the trail, smiling broadly as he approached.

"Do you want me to take a picture of you with the view behind you?" he asked in a cordial tone.

Hayden hesitated. She didn't want anyone nudging her along or she could panic. "No, but thanks anyway."

He offered her his hand. "Come on. There's nothing to be afraid of." He made a swooping gesture with his arm. "You've got at least ten feet before the edge." The intensity in his dark blue eyes mesmerized her. She took his hand and slid off the outcrop without taking her eyes off them.

"There. Now give me your camera."

She handed it to him and barely smiled. He led her back toward the cliff a couple of steps and told her to turn and look out and he'd get a good shot of her with the west end of the gorge in the background.

Hayden felt her knees get wobbly, but bit her lip and turned. She got her first clear view of the bottom of the gorge four hundred feet below. The village looked like a toy town on a child's train set. Darkness suffocated her. A sharp pain in her elbow, then her head. She felt an impact on her leg as if she were being kicked and could hear grunts and the shuffling of feet somewhere off in the distance, then a few moments later slaps on her face. She opened her eyes. Johnny Reb knelt by her side.

"Are you all right?"

She sat upright, dazed. "What happened?"

"You fainted." He reached over and picked her camera off the ground and put it in his pocket.

"Where's the man who was going to take my picture?"

"There'll be plenty of time for pictures later. Right now we've got to get off this mountain."

He helped her to her feet, his arm around her waist. "Don't look to your left. Just hold on to me and keep moving."

The two made their way down the path with Hayden stumbling and tripping and Johnny pulling her along. They reached the first major bank of steps going down. Johnny leaned Hayden against the railing and brushed her off. "Listen to me, girl. We're going to go down this trail to the lounge and we're going to look like nothing has happened. Do you understand?"

"But nothing has happened." She looked up at him questioningly. "Has it?"

He grabbed her shoulders. "You've got to trust me. We've got to get down this trail as fast as we can. Do you understand?"

She nodded. He untied the caution tape, they slipped through, and he quickly retied it; then, they both started down the stairs. The two took on the steps and rock strewn path aggressively, Hayden with her agile body easily in the lead, sometimes waiting up for Johnny. When they approached the final set of staircases cantilevered off the cliff and leading down to the bridge, Hayden eyed the gorge sprawled below and froze.

"Johnny, I can't do it. I just can't."

He clutched her shoulder with a strong hand. Calm, measured, efficient like the authoritative voice of a military leader, he commanded, "Don't look over the railing. Keep your eyes on the steps." He pushed her forward and shouted, "Go!"

Hayden grasped the handrail and took the stairs like a zombie until they reached the bottom. Luckily no one was around and there was a space they could squeeze through without disturbing the tape. Johnny took her by the arm and walked her to the bridge railing where they looked out at the view like tourists.

"We're going to walk through that lounge to the elevator like nothing's happened. Can you handle that?"

She nodded. "But I need a drink of water."

"There's no time. Are you ready?"

She nodded again.

They walked through the lounge and straight into a waiting elevator. Hayden sank against the back while Johnny cheerfully chatted with the young operator, even managing to joke a little. The door opened and they made their way down the tunnel and out into the open.

"Where's your truck?" asked Hayden.

Johnny tossed his head. "Over there, next to your car. Why?"

"Johnny, I can't drive down. I'll never make it."

"Listen to me, girl. I don't want your car left behind. At the end of the day they'll be asking questions about it. I want you to get in it and drive down right behind me. Do you hear?"

She closed her eyes tight and nodded.

They walked to Hayden's car through a boisterous group of school kids spilling out of a bus. Just before she got in her car, Hayden glanced over at Johnny who gave her a thumbs up.

"I DID TOO, DADDY! I did too!"

The mother came out of The Chimney Sweeps store on Main Street. "What's that boy fussin' about now? Can't you watch him for five minutes without causin' a rumpus?" she yelled at her husband.

"He's got to stop his lying. Now he says someone jumped off that there cliff."

NUMB ALL OVER, Hayden followed Johnny to the house and was thankful Addie wasn't there.

"I'll get you a drink," said Johnny as Hayden flopped into an easy chair." He came out of the kitchen with two glasses of water and sat across from her. "Hayden, I should have told you this earlier but I never dreamed it would go this far. The man that wanted to take your picture is the same one I asked you about the other day. I had his file pulled by a friend of mine in the sheriff's office, and he's a real bad character. He went to Pratt with your father, and I suspect he's after the three paintings you found here at the house."

Hayden sat in shocked silence.

"Where are they?" Johnny asked.

"What?"

"The paintings."

"Upstairs… in the attic."

"Are you sure?"

"Yes. I've only been up there once."

He rose and reached for Hayden's hand. "Show me."

The way things had been swiped off the table in the attic and lay all over the floor, Hayden knew things had been disturbed, then she noticed the watercolor board she had slid back into the last slot was gone and lying on the floor with the painting stripped off. She looked at Johnny and frowned. "Someone's been up here."

She remembered putting the portfolio with the other two paintings against the wall next to the hatch so she could easily retrieve it, but it was missing, too. She gave the place a thorough search before conceding that the paintings weren't there.

They heard the sound of sirens passing on the road leading up to Chimney Rock just above them and looked into each other's eyes. Hayden sank onto the desk and listened to a second series of sirens go past. They got louder, then faded, then louder again in waves as the emergency trucks weaved upward on the mountain.

Johnny put a foot up on a chair, rested an arm on his leg and leaned toward her. "He went over, Hayden. It'll take them a couple of hours to bring him out. The minute I saw him try to push you off, I figured he had the paintings. I hate to tell you this, but all indications are that he's been up here before, and got into a fight with your father over the paintings. That's probably what did your father in, not a fall down the stairs."

"But I don't understand. If this man already had the paintings, why would he want to kill me?"

"First of all, you have to remember this Freddy Lucas was in deep trouble. He was out on bail for an assault and rape charge in Cherokee. A pretty brutal assault at that. And was going to end up doing at least five years for it. He needed a lot of money fast if he wanted to skip bail and live out of the country. I bet you anything they're going to find a passport on him."

His eyes squinted and he looked ahead, thoughtfully. "That fella in New York must have told him you wanted all the paintings back, and that he didn't want to buy any more. The only way for Freddy to keep the sales channel open was to get rid of you."

"Where do you think the paintings are now?" asked Hayden.

"That's why we had to get out of there so fast. He's been staying in a motel in Black Mountain. They're probably there.

He's evidently changed cars, but I doubt he's checked out of his room yet. It's just a matter of hours before the lot is cleared and they associate him with whatever car is left. That's, by the way, why I didn't want you to leave yours.

"Once they find the body, he'll probably have enough identification on him to trace him to the motel. If they discover three Winslow Homer masterpieces... hell... it'll spark all kinds of investigations that will in all probability lead to your father."

He stood up and put a hand on her shoulder. "I know that's not what you want. Nor do I. I'm going to Black Mountain to get 'em, then come back and tell the authorities I saw him jump. I don't want you drawn into this messy business unless it's necessary. I'm sure they'll believe me. After all, I have no motive for pushing him, and there is nothing connecting him to me... or to you for that matter... *once we get the paintings.*"

CHAPTER TWENTY-SIX

A DDIE WAS SLEEPING IN LATER AND LATER, so Hayden dressed as quietly as she could. Jack and Barbara would be there late in the afternoon and take her back to the beach in the morning. Meanwhile the ten o'clock press conference announcing that the gallery was being turned into a co-op would be the last time she'd see everyone until she came back for the baby.

Jack had finally warmed up to the idea once she took Addie to get a sonogram and found out it was a boy. When she talked with him the other day, she was surprised to hear he had already contacted his lawyer about the adoption; but why, she wondered, wouldn't he bring Barbara a day earlier so she could be included in the ceremony turning the gallery over to the co-op? To make the day special and erase her disappointment, she'd invited Ben to lunch instead.

She finished putting on her pantyhose, picked up the dress lying across the bed, and pulled the clingy cashmere sheath over her head. Then, she went over to the dresser and carefully lifted the gold necklace off the velvet bust, put it on, and ran her hand over the dozens of fine gold chains. A finger traced the jeweled collar. The outfit was on the dressy side for the press conference, but she wanted to give all the friends she had made something to remember. She took a look at herself in the mirror and admitted that she mostly wanted Ben to remember her looking that way.

She slipped into her cashmere coat, then picked up her heels and tiptoed down the stairs in her stocking feet. She put on her shoes, picked up a portfolio leaning against the wall next to the door that held one of the Winslow Homer paintings, and carried it to her car.

Frost had settled on the window, so she foraged through her purse for a credit card and scraped it off. She laughed to herself, thinking the gallery's future wasn't going to have to depend on that piece of plastic anymore.

She started to back the car out and thought for a moment. She couldn't leave without giving some personal memento of her father's to Judy. But what? She remembered her mentioning blue was her favorite color. There was a lovely piece of hand-blown blue glass her father kept on his desk upstairs as a paperweight. She left the engine running and went back inside, stepped out of her shoes, and started back up the stairs.

The sound of Addie talking sweetly to someone made her stop for a moment. Curious, she tiptoed up the stairs and crept up next to her room, keeping flat against the wall and out of sight as she listened.

"My darlin' baby boy is gonna' have a right proper home with a handsome daddy and beautiful mommy."

Hayden heard the rocker creak on the floor to the rhythm of her singing.

"You're my darlin', you're my darlin', you're my darlin' baby boy. You'll be lost and gone forever, you're my darlin' baby boy."

Hayden put a hand to her mouth to silence a cry, then hurried down the stairs and into her shoes and out the door. Her ears burned as she drove out of town. How could she have gotten Addie so wrong? Addie had always talked about the baby as if it were something she wanted to toss out. When she mentioned she might want to adopt it, Addie had said, "Sure. You might as well git it as much as anyone else. I ain't keepin' it." It was confusing. How could anyone talk that way about someone they loved?

The words to Addie's lullaby swam through Hayden's brain

281

and stabbed her in the heart. Now, well out of town, she pulled off the road, covered her face and sobbed. *Gone forever. My darling baby Carrie. Gone forever.*

She didn't know how long she had sat crying as she studied her puffy red face in the mirror. She wondered how many women over the centuries had lost a child and gone on with their lives? Thousands. Millions. She'd known for a while now that she would be one of them. Addie's tender words floated through her brain again. She covered her face and sobbed like her heart would break. How could she do to Addie what had been done to her?

A passing car slowed down and a woman passenger looked at her, concern on her face. Hayden quickly smiled and threw a slight wave. She hastily wiped her eyes and got back on the road. Everyone was waiting for her at the gallery.

She decided to drive Addie's lament out of her head by mulling over all the things that had gone right. Something she was doing more and more of these days. All six paintings were in her possession and she had taken the liberty of putting "Interpreted by Hayden Taylor" across every Winslow Homer signature, all in indelible ink. Barbara was getting two of them, as was she, Johnny Reb one, and the last one was going to Ben. She'd give it to him after the press conference, before they left for lunch. He hadn't seen any of her father's paintings yet and she couldn't wait to hear what he thought of them.

Her business with Sal had gone surprising smoothly. After she paid him in cash for the first painting and turned around and asked him to ship it to the gallery, their relationship mellowed. When the other two arrived from Dubai, he phoned her and said he'd accept her check and ship them to the gallery also. He seemed to be as relieved to get them out of circulation as she. When she got an invitation in the mail to one of his openings, she had to laugh. He'd actually put her on his client mailing list.

The smell of coffee wafted out of the gallery the minute she opened the door. She quickly slipped into the office with the portfolio and hung up her coat before going back out.

Ruth Summers, the executive director of the Arcade, stood

with a cup of coffee, waving a greeting as Karen and Terri gave Hayden a big hug. Hayden went around shaking hands. She spotted Judy in the crowd and laughed to herself. She would have been offended if she hadn't been sniffling into a tissue.

Someone came up to Hayden with a tray of small cakes. She took one as her eyes wandered over to the door hoping for someone else to appear. She smiled broadly and filled with emotion when Ben came in. He looked so handsome and sure of himself.

The reception was followed by a formal announcement that the gallery was turning into a co-op with Karen and Terri as the co-managers. Karen proudly read off a list of directors including Hayden and Ben, and Terri thanked the Grove Arcade Public Market Foundation for its support. A reporter from a local television station interviewed Hayden and referred to her as the daughter of the founder who was respected and revered by the art community before his untimely death, not knowing how much that phrase meant to her.

BEN HUNG BACK AND WAITED to go to lunch with Hayden. Everyone was pretty much gone and the afternoon classes were setting up. They hadn't had much of a chance to talk, but he caught her looking at him several times during the reception. Maybe because she felt his gaze. He couldn't take his eyes off her.

He watched her walk the Arcade director out, then lean with her back against the door once it closed, a mixture of pride and satisfaction on her features. She came toward him smiling.

"Now, it's your turn," she said.

The playful grin on the beautiful face warmed him to his toes.

She took his hand and led him into the office where the portfolio lay on the desk. She folded her arms and tapped her foot.

"Open it."

He shook his head and smiled at her kittenish expression, then unzipped the case and opened it flat. He couldn't keep the shock off his face as he picked up the sheet of watercolor paper and ran his eyes across the image. He looked at Hayden. "I'd of sworn this was an original."

She pointed to the signature with her father's name across it.

He nodded. "That ought to do it."

"Aren't you going to thank me?" she asked.

"You're giving me this?"

"Uh huh."

He scratched his head. "I don't know what to say; but, thank you. Thank you very much."

"Surely you can do better than that. Aren't you going to give me a hug or anything?"

Ben gave her a long look. "Darlin', in that outfit you're wearing, if I laid one hand on you, I'd have to pick you up and run right out with you in my arms, husband or no husband."

She laughed, then her face took on a serious expression. "I can't thank you enough, Ben, for all your help."

"I didn't do that much."

"You were there when I needed a friend."

Ben wanted to put his arms around her and never let go.

"Let's get out of here," he said.

They stopped and locked the portfolio in his SUV, then crossed the street arm-in-arm. He could feel her bury her face in his coat every time the wind kicked up. They reached the restaurant with Ben wanting to walk to the ends of the earth with her pressed against him.

Out of the wind, she shook her head and her golden hair tumbled over her shoulders. He brushed a lock from her cheek and smiled as he remembered how she had braided it for the climb up Little Pisgah. She smiled back and looked into his eyes. He couldn't stand it and started helping her with her coat.

He'd picked this place special because it was perfect for a quiet lunch. He wasn't going to let her go without telling her something. The hostess appeared and Ben pointed to a table in the corner. "How about that one?" The hostess obligingly walked over and pulled out a chair for Hayden.

Hayden looked over the wine list and ordered a chardonnay, Ben a martini. When he noticed her brow rise a tad, he wanted to tell her she hadn't seen anything yet. It was going to take more than one drink to get him through this lunch. She looked over the menu and he looked over her. He wasn't accustomed to seeing her in such a revealing outfit, especially the way the necklace called attention to her breasts. He couldn't help wondering if she dressed with that in mind. Damn! He had to stop reading things into everything she said or did. He reminded himself of how he got carried away over the dinner invitation.

She rested a hand on the table, and in a reflex motion he put his hand over hers and squeezed. The drinks arrived and they both pulled their hands away.

Yesterday, he knew he'd make a fool out of himself if he accepted her invitation to lunch, but he couldn't stop himself. The main reason he accepted the position on the co-op board was to get news of her from time to time, since they all knew they weren't going to see much of her once she went home and got her hands on that baby. He tossed down the martini, looked around for the waiter, and motioned for another.

Hayden put her hand on the table again. Ben massaged his jaw. Was she flirting with him, or was he going off the deep end again. He better keep the conversation on safe ground. He looked her in the eyes. "You've come a long way since I met you at the visitation."

Her smile was slight, but broad enough to show the two crowded eye teeth. "I have, haven't I?"

He studied her face and hoped the memory would last a lifetime. The delicate features that masked an iron will made him smile to himself. "When do think you'll get the baby?"

"Next month."

Sensing a lack of enthusiasm, Ben asked, "That's what you wanted, isn't it?"

She stared at her wine glass, running her finger along the stem. She stopped and looked up at him and said matter-of-factly, "Yes. It was."

Ben wanted to tell her she was making a mistake. That she couldn't cheat fate by pretending it never kicked her in the gut so hard it took everything she had to get over it, by it, and around it. This baby was never going to erase what happened to her. Hayden, he pleaded in his head, this isn't the way to go. Make yourself a good life first, and then if you want a baby, may God help you get one.

Most of all, he wanted to beg her to make that good life with him. His drink arrived and he took a gulp. He'd better get his mind on something else.

"It's good about what's happening to the gallery. Karen and Terri will do a good job," he said.

"Yes. I'm sorry I can't be there tomorrow to help re-hang all the paintings."

"Well, I'll do a little extra for you."

"You mean to tell me you're going to help?"

He tossed his head. "Yep. I'm going to miss a couple of games, too." That was his punishment, he said to himself. The only reason he offered was because he thought Hayden might be there.

Throughout the meal, he did his best at small talk. "Were you on the trail when that guy jumped off the cliff at Chimney Rock?" he asked as he put a forkful of salad in his mouth.

Hayden didn't respond.

He reached for a roll. "The paper said he was out on bail and could have gotten twenty years." He looked up and could see Hayden didn't want to talk about it. "Sorry. Didn't mean to bring up such a gory story. What time tomorrow are you leaving?"

"I don't know yet."

Ben dragged the meal out as long as he could. Finally, the waiter took his empty plate and asked if they wanted coffee and dessert. Hayden dabbed a napkin against her lips and said she had better be getting along.

"Oh, no you don't. You invited me to lunch and I'm not leavin' 'til I get my piece of pie." He looked up at the waiter. "You got apple?" The waiter nodded. "I'll take a piece with coffee."

Hayden put both elbows on the table and clasped her hands under her chin. An eyebrow rose slightly, and he suspected she knew he couldn't let her go. He ate the pie without looking at her, for he was starting to get teary eyed.

She reached across the table and squeezed his hand.

"I'm going to miss you too, Ben."

If he was going to say anything, he had to do it now. He couldn't stall any longer. "Hayden, it's probably pretty obvious how I feel about you. Promise me if things don't work out... at home, that is... you know what I mean... I hope it does and wish you all the happiness in the world... but if it doesn't, promise you'll give me a chance."

There! He went and said it and made an ass out of himself. He threw his napkin on the table and signaled for his check, avoiding her eyes. The walk to her car was awkward, both of them not speaking. He opened her door and started to help her in when she threw her arms around him. He put his arms around her and buried his face in her sweet smelling hair. The wind kicked up and her golden locks swirled about his face. She looked up at him with the strange gray eyes and he framed her face with his hands.

"Will you?" he asked again.

"Yes. I will."

She pulled away and slid onto the seat. He closed her door and watched until the car disappeared in traffic.

CHAPTER TWENTY-SEVEN

J ACK SWUNG OFF ROUTE 26 in Columbus and started the climb to Chimney Rock. Barbara sat quietly filing her nails. He'd been waiting for her to mention Hayden for the past four hours and wondered if she was ever going to get around to it. He had an inkling she might be annoyed he didn't make the trip yesterday so she could go to her sister's press conference.

She opened her purse, threw the file in, and took out a candy bar, something he knew she did when she was nervous.

"You can talk to me, Barbara. Are you worried about Hayden?"

"It's none of my business."

"What do you mean, it's none of your business? You're the only mother she's ever known."

As usual he was being shut out. Let them have their little secrets, he thought. It was just that he was dying to know how Hayden got her hands on her estate. Not even Russell could tell him. Not that he cared about the money either way; it must have been a masterful feat was all. He'd always known Hayden had what it took to face her mother down.

"How'd she pull off getting her estate away from ole Liz?" he asked.

"I wish I knew."

"You mean she didn't tell you?"

"No. I was sitting there expecting her to ask me to sell our father's property so she could keep his gallery going, and just like that..." She snapped her fingers. "...she calls and says she coming home. Then my mother casually lets it drop that she's letting us handle our own affairs. The next thing I know, Hayden's adopting Addie's baby."

"Did you know she was at the beach two weeks ago?"

Barbara turned to him, her mouth open.

"Isn't that when your mother took the sudden change of heart?" he added.

The land was starting to rise in gentle rolling hills from out of the piedmont. The Blue Ridge loomed up ahead.

Barbara sat quietly munching on her candy bar. Finally, she scrunched up the wrapper and tossed it in her purse. "I'm worried about this baby, Jack. I don't trust this Addie. She's the kind that would take advantage of Hayden. If that greedy little opportunist changes her mind in a couple of months, you know what it would do to my sister."

"Don't worry. My attorney's aware of the circumstances here, and he's in touch with the best adoption lawyer in North Carolina. He's going to make sure we're locked in solid before we bring the boy home."

"I'm sure he will, Jack. But that woman is insidious. I can see her hanging onto Hayden like a parasite. Jack, I can't understand why you're going along with this?"

Jack said nothing. He understood all too well. Hayden had sounded so hopeful on the phone when she told him about the baby, he couldn't say no.

"I thought she was getting better," said Barbara. "Everything seemed to be working out so well, and now this. Why can't she let go, for God's sake?"

As the mountains rose in front of him, Jack started to dread seeing Hayden. He didn't think he could stand to be rejected one more time. He was hurt when a neighbor told him he had seen her coming out of the beach house two weeks earlier. When she asked him about the baby on the phone, she had said she wanted to start over; but if that were the case, why hadn't she missed him enough in all these weeks to want to spend one evening alone with him.

She'd obviously accomplished some life-changing feat when she was at the beach and didn't feel an urge to share it with him. Why would she? He'd dealt himself out of her life by not running up there after her. He should have stood by her side and slugged it out with her, doing whatever it took to help get the gallery going if that's what she needed.

A few weeks before that, when she phoned to thank him for paying her credit card bills, she sounded so grateful. He should have asked her right then and there if she needed anything else, but instead he settled for a friendly chat. He didn't want to take the gamble of being hurt again, so he let another opportunity to get close to her slip through his fingers.

What amazed him most about the conversation was her uttering Carrie's name when she asked him to Fed Ex the picture of her she kept in her dresser drawer. She wanted to show it to Addie. It was as if she were finally starting to let Carrie die. At the time, it made him wonder if she might be ready to let him go, too; but her latest call about Addie's baby, dashed all hopes of that coming about. Maybe they could make it work out.

HAYDEN STOPPED AT THE GROCERY STORE to shop for the night's dinner. There was plenty in the fridge, but everything had to be fresh. She came around the final curve into Chimney Rock, and looked up at the ridge. She shuddered. Suicide the papers said.

When Johnny came back with the paintings, he had told her, "I reached Lucas just as he was about to push you over the cliff, but he was comin' at you with such a force, when you fainted he flew right over instead." Hayden remembered hearing the shuffling of feet and feeling the kick on her leg, and couldn't help wondering if Johnny hadn't given him a little help. She remembered his house... practically a shrine to his Vietnam buddies. She was convinced he was capable of avenging the murder of any one of them.

She pulled in front of the cabin, quickly unpacked, and started in on the meal. It was a while before she spotted Jack and Barbara drive up. She was excited. They arrived just in time to watch her on the six o'clock news. She ran out and gave Jack a big hug. It felt strange. Had to be the first time she'd done that in over a year.

They rushed into the house just as she appeared on the TV screen. Jack started to reach for her, then pulled back and folded his arms across his chest.

"You look like a movie star." He winked. "You want a job at the theater?"

Hayden was pleased. Everything was going smoothly. She got a little nervous as Addie came down to join them for dinner, and worried she might have offended her. A few days ago, wanting her to make a good impression on Jack, she had made her promise not to say a word during the dinner, except for a few pleasantries about the weather. Especially nothing about her staying on at the cabin indefinitely, or getting contractors to do some work.

The dinner went well, and when it ended, Jack got up and began packing all the things she had stacked at the door into his car, while she and Barbara did the dishes. Finished, Hayden shepherded everyone into the living room, and prepared the coffee. She could tell from the conversation drifting into the kitchen that Addie was nervous. Maybe she had been too hard on her about not saying anything. Hayden picked up the tray and went in, interrupting an awkward silence. She noticed Addie staring at her like she wanted to be excused.

"You look tired, Addie. Why don't you go on up and rest."

Minutes after Addie left, Barbara rose and said she was heading to bed, too. It wasn't like Barbara, and Hayden wondered if something was worrying her.

Hayden sipped her coffee. Jack looked handsome lounging on the couch. His light blue sweater made his eyes look bluer than ever. She could tell he liked the place. She wished her father and Carrie were alive and they were visiting for the holidays. That would have been so wonderful.

He scooted over and patted the seat. "Come on, Angel Face. If we're going to start all over, there's no time like the present."

Hayden kicked off her heels and lay down next to him.

He ran his hand over the gold necklace, feeling the contours of her breasts. "You look like a million dollars in that outfit. And, by the way, did anyone ever tell you that you are one hell of a cook?"

Hayden suddenly felt very sad. She took his hand from her breast and gently put it to his side. "I want to make a go of this, Jack, but I'm not ready yet. Are you all right with that?"

"As long as you will be."

She put her arm across his chest and nestled her head in the crook of his arm. He was such a handsome figure of a man. But mostly kind. Tears ran down her cheeks as she remembered how happy they had been. She ran a hand along his sweater and closed her eyes tight. *Oh Jack, you deserve someone better than me. Someone who will want you more than anything in the world. Someone whose passion will enflame your manhood until you're too old to remember.*

Then she thought about herself. She knew she could feel passion again. She'd been fighting it from the first time she laid eyes on Ben. She pictured the joyous wedding couple in the frame on her dresser. *Oh Jack, I'm a different person now.* She saw Carrie's darling dimpled grin. The hurt had finally become muted enough for her to find a little pleasure in the warm glow of her memory.

The touching sympathy card her father had tucked in his drawer lingered in her thoughts. Maybe that's what changed her. She remembered how it started to make her feel whole again. She wondered. Maybe it was this strange gorge chiseled out of granite. It called out to her from the first time she stood at the cabin's window and watched the shadow of Chimney Rock creep up Round Top. She recalled how the timeless display made her feel connected to all the generations of Taylors who must have stood at that window witnessing the same eternal rhythm of the sun setting behind the mountain. Standing there, she had finally felt the warmth of her father's breath and the comfort of being drawn to the bosom of the gorge.

HAYDEN WOKE BEFORE THE SUN ROSE. She scooped up the blankets and stuffed them in the closet so no one would know she'd slept on the couch, then put on the coffee. Barbara was going to drive her car and she was to ride with Jack.

After breakfast, Barbara and Jack stood at the door, prepared to go, when Addie waddled out to the living room to say her goodbyes. Barbara and Jack looked on as Hayden helped her sit down. Hayden went over to the table and brought her something wrapped in a silk scarf. "This is for you."

Addie looked from face to face. Puzzled.

"Go on, take a look at it," Hayden coaxed, her voice soft.

Addie appeared reluctant. Like she knew what was inside and didn't want it. She unfolded the scarf and slowly pulled out a delicate handspun yellow baby blanket. She looked up at Hayden, confused.

"I want little Hayden to have it."

Addie looked at her for a long moment. The sneer dissolved.

"You're not going to take him, are you?"

"No, Addie, I'm not."

"Why? This baby needs what you can give it."

"No, Addie. What this baby needs is his mother."

Addie flailed her arms. "But you've got to take him! I don't want my baby to end up white trash like me. I want him to have class. To be decent and kind to people like you and your pa was to me." She put her face in her hands. "Not ugly mean like his good for nothin' mother."

Hayden sat down and put an arm around her; then, she glanced up and looked into Jack's eyes for a long moment. Her gaze roamed over to Barbara who was wiping a tear from her cheek.

She looked back at Addie and tenderly brushed aside the stray strands of hair from her face. "You're not good for nothin', Addie. Remember how you took care of your sisters? No baby could have a better mother than that." She wrapped an arm around Addie and squeezed. "And, Addie, I want you to know something. This baby's going to have the kindest, most generous aunt anyone's ever had."

BEN ROLLED INTO THE GALLERY AROUND NOON. He had programmed his DVR to record all the games, but it wouldn't be the same. He looked around the gallery. There had to be at least two dozen co-op members assembled, with home baked cakes and cookies lying all over the place. He glanced around at all the men with potbellies and shuddered to think how close he was to looking forward to food for contentment.

Karen and Terri arranged everyone in teams, assigning Ben to the sculpture. They quickly stripped all the tables, cleared the floor and got started. Ben's team, consisting of a married couple in their sixties, began by placing two small pieces facing the wall.

"No, no! Not like that," Ben shouted as he ran over and turned them around.

Judy rushed over, placed a hand on his shoulder and gently whispered, "Ben, why don't you go over to the Flying Frog and chill out. Watch the game at the bar. You can come back after we're done and check everything out."

Ben apologized to the couple and said he'd be back later. He had no business coming to the gallery. He'd been in a rotten mood from the moment he woke. He put on his old Penn State letterman's jacket and started up Battery Park toward Haywood. The wind whistled through the buildings and swept leaves and debris through the streets, reminding him of his last walk with Hayden and adding to his melancholia.

Ahead, he saw a woman coming around the corner from Haywood, her golden hair flying in the wind. Ben shook his head. He never wanted to lay eyes on another flaxen-haired female as long as he lived. Another half a block and he'd reach the bar. He could almost feel the drink in his hand.

He noticed the blond cross to his side of the street. The after-church throngs swarmed all over the sidewalk, but every once in a while he caught sight of the bobbing blond head in the distance. He slowed and let the crowd stream by. A teenager jerked away from his mother's grip and bumped against him, but his gaze held firm.

He stopped breathing and fixed his eyes on the oncoming crowd. The beautiful alabaster face appeared from behind a couple pushing a stroller. His heart stopped. She came close enough to touch. They stood, eyes locked. Hers were the same strange color he remembered, but set firm, like she finally knew what she wanted.

"I thought you were going home," Ben said.

She barely shook her head. Her lips teased with a hint of playfulness. "I couldn't."

Ben could feel his throat tighten and his eyes fill with tears. "Why not?"

Her voice was soft and steady. "Darlin', how could I? You still haven't shown me the granite dome goldenrod."

෧෨

ACKNOWLEDGEMENTS

I am deeply grateful to the many people who have helped in my research for this novel. One of my favorite resources which I have drawn from in this novel is the series written by Frank L. FitzSimons Sr., 1897-1980. This local historian's three books, *From the Banks of the Oklawaha, Vol. I, 1976, Vol. 2, 1977, and Vol. 3, 1979,* are filled with local lore and historical anecdotes.

I can't thank the dedicated professionals at the Carolina Mountain Land Conservancy enough. Their achievements will go down in history as the pivotal point in turning around the runaway over-development and defacing of the mountain and farm lands of this section of Western North Carolina. Amongst them are Kieran Roe, Executive Director; Tom Fanslow, Land Protection Director; Suzanne Hohn, Outreach Coordinator; and Bill McAninch, trustee. The story in this book of how the conservancy helped acquire The World's Edge property is true, and one of the most inspiring events to come about in the gorge.

I want to especially thank Linda Ketron, who established the Art Works, a gallery that also offers classes in art in Pawleys Island, SC, and was my inspiration for the story's plot.

I'm grateful to all my friends in Chimney Rock, Lake Lure and Pawleys Island who offered support and assistance during the year it took to write this book, including Nikki Gordon, Becky and Danny Holland, Galen Reuther, Ann and Peter O'Leary, Jim Proctor, Bess Miles, Deborah Chalk, John Benick, Charles F. Hicks, Melanie Greenway, Linda Turner, Joselyn Watkins, Saundra Nelson, Lou Pfeifle, Valerie Griswold, and Marianne Flanders.

BLUE RIDGE SERIES of Stand-Alone Books

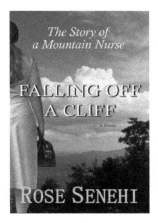

Falling Off a Cliff. Two women a generation apart and from two different worlds, are driven by a passion to heal. Will one have her innocence shattered and the other be forever haunted by an unanswered mystery? In the 1920s, Lula Mae clings to a doctor woman as they gallop horseback all over the steep, harsh Blue Ridge Mountains. In the 1960s, Home Nurse Holly travels the same mountain paths to reach the ill and search for the mother she's never known.

Winner, 2019 Historic Book Award, N.C. Society of Historians, Inc.

Catching Fire. With over 20 fires ranging in the North Carolina mountains, how does an emergency response network pushed to the breaking point respond to a fire threatening to devour 4 mountain communities? Annie Simms, a volunteer firefighter and biologist becomes embroiled in the fire that initiated the largest request for mutual aid the state had ever seen. Woven throughout this tale of two firefighters in love, yet, torn apart by swirling suspicions and mistrust, is the story of a family is crisis.

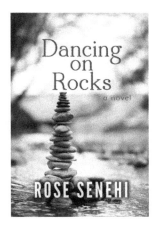

Winner of the 2014 Indie Reader Discovery Award

Dancing on Rocks. Nursing her mother back to health wasn't all that drew Georgie Haydock back to the little mountain tourist town. Hiding around every corner, are a family's painful memories of a child who disappeared in the middle of the night 25 years ago. The summer roils as her mother thrashes in her bed, insisting that the woman stalking her store downstairs is the missing sister. Meanwhile, Georgie aches to reunite with the hometown boy she never forgot.

Winner of the 2012 IPPY Gold Medal Fiction-Southeast

Render Unto the Valley. *Karen Godwell isn't as much ashamed of her mountain heritage as of what she once had to do to preserve it.* She reinvents herself at college and doesn't look back till her clan's historic farm is threatened. She returns only to come face to face with who she was and what she did. Cousin Bruce sees life through the family's colorful two-hundred-year past; Tom Gibbons, a local conservationist, keeps one eye on the mountains and the other on Karen. Her nine-year-old daughter is on the mission her dying father sent her on.

Carolina Belle. Belle McKenzie is obsessed with finding the best apple anyone ever bit into and determined to rekindle the love this obsession almost destroyed. She risks her life rescuing four hundred antique apple trees her neighbor has collected from all over the South, and from which she plans to create a "billion dollar" apple she'll call the Carolina Belle. Pap thinks of Matt as a son, but Belle as the man she loved and who betrayed her.

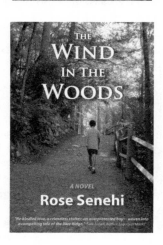

The Wind in the Woods. A romantic thriller that reveals a man's devotion to North Carolina's Green River Valley and the camp he built to share its wonders; his daughter's determination to hike the Blue Ridge—unaware that a serial killer is stalking her; and nine-year-old Alvin Magee's heart-warming discovery of freedom and responsibility in a place apart from his adult world.

Other Novels by Rose Senehi

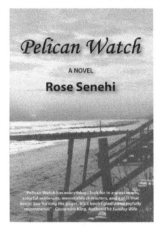

Pelican Watch. *Laced with the flavor of South Carolina's low country, this love story is told against a backdrop of murder and suspense.* Nicky Sullivan always nurses injured animals, but this time she's going to heal herself. She flees to a SC barrier island and discovers a kindred spirit in Mac Moultrie, a salty retired fisherman. From the moment she meets Trippett Alston, she's smitten, but the dark forces swirling around the island threaten to keep them apart.

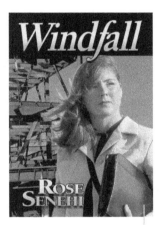

Windfall. *Meet Lisa Barron, a savvy marketing executive with a kid and a crazy career in the mall business.* Everyone knows she's driven, but not the dark secret she's hiding. She's keeping one step ahead of the FBI and a gang of twisted peace activists who screwed up her life in the sixties, while trying not to fall in love with one of the driven men who make these massive projects rise from the ground. What will she do if her past catches up with her? Grab her daughter and run, or face disgrace and a possible murder charge?

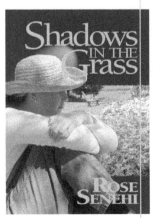

Shadows in the Grass. Striving desperately to hold onto the farm for her son, a widow comes into conflict with the handsome composer who builds a mansion on the hill overlooking her nursery. All the while, she never suspects that the man who moves into the rundown farm behind her has anything to do with the missing children.

ABOUT THE AUTHOR

"WHEN I STARTED developing a plot for my fourth novel in 2005, I needed to find a small town in the mountains where my heroine's father lived, so I took off from Pawleys Island and started my search in North Carolina. When I came upon the village of Chimney Rock I was so struck by its rustic charm that I decided to buy, as a vacation place, one of the cottages nestled in the mountainside behind the little downtown.

"That story turned out to be *In the Shadows of Chimney Rock* and the first "stand alone" novel of what would be my Blue Ridge Series. All the books can be read in any order since they have separate plots—they all just take place in the Hickory Nut Gorge area.

When it kept breaking my heart every time I left Chimney Rock to go back to the beach, my vacation place slowly evolved into my permanent residence. However, South Carolina's Low-country and its people will always have a special place in my heart.

The Wind in the Woods is the second book in the "stand alone" series. I was thrilled when *Render Unto the Valley,* the third novel in the series, was awarded the 2012 IPPY Gold Medal for Fiction-Southeast. *Dancing on Rocks,* my seventh novel and the fourth "stand alone" book in the series, was given the 2014 Indie-Reader Discovery Award for Popular Fiction.

"Researching the history of the Hickory Nut Gorge and weaving stories around it, has been a wonderful experience. Throughout them, I have strived to paint a portrait of the mountain culture I have fallen in love with and portray historical events as accurately as possible. I do hope you enjoy them."

P.S. I especially enjoy leading discussion groups with book clubs, and would greatly appreciate your reviewing my books on Amazon and Good Reads. Thank you.

rsenehi@earthlink.net
www.rosesenehi.com